Looking for a session of spine-tingling suspense? How about bone-chilling, hands-on murder? Stop looking. You've got it in your hands. *Beast of Bengal* is a well-written, tightly-plotted, skin-prickling tale. Take Elaine Pinkerton's book home. Read it tonight by candlelight.

-James D. Doss, author of Charlie Moon/Shaman
mystery series

Elaine Pinkerton's *Beast of Bengal* is the perfect read for armchair travelers who are instantly transported to exotic Calcutta, India. The suspense novel should be on the do-not-miss reading list for history and WWII buffs: one always learns from Pinkerton's fact-filled novels.

-Peggy van Hulsteyn, author of *Sleeping With Literary Lions*

A wonderful snapshot from World War II—full of depth, color, and resonance.

-Steve Berry, national bestselling author of
The Romanov Prophecy

Beast of Bengal

A Novel

Elaine Pinkerton

Elaine Pinkerton

Pocol Press

POCOL PRESS

Published in the United States of America
by Pocol Press
6023 Pocol Drive
Clifton, VA 20124
www.pocolpress.com

Publisher's Cataloguing-in-Publication

Pinkerton, Elaine.

Beast of Bengal / Elaine Pinkerton. – 1st ed. – Clifton,
VA : Pocol Press, 2005.

p. ; cm

ISBN: 1-929763-18-2

1. World War, 1939-1945—Campaigns—Burma
— Fiction. 2. Wold War, 1939-1945—Campaigns
— India—Fiction. 3. India—History—British
Occupation, 1765-1947—Fiction. 4. Historical fiction.
I. Title.

PS3566.I544 B43 2005
813.54—dc22   0503

Excerpts of Gandhi's "Quit India" speech are reprinted from the *New
York Times*.

Acknowledgments

Thanks to the kind people who helped make this novel happen. Writing mentor Bob Mayer and thoughtful readers Karen Russell, Jann Arrington Wolcott, Marty Reiner, Erica P. Cooper and Marianne Creamer helped me more than words can say. Neela Ladd of India Tourism and Hauke Wiebe of the Calcutta 1940s website provided important background information. Jane Gee led me to further insight into the life of Mohandas Gandhi. Diane Barnes lent superb editorial talent. Valuable support came from Martha Davis, Julie Weston and Kathie Carlson. Shirley Taylor deserves special credit for sharing her computer and Photoshop expertise. Kudos to Janice Boyd and Katil K. Goyal for their translations. Praise goes to the Los Alamos Writers Group for insight and ideas. To these and all others who assisted me along the way, my deepest gratitude.

Tiger! tiger! burning bright
In the forests of the night,
What immortal hand or eye
Dare frame thy fearful symmetry?

-William Blake

Prologue

Midnight in the Burmese jungle was sweltering hot. They had to move fast. Most soldiers in the unit, following Mac's orders, walked steadily north to their destination outside Myitkyina. All but the private who refused to move. The sorry devil argued that they should take a different route, they should wait until morning, they should try to establish communication with the medical unit before relocating. The private kept talking, arguing, cursing.

Mac would teach that son-of-a-bitch to defy orders. His hands grabbed the soldier's neck, gripping tighter and tighter. He felt the skin swell. The private crumpled at his feet just as an explosion of enemy fire seared the terrain. Mac fell to the ground on top of the dead body. He heard moans and cries from the wounded soldiers ahead.

Colonel James "Mac" McDermott awoke in a cold sweat from another nightmare about that horrific night in the jungle. He thought of the soldier who'd died at his hands and told himself— as he had countless times before—that it had been an accident.

Once again he hashed over the account he'd given to his superior officer, General Peterson. Mac was the leader of a surveillance unit. He and a small group of soldiers were ordered to reach Myitkyina before dawn. It was imperative to keep walking the thin path through trees and vines. Four men had traveled ahead. One insubordinate bastard, though perfectly healthy, refused to move. A sixth, plagued by dysentery, was lagging somewhere behind. Mac shouted for the others to continue walking while he stayed back to deal with the sluggard.

Mac had intended to just threaten. In the report to Peterson, he'd downplayed the strangling. He'd stressed his philosophy that discipline was necessary at any cost. It was not his fault he'd accidentally gone too far. Surely Peterson would agree that, after all, he and the other survivors made it to Myitkyina by morning and rescued the medical unit. In a way, they were heroes. Mac was now in Calcutta, India, assigned to direct the 142nd General, one of the city's three military rehabilitation hospitals.

In Calcutta, miles from the steamy jungles of Burma, everything was fine until the arrival of a new patient at the 142nd. Private Calvin Brothers had been under Mac's command in the Myitkyina mission. It was assumed that he failed to survive the explosion. He'd been declared missing in action.

The assumption was wrong. Brothers was very much alive, and he had ended up at the 142nd. Mac thought about possible outcomes of this ironic quirk of fate. Finally he decided that Brothers, companion of the soldier Mac accidentally killed, *had* witnessed the strangling.

There was no immediate cause for worry, as Brothers had lost his ability to speak, a condition termed *mutism*. However, as the soldier began to recover from the Burmese ordeal, he would likely reclaim his voice. He would summon up the sight of Mac "disciplining" the rebellious soldier. As soon as he could talk, he would tell. Mac would be court-martialed and sent to prison.

As Colonel McDermott lay in bed listening to night birds cawing and jackals keening in the distance, he realized it was time to put his plan into action. He dressed hastily in old khakis, leaving his feet bare, native style. Stuffing a few supplies in his pocket, he walked to the wards, unlocked the door, and went directly to the bedside of Calvin Brothers.

He clutched the private's shoulder and whispered in his ear. "Brothers, wake up. There's something you've got to see."

The private blinked his eyes and stared at Mac with a puzzled expression.

"There's a meteorite shower tonight, the most spectacular of the decade. Who knows—the sight might just shock you out of your mutism." A ludicrous suggestion, but to Mac's relief, Brothers seemed to be going along with it. If the situation hadn't been so desperate, he would have laughed at his own inventiveness.

Mac pushed Brothers ahead of him. They stepped outside the hospital ward building. He walked arm in arm with the private until they reached the latrine.

"Just keep calm," Mac said. "There's something we need to get in here before we go view the stars. You'll see."

Brothers shook his head and tried to remove his arm from the Colonel's grasp.

Mac got out a revolver and pointed it at the private. "I know you don't want me to use this. Just do as you're told and you won't get hurt."

He pushed the barrel of his gun against the other man's spine and walked him into the depths of the concrete building. At the end of the hall was a small windowless room. Mac pulled a dirty cord to switch on a single overhead light bulb.

Brothers made terrified, guttural sounds. He got down on his knees and tried to hug the colonel's legs.

"Well, here we are again, Private Calvin Brothers. Remember that night we shared in the jungle? Did you witness my disciplinary action with that poor schmuck? You may have, you may not have, but in case you did, we can't let the cat out of the bag, can we?"

Tears streaming down his face, Brothers found his voice at last. "Noooo. Please, no."

He leaped to his feet and punched Mac in the face and stomach. He kicked at the larger man and tried to bite. The two fell to the ground in a wrestling match. It took less than five minutes for Mac to overpower Brothers.

Mac roared with anger. "Cut it out, goddamit. You're just like that worthless friend of yours, no respect for authority. You saw what happened to him and you still didn't learn?" With a vicious shove, he pushed the now hysterical Sergeant to the floor. He smiled and took a deep breath.

"See," Mac said. "I'm putting my gun down. I'm not going to shoot you after all. That would be too messy." He put on a pair of white gloves he'd taken from his pocket.

Crawling on his hands and knees, Brothers made a last wild protest. "I won't tell. Saw nothing. Please, NOOOO."

Mac kicked his victim in the ribs and face.

"It's a shame you couldn't have told me sooner, but now it's too late. And now Private Brothers, I have a final treatment for you. You just might see stars, and you'll have no more mutism, no more anything."

Feeling energized, Mac placed his hands in a ring around the private's neck. His grip tightened. The private twitched and clawed wildly. Finally, Brothers went limp.

It took no time at all to secure a rope around the lifeless neck. Using a wooden box to stand on, Mac strung Brothers from a rafter directly above the shower head, silently congratulating himself on all the preparation he'd done before tonight. "Goodbye, Private Brothers," he said. "I'll turn off the light so you can get a good night's sleep."

August 8, 1942
Bombay, India

The All-India Congress Committee was about to commence the day's business. As dawn turned the sky from black to silvery gray, then to blue, people filtered into a large grassy area known as Gowalia Tank Maidan. The morning air was cold, so most wore shawls over their thin cotton garments. At the maidan's center was a large raised stage and podium. This arrangement was flanked by rows of wooden chairs. Congress *Wallah's* in white caps stood along the roped off area to keep mere onlookers from sweeping into the reserved section.

Two visitors to Bombay, Ravi Ghosh and his friend Sanjay Roy, slipped into the growing crowd. Like most of the others, Ravi and Sanjay felt that it was time for the British to quit India forever. Everyone was curious about what Gandhi, the advocate of *Satyagraha*, would say. It was felt that Gandhi's words about peaceful resistance would surely influence the outcome of this congressional gathering. Indeed, they would shape the future of the subcontinent.

Ravi was a man of the world, a businessman—or so he claimed. Sanjay, until dropping out to help fight for Indian independence, was a student at St. Xavier's College. In his heart, Sanjay agreed with *Satyagraha*. A word coined by Gandhi, *Satyagraha* literally meant a fierce demand for truth. Gandhi believed in winning freedom from British rule without resorting to physical battles. His devotees believed that adherence to *Satyagraha* would succeed. Sanjay feared that Gandhi's nonviolent way of fighting oppression might not work for the masses.

Ravi, who was a foot taller, looked down at Sanjay to continue their ongoing debate. "There is little possibility," he announced, "that the British government will peacefully release our beloved Mother India from its control."

"Nonetheless," argued Sanjay, "If anyone can keep violence from erupting and staining our motherland, it is Gandhiji. People listen to his words and many will sincerely try to follow his peaceful example." As though doubting the truth of what he'd just said, Sanjay added, "At least...one can hope."

"My unseasoned young friend," said Ravi, "you are idealistic to a fault. I'm saying that people are not willing to wait any longer for freedom from slavery and submission. Even at the cost of lives, the

4

British tyrants must vacate our land. If men were all saints like Gandhi, there would be no bloodshed and we would..."

"Look!" interrupted Sanjay. He pointed to the far end of the maidan. "The speakers are arriving."

Cries and chants arose from the growing mob...

Mahatma Gandhi Ki jai! (Victory to Mahatma Gandhi!)
Mahatma Gandhi amar hai! (Mahatma Gandhi will never die!)

The adulation of Gandhi was seductive, and many of Sanjay's friends literally worshipped the Hindu spiritual leader, but the young man was undecided on the right path. In the same way that the believers in *Satyagraha* or "truth force" were devoted to Gandhi, Sanjay was intensely committed to learning from Ravi Ghosh.

The cheers grew louder: *Mahatma Gandhi Ki jai! Mahatma Gandhi amar hai!*

Only a fierce effort by the stewards kept Gandhi's devotees from breaking through the guard ropes. Nearly all of the chanters aspired for *darshan*, the supreme happiness that came to anyone in the presence of the Holy One.

Sunlight illuminated the maidan grounds and warmed the air. Prominent Congressional Committee members Abul Kalam Azad and Kripalani climbed stairs to the raised wooden stage. Following Azad was Mohandas K. Gandhi, a small man wearing a white dhoti and a shawl, smiling radiantly and holding a bamboo cane. To his devotees, he was "Mahatma," the Holy One, or "Gandhiji," the Beloved. A hush fell over the crowd as Ghandi began to speak.

There are people who have hatred in their hearts for the British, he began. *I have heard of people saying that they are disgusted with them. The common people's mind does not differentiate between a Britisher and the imperialist form of their government. To them both are the same. There are people who do not mind the advent of the Japanese. To them, perhaps, it would mean a change of masters.*

But it is a dangerous thing. You must remove it from your minds. This is a crucial hour. If we keep quiet and do not play our part, it will not be right...

I know full well that the British will have to give us our freedom when we have made sufficient sacrifices and proven our strength. We must remove the hatred for the British from our hearts. At least, in my heart there is no such hatred. As a matter of fact, I am a greater friend of the British now than I ever was...

5

"Only a saint could feel that way," Ravi whispered to his friend. "Gandhi is wrong to think that the people agree with him about the British. They are not ready to follow the demands of *Satyagraha*. They lack the discipline, the self-denial."

"Shhh, quiet please, *sahib*," hissed Sanjay. "I want to hear what Gandhi is trying to tell us."

I know (the British) are on the brink of the ditch, and are about to fall into it. Therefore, even if they want to cut off my hands, my friendship demands that I should try to pull them out of that ditch. This is my claim, at which many people may laugh, but all the same, I say this is true.

At the time when I am about to launch the biggest front in my life, there can be no hatred for the British in my heart. ...It may be that, in a moment of anger, they might do things that might provoke you. Nevertheless, you should not resort to violence; that would put non-violence to shame...It may be that wisdom will dawn on the British and they will understand that it would be wrong for them to put in jail the very people who want to fight for them....

Non-violence is a matchless weapon, which can help every one. I know we have not done much by way of non-violence and therefore, if such changes come about, I will take it that it is the result of our labors during the last twenty-two years and that God has helped us to achieve it.

When I raised the slogan "Quit India" the people in India, who were then feeling despondent, I felt that I had placed before them a new thing. If you want real freedom, you will have to come together, and such a coming together will create true democracy—the like of which has not so far been witnessed or attempted.

I have read a good deal about the French Revolution. Carlyle's work I read while in jail. I have great admiration for the French people, and Jawaharlal has told me all about the Russian Revolution.

...Once you understand these things you will forget the differences between the Hindus and Moslems.

Sanjay nudged Ravi's arm to get his attention. "How many of these people have read about the French Revolution?" he whispered. "They can't even read! How can most Indian people 'just forget' the differences between Hindus and Muslims. They won't!"

Ravi nodded in silent agreement.

In Satyagraha, Gandhi continued, *there is no place for fraud or falsehood, or any kind of untruth. Fraud and untruth today are stalking the world. I cannot be a helpless witness to such a situation. I have traveled all over India as perhaps nobody in the present age has. The voiceless millions of the land saw in me their friend and representative, and I identified myself with them to an extent it was possible for a human being to do. I say trust in their eyes, which I now want to turn to good account in fighting this empire upheld on untruth and violence. However gigantic the preparations that the empire has made, we must get out of its clutches. How can I remain silent at this supreme hour and hide my light under the bushel?...*

Every one of you should, from this moment onwards, consider yourself a free man or woman, and act as if you are free and are no longer under the heel of this imperialism....

It is not make-believe that I am suggesting to you. It is the very essence of freedom. The bond of the slave is snapped the moment he considers himself to be a free being. He will plainly tell the master: "I was your bond slave till this moment, but I am a slave no longer...".

Here is a mantra, a short one, that I give you. You may imprint it on your hearts and let every breath of yours give expression to it. The mantra is: DO OR DIE. We shall either free India or die in the attempt; we shall not live to see the perpetuation of our slavery. Every true Congressman or woman will join the struggle with an inflexible determination not to remain alive to see the country in bondage and slavery. Let that be your pledge...Freedom is not for the coward or the faint-hearted...

The day's meeting was nearing a conclusion, and the crowd of onlookers drifted away from the maidan *en masse.* Ravi and Sanjay, wishing to avoid the crush of humanity, began walking toward Cruikshank Road.

"There's a small cafe at the Shivaji Hindu Hotel, where I'm staying," Sanjay told his friend. "We can have some tandoori chicken and try to find out where Gandhi is staying. At dinner, we will be able to overhear conversations of the *Satyagrahis* about Gandhi's overnight whereabouts, and we can go wherever it turns out to be so as to catch a glimpse of him in the morning."

When Ravi said nothing, Sanjay added "I have mats and blankets enough for us both. It might be an adventure."

Ravi valued Sanjay's allegiance. Even though his tentative plan was to align himself with the Indian Independence Movement, he would spend a few days with the younger man to learn more about his character. He needed to surround himself with allies, and he sensed that Sanjay, at some point in the future, might prove to be a reliable accomplice.

"Well, why not," Ravi answered at last. "It will give us time, Sanjay, to finish what we began discussing a few days back. The Congress meeting took our thoughts away from immediate plans."

"Yes," said Sanjay "but at the maidan, we witnessed history in the making. We *needed* to be there."

"I'm not sure what kind of history was being made," Ravi said. "India demands home rule. It is overdue. Even Gandhiji seems aware that our country's need for self-respect has gone beyond mere passive resistance. Like everyone, I want India for Indians, but the more I learn, the more I believe there are stronger paths than that of *Satyagraha* ."

"I live nearby, Ravi. Why don't we walk rather than go by bus? It is safer to speak about private matters in the open air."

"As we do," said Ravi, "we can work up an appetite for a fine dinner."

As the sun was going down, the two men arrived at Sanjay's apartment. They shared dinner at the Shaivaji's small restaurant. It was run down, and they sat on crude wooden benches, but the place seemed clean and the food was good. Later, along with hundreds of others, they camped in a large city park near Mani Bhaven, where Gandhi and his wife Kasturbai were staying. Early on the following morning, they walked to the railroad station, then joined in with other pedestrians following Gandhi and his entourage. It was common knowledge that Gandhi would be returning to his *ashram*, where he lived the simple life that he preferred. Thanks in part to Ravi's commanding height, they were able to get quite near.

"Ravi, look behind us," Sanjay whispered. "There's a British officer, and a pack of sergeants and constables. What on earth are they doing here?"

"Shhh. Just be inconspicuous and listen. I think we are about to see more history in the making."

The cadre of British and Indian officers walked briskly by Ravi and Sanjay and stopped directly in front of Gandhi.

The chief officer, a florid, overweight Brit with several chins and small, squinty eyes, blocked Gandhi from walking any further.

8

"What are you planning to speak on at the meeting next week?" he asked.

Gandhi held himself in a proud, upright position. The sun glinted against his round spectacles as he replied. "Why, my subject will be the value of goat's milk in one's daily diet. I will also speak against the war to prevent a free India."

"Sir, I'm sorry," said the chief officer, "but that can't be permitted. I have orders for your arrest. You must come with me." Kasturbai and Mirabel, the Gandhi's adopted daughter, moved closer to their beloved husband and father.

"Mrs. Gandhi," said the officer, "I have orders to return you and your companion to the ashram.

"If my husband is arrested, I will speak in his place." Gandhi smiled proudly at his wife's answer. Kasturbai, however, was arrested with her husband.

In the next day's *India Times*, it was announced that Gandhi and Kasturbai were interned near Poona at the palace of Aga Khan. The stately building, surrounded by palm trees, had for several years served as a prison and detention camp. Nehru and nearly all the other congressional committee members were also imprisoned.

The reunion of Ravi and Sanjay ended the same day. Ravi proclaimed that *he* was going to "quit India," and would be spending time out of the country. "I am filled with outrage," he proclaimed. "When I return to India, I will be needing your help."

Sanjay would leave the next day for Calcutta, the city in which he had relatives who promised to help him find work. It would be nearly two years before he and Ravi would meet again.

1

Before he left for India in August of 1944, Lieutenant Richard Benet promised his young wife a daily letter. On this muggy Calcutta evening, he placed Rita's snapshot against some books. The photograph was taken on their honeymoon at Niagara Falls. His wife's black hair was parted in the middle and pulled back behind her ears. Her dark eyes, wide set and perfectly symmetrical, seemed to glow with love and happiness. Her smile was just for him.

His first week at the 142nd General Hospital kept him so busy that he could write only a paragraph or two at a time. Earlier that day he'd started the daily "Rita letter." Tonight he would finish it no matter what.

At 2100 hours the electric lights dimmed. Lt. Benet could barely see what he was writing. He lit an oil lamp, penned a numeral five at the top of a fresh onionskin page and continued where he left off.

...My darling, it is much later now, and I think the training sessions are nearly over. The army batters one with policies and procedures. They love their regulations and the chance to catch a man breaking one. The commanding officer of the 142nd is a sour colonel named James McDermott, 'Mac' to the fellas. The only time he says anything is when he's finding something wrong or when he's giving orders. Talk about Hitler: Mac is like him only not as smart. I plan to avoid this jackass whenever possible.

I'm creating this message to snores of soldiers and the rat-a-tat of bugs bombing against the basha walls. Andy and Silas have been sawing wood for the past two hours and your weary boy is writing to you by lantern. As I calculate the time between us, my princess, you are now teaching those lucky Washington Elementary School children. No wonder they always bring you presents. How happy they must be to have such a charmer for their teacher.

I think this assignment will allow plenty of opportunities to apply my study of psychology and explore Calcutta. The main objective of the hospital is to rehabilitate the physically, mentally, and emotionally wounded. The patients are declared "well," then sent back to the front lines as soon as possible. The cure might be superficial and a patient might need more time for healing, but to the Army the soldier is a mere cog in the machine, an expendable part. It's the cogs that count, not the humans.

10

Those cases who seem to be recovering, I will take for jaunts to the open-air markets. To a man, they have sweethearts, wives, daughters, aunts or grandmothers who would be happy to receive souvenirs from India.

Even though it is only September, I am shopping for your Christmas gifts. The New Market shops offer the most beautiful goods in the world—ivory necklaces and pins, silk saris, handbags, marble boxes inlaid with semi-precious stones. Usually, the maker of whatever item is for sale creates wares in the back of his store. Often the entire family—a wife and children of all ages—is crammed into a small area and working most diligently.

As the oil lamp flickered and shadows danced on the walls, Benet wrote all this and more. An hour later, he sealed the letter and left it on the table for Sanjay, his bearer, to mail tomorrow. The Army assigned personal helpers, known as bearers, to officers at the hospital. Though some of his colleagues thought of their bearers as servants and treated them accordingly, Benet considered Sanjay to be a solicitous friend.

Drunk with fatigue, Benet staggered out of his clothes and dropped into bed, a hard, narrow platform parallel with those of his *basha* mates. Once inside the mosquito netting, he snapped it tight.

Some of the hospital staff would soon be transferred to Burma, another part of this China-Burma-India theater of World War II, and the officers were promised private quarters in a week. Benet really didn't mind sharing his territory. In a way, it kept him sane. Let Si and Andy snore to their heart's content; exhaustion worked better than earplugs.

A fleeting image of Rita passed through his mind. What might she be doing on her side of the world? Perhaps she was going to a friend's house to play cards. The teachers were all learning to play bridge, and Rita often wrote to Richard about the points she'd been dealt in a certain game or her delight at mastering no trump bidding. Seeing Rita holding a hand of cards at the bridge table, he drifted off.

...He could see the landscape of an impressionist painting. The colors were sizzling green, blue, and vibrant pastels. A couple were boating on a turquoise lake. They were far away, then closer. Why, he and Rita were the boaters! Cloudless azure sky loomed over them, and Rita wore a white summer dress that managed to look both sensuous and refined. Her luxuriant black hair flowed out from

under a wide-brimmed straw hat. Richard did all the rowing as she lazily dipped her fingertips in the water. Now was the time to express his love. He fingered the emerald ring in his pocket. The oar strokes grew louder.

Thump...thump...thump.

It grew darker as black clouds swept across the sky. Something was wrong. The paddles were banging against the side of the boat. As the lake grew rougher, angry whitecaps formed.

Thump...thump...thump.

The boat rocked violently and he was tossed out into the roiling lake...

Richard awakened. The lake became the wooden *basha* floor. The thumping was now loud, frantic: someone was at the door. He hadn't fallen out of bed since boyhood. Feeling like a fool and hoping that Si and Andy were still asleep, he sat up and rubbed the bump on his forehead.

"*Sahib, sahib,*" beseeched a soft male voice. "Please come with me to the shower rooms. Something is very, very wrong, *sahib.*"

Benet untangled himself from the mosquito netting, stood up, and pulled on his khaki pants. He unlatched the *basha* door to find a perspiring Sanjay, who was wearing only a white jodhpur-like garment and turban. His skin glistened in the moonlight.

The bearer pressed flattened palms together at his chin and bowed his head toward Richard. "*Namaste, sahib.* Please forgive me for awakening you at this fearsome hour. I know it is three o'clock but when I make a walk around the *bashas* I see that coming from the showers and latrine are jackals. One has meat hanging from its mouth. I go closer and see that it is the foot of a person. The jackals run away and I go inside." Sanjay was chattering nonstop.

Benet stepped outside the *basha* and closed the door. Though he was barely six feet tall, he stood more than a foot taller than Sanjay.

"*Sahib,* you must see for yourself. I take you and show." He shook his head. "Is very, very bad."

"Yes, you take and show me. Wait here one minute." Benet tiptoed into the bedroom to get shoes, shirt, and a flashlight. Amazingly, his colleagues were still snoring. Now that he thought about it, both had probably come back from the club drunk as skunks and passed out. He would hear their bellyaching in the morning about hangovers.

An impatient cough sounded from the entrance. Benet closed the *basha* door quietly and stepped outside to join Sanjay. They walked for five minutes, the Tamil native leading the American to a rambling, decrepit cinderblock building. Mostly, it housed showers and toilets; part of it was abandoned. Their soundless footsteps left clear impressions in the dirt. A huge silver moon illuminated the terrain.

At night, sounds traveled from the strip of jungle not too far from the *bashas*. Hearing the roar of a large cat, Benet remembered that man-eating tigers were rumored to be increasing in numbers. The men were warned not to walk about at night without a flashlight, an admonition most of them ignored.

By now Benet was well aware of the Army's practice of shutting off most of their generators at night. During the dark hours, only the Central Administrative Center had lights on between 2000 and 0600 hours. Other areas were either dimmed or black. Under the moon, the thatched *basha* roofs shone silver and the dirt paths gleamed with a mysterious sheen.

"OK, *sahib*, here we are. I go first, I lead you. Is bad to see this." Sanjay seemed to be apologizing. It was totally black inside the shower rooms and they moved cautiously.

"Here, take this." Benet thrust his flashlight into Sanjay's hand.

The psychologist felt queasy. A fetid odor assaulted his nostrils, the smell of rotting flesh. They walked on. He strained his eyes to pierce the darkness but could discern only Sanjay's white garments. Beginning to feel the bruises from his earlier fall, Benet wobbled a bit.

Sanjay waved the flashlight down the hall. "*Sahib*, we have gone too far. I believe the room we are seeking is at the opposite end of this place. You see, when I first saw such an evil sight, so horrified was I that I became confused. I turned in several directions before I found the door to outside and rushed to your *basha*. I ran very, very quickly to you for I knew that you, *sahib*, would know what to do."

But would he know what to do, Benet wondered. He kept his eyes on Sanjay's white turban as they seemed to be retracing their steps. They were headed down the concrete tunnel toward the door that a few minutes earlier they had entered.

"Yes, *sahib*. This is it. Here we are. Please to prepare yourself."

Moving slowly, flashlight beaming ahead, Sanjay guided Benet into a bare cement room with a drain in the center and shower heads

13

on the walls at regular intervals. Sanjay moved the flashlight around like a searchlight.

"God Almighty!" shouted Benet.

One of the showerheads had a person underneath it. He was not taking a shower, however. He was hanging by a rope.

2

Flies swarmed thickly around the footless corpse. Had the men not arrived, the jackals would probably have finished their job. While Sanjay, following orders, ran to the *basha* of Colonel Mac McDermott, Benet stationed himself beside the poor fellow whom, he assumed, had lost the will to live. The psychologist averted his eyes from the dead man. If he'd been religious, he would have said a prayer.

Even with a handkerchief held tightly to his nose, Lt. Benet could smell rot. Groping wildly, he found a light bulb cord and pulled it down. He spotted a toilet and raced to it. On hands and knees, kneeling over the bowl, he vomited until he thought his guts would spew out. As he was dousing his face with cold water in a nearby basin, he heard two voices. Sanjay and the colonel were already back.

It would not do to be caught sick on the job. Benet turned on the faucet to rinse out his mouth. He made it back to the corpse before Mac and Sanjay reached the room. A rat went squealing away as Benet took a sentinel's position next to the hanging man.

Slowing his breathing, he tried to look calm as the colonel approached. He fervently hoped that his sickness of a few minutes earlier would not be detected. A saving grace might be the dead body's odor of putrefaction.

Mac walked within five feet of the body and stopped in his tracks. "Lieutenant," he barked, "what the hell is going on? Was this one of your patients? Weren't you aware of his mental state? Why didn't you report his suicidal tendencies to me?"

Benet saluted. "Colonel McDermott, he was not in my care. I've never seen this soldier before. The first time I knew about this was when Sanjay woke me up in the middle of the night and brought me here."

The colonel stood glaring, arms crossed and chin jutting out. "Benet, there will be an investigation and you must be prepared to account for your actions, or should I say 'lack of actions'? Your bearer, Sanjay, seems to be the only one around here doing a decent job. I've sent him for the MPs so we can identify the deceased, prepare a notification for his family and bury him as quickly as possible. In this starving country, which produces many corpses of its own, dead bodies are a source of pestilence. Do you understand, Benet?"

"Yes sir, I realize that we must keep up morale. But sir, won't there be some kind of detective work? I mean, are we sure this was a suicide?"

Mac aimed a mean look at Benet. "Don't be insulting, Doctor." Richard caught the sarcastic intonation when Mac used the title *Doctor.* "You fool, of course there will be an investigation, but that is my business. The information that comes out of this incident is my business. It is also classified business and since this was not your case, as you pointed out, you are not privy to the report."

Richard Benet had the uneasy feeling that this conversation was moving too fast. Why was the suicide of an enlisted man classified, and why was Mac questioning him if he wasn't interested in his answers? On the other hand, he wasn't sure he really wanted to know.

The colonel's voice cut into Benet's thoughts. "I will not have you questioning my handling of this crises. Your job is to rehabilitate the patients under your care. *They* are your business."

Mac's dressing down of the psychologist was interrupted by the arrival of several MPs. They laid out a body bag and went to work removing the corpse. Mac ordered Benet to take the rest of the morning off, clean up, and get some sleep.

"I will handle this," the colonel said in a steely voice. "You report to the Q Building, room 101, at 1600 hours for a meeting with me and several others in the administration. I realize that this is your first experience in a military hospital, Lieutenant, but this is not your university; this is the Army. Your commanding officers are not to be questioned."

"Yes sir." Benet saluted. "Am I dismissed now?"

"You are ordered to go to your *basha*, rest up, and—as I said—report to me at 1600 hours. Not a word to your mates about this. Just say you were called out on an emergency by me. I will see to it that you have private quarters before the week is over."

Sanjay was to stay and help the clean-up crew. Benet walked back to his *basha* alone. The sky had lightened from black to gray. Andy and Silas had already left for the morning drill. The solitude was a welcome relief. No explanations would be needed, at least not right away. After undressing, Benet set the alarm clock, collapsed into bed, and instantly fell to sleep.

16

Raucous clanging interrupted what seemed like just a few minutes of sleep, although it had actually been four hours. Benet found the note Andy had left for him on the community table in the *basha's* foyer.

Dick: Mac sent a courier to me explaining that I was to take over your group therapy session this morning. He told me to cover for you all day and that the situation was classified. I was 'not to ask questions.' Don't worry. I won't. I don't want Mac's knife aimed at me! Andy.

Lt. Richard Benet knew that Andy referred to Mac's nasty tongue-lashings. But he could imagine the colonel carrying an actual knife in a leather case close to his chest. He always seemed on the verge of an attack.

Dressed in fresh khakis, Benet entered the mess hall. It was 1300 hours, just time for lunch before the briefing. There was Andy, sitting alone and eating pork and beans. A lifetime of having to adjust his six and a half feet to furniture too low for him resulted in a permanent slouch. The Army's mess tables were even lower than most so Benet couldn't see the Lieutenant's face. He knew it was Andy, however, because of his sandy curls.

Andy swilled coffee and looked quizzically at his friend. "What's up? Mac told me you were involved in some kind of emergency and that I needed to cover for you, but when I came to the *basha* after breakfast, you were sawing wood. Seems more like a vacation than an emergency. How do you rate time to catch a nap?"

"Yeah, some strange things are happening around here," Benet said, "but they're classified. I got pulled into it sort of by accident. I'm not able to talk about it." The psychologist drew his index finger across his neck as though his throat were being slit. "I've got to report to Mac in an hour."

"Your bed-ridden patient Warren seemed upset that you weren't there this morning," Andy said. "His dysentery is letting up, but he's becoming more unraveled. Apparently he felt his illness was going to be his ticket home."

Benet sighed. "Warren's been trying to work the system for weeks. He told me that if he didn't get a discharge, he was going to kill himself. I was alarmed when I first heard this, but Mac told me that he's said that frequently. I think his basic problem is that he got a letter from the girl back home breaking their engagement."

"Ah, that'll do it every time. I can't tell you how often I've seen a man crumble when he's cut off from his sweetheart. Enemy fire, mine fields, nighttime raids in the jungle are something they can endure, but there's nothing worse than a 'Dear John' letter."

"Tell Warren I'll come see him after my briefing, if not right before supper then afterwards. I owe you a big favor, Andy. I'll be glad to cover for you if you ever need it."

Benet hurried to the designated meeting room. Mac was already there, seated at a long rectangular wooden table. Next to him was a square-shouldered blond man with a ruddy face. For a moment Benet thought he was one of the British liaison officers. He looked as though he should have been wearing an ascot. His hair was tousled, as though he'd been out yachting. It was not uncommon to see a few British officers parading about the hospital. Calcutta was still considered a jewel in the necklace that was once the British Empire.

When Mac introduced Benet to Brigadier General Peterson, however, the illusion of Britishness vanished.

"Howdy, Lieutenant," Peterson said. "I heard ya work mighty well with the men. Pleased to meet ya."

"Benet, close the door behind you," Mac ordered. "The General here will give you some background on the suicide case and, as you're new on the scene, he'll be presenting some nuances that your psychology classes at Ohio State may not have covered."

"Yes, sir, I appreciate that."

Peterson looked at Benet with a faint smile. He sounded almost pleasant. "'Fore we begin, Lieutenant, do ya have any questions?"

Deciding to risk insubordination, Benet burst forth. "Well, yes. Who was this man, and is it always customary to treat fatalities like this one with secrecy? No disrespect intended, sir, but I am dealing with the mental health of patients here at the hospital. Surely I ought to be informed as to what really happened."

"Why, course ya'd feel that way, Lieutenant," Peterson said pleasantly. "For security purposes, howevah, we mus keep our investigation classified, top secret. There are mattahs involved that ya'll er not privy to."

"But," protested Benet, "I can be trusted to keep things confidential. I can actually help you solve..."

Peterson cut him off. "Ya heard of the 'need to know' rule, Lieutenant. If there's anything ya need t' know 'bout this case, I'll inform ya."

18

Mac was scowling. Benet was now certain that this session was to be more of an 'attitude adjustment' session than an opportunity for him to ask questions. The meeting was destined to be one-sided. Mac's face said it all.

"I'd never even met the soldier," Mac lied. "I'll defer to you, Peterson."

The General cleared his throat. "Tha suicide victim waz Calvin Brothers, a private in Merrill's Marauders who waz injud in uh night raid by tha Japanese. He'd been lost 'n wanderin' for a month, and finally air lifted to tha Twentieth General Hospital to recovah from malnutrition 'n malaria. Brothers waz plagued by nightmares 'n began actin' strange. He waz in our gen'ral ward, as we had no Neuro-Psychiatric division jus at tha moment. When he developed mutism, we transfud the luckless fella to tha 142nd."

Peterson continued, "He was here jest a day when he disappeared. We all thot he'd gone AWOL. It wasn't until your bearer found his corpse that we knew 'bout his suicide. As ya know, the other half of the latrine buildin' is nevah used. There wudda been no reason fer anyone to go back there.

"Lieutenant, I understand yer doubts," Peterson said. "Ya see, part of our mission is to rehabilitate these patients in spirit as well as body. Tha men stationed here in Calcutta are already sufferin' from boredom 'n lack ah spirit. As ya know, or at least ya should know, we're playing a crucial role in this China-Burma-India theater. Are ya with me?"

"Yes, of course," Benet said. "General Peterson, sir, I'm aware that Assam, to our west, is a region filled with staging areas, a veritable launching pad to get munitions to Kunming. I'm also aware of the responsibilities of our general hospitals here in Calcutta."

Both Mac and Peterson deflected Benet's questions about the late Private Brothers. Peterson continued lecturing about the psychiatric costs of war, as though Richard had been summoned to hone his skills as a psychologist.

"Lieutenant," General Peterson pontificated, "yer tha psychologist. Surely yer aware that in uh war, men have limits of psychological endurance. Fear 'n yes, evin madness are constant companions."

Mac broke into the presentation. "As you must know, Benet, from your initial briefing, the major challenge of our Neuro-Psychiatric Ward doctors—both Ph.D.'s and M.D.'s—is to distinguish imaginary ailments from genuine psychoses. It's never

19

good when a soldier decides to end his own life, but it happens—not just in the NP wards of military hospitals, but on the battlefield."

Peterson lit a cigarette. "Every day we see men killin' themselves rather than waiting fer the enemy to do it. Sometimes it's from sheer disgrace: a soldier blames himself for cowardice or can't tol'rate the thought a livin' when all his buddies have died. Sometimes, as 'n the case of Brothers, a man jes loses his will ta live. Brothers had been through too much, and since his speech fer sum reason jes vanished, the usual remedy of talk therapy wasn't available."

"But...," said Benet.

"Lieutenant, apparently mah message is not getting through ta ya. Is not yer 'sponsibility to investigate the unfortunate suicide a Private Brothers. The Colonel waz with Brothers in the jungle; he's detailed tha man's past behavior t'me."

Peterson ground the butt of his cigarette in an ashtray. "You mus' think of the well-bein' of the living, those under your care, those men who have sum hope a regainin' their mental health. Tha's yer special talent. This is a complicated situation, Lieutenant, 'n we will take care of it."

Benet felt heat rising from his neck, the same reaction he'd had years ago when facing bullies on the playground. "General Peterson," he said, trying to mask his indignation, "I have spent considerable time learning about the situation of our neuro-psychiatric patients. I know that some fellows have experienced the horror of being prisoners in Rangoon; I'm aware others have lost all their buddies when a plane went down flying the hump. I know—"

Mac broke in. "Yes, yes, we know you know. All our medical staff have heard tales of men who've shot off their toes or quit taking their atabrine rather than face night raids. We're not saying that you aren't well informed. Just listen and quit being so defensive."

"Sir, I'm not defensive, I'm aghast. I can hardly believe Brothers wasn't missed before he managed to hang himself in the unused part of the latrine building."

Mac jabbed his index finger in the air as he made a point. "Your task, doctor, is to distinguish genuine ailments from those that are stress induced."

He pulled a textbook out of his briefcase and opened it, referring to a symptom indicator chart. "Let me remind you that neurosis manifests as irritability, fatigue, phobia, anxiety, insomnia, nervousness, hypochondria, and obsession."

20

"Sir, I'm familiar with the difference between soldiers who just need rest and relaxation and those who are psychotic. You don't need to review all this."

Mac glared at Benet. "Shut up and listen. I'm reminding you that your job is not to be a detective but to analyze and treat soldiers." He turned back to his text. "To continue, psychosis, on the other hand, is recognized as extreme anxiety, depersonalization, depression, abulia, melancholia, apathy, stupor, hallucination, delusion, compulsion and agitation. There is also a condition that we've come to call 'post-traumatic stress disorder.' Your job is clearly to analyze, categorize, and treat these ailments."

The lecture ended at last. Mac told Benet he would let him know if anything emerged about the suicide case. "That is—anything necessary for you to perform your job." It was 1900 hours when Benet finally escaped into the muggy night and hurried to the Neuro-Psychiatric Ward.

He was too late to be of any help to Warren. The disturbed young man was fast asleep.

3

...They were in the luxurious bedroom of a strange house. She sat at the wicker dressing table, dressed in a black satin slip. Richard watched as she brushed her hair and swept it up into a chignon. An ocean breeze ruffled the curtains at the window and a light, chilly rain blew into their faces. They embraced.

Just as they were about to kiss, Rita awakened to Monday morning of another school week.

In the real world, Richard was on the other side of the globe, 6,000 miles away and serving in India. Here in Findlay, Ohio, twenty-six-year-old Rita was living at the home of her parents. In some ways, she thought, it was as though she had never married. It could have been worse, however. Because she was teaching school this year, she was able to pay some rent to her parents. What's more, for at least seven hours a day, when she was busy with her students, she had little time to miss Richard.

Rita dressed in a black and red crepe sheath dress, one that Richard loved. She looked in the mirror and knew that he would approve. Sitting at her vanity table, she applied bright red lipstick and a dash of powder. Leaning her head over her knees, she brushed her jet black hair and pulled it back into a bun, the style that she usually wore for school days.

She stood up for a full view and noticed that her dress, formerly snug across the hips, was now loose. Richard loved her being slender, but of course he wasn't here to notice. Nor was he here on this late September day to celebrate their first wedding anniversary.

Rita felt a lump forming in her throat and held back tears. If only she could just forget the date. Somehow she knew the anniversary would be on her mind all day. The gift Richard mentioned in several letters had yet to arrive. In fact, no mail had come from India in nearly a week. It should have been a joyous day, one in which they celebrated their year-old marriage. Instead, Rita thought grimly, the challenge would be just to get through this dour Monday. That's what life had come to: just getting through one day, then another.

"No thanks, Mama, I don't have time for breakfast," Rita called in answer to her mother's invitation to come eat. She hurried through the kitchen with a quick hug for her mother. "Goodbye, Ma," she yelled on her way out the front door. "I have a meeting after school, so don't wait supper for me."

A light drizzle was falling. The green Packard was parked by the curb. Her father must have brought it out of the garage before he left for the office. The family was being wonderful, Rita reminded herself. With gas at such a premium, it was real luxury to be able to drive. Some of the teachers had to take the bus or walk. She couldn't complain.

She drove the sedan cautiously over the rain slick streets. World War II interrupted what should have been the best time in her life, Rita mused. She was just sixteen when she first met Richard. He was four years her senior, and she had never loved anyone else. Sometimes she wondered what she'd do if he didn't come back, if the war kept them apart forever. One thing she knew for sure: no matter how long it took for Richard's return, she would never love anyone else.

Washington Elementary School loomed just ahead, a massive square brick building with gray stone trim. Inside, twenty-five children awaited. Though sometimes unruly, they were basically sweet kids. Each day she spent with them reminded Rita of how much she wanted children of her own.

On many days, they seemed like her very own. Every morning she hoped that this would be the day that her student Robert would learn to read. She'd worked with this small, shy boy to bring him out, but he refused to speak a word in class. It was as though he never learned to talk. The harder she tried to coax him to participate, the more he withdrew. Finally one of the girls in the class said that Robert really did know how to read, but that he could only do it in private. Maybe she would work with him during lunch or after school.

"Morning, Mrs. Benet. You must have gotten that car fixed."

Fred Eckles, principal of Washington Elementary, was always the first person Rita saw when she walked the school's broad stone entrance steps. She'd made the mistake of asking Eckles to let her have a substitute one day so she could take her old Packard to the garage to be examined. Ever since then he'd been acting familiar and obnoxiously flirtatious. Rumors floated among the teachers that Eckles' wife had left him because he cheated on her.

"You know it was really just a little problem, hardly anything to repair," Rita said. She barely came up to Eckles broad shoulders. "I know you don't need your teachers complaining about how much trouble it is to get to and from school." Good jobs were hard to come by, she silently reminded herself, and teaching at Washington was far better than clerking in a store.

"Mr. Eckles," Rita continued, "I hope you can come by Room Three tomorrow afternoon to hear our poetry recital. The children got to pick what they wanted to learn and they have practiced for the entire six-week period. Today is our dress rehearsal, you might say. It would be wonderful if you could come listen. The children always do better with an audience."

Rita walked into Room Three, past the neat sign announcing "Miss Benet's Third Grade." The room smelled of freshly waxed linoleum, chalk dust, and the ancient radiator's hot, dusty fumes. The odors were comforting in their familiarity, as was the arrival of Sharon Mullins. As she did every Monday, Sharon brought Rita an apple.

When the bell rang, the rest of the students clamored into the room, several bringing apples, oranges or other small gifts. In minutes, they were seated and looking expectantly at her. When she talked to the children, Rita was able to keep thoughts of her wedding anniversary at bay.

Her cheerfulness didn't last. Rita moved through the lessons only half paying attention, disciplining when necessary, following the teaching plan she'd devised a month earlier. Mr. Eckles made his staff submit detailed outlines of what they'd be teaching far ahead of time. For once, she was grateful.

"OK, Donald, your turn to recite." She had asked each student to memorize a favorite poem, at least one stanza. They'd been encouraged to ask their parents for assistance in selecting a poem. Donald's grandfather and father were blacksmiths, so Rita was not surprised when the pudgy, red-haired boy recited,

"Under uh spreading chesna tree
The village smith he stands
The smith, a mighty man is he,
With large and sinwe hand;
And the muscles of his bwawny arms
Are strong us iron bands."

Donald grinned, bowed to the class, and looked to Rita for approval. He enjoyed being in front of the other children.

She didn't bother to correct his mispronunciations. That would come later. Instead, she asked, "Do you know who wrote 'The Village Blacksmith'?"

"My mom. She wrote my verse on my tablet so I cud mem'rize it." Donald was squirming now, shifting from one leg to another.

"I mean the poet who put down the words in the first place." Rita smiled as she said this, trying to sound kind. "Does anyone know who this great American poet was? We talked about him in our lesson about Hiawatha and the Indians."

Rita ended the silence: "Longfellow, remember? OK, Donald, you may sit down. That was very good. Let's applaud Donald." She led the class in a loud, enthusiastic round of applause.

Still Donald stood there. "Um, Miss Benet, may I go to the restroom?"

"Why of course, Donald. Here's the hall pass." Rita handed her student the large, worn wooden paddle. Painted in white letters was the label "Room Three."

Donald grabbed the pass and hurried out of the room. The day wore on, and with every hour she could feel her shoulders slumping and her frown lines growing deeper. The student performances which followed were not as good as Donald's, but Rita praised each effort with cheerful remarks: "You pronounced your words quite clearly, Mary Jane;" "I can tell you liked this poem, Susan;" "Good poem selection, Johnny." As she'd left home without breakfast, her stomach began to growl loudly. By the lunch bell at 11:45, she was weak with hunger.

Heavy-hearted, she escaped into the teachers' lounge and opened the sack her mother had packed the night before. The usual contents: a liverwurst sandwich, carrot sticks, and several walnut cookies. Some anniversary luncheon, she mused glumly.

"Hiya, Rita," science teacher Marv Thompson called out to her. "What's up, kid? You look like you just came from a funeral."

"Nah, Marv, I'm just hoping I get a letter from Richard today. It's our first wedding anniversary. Richard fills his letters with descriptions of temples and burning *ghats*, adorable Indian children crowding the streets, and animals right in the city. I don't have much to write about."

Marvin smiled and patted Rita's shoulder. "Hey, it's your anniversary whether Richard is here or not. You can be sure he's thinking of you over there in India. Brighten up—there's people a lot worse off than you. My cousin, for example. Her husband is on the front lines in Italy. He lost his two best friends in gunfire."

Several other teachers sitting around the lunch table chimed in with stories of their husbands, uncles, brothers or cousins. The main idea shared by all was first the importance of the loved one returning alive; secondly, of winning the war. Evelyn, the fifth grade teacher, shed the tears that Rita felt.

Rita reached over to put her arm around Evelyn, whose husband was flying the Himalayan Hump. These brave fliers, Chennault's "Flying Tigers," were national heroes. Newspaper reports depicted this assignment as a virtual suicide mission. Evelyn had two small children at home and no family living nearby. Rita's heart went out to her.

After lunch it was raining hard. When they would normally be running around the playground, the children had to play in the gymnasium. They would be restless all afternoon. Hoping to get them involved in art projects, Rita passed out crayons and construction paper.

"OK, kiddos, now all of you can make drawings to go with the poems you've memorized. Does anyone know what it's called when pictures go with words, as they do in your reading book?"

Patricia, a pudgy girl with curly red hair and freckles, waved her hand. "Billistrate?" she asked. "I mean illustrate."

"Yes, very good. We are going to *illustrate* our poems. The pictures you draw are called 'illustrations.' Parents' night is coming up in two weeks, and I want our classroom to be adorned— decorated—with your pictures. You may go ahead and start."

This was a favorite activity. As her twenty-five students drew and colored, Rita walked up and down the aisles, commenting on each child's work.

Sarah, a pretty brunette with long, silky hair and large blue eyes, was one of Rita's favorites. She could imagine having a daughter just like Sarah. "Is that the 'ancient mariner'?" Rita asked the girl. "He might look even more ancient if you added whiskers."

"What about a long gray beard?" asked Sarah.

"Oh, that would be perfect. By the way, I like his ship, and you've made the ocean look vast and stormy."

"Those are beautiful daffodils, Alvin. Is there going to be a person wandering among them? Will it be you?"

Alvin giggled and started drawing himself into the picture.

"Donald, that chestnut tree looks mighty indeed. Now are you going to add a village blacksmith standing underneath?"

Each student's picture had been praised. The sound of scribbling crayons mingled with an occasional rustling of paper. Heads bent down, fingers busy with crayons, the class was fully absorbed. Rita might have walked out of the classroom and the children would not have noticed.

The idea of walking out was tempting. As much as Rita enjoyed her class and hoped—when an adoption came through—to be a mother, she was bone tired. Half the time she was only present in school in body. Without her husband, she felt terribly alone. She was wasting precious weeks and months of her life.

At least she had the students to occupy the day. She loved the little rascals and could pretend to be lighthearted for their sakes. In Richard's letters, he urged her, "Hold your head high." She wanted to set a good example.

"See, here I am, teacher, walking in the yellow flowers, the daffydills." Like the boy himself, the crayoned Alvin was spindly, a stick figure. "What are *you* drawing, Miz Benet?"

By now, the students were all looking at her and starting to talk among themselves.

Rita held up her sketch of an envelope with wings. "It's a letter from my favorite soldier, Lieutenant Benet. But it's not time to talk now. I'm passing out more paper for you to make a second drawing to take home for your Moms." She deliberately avoided saying "Mom and Dad," as most of the dads were away at war.

"OK, class, we will take ten more minutes to draw, until the bell rings. If you've already finished two pictures, you can do a third one. Before you continue, let me tell you about my drawing. Lieutenant Benet is serving in the China-Burma-India Theatre of operations. He's in a city on the other side of the world—Calcutta, India. He works in a big army hospital helping soldiers who have ended up in the Neuro-Psychiatric Ward."

"Nero what?" asked Alvin.

"I'll explain later," Rita answered. "No one asked me what my drawing illustrates. Any ideas?" No one responded.

"Well, I'll just tell you. My poem is actually a song, and it begins like this: 'Love letters straight from the heart keep us so near though apart'."

Rita felt she'd revealed too much. Even though her students loved it when she talked with them like an adult friend, maybe it was

27

better for her emotional well-being not to share this part of her life. "Now, get back to work on your pictures. We're going to have the best display in the third grade." The radiator sizzled, as though confirming her statement.

The children responded to her very well. Her kindness, inspiration and discipline were paying off. As the recess bell rang, she thought of a perfect idea for later in the week. At the beginning of the school year, Richard sent her class a letter about the life of children in Calcutta. Unlike young children in Findlay, she would explain to them, Indian children didn't have to go to school. It was so hot, they didn't need many clothes; the littlest ones wore nothing but a string around their waists. They had no toys but played with sticks and stones.

After a dreary but mercifully short faculty meeting, the school day was over. Rita's first wedding anniversary would soon be history. Five minutes after leaving school, she drove into the wide driveway on Center Street to the white house with green trim. It was 4:15 p.m., the usual time of her homecoming. To Rita's astonishment, the mailman, who normally delivered letters in the morning, was walking toward her parents' front door. He reached it before she did.

4

On the outskirts of Calcutta, under an orange moon, hyenas howled and the big cats roamed. A band of Indian independence fighters pitched tents. Hoping for a good night's rest before they began their campaign to oust foreigners, the men fell asleep on their mats just as the constellations appeared over East Bengal.

A few hundred feet from the sleepers, two men stood talking under a palm tree. One was East Bengal native Ravi Ghosh, Hindu leader of an extremist splinter group of the Indian Independence Movement. The other was a diminutive Tamil named Sanjay Roy. Exhaustion covered Sanjay like a shroud, as he'd walked all day to come to the insurrection camp from the Alipore District. He'd made the three-hour journey from the 142nd General Hospital, where he worked as a bearer. There had been no time to prepare; he made the journey without food, water or shoes. The latter item he'd loaned to his twin, Shubi, to wear at the army hospital. During Sanjay's mission, Shubi would fill in for him as bearer. The brothers had often made a switch before, but it had been a joke. This time was different. This time it was dead serious.

The tree's fronds cast spidery shadows that matched the hushed, furtive tones of the conspirators. Ravi was slightly worried about employing Sanjay as a spy at the hospital. True, as a bearer for the American officer, he was ideally positioned to gain information. Young and generally quiet, Sanjay would fit in perfectly with the hospital's Indian staff. However, they hadn't seen one another since the Mahatma's "quit India" speech.

"You say you have a plan, Sanjay? Please do tell how we are to infiltrate this giant military complex that is so well guarded day and night." Ghosh knew that without inside help, it would be impossible to regain the municipal property. The respected Calcutta hospital had been taken over by an Army Air Force medical facility imported to India from Fiji. It was needed for Ravi's headquarters, for the cause. Nothing less than Indian independence was at stake.

As the shorter man shifted from foot to foot, Ravi spoke to him in tones of civility based more on their past friendship than his present agitated state of mind.

"Sanjay, you must know that even as the British no longer reign supreme in India, so must these Americans be sent packing."

Sanjay noticed a cloud passing across the moon above the tall man's turban and took it as a sign for him to speak.

"Most honored sir, I have no doubt we can in time take back our *bashas* in Alipore. Though I have yet to learn about all of the men at the American hospital, I have already seen that the Americans are very careless. They do not look with sharp eyes; they think that because they are not fighting in the war but are here behind the lines, this allows them *saat kohn maph*."

Ravi massaged his temples with the fingers of one hand. "This is an auspicious situation, yes, but unless we use it to our advantage, it does no good whatsoever. We don't have weeks or months, so we must find a way immediately. It would be well to use our stash of opium from General Aikido to buy an advantage."

Sanjay did not know what Ravi meant but he did not want to show his ignorance. Two years ago, when they attended Gandhi's "quit India" speech, he agreed to work with the tall Bengali as a patriotic gesture. He was willing to do whatever it took to rid his country of the foreign blight.

Inspired by Mohandas Gandhi, he and his friends had always joined in whenever the people chanted their beliefs to the British and Americans, "Quit India," or "India for Indians." Originally intended for the British, the slogan now indicated Americans as well.

If Sanjay had his way, the ousting would be nonviolent. Ravi, however, would train a small volunteer army and have explosives prepared should either be needed. He was a man who left nothing to chance. Educated in England and an ardent admirer of Bengali hero Subas Chandra Bose, Ravi had cleverly worked his way up the movement's ranks. His plan was simple but risky. Close association with the American military personnel stationed at the hospital in Alipore gave him an advantage over equally ambitious colleagues.

His secret allies worked as orderlies and bearers for the American officers—doctors who treated the diseased or shell-shocked American soldiers from Burma. They would keep him supplied with the pharmaceuticals he needed to finance his plans for independence. In return for a steady supply of drugs to keep their troops in fighting condition in Burmese forests and jungles, the Japanese generals paid him handsomely—hundreds of *rupees*, which he would use to feed his men and ultimately overtake the hospital. The 142nd had been a respected Indian hospital before the unfortunate arrival of Americans, and Ravi was determined to return the property to his own people for its rightful use. Long after Sanjay

30

retreated to his tent, the lanky Bengali sat under the full moon, planning, his back against the trunk of a palm tree.

5

The morning began on a harsh note. Benet's optimistic mood was undermined by Warren Blackwell. He'd been assigned to Warren's case on his second day at the hospital. But instead of making progress, Benet sensed that he was losing ground. As he stepped into Blackwell's hospital room, this feeling was confirmed.

The disheveled patient glared at him. "You're no psychologist— I wouldn't let you analyze my cows!"

Benet was prepared for such a reaction. "I wouldn't have time to, seeing as I'd have my hands full with their owner," he replied in a cool tone.

Fist curled, Warren punched his right arm through the air toward Benet. "You stupid bastard, you're the one who should be locked up."

"Sit down," Benet ordered. Despite his small stature, the Army psychologist handled bullies well. He knew that men like Warren were often all show. He'd learned to use his wits in the one room schoolhouse of his childhood, and those early lessons served him well.

Today's thwarted knife attack was the last straw. Bayliss Kennedy, Warren's intended victim, was fearful enough without the latest trauma. Warren walked backwards, away from Benet and collapsed on the edge of the bed. "Damn you to hell," he sputtered. "I don't belong in the nut ward. Kennedy cheated me. He asked for it." Like everything else in this godforsaken theater of the war, Benet mused, even the poker games had turned rotten.

Warren had been trying for weeks to manipulate the Army's release system. He would do anything to go home. Ironically, on the day before he was scheduled to ship out, Warren was involved in a car accident that killed a Hindu boy. Following that, Warren exploded and tried to stab Bayliss Kennedy.

"Lt. Benet, you're being paged," called Nurse Clara Jacobs from the Neuro-Psychiatric Ward's central desk. "Report to Captain McDermott. Lt. Benet, report to Captain McDermott ASAP." Clara, who ruled Ward 51 as directed by McDermott, expected crisp efficiency from everyone around her.

Benet groaned inwardly. How many times had he asked Clara to quietly come and tap him on the shoulder rather than blaring out a summons? Though often called "Mother Jacobs" by the fellows, she could be insensitive as a stone.

Benet signaled to the orderly on duty, a swarthy Bengali. Mahmood was new on the job but seemed to be a fast learner. He wore the white pajama-like uniform of the hospital attendants with a certain regal bearing. His eyes sparkled, which Richard interpreted as a sign of intelligence. Like most of his people, he was polite and slightly deferential.

"You'll have to take over, Mahmood. Give this belligerent fella a sedative if you have to, but make sure he goes to sleep."

Benet nodded his head in Warren's direction. "If you need to, strap him to the bed." He was only half joking about that. Warren was affecting the morale of the entire ward. The psychologist's main task was to rehabilitate soldiers before they were sent back to the front or were be shipped home to the States. It should have been easier. Instead, the ward—indeed, the entire hospital, seemed to be falling apart.

"Ay, *sahib*." Mahmood bowed slightly, his flattened palms held together and barely touching his chin. He sat next to Warren, who seemed frozen, his eyes two narrow slits. Ignoring the Indian, Warren concentrated on sending poisonous looks the psychologist's way.

Benet had an appointment for a "private conversation" with his boss at twenty hundred hours. Glad to escape from the Neuro-Psychiatric Ward, if only for a meeting with McDermott, he stepped out into the furnace of a Calcutta night. The slight breeze that rustled the palm trees was the only other sound besides that of his footsteps on gravel. A few monkeys chattered at each crunch. Ordinarily, Benet, a great animal lover, would have talked some nonsense to them.

Perhaps because he could not communicate with most of India's human inhabitants, he made it a practice to talk with giant crows, monkeys, and even snakes. Tonight, however, he was too worried for such silliness. His mind flashed back to the dangling corpse. Mac dismissed the hanging as a suicide, but how could he have known for sure?

Benet recalled probing for more information. A security official had filed the final report. When Benet questioned the hospital colonel, he was yelled at. Mac's words haunted him: "The case is closed. Do you understand? Any more meddling will be considered a direct flouting of my orders and you will be cited for insubordination. Now, if you know what's good for you, just drop it."

Questions gnawed at Benet. Though it wasn't his job to play detective, the death had been brushed aside too quickly. Something wasn't right.

To make matters worse, he hadn't heard from Rita in three days. Benet consoled himself with the fact that his bride wrote every day, as he did. He told Rita that their letter writing kept him from ending up like his patients. As Benet walked the quarter mile to McDermott's office, he counted the weeks he'd been stuck in this rat's warren, this armpit of the world. Ten... twelve... thirteen.

Lost in thought, he nearly walked by McDermott's *basha*. In the short time since he'd been here, he'd grown to detest *bashas*. Though the word sounded romantic, like something out of Rudyard Kipling, in reality the *bashas* stunk. Straw huts, mused Benet, that's what they had lived in, exposed to dust, bugs, fierce heat. The game here, however, was to act as if none of that mattered. Those who planned to make a career of the United States Army Air Force maintained the farce.

Benet could hardly wait to return home to wife and love. So, he just pretended, for self-protection, to be serious about an Army career. Underneath he felt himself coming unraveled. Though he considered himself a patriot and loyal citizen, he detested the military and everything about it. The past few, weary months had turned him into a cynic.

McDermott was sitting in a rattan rocking chair next to a crystal decanter of sherry. Despite the heat outside, a small blaze burned in the fireplace. McDermott's attendant emerged from the shadows with a fresh armload of wood. A small man, who might well be Sanjay's double, the servant gracefully deposited more fuel in the basket next to the hearth, then added more logs to the fire. The servant slipped out of the room on silent feet. Benet began to suspect that this meeting had nothing to do with the dead body, just as though it never happened. Benet thought to himself.

"Well, well, Benet. What took you so long?" James McDermott motioned for Benet to sit in the rocker opposite him. "I'm afraid we have a bit of a situation here. Mohandas K. Gandhi is stirring up anti-British fervor among the natives, and that's overflowed to the Americans here. Right here in Alipore, one of our men was caught in a barrage of rocks. The chant goes 'Quit India, quit India, quit India.' I know you take your therapy groups to New Market. I'm not sure it's safe anymore. I trust you to use caution. If anything happens, you'll be held responsible."

Mac had a well-deserved reputation as a tyrant. Once his mind was made up, he closed his ears to opposing arguments. Any comments were interpreted by Mac as "insubordination."

Benet perched uneasily in the chair opposite his heavyset supervisor. He noticed two details. McDermott's flinty blue eyes were more sunken than usual, and his oiled black hair, slicked back away from his brow, looked like a wig.

"Have some sherry," offered the older man. Before he could answer, McDermott poured a small glass and handed it over. Despite his contempt of Mac, Benet wanted to believe that his boss liked him and respected the work he did with patients. He knew that McDermott considered him naive. In contrast to his impatience to leave the subcontinent, Benet tended to romanticize India.

Mac began a lecture about Indian unrest and the need for more security. As the older man rambled on, Benet found his mind wandering. Instead of listening, the psychologist recalled in detail General Joseph Stilwell's visit to the hospital base.

At the Saturday officers' banquet, Benet was seated next to "Vinegar Joe." He recalled blurting out, "The vine-covered ruins I discovered by the Hoogly River were a vision out of Coleridge." Benet had boldly gone on to quote lines from "Kubla Khan." While most of the dinner guests had stared at Benet with puzzled expressions, the usually crusty General looked amused.

Emboldened, Benet continued, "It is more fascinating than disgusting to wander through the burning *ghats*...I'm amazed at the pageantry of women doing laundry out on the sidewalk, using a spout of cold running water. One wonders how they can get anything at all clean."

After the dinner, Mac had snapped at Benet and apologized to the General for what he called "foolishness." Benet suspected that his commanding officer hated being upstaged. Though the Stilwell episode happened over a week earlier, Benet recalled every detail.

Suddenly Benet realized that he was being addressed.

"Don't you agree, Lieutenant?" McDermott asked. He was leaning toward the fire, elbow on one knee, rubbing his unshaven chin. McDermott's brow furrowed, as though he were trying to find the answer to an algebraic problem. Benet had no idea what Mac was talking about, but he decided to fake it.

"Umm, yes, you're absolutely right, sir," Benet said. Jolted back from imagining his last trip to the banks of the Hoogly River, he tried to recall what McDermott had been droning on about. Unlike most soldiers who were "stuck" in Calcutta, Benet drank lightly, if at all. Ironically, the tiny glass of sherry he'd drunk had clouded his mind. That, and the enervating heat.

Benet pretended that he'd been following the conversation. "Any reasonable man would come to the very same conclusion," he assured McDermott.

"Well then, what should we do?" The hospital supervisor sat up straight and probed Richard's face with his eyes.

"What do *you* think would be best?" Benet questioned. He emphasized the "you," his deep, rich baritone voice making it sound almost reverent.

A log fell into the grate, causing the fire to burn more vigorously. By now, Benet was bathed in sweat, but McDermott seemed oblivious to the heat. It was all Richard could do not to tear off his shirt or open the *basha* door. The latter action would invite a horde of stinging, biting insects, monkeys, birds, and cats. Calcutta teemed with an overabundance of all living things.

"We need to distract the patients from this growing menace," said Mac. "Keep them occupied and continue efforts to rehabilitate. Who knows when we will get out of here? While your personal wandering might be considered permissible, individual outings by our charges must be prohibited. It's necessary to contain the men. It used to be the case that Alipore was safe, considered the 'nicer' part of Calcutta. But the masses are eroding. It's going to get worse before it gets better." McDermott downed another glass. "More sherry, old man?"

"Ah, no thank you, sir. Some of my patients have been keeping me up all night, and I need to retire early." He thought about Warren, hoping that the troubled boy was sedated for the night. "I will go back to my *basha* and work out a new recreation plan that keeps our neuro-psychiatric cases within bounds. Many thanks for your hospitality, sir, and good night."

McDermott harumphed. "Containment. Except for your therapeutic outings, keep the men within limits." Mac waved Benet toward the door with a phony smile. Once his visitor was gone, the Colonel slumped back in his chair and passed out.

Sanjay's lookalike, appearing from nowhere, opened the door just enough for Benet to slip through and closed it tightly behind him. Evening breezes offered a welcome contrast to the inferno of McDermott's quarters. Benet breathed in deeply as he walked briskly down the dirt path that led to his basha. He looked up at the vast sky over Bengal. As though swept out by earlier gales, clouds dispersed to reveal a three-quarter moon and brilliant stars.

Rita would be in her classroom. Back in Ohio, it would be ten in the morning, Benet calculated. Her letters usually came every day, but this week was a virtual drought. Letters were everything. He knew it was the same for Rita and that she needed to hear from him every day. Ruth and Gale, her parents, were kind people, but very strict. Rita must long for privacy almost as much as she ached for her husband.

Benet's footsteps led him past the turnoff to his *basha*. He reminded himself that McDermott's ultimatum to keep within hospital boundaries was for enlisted men only. Didn't Mac more or less say that he, Benet, was exempt? After all, without doing "on-foot research," how would he learn where best to take his patients? Hoping to satisfy his curiosity about a ruin he discovered in the past week, the psychologist headed toward the Hoogly River.

Benet felt a surge of energy, enough to walk for several more hours. He needed these private outings. They were essential to his own mental health. The further he got from the hospital territory, the better he felt. Striding toward the Hoogly River, Benet felt anonymous and almost euphoric.

Not only were these adventures fascinating, they gave him something to include in daily letters to Rita. How many paragraphs could he write about the nightly poker games, the putrid Vienna sausages that sometimes passed for dinner, or the humdrum tasks that filled most of his day?

Leaving the hospital's north boundary behind him, Benet checked his watch. It was past nine, but Andy Anderson, the other clinical psychologist on Ward 53, came on duty promptly at 8:30 every night.

Benet felt a pang of guilt for not explaining Warren's latest episode to Anderson. If Warren awakened, the First Lieutenant would learn soon enough. Insulting remarks were nothing new in Benet's patients, but something in Warren wrenched at his guts. He could still see the meanness of Warren's look as they'd faced down. He would try to put the hospital out of his mind, at least for a few hours.

6

Benet passed stone walls, barricades enclosing the homes of diplomats, civil servants, and officers of the Indian Army. Flowering trees drooped over the walls, spreading their fragrance out into the night air. Amazing, these pockets of beauty and luxury in the midst of a city filled with squalor.

A beggar with no legs scooted over to Benet on a self-propelled wagon. "*Baksheesh, sahib, baksheesh?*" he whined. A thin, gnarled arm thrust in front of Benet's knees. "No family, no work, *sahib*, please *baksheesh* please?"

Under his rags, the man looked to be about 50 or 60 years old. That might be deceptive, however. Malnutrition and disease aged the street people. This wretched soul might be in his twenties or thirties. Most likely he was deformed at birth and trained to beg. He probably supported a family with his meager earnings.

Benet replied, "Nay, *sahib*, nay." Inured to such petitions, he walked briskly on his way. He'd picked up a little Hindi since living in Calcutta and understood the soft curses that followed him. So many hungry mouths in the world, so little one could do.

After going a block west on Judge's Court Road, he turned at Tollys Mala, and wound north on Kidderpore Road. He thought of McDermott's warning about safety, but if he had to stay cooped up in his *basha*, time would weigh more heavily than he could bear. Like one listening to a familiar melody, Benet opened up his senses to the kaleidoscope of the street. Walking in Calcutta, or anywhere in India, a person became part of a vast human river. Barefooted Indian men hurried by with bundles and baskets. Were these delivery men or were they simply carrying all their worldly possessions with them?

Women in brilliant *saris* and gold bracelets, stunning in their dark beauty, drifted by Benet. They traveled in twos and threes. Benet wondered if they were prostitutes, then reprimanded himself for the thought. Though most of the officers visited brothels, he steeled himself against such temptation. Rita was worth everything. He would no more be unfaithful than he would cut out his eyes. Most Indian girls were married off, in a most businesslike manner, as soon as they entered puberty. So why were these women out strolling?

On he wandered, feeling conspicuous and invisible at the same time. Everything was alien to all he'd known or even imagined. It seemed as though he were watching a movie in which he also played a part. If he disappeared into the depths of Calcutta, would anyone have the slightest idea of where he'd gone? Only his roommate Andy might have some notion. When he took the trouble and was sober, Andy was a crackerjack photographer. Just last week, when Benet regaled Andy with tales of the sights he'd seen, the latter declared he would come along and take photographs. Sanjay might miss him. But if he returned before morning, neither one would know.

The moon hung behind the clouds as Benet side-stepped people carrying all manner of bundles. Only the cattle seemed unburdened. As abruptly as it started, the block of relative luxury stopped. Once more, the street was lined with signs of desperate poverty. Ragged people held out gnarled hands for alms. Among the begging throng were children, and they troubled Benet the most. A few of the children were playing musical instruments or dancing. A boy of ten or twelve passed around a cup for coins. A vile stench, wafting east from the Hoogly River blended with odors from the garbage heaps along the road. A human figure struggled to its elbows from one of the heaps, built a small bonfire, and appeared to be cooking a miserable supper.

Benet stepped carefully, dodging cattle, carts, people, and an occasional car. He avoided stepping on feces, trash or lifeless human forms by treading between street and sidewalk. The flow of people grew denser. A man in ashy gray rags hurled himself in Benet's path. Overhead, the moon had come out from the drifting clouds, giving the scene an eerie silver cast.

Benet stumbled over a dead dog, nearly falling into the detritus beneath his feet. He was beginning to give up the hope of finding picturesque ruins or abandoned temples tonight, and the thought of Warren under Mahmood's "care" nagged like a dull headache. He had no doubt that Mahmood would try to follow orders, but there was always a chance that Warren could leave for the latrine and go AWOL. All the blame would go to Benet, of course, and in addition to other punishments, such a snafu would put an end to his nighttime wandering. He felt drained. The combination of fatigue and the sherry he'd consumed with McDermott was taking its toll.

Suddenly Benet grew aware of a low rumble of many voices chanting and wailing. It was a mob, not an unusual event in this teeming country, but surprising at this hour of the night. Usually a crowd meant one of the interminable parades or never-ending religious festivals.

Benet was swept along in a flow of people. Backtracking to the 142nd hospital was now out of the question. He found himself ascending a stone pathway to the Hoogly. At the top of the path, a vast concrete field provided spectators with a view of burning funeral pyres, the *ghats* that Benet had heard so much about. Flames roared fiercely, turning both corpses and their wooden platforms to ashes. He was bathed in sweat. Everyone around him seemed to be in a festive mood, families and groups in animated conversation. In contrast to brown-skinned men wearing *salwar kameezes*, *saris*, or white loincloths, there stood a slender, blond man in olive slacks and a white shirt—another American, or perhaps a European. The fellow scribbled furiously in a notebook, then looked up at Benet.

"Howdy, I'm Chris Shallet, reporter for the *Saturday Evening Post*. I thought I'd be the only foreigner here for the roasting. You look like an Army Air Force type. Aren't you supposed to be back on base at this hour?"

"Yes, it is after hours but things are a bit lax back at the hospital. I'm one of the psychologists heading up the Neuro-Psychiatric Ward, 142nd General in Alipore. Walking around the city keeps me from ending up like my patients, the emotionally unbalanced and psychically shattered."

Benet was careful not to reveal his name. Though Mac was a slacker, he didn't want his other superior officers to know about this evening.

The two men stood for a long moment looking at the scene ahead. Being the only Americans in a sea of Indians created an unspoken camaraderie. Sparks drifted upward into jagged patterns into an inky sky, seeming to blend with the stars. Shallet stopped writing in a pocket-sized spiral notebook and mused aloud, "Those souls are going to the next life. They've just been released to take another form. You know, of course, that according to Hindu belief, ones deeds in this life determine whether he goes to a lower or higher caste."

"You really think so?" Benet asked. "I'm not sure I believe that there's anything at all after death. I decided long ago that I was an agnostic, despite attempts by many to take me to church. I've seen too many so-called religious people who are hypocrites."

"Yeah," Shallet agreed. "I know what you mean. However, I'm here to get a story for the magazine and I've decided to see everything with a 'willing suspension of disbelief.' I'm also conducting my own private cultural survey, gathering material for a book I plan to write when I get back home. That is, if I get back home."

"What do you mean, 'if'? We're all going to get out of this hell hole. This is not even where the real war is being fought. We're just backups. The Army never needed most of us in the first place."

"Oh?" Shallet looked at him wryly. "According to the Indians, none of us should be here. You've heard about the stonings? In the off-limits areas of Calcutta, you know, where the fellas go for brothels, the Independence fighters are throwing rocks and heckling. Last month, a Brit suffered a concussion. Nearly died, so I heard."

Wanting to learn more, Benet pretended that he'd heard nothing about Calcutta's growing unrest. "Has this been going on for long?"

"I heard about it for the first time tonight. I'm sure the brass are trying to keep it hush-hush. You work with the disturbed, the mental cases. I can hardly imagine what this kind of news would do to those fellas who are already on the edge."

"What was the soldier doing, the one who got clobbered?"

"You mean the Brit? If you think he did anything that invited disaster, you're mistaken. He was trying to buy some semi-precious jewels from a licensed vendor. Everyone knows that they're practically giving merchandise away.' The chap was shopping. He's in bad condition at the 20th General Hospital. I heard he might not make it."

Benet absorbed the news and thought for a moment about his own safety. He would never dream of going near the off-limits area, especially not to a shop or business.

"So are you going to write this up in your news report for the folks back home?" Rita would hear about the unrest and worry about him. Benet's worst fear was that his wife would get discouraged and tired of waiting for him, that she might lose her vivacious spirit before he got out of this mess.

"Hey are you all right, man? You look a little stunned. I guess it comes as a nasty surprise to soldiers here in this forgotten theater that they're not being given the full story. Hell, they don't know what's going on in their own areas. Can't see the forest for the trees. There's something else you boys at the 142nd would be shocked to hear. Not sure I should tell you, however."

"I need to know. You said it yourself. My patients are not the most stable human beings. Some of them are right on the edge. If they hear rumors, I have to be prepared to deal with them. It's my duty to stay one step ahead at all times. Besides, how do I know I can believe you?"

"This ain't no rumor, man. It's God's truth. The Indian Independence members here in this black hole of Calcutta are allied with the Japs—they are trying to help them drive out the Brits and also the Americans. They figure it makes no difference to them who comes out ahead. They just want their country back. India for Indians, Yankee go home, and all that jazz."

"So, what's surprising about that? It's what I would expect."

"These Indians are stealing from Army bases and selling black market wares to the Indians who in turn sell them to the Japanese."

"Stealing?" Benet echoed. "Well, I can believe it, but I don't exactly see how."

Shallet kept walking as he talked. Benet followed along, not asking nor particularly caring where they were headed. He was in no hurry to return to the hospital.

"It has to do with territory," began Shallet. "Your hospital occupies an area that used to house the most popular medical center in all of Calcutta. Many of their former staff members are now involved in the Indian Independence Movement. They need headquarters and feel that the hospital would be a perfect locale. They want the building and grounds back, and they'll do anything to get them."

The two men crossed Circular Road on Chowringhee and headed toward the maidan. "Let me get this straight," said Benet. "The natives feel we should move out of their buildings even though the British are already quitting India, which I thought was what they wanted. We Americans aren't arrogant or cruel like the Brits."

"Well, not exactly," Shallet replied. "Maybe you treat Indians well; maybe I do, but many military people act like the natives are just another form of cattle. I've heard reports of Indian civilians getting hit by military vehicles, about officers lifting bananas from the fruit stalls and not bothering to pay for them."

Benet was getting impatient. "Dammit, man, what is this about the hospital and an illegal market? I always treat the Indians who work for our ward very well, and I trust them. No one has ever stolen from me."

"Have you checked your medical supplies? I'm not sure I should be telling you this, but I hear that the Japanese have won over the more radical fringes of Indian Independence leaders. They've convinced them to smuggle out malaria prevention medications, morphine and other pharmaceutical supplies and to sell it to their colonels."

"My God," said Benet. "I had no idea, but now that you mention it..."

"This is how it works: the Indian workers at American hospitals sneak into the cabinets and pilfer; they take the drugs home and then command a very high price from the Japanese. In return, the workers receive money for food and shelter. This supplements the pittance they earn in legitimate wages."

As the two men crossed Lindsay Street, they were back in what resembled the western world, not in America but in England. Well dressed men and women were queuing up outside the Globe Movie Theater, where a neon marquee announced *Ali Baba and the Forty Thieves*, an exotic adventure filled with fantasy.

"What do you say?" asked Shallit. "Let's forget this heinous situation and go to the movie."

"Great suggestion. I'm always listening to the woes of my patients. Escaping for a couple hours sounds like great therapy."

7

Assigning Kopriva to be the acting officer on duty was not a wise move, but Colonel James McDermott was beyond caring. In the correct order of things, it should have been the new man, Richard Benet. Mac had taken an immediate dislike to Benet, and he always trusted his dislikes. Kopriva was a known factor and his loyalty to Mac was almost bizarre. Kopriva was a bit of a dope. He lacked the background to run the 142nd, but given recent carelessness on the part of everyone, things would probably be just about as usual. McDermott admonished Kopriva not to let anyone know his whereabouts, then walked briskly to his well-furnished *basha* on the outskirts of the medical installation grounds. Fortunately, it appeared that none of his colleagues had seen him.

Shoulders slumped and hair awry, McDermott stared into a blackened fireplace. He couldn't remember when he started drinking. It was sometime that day, or was it yesterday? The depression that set in after a fruitless talk with Richard Benet had worsened with each passing hour. As the vodka took effect, his mental anguish diminished. Mac didn't care that the men were beginning to call him an "empty uniform." Thanks to his careful planning, his actual time at the hospital was extremely scarce. How wise he'd been to establish a chain of command that made it easy to delegate responsibility.

Being stuck in this Godawful black hole of India had its advantages, Mac told himself. In the periphery of the "forgotten theater" of war, military rules and procedures that applied elsewhere could be twisted, adapted, and shaped to individual whim.

Slouched in a chair, Mac sank deeper into reflection. He tried to remember the events of yesterday and earlier today. Many were fuzzy memories, but he clearly remembered seeing a dog. Yes, it was a damn dog that shattered his intentions; his recent drunken binge was the dog's fault.

When had he started to slide downhill? It was right after his talk with that horse's ass, Benet. Wasn't that just yesterday? Today began with an intention to stay sober, but by ten o'clock in the morning, he gave in. The mangy dog reminded him of a train accident years ago. If not for the dog, he might have avoided remembering Jessie. The dog brought back that hideous day in 1935 when Jessie ran ahead after his new puppy, Lucifer, and when the train came out of nowhere. Jessie was his brother's son, but Mac had adopted the boy when he was five.

Like a record player needle stuck in a groove, Mac recounted the disaster over and over. Jessie had been especially happy that day because of his new puppy. The boy hadn't let Lucifer out of his sight for a week. He, the dog and Uncle Mac were walking toward the quarry, taking a path along the railroad tracks. When Lucifer sighted a rabbit, he leapt out of the boy's arms, and raced for the rabbit. Like a shot, Jessie ran in hot pursuit. The boy disappeared. McDermott remembered shouting, running so fast he thought his heart would burst, and falling, wrenched with sobs. The train roared by and it was clear that he was too late. Even though May, Jessie's mother, did not blame her brother-in-law, he never forgave himself. A major responsibility, the young life in his hands, and he failed the test.

The vodka bottle was empty; the sun had set. Sitting in the dark, McDermott continued his self punishing trip down a grim path of memories. After Jessie was run over by the train, Mac wanted to die, to trade his worthless life for that of Jessie. He drank to numb his sense of guilt.

When he met a woman named June, warm and soft as her name, Mac sobered up. They fell in love after their second date. June agreed to marry Mac if and when he quit drinking. Vowing to make a fresh start, he lifted weights, bicycled five miles a day, and tried to quit blaming himself for Jessie's death. He finished college and started medical school. June was committed to caring for her aging father, so they agreed on a long engagement.

When America entered World War II, Mac volunteered. He was ten years older than most of the men, but his medical background was much needed in the remote China-Burma-India Theater. In far-flung CBI, the worst diseases and the worst weather in the world, along with suicide missions of flying the Hump or hacking a road through jungles in Burma, had taken a toll. Even though the Army Air Force might have preferred a full-fledged M.D. to head up the field medical unit, they were willing to take what they could get. McDermott sailed for the CBI theater in 1942, serving as a field surgeon in Burma's outposts.

He received a letter from June telling him that she could not wait for him. She was engaged to marry someone else. The rejection threw Mac into despair. Once the 142nd General Hospital had been transported from Fiji to Calcutta, he was transferred to the hospital as a Colonel.

The fieldwork had been so demanding that it left no time to think. For many months, it had been possible for McDermott to keep thoughts of Jessie out of his mind. Here in Calcutta, however, he had more time on his hands. In a matter of days, he relegated the endless paperwork to underlings and started drinking again. He hardened his heart to the softer emotions, to mushy remembrances of the sweetheart who had thrown him over to marry his best friend. It was hard at times even to remember her name. But he could never forget the child he'd adopted as a son. Guilt about Jessie invaded his dreams and lurked deep in his heart.

McDermott had no idea how long he'd been sitting alone in the *basha*, staring into the ashes. There may or may not have been flames in the fireplace just a bit ago. Hoping to unearth some embers, he stirred a poker through the ashes. He roused not even a spark. That's just how I'll be, thought the Colonel, a dying ember, and the sooner the better. Hospital doctors and nurses talked about the loneliness of being stuck in India, ironic since they were surrounded by millions of people. McDermott's loneliness and isolation, however, began long before he was assigned to this forlorn post.

God, would he even be able to stand up after so much vodka? He was pleased to realize that he didn't care one way or the other. Not caring had a liberating effect. In a way, it was relaxing.

He was nearly asleep when Shubi appeared from the shadows. "*Sahib*, would you please for me to build a fire and serve your supper in here?" The Indian bowed his head ever so slightly, then, without waiting for an answer, placed a log on the embers. He poked the log until it crackled and blazed. So, thought the colonel, there were live embers after all.

McDermott pulled himself out of his stupor enough to reply, "No, Shubi, I need nothing. Go." Shubi had been carefully groomed for household work by the owner of a British tobacco company. When his previous employers, the baron and baroness moved back to England, he had found work with the American military installation in Calcutta. Though he at first enjoyed the attention, now McDermott found Shubi's gracious manner irritating.

"Good night, *sahib*."

Shubi vanished into a corner of the room, reminding Mac of the Cheshire cat in *Alice in Wonderland*. Now you saw him, now you didn't. They must take "stealth lessons," these damn natives, he thought to himself. They were beginning to give him the creeps. They were oh so pleasant, ever polite in their oily way. He, for one, wasn't fooled. The natives hated not only the Brits but also the Americans. They were not to be trusted at all. And speaking of trust, he doubted if he could trust that head shrinker Benet to follow orders about staying in bounds or reporting only to him about medical supply levels.

McDermott continued drinking, all the while carrying on a dialogue with himself. Benet was an arrogant bastard. How dare he assume that because he was a psychologist, he was smarter than his Colonel? He yammered on about his Calcutta perspectives, as though he was over here to be a damn travel writer. Just who the hell did he think he was anyway?

The night before, McDermott had walked into the Officer's Club to find Benet entertaining the men with his observations of Calcutta's street life. The so-called psychologist was laughing at his own impressions of human "beasts of burden" carrying a piano on their collective backs. The audience was entranced. As McDermott approached this cozy bunch, he'd heard his name followed by raucous laughter. Making fun of him behind his back, were they?

As his internal monologue raged on, anger roused the hulk of a man to his feet. A smile crept across his face. He would take his own "tour," following a route such as Benet would take. Fortunately, Benet had spoken quite publicly about exactly where he liked to walk.

Tonight something told him that Benet might have ignored his suggestion to stay in bounds. Men like that often lacked backbone. If Mac's suspicions proved correct and he caught the psychologist out of bounds, he would need to discipline him severely.

First things first, however. Mac badly needed to empty his bladder. Before reaching the door to the bathroom, he staggered and nearly fell. His head was pounding, but so what? He refused to let some snotty little fruitcake make him look bad.

He'd take a hike, that's what he would do. After relieving himself, McDermott tore off his clothes and turned on the shower full blast. His heart pounded as he stepped under a cold stream and turned around three times until his skin was soaked. He put his head under the spigot and felt icy water pouring through his thick mane of black wavy hair.

8

After five minutes under an icy spray of water, Mac dried off, put on fresh khakis, and gulped a couple aspirin. He reheated a pan of strong coffee and drank it, burning his lips and tongue. He chuckled at the thought of putting Benet in his place. He'd see to it that that arrogant fool would never again be able to sit at a table next to General Stilwell. He wasn't quite sure how, but Mac felt that his walk "out on the town" would give him an advantage.

When the hospital commander stepped out of his *basha* into the steamy Calcutta night, he saw Shubi walking along the main path that ran throughout the rambling complex of *bashas* and wooden buildings.

Mac hid behind a palm tree and waited until the Indian was out of sight. Five minutes of silence assured him that there were no passersby to notice him. Mac strode briskly out of the Army Air Force complex onto Chowringee and toward the off-limits area. He ignored the throbbing of his temples and the waves of nausea churning through his stomach. *Damn fool, you should know better than to drink yourself stupid.* None of the McDermotts could hold their liquor. His own worthless father had died from cirrhosis of the liver.

A whiff of fruity perfume drew Mac's attention to several women walking across the street in the opposite direction. Their brilliant silk *saris* dazzled him—saffron yellow, royal blue, scarlet, and kelly green, all of the garments trimmed in gold or silver. Little could be seen of the actual women inside these garments. It was obvious, however, that they were young and slender. Their faces, the color of *cafe au lait*, were exquisite, their eyes dark and soulful.

Though Mac didn't know for sure, he assumed that these were young widows who had been ousted by their families. In this country, women were married off at thirteen to a husband chosen by the family and very soon started bearing children. Widows often had to sell their bodies in order to live. Their beauty would fade rapidly and life on the streets would soon kill them, but for now, they were like beautiful new butterflies.

The girl in royal blue brushed next to him, looking up with a smile. "What you want, you buy, *sahib*. You name, I do. Anything you like, five *rupee* only." She took his gnarled hand in her tiny one and tried to lead him to a low door in the nearby stone wall. Her skin felt like velvet and her grip was cool and firm. *She must be about fifteen, maybe even twelve.*

"Nay, *memsahib*, nay." He brushed the girl aside and strode on quickly. Fortunately, the women walked the other direction in search of customers. He'd heard stories of the Indian pimps beating up men who refused their prostitutes.

In his haste, he'd failed to apply bug spray. He slapped in vain as mosquitoes bit his neck and ankles. *Forget about the cultural tour; I've got to get inside somewhere, anywhere.* As if reading his mind, a tall Hindu in a billowy white *curta* and jodhpurs appeared alongside and asked, "*Sahib*, where is it you would like to go? Please let me help you find your location." The man seemed too aristocratic to be on the streets wandering around homeless. But then he, McDermott, was out here as well.

The Hindu apparently knew western ways. He held out his right hand to Mac.

"My name is Ravi Ghosh," he said. "I usually am called just 'Ravi.' Calcutta is my home and my place of business. I'm what you might call an entrepreneur. Having said that, I am free this evening to escort you. Calcutta is a vast city, and many parts of it are dangerous."

Mac felt he must explain his presence as something other than a desire to bring back impressive stories for the hospital staff. "Uh, well, I was looking for a well-known Chinese restaurant somewhere in this neighborhood ... um, the name escapes me. I'm Colonel James McDermott of the 142nd General Hospital, United States Army Air Force."

Until the words came out of his mouth, McDermott didn't realize that he was starving. Because of his drinking session and the funk he'd fallen into, he'd missed the last several meals. *Damn jackass. Get a grip, man, get a grip.*

The stranger reminded Mac of his father's brother, Uncle Leonard, who'd been like a father to him. His biological father, Thomas, was a sad excuse for a parent. The old sot used to ask Mac to hide his empty whiskey bottles under the house.

The irony of his own drunken state did not escape Mac. He was just sober enough to keep up with the swift walking of his Bengali companion. He wasn't quite sure why, but Ghosh put him at ease. There was none of the usual skepticism Mac would feel toward a stranger.

Mac was pleased. This was the first time since his arrival in Calcutta that an Indian had been anything other than formal. Though he hadn't planned on going to dinner, why not ask this fellow to join him? Later, he would be able to irritate Benet by relating the entire evening. Benet constantly boasted about his "just wandering around, a stranger in a strange land." But here he was, U.S. Army Air Force Colonel McDermott, actually socializing with a native.

The hospital director and the Indian independence leader walked in silence toward the maidan. "Well, here we are," said the Indian. Mac looked around: no restaurant in sight. They were standing in front of a residence with high white stuccoed walls and a gate of dark carved wood. Palm trees peeked out over the walls.

Ghosh smiled at McDermott's confusion. "I think you will find the dinner at my home better than any of the restaurants in Alipore. I hope you brought with you a large appetite."

Mac was amazed at the warmth of Ghosh's invitation. As curious as he was about seeing an Indian home, however, he put up a show of polite resistance. "I'm sorry, but I don't understand. We only just met. I think I'd best not accept your invitation just now. Perhaps when we know one another better, it would be more appropriate. I must get back to the hospital." From everything Mac had been told, Indians stood upon formality. It took weeks, months, years to gain a dinner invitation. Why was he being welcomed at such an early stage? Either Ghosh's gesture was wildly inappropriate or Mac was misinformed.

"Oh, but of course you think this too forward of me." Ghosh had pressed a buzzer and the wooden gate opened slowly to what looked like a miniature version of the Taj Mahal. "But I assure you, such hospitality to foreigners does exist in my city."

"Do you mean to tell me that this is your home?" Mac asked.

"I must explain. My beloved wife Uma died of cholera recently. For now, I am living with her parents. Uma's younger brother Narendra has just been accepted to an American school but he is refusing to go. He fears his English is not good enough. We tell him that his speaking is quite good enough, but he will not listen. If you converse with him and compliment him on his English, I feel sure that he will be convinced. What's more, I am not one of those Indians frozen in time and refusing to change. I like the modern ways. My friends will most certainly envy me for having entertained an important American official."

Mac accompanied Ravi Ghosh to the front door. "Pardon me for asking, but what if Narendra's English is not good? What do I say then?"

"Oh, not to worry. You will see. My nephew attended a British school and he speaks very correct English. He simply needs to gain confidence. When he sees your uniform and learns that an officer from the American military hospital approves of his speaking, that is all it will take to, how do you say it, 'muster his courage'."

Once inside, Mac was captivated. The American swung his head around, toward the mirrored walls, down to the gleaming gray and white marble floor, overhead toward the series of rotundas inlaid with brilliant mosaics.

"I've never seen such grandeur."

"Ah yes, I see that you admire my late wife's family home. It has been theirs for generations and alas is only a shadow of its former splendor." Ghosh did not explain what had happened to cause the decline.

"The women have retired to their quarters for the evening as they are preparing for the wedding tomorrow of a young cousin. They are sewing her wedding garments. So it will just be you, Narendra and I for dinner. But of course in the military, you must be accustomed to being with men only."

Ravi and Mac entered a small dining room adjoined by a sitting area. A fire burned in the marble fireplace. Servants brought out glasses of hot tea. One of them whispered in Ghosh's ear.

"Ali wants me to tell you that our religion does not allow alcohol," said Ghosh. "He fears that you Americans do not like to drink tea."

"Not true," Mac lied, "I like tea very much."

The rich, spicy aroma of curry wafted through the air. "I hope you like our cuisine," said Ghosh. "Shrimp Curry is our chef's specialty, and—fortunately for you—he has not made it extremely spicy tonight. I'm told it will be ready in about ten minutes. In the meantime, have more tea."

"So where is your nephew?" Mac inquired after the third cup of tea.

"Ah, yes, my nephew Narendra," said Ghosh. He spoke in Hindi to one of the servants who nodded and after a few minutes ushered in a svelte young man in a white linen suit of European cut. Mac guessed that the lad was around twenty years old. He had a full head of glossy black curls. His eyes were a deep brownish gold.

51

"My new friend, Colonel James McDermott," said Ghosh. "Meet Narendra Chatterjee, my extremely intelligent and ambitious nephew. He has been accepted at Columbia University in the United States to begin pre-medical studies. Colonel McDermott is the chief officer at the 142nd General Hospital for the U.S. Army Air Force and he will be joining us for dinner tonight."

Narendra and McDermott shook hands. The young man had a firm, cool grip. "Honored, I'm sure," he said to the older man, with a slight bow of his head. Like his uncle, he was darkly handsome. He resembled a movie star that Mac couldn't quite name. The young Indian spoke English with a British accent.

In the luxurious surroundings of Ravi Ghosh's home, Mac felt himself relaxing. It was good to be away from the hospital, the patients, and the officers both below and above him in rank. *Amazing*, he thought to himself. He'd just met these people and yet here he was, enjoying the best evening since he'd arrived in India. A real advantage of being hospital commander was the relative freedom the position allowed. No one knew he was here, nor would they—unless he chose to tell them.

Ravi, Narendra, and Mac sat at a sleek table of dark wood. They were far apart on three sides of the large rectangle. A centerpiece of intricately patterned brass held dozens of candles. Mac could see very little of his companions' expressions; only their dark eyes were distinct. The rotating overhead fans—with their "swoop, swoop, swoop"—were hypnotizing him.

Silence was broken by occasional polite conversation. Heavy incense wafted from the room's dark corners along with an odd aroma that Mac could not identify. The fans' rhythmical fluttering reminded Mac of jungle breezes flapping huge leaves in the Burmese forest near Rangoon. What a contrast, he mused. This wasn't a jungle, but a dinner party.

At last the food, in great abundance, began to arrive. Men in turbans served platters of curry, rice, tandoori chicken, several kinds of flat bread, and a multitude of sauces and chutneys.

"Yes, I'll take more tea," Mac said to the waiter hovering over him.

Eventually, small talk began to flow. "I'm a loner," the American confided. "I run the hospital with an iron hand, and to do that, I must distance myself from the other men. It's lonely but effective."

"As for me," Ghosh said, "I am a businessman, or as you Americans put it, an 'entrepreneur.' I went to Calcutta University for a year but the life of a student was not for me. My skills were best suited to managing."

"Managing what...?" Mac started to ask. As if he hadn't heard, Ghosh arose and walked to a cherry cabinet against the wall. He opened the top, which held a record player.

"I thought we might enjoy a little dinner music," he said, placing a 78 record on the spindle. "This is my favorite sitar player. Ishmael Roy is his name."

Ghosh indicated to one of the servants to turn off the player after the record finished, then he rejoined Mac at the dinner table.

Though the Bengali had mentioned his daughters Chitra and Arundati being somewhere in another room, there was no sign of them. McDermott was hoping to at least catch a glimpse. He imagined them in an ornate women's quarter with silken draperies, brocade-covered overstuffed chairs and servants pouring tea. He'd especially hoped to meet the daughters.

Compared to the stark atmosphere of the barracks, the dinner party seemed like number one in *1,001 Arabian Nights*. Though the alcohol of the earlier bender had worn away, Mac felt lightheaded.

People often accused him of being a Jekyll and Hyde, and tonight that's just how he felt. The man who dealt harshly with underlings at the hospital was gone. The beastly superior who delighted in making Richard Benet feel stupid was but a memory. In his place was a transformed Colonel Mac McDermott, a gracious *bon vivant* who mingled well with upper class Calcutta natives.

A mango pudding was served for dessert. "Everything tastes wonderful, and I really have not had the chance to try authentic Indian cuisine until now," Mac said to his host. He wanted to add, "To what do I owe this enormous favor?" but he decided to put off questioning. The strings would, no doubt, appear.

Once again, Ghosh seemed to read his guest's mind.

"Ah yes, the possible exchange, which is by now what you must suspect was behind my invitation. You Americans are—how shall I put it—predictable. You always imagine that life is a ledger sheet, when it is not at all that simple. Before we talk business, won't you join me for something quite special, a little sample of Bengali hospitality?"

Mac didn't know what to say. He didn't want this evening to end, so he remained silent. Narendra pulled his chair out from the table, stood up and, touching his fingers to his chin, put his palms together. He bowed his head slightly.

"Excuse me, Uncle Ravi, Colonel McDermott. I must leave you gentlemen for an appointment with my medical textbooks. Colonel *Sahib*, thank you for gracing our household with your presence."

Mac remembered the earlier matter of Narendra's English pronunciation. It was odd that no one had mentioned it. "The pleasure was mine, Narendra. You should do very well in American college from what your uncle has told me. You speak English fluently and with perfect correctness. Best of luck with your studies."

Narendra bowed again, and with a final "*Namaste*," was gone.

"And now, *sahib*," said Ghosh, "please follow me to the den. If you do not wish to partake, that is up to you, but I urge you to experience one of India's most sensuous pastimes. Very few Americans are invited into the inner chamber."

"Do you mean sex? I'm well supplied with *rupees*," Mac asked. Immediately he realized how inappropriately he'd spoken. But it was too late; the words were out.

Ravi Ghosh turned around and grinned. Though the light was very dim, Mac detected a slight, knowing nod of the head. Sweeping aside any doubts, he suddenly felt happy. Maybe he would be able to enjoy India at last. He walked faster.

The house comprised a far-reaching maze of rooms. Mac imagined silken bedrooms where the Indian women of this charming family must be residing. Perhaps there was another chamber for the concubines. Not wanting to appear unsophisticated, he refrained from asking exactly what the "pastime" was. He merely followed the Bengali through yet another dark hallway.

The American felt a stirring in his loins. How very kind it would be of Ravi Ghosh to share a mistress with his new friend, a lonely, sex-deprived soldier. After all, wasn't sex a universal language? Even if he had to pay, there was nothing so bad about that. He could afford it and no one at the hospital would ever find out a thing.

The sounds of sitar music wafted through the hall. Ahead was a door outlined in thin shafts of light. "Enter the den of paradise," Ravi announced as he ushered his guest to the strange room.

The occupants were not women but men of various ages, all reclining on little couches and smoking pipes. Most appeared half asleep; some were catatonic.

"Can you sense it," asked Ghosh, "this feeling of drowsy bliss? Yes, it is bliss, but to quote that famous English opium eater,

Thomas DeQuincey, 'These men have found a panacea for human woes, the secret for happiness, peace of mind and the key to enhancing one's mental faculties. Wine robs a man of his self-possession; opium greatly invigorates it.' Shall we join them, my astonished American friend? Shall we too be invigorated?"

McDermott stifled a gasp. He tried to think of a way to leave, something he should have done hours ago. He was curious, of course, but he could not risk losing his position as hospital director. His rank was all he had; detest it though he often did, the military was his life. And yet, Ravi Ghosh was beckoning him to a lounging couch.

"Please get comfortable. Don't worry if this is your first taste of paradise on earth. I will be here to help you and all you need to do is ask. You might want to loosen any clothing that is tight or binding so that absolutely nothing impairs your enjoyment."

"Thank you so very much, but I must decline your kind offer." Looking at his watch, Mac moved with small steps toward the door. "The dinner was glorious. I enjoyed it; I was happy to meet your nephew Narendra and have no doubt that he will be very successful in college. His English is top notch."

The smile was gone from Ravi's face. "But you cannot go now. It would be an insult to me and everyone in my family. Besides, as you will see, it is not possible for you to leave."

A giant of a man dressed in khaki *curta* and leggings stood by the door. He was wearing a gun belt and a menacing expression. A black turban, heavy sideburns, mustache, and beard added to his sinister appearance. McDermott recalled hearing something about the wearing of a black turban, but he couldn't remember its significance. Losing all hope for an escape, he tried to think of what to do. If he revealed his distress, it would make matters worse. So, he would have to smoke opium to get out of this mess. For the first time in a couple hours, Mac recalled his original purpose, gaining a cultural perspective and possibly finding Benet. If ever a mission had gone awry, this was it. His thoughts had become muddled. For one of the few times in his life, Mac wasn't sure what to do.

Walking away from the exit door with a falsely casual air, Mac resumed talking with Ravi. If only he hadn't looked frightened at seeing the armed guard, he could pull this off. There was no way to tell from the Indian's face if he suspected that his "guest" had tried to make a getaway. To heighten the air of nonchalance, Mac loosened his shirt collar. He and his host walked back toward the dim light of the "smoking section," the Indian in the lead.

Clearly there was no escape now that he was actually going to indulge. Mac let go of his doubts and decided he might as well pretend to enjoy it. In truth, he was growing curious. "I must tell you, I'm totally ignorant of the mystery and art of opium-taking."

Guided by his host, Mac reclined on a chaise lounge. He took a long puff of the opium pipe that several devotees of the drug were also sharing. Instantly, he forgot about everything else; he was flooded with an incredible sense of mental exhilaration.

Time passed, and it all began to seem perfectly natural. Why shouldn't he be right here at this very moment, sharing the pipe with his new friends? Mac was privileged, an honored guest. He owed it all to Ravi Ghosh, a man he'd never seen before this morning but who would surely be part of his life from now on.

His immediate companions, strangers just a bit earlier, were his new best friends. Wordlessly they puffed on various opium pipes, communicating by thoughts and subtle nuances of movement: the brush of a hand, nod of the head, a sigh or shift in position. All around Mac floated musical utterances in a language that he assumed was Hindi. He lay, at rest, smoking and listening.

"How are you, my friend?" Ghosh appeared at the side of his couch and gazed down at the limp, dazed American. "It appears that you like our after-dinner custom. I will desire very much to know how you feel tomorrow. I have found that the day succeeding my indulgence in this luxury is invariably a day of amazingly good spirits."

"Fine. I'm very good. I can't remember feeling this happy for years. I like listening to your servants talking in their native tongue. You know, don't you, that the less you understand of a language, the more you hear the melody of its sounds." It was impossible to speak further. Mac closed his eyes and sank into a dream.

9

The hours floated by, as did Mac's childhood. He saw himself at seven years old, when his mother died of tuberculosis and his father hired a housekeeper to take care of the children. He remembered how the housekeeper stinted on the food she allowed Little Jimmy to eat. That was his nickname, Little Jimmy. He recalled the horrific stomach pains that plagued him and the feelings of unworthiness he suffered because of his father's neglect. Once again he replayed his shock and sadness at the death of Jessie, a loss that he felt he had caused. Every memory was fraught with pain, and yet he was able to review these events dispassionately, to merely observe and let them go. He was floating, flowing outside his body, looking down at himself.

Figures drifted in and out of his consciousness. Ravi—he could call him "Ravi," for surely by now they were on a first name basis— was just one of the Indians who made sure he was comfortable. Another brought him a goblet of water to drink. The Indians became tiny figures in a vast panorama, and it seemed to Mac that they comprised a frieze of tiny Asian potentates, painted in miniature and portrayed on intricately detailed wallpaper. As the figures became smaller, he could hear his own breathing.

It seemed that he had never breathed in life as he did now. With each breath, something new appeared on the blackboard of his mind. Lurid scenes from his past returned to Mac as vividly as though they were yesterday. He saw through ugly gray dust to the home of his childhood, a small coal town in West Virginia. He saw himself as a little boy in overalls treated as a burden by the adults around him. He realized now that his father blamed him for the family's problems. He felt the ache in his buttocks from being whipped, remembered the panic as he attempted to hide. He ached for the little boy who felt such a desperate inner loneliness. Tears flowed down his cheeks. Ravi came forth from the wallpaper with a soft handkerchief. In real life, Mac would have been embarrassed to share such a personal moment. But this was not real life.

Mac puffed on the opium pipe. When he was too lethargic to do it on his own, hands reached out to help him.

He saw himself as a young Army Air Force reserve officer, felt the enthusiasm of the day he volunteered and was picked to serve in the medical corps. Thrilled at the approval he gained at following orders and being an important cog in the machine, he rose quickly through the ranks and became a Colonel after heading up the 142nd General Hospital in Fiji. It was only when the hospital staff was ordered to transfer to Calcutta that things began to unravel. Not wanting to dwell on that chapter of his life, Mac ceased reviewing his past and relished the halcyon tranquility brought by the pipe. Days and months, weeks and countries flowed through his mind.

The next reverie took him to the greenest of jungles. He was walking on a path surrounded by roots and the mossy trunks of huge trees. Branches and dense vines draped over each side of the path. He walked alone, not knowing exactly where he was going but drawn forward with an almost sexual feeling of anticipation. Ravi was here again. Ravi, it seemed, was a friend he could trust completely, someone who had his best interests at heart. He would never be alone again.

In Mac's forest, the trees grew closer together. Greens turned darker, almost black. A chill had arisen and he began to shiver. Overhead, a monkey shrieked, a doleful sound of warning. Monkey sounds answered from every tree. Mac's feelings of anticipation changed to dread. Perhaps it was not a friend he'd met, but a sly enemy. Now, instead of feeling cold, he began to sweat.

The monkey sounds ended abruptly and were followed by an ominous silence. Mac could barely see the path. He walked anxiously to avoid tripping on roots or rocks; he placed his feet very carefully on the dirt, one in front of the other. The new friend had been a figment of his imagination, wishful thinking. The silence was replaced by a loud wind, and he felt incredibly alone and vulnerable. He put his hands out to feel the wall but his fingers met vines and hanging moss.

A bloodcurdling snarl echoed through the air. He looked up just in time to see a huge tiger crouched on a boulder just a few yards ahead. The enormous beast was brilliant orange, its black stripes dark as tar. Angry at Mac's intrusion into its world, the tiger bared its fangs and snarled. Mac made himself invisible. Now he could see without being seen.

Somewhere outside him, a voice recited the poem he'd memorized in high school. "Tiger, tiger burning bright, in the forests of the night." Once he had known the entire poem, but this was all that came back to him. The glimmer of happiness brought by just that one line vanished in the pain of forgetting the rest of them. The missing words expressed something about symmetry, burning fires, stars throwing down their spears.

Struggling, Mac retrieved one line, then another, trying in vain to put them in the proper order. In the process, he lost the tiger. The jungle was gone, the opium den had disappeared. Maybe they had never existed. He blacked out.

The next thing Mac knew, it was dawn, and he was somewhere in Calcutta. From the back seat of a moving car, he could hear Ravi's voice and that of a stranger. They spoke Hindi, so there was no way to discern anything from their conversation. Where were they? Were they taking him back to the base?

Mac lay on the back seat trying to put together the pieces of the night before. He remembered nothing of getting into the car. He'd have to ask Ravi what was going on. Very slowly he rose to a sitting position, nearly bumping his head on the metal grating separating him from the front seat. The man with Ravi wore a black turban exactly like that worn by the guard at Ravi's opium salon.

Mac's head was throbbing and his mouth felt as though he had walked for hours in a desert. He cleared his throat, affecting a calm he did not feel. "Um, how long have I been asleep and where are we going? You're taking me to the 142nd, right?"

The two men in the front seat glanced at one another. Mac heard a metallic click and strained to look over the back seat. The turbaned one was checking his gun. Maybe he should offer them money. On the other hand, from the looks of Ravi's dwelling, it did not seem that money could be his objective. Despite his determination not to panic, Mac broke into a sweat. No one knew where he was. He could simply disappear into the murky, chaotic depths of Calcutta.

As his escorts continued to talk heatedly, Mac heard them repeat the word "morphine." When the car passed the Royal Calcutta Turf Club and cut over on Circular Road to Russia Avenue, he realized they were headed toward Alipore District and the hospital. They stopped a couple blocks away from the *bashas*. Ravi spoke at last.

"*Sahib*, you had a quite interesting journey, and lucky for you, we are looking out for your best interests. We are nearly at your headquarters. No one will know that you have been smoking opium. But before we deliver you to your door, I must ask you one small favor. It is not really a favor, for if you comply, I promise that you will be able to once again be transported into that most pleasant blissful state. I will be blunt. Allies of our independence fighters are sick and dying in the jungles of Burma. We need morphine and a lot of it. You will supply us and we will provide not only generous payment in *rupees* but all the opium you desire. Our transaction will be completely confidential." He paused, "You may take your time to answer and when you do, speak very carefully."

Slowly, Mac thought over Ravi's words. He lay down and pretended to doze. Dawn was ending. It was growing lighter outside. The hot Indian sun would soon turn the car into an oven. Mac apparently left his watch somewhere, but time didn't matter. Because he was known to be a loner, he probably would not be missed. The challenge was to rid himself of his two Indian escorts.

Sitting up, he rolled down the back seat windows, filled his lungs with the damp morning air and returned Ravi's bold stare with an insincere smile. The guard clicked his revolver trigger once again, making it clear that Mac was a prisoner and that if he wanted to escape alive, he had no choice but to cooperate.

Ravi drove the car very slowly toward the hospital grounds. "You see, I am taking you right to your door, *sahib*, but you will not be released until we are sure you will help us. Unless you bring us several hundred milligrams of morphine, my brother Ashok is prepared to shoot you."

"But this is blackmail," Mac said. "I was simply accepting your hospitality. You can't force me to play your game. Release me this minute!" He tried the handle to the car door next to him, but it was locked. Ravi had stopped the car and Ashok was pointing the revolver through the grating directly at Mac's head. Unlike Ravi, he was not smiling.

Both Ravi and Ashok stared at him expectantly. Even though the pre-dawn air was cold, sweat continued to pour down Mac's brow. Once the sun was up, it would be harder to slip into the hospital unseen, remove the morphine from the locked medical supplies, and appear at the officer's mess in time for breakfast. He could not let anyone know about last night. He could be court marshaled, expelled, sent to prison.

By this time Ravi had driven the car to the hospital grounds entrance. "I see your reasoning," Mac said. "You just wait out here and I will quickly bring back the morphine you need." Maybe he could alert the Military Police and make up a story about being forced to join in the opium den; they could come back and arrest the two Indians. Who was he kidding? He might never move beyond this whole rotten mess.

"Not so fast, *sahib* McDermott," said Ravi. I will go with you and no one will take notice. As I have relatives who work at the hospital, I am often here to bring them food or clothing. You see, with my flowing garments, I can more easily carry our medication out. Also, I have so much room in my *curta* that I can even carry a knife." He lifted his tunic and opened a leather case. The knife gleamed in the sunlight. Ravi placed the knife by Mac's Adam's apple and drew a thin line of blood, then grinned.

"I will walk with you, understand? Or perhaps slightly behind you."

Feeling nauseated, Mac nodded his agreement. He suppressed the urge to vomit. "Yes, of course. But if we do not move quickly, it will be more difficult. We will arouse suspicion. Let's just get on with it."

Ashok opened the back door, his gun held in one hand. Ravi was right by his side. Mac nearly fell out onto the pavement as he got out of the car, then began walking. He could feel Ravi right behind him. He waved past the guard and continued toward the hospital's main building. Thank God, the morning wakeup alert had not yet sounded and the grounds were still empty.

Having felt nearly comatose in the car, frightened during the interrogation and the forced "deal," Mac was now filled with relief. He was beginning to hope he could put this unfortunate episode behind him. Ashok stayed in the car as Ravi escorted him through the hospital entrance. The two men, Mac reflected, did not look at all like brothers.

Ravi was tall and lean, aristocratic in appearance. The truth slowly dawned on Mac. Ashok was short and quite stocky; his skin was much darker. No doubt the entire "family" story was a hoax, a masquerade. Narendra, the hidden wife and daughters—it was all pretense. Ravi was probably a political activist, a chameleon who changed skins whenever he needed to hide.

Mac cursed himself for getting snared. If only he'd stayed on the base, he might have avoided the entire debacle. However, what was done could not be undone. It was just as well to get the requested medicine and get the Indians out as quickly as possible. He had no idea if or how soon he would be "paid." The fact that they would be reimbursing him primarily with opium rather than money made the transaction seem legitimate. He could justify medicating himself. He could no longer endure the hospital, Calcutta, and India's horrific climate without an "attitude adjustment."

Mac had seen men drift into madness just from being here. Madness and suicide: they were not that uncommon. But now he could transcend such mental weakness. How long would it be before he could again move so smoothly from pain to Nirvana? He walked slowly, anxious about the theft he was about to commit. What if someone saw him? It would be just like that jackass Benet to pop up out of nowhere.

"Just keep moving," hissed a voice. Ravi pressed the blade of his knife next to Mac's neck. All illusions of freedom vanished. Mac was a prisoner, a victim of his own stupidity. He could do nothing but comply with the wishes of Ravi and his minions. The only way out of this nasty situation would be for the war to end with orders for shipping out. As soon as the hospital was demobilized, the Indians would lose interest in him and what he could supply.

The rising sun was beginning to warm the soggy air. Monkeys shrieked from the treetops. Although becoming more visible in the growing light, the *bashas* remained silent. The hospital commander and the Indian reached the brick building that served as the hospital's headquarters. A *Gurkha* kept watch at the door. When he saw McDermott, he saluted. A puzzled expression swept over his features at the sight of the colonel's disheveled appearance and the tall Hindu following so closely behind.

"At ease, Ram. This is my friend, Ravi Ghosh. He's from the Independence Planning League, here to inspect the hospital. He'll make sure any changes headquarters have made will not affect conversion to peacetime use for the 142nd. That is, when peace finally arrives."

Ram, who knew very little English, bowed his head in deference and opened the door for the two men. Mac's bogus explanation had been for the benefit of Ravi. It was very important not to arouse suspicion. In the future, Mac thought to himself, he would have to think of another way to get supplies to the Indian. They would have to devise a system. He was not a man used to being controlled in such a way. How could he have been so trapped? If only this were a bad dream from which he could awaken.

Walking in tandem, Ravi and Mac reached the hospital's supply wing. Mac produced a ring of keys from his pants pocket. Morphine syringes and refills were kept in a separate refrigerated room, along with perishable medications and blood for transfusions. For a brief moment, he considered pushing Ravi into the room, locking the door and calling for help. The thought quickly died. Ravi's greater height and strength would make him the winner in any contest. Mac, not Ravi, would be trapped in the refrigerator room. What's more, once Ravi told Peterson or Stilwell about the opium den experience, Mac's credibility would vanish.

They entered the medicine room's arctic chill and Mac started putting vials into a cloth pouch. "How much did you say you need? Or did you say? It might be better to start with a small amount, as it will arouse less suspicion."

Ravi's thin cotton garments were completely inadequate in the cold. The Indian was shivering. "If you can promise to increase your supply by ordering more, why don't we begin with three dozen vials?"

McDermott was enjoying the Indian's discomfort, so he moved slowly in filling a cotton pouch with the morphine vials. "I'll send a telegram to Bombay tomorrow to double our supply. I can blame it on an epidemic here in Calcutta. For all I know, there might really be an epidemic."

Ravi unsheathed his knife and polished the blade on his tunic. "Hurry up," he growled. He touched Mac's jugular vein with his knife tip. "If you don't hurry up, I'll do more than nick you. Just give me the morphine and let me get out of here." He held up the knife and returned it with a flourish to a leather sheath. "I love to use this, but I'd hate to use it on you. Just do what I tell you and I'll never have to."

Furious, Mac gritted his teeth. There was nothing he could say. He handed the bag to Ravi and watched as the Indian tied the top of the pouch to the drawstring on his trousers. Covered with his billowy tunic, the extra baggage did not show. It was impossible to tell that he was carrying anything.

Back out in the hallway, the two men parted with grim expressions. Ravi strode outdoors and across the hospital grounds. Ashok was ready for him. He revved up the black Ford coupe, Ravi folded his long limbs into it, and they shot off into the awakening streets of Calcutta. Mac watched the Indians drive away, then sought out Lieutenant Kopriva at the officers' mess.

A low edifice near the administrative headquarters served as cafeteria, Officer's Club, and (when rain drove the evening entertainment under cover) a movie theatre. Mac's head was pounding and he was beginning to shake violently. The day was growing hot, but he had chills. Stomach pains warned him of impending diarrhea. It would be necessary to find a bathroom soon or he would disgrace himself in front of everyone.

Kopriva, a man Mac liked as much as he detested Benet, was sitting at a table with several pals. Intent on chow, the soldiers were plunging forks into steaming platters of scrambled eggs and bacon. Kopriva was startled at McDermott's wild disarray. He jumped up quickly when the colonel called him for "a word in private."

A few stares followed them as they walked out of the main dining hall into the foyer.

"Look, old man, I'm not feeling too well. I accepted a native's invitation to dinner and I think I got some food poisoning. Either that or I forgot to take my Atabrine and have a touch of malaria. Can you fill in as officer on duty until further notice?"

Kopriva could hardly contain his delight. He hopped about like a bantam rooster. What good fortune to hold a position of authority, even if it was temporary. He liked and admired McDermott and had tried in vain to win his approval. This was the opportunity he'd hoped for.

"Yes sir, thank you sir. I will be diligent and watchful, stern and authoritative, and though no one could ever fill your shoes, I will keep things in ship shape until you are back at the helm. But, sir, are you OK? You look sick. Are you sure we shouldn't call a medical officer from the wards to come take care of you? Shall I escort you to your *basha*?"

"No, Kopriva, I'll be fine," said Mac. "I just need a few hours sleep. My bearer takes good care of me. If you want to send a nurse to check on me this afternoon, that would be fine. What about that new woman, Clara Jacobs? Just don't let that jackass Benet start making decisions. He's the type that likes to run things. He doesn't know how to stay within his boundaries and I think he's taken a great dislike to me. I know I can count on you, and I'll see that your extra responsibility will be aptly credited at promotion time. Just proceed to the headquarters and place yourself in charge. You have my full authorization to make decisions."

"Yes sir, thank you sir," Kopriva repeated. He stood taller and walked briskly in the direction of the hospital's main building.

As soon as his junior officer was out of sight, Mac leaned against a tree and retched. Everything from the night before—the dal, curry, tandoori chicken, pickled melon, mango pudding, and rice—all came up. Next, he raced to the latrine and released his bowels. He was dizzy and covered with sweat when he finally emerged.

Thankfully, no one was around to witness Mac's suffering. Though Mac was tempted to call Kopriva back to escort him to his quarters, he thought better of it. He needed to be alone. If anyone at all detected signs of his opium indulgence, this whole miserable situation would blow up in his face. As it was, things were just barely manageable. It was all he could do to stagger into his *basha*, lock the door behind him and stagger to the toilet to once again relieve his bowels. He crawled on hands and knees to his bed. The chills had returned. He let Shubi remove his shoes and cover him with several blankets. The last thing he remembered hearing before passing out was the crackle of a fire in the hearth.

10

Benet awakened on Monday trying to remember the name of the reporter he'd spent a rather odd evening with the previous weekend. Was it Mallard, Shifflet, or something like Pallet? Finally it came to him: Shallet. He'd enjoyed the man, especially when Shallet wanted him to share his impressions of Calcutta for a newspaper story, "East meets West: American G.I.s in India."

As was his custom, Benet mentally composed the day's letter to Rita. He would describe the entire evening to his wife, and he'd tell her to look for his name in a *Saturday Evening Post* article sometime in May of '45. Writing was his therapy. Though he probably wouldn't be able to actually write his letter until tonight, even imagining pen to paper brought him solace.

Enough of such thoughts, Benet told himself. The Army left no time for one's personal life. Slapping his bare feet on the wooden floor, he stood up, stretched, and quickly pulled on his khakis. Soon, maybe by next week, he would move to better quarters, and to his relief he would be able to take Sanjay along. Despite their cultural differences, he'd grown to depend on the quick-witted little man.

"*Sahib*, do you have mail for me to post?" Sanjay appeared just as Benet adjusted his CBI shoulder patch and straightened his cap. As always, the Indian's appearance seemed abrupt. No slamming of a door, not a click or knock. He was simply there. Benet genuinely liked his bearer, but this trait was most annoying. Indians, he decided, simply did not make a production of arriving or departing.

Benet wondered if he would ever understand these natives? They moved like cats, but that didn't mean they had anything to hide. No matter what happened he was determined to like the Indians. It was a matter of pride that he rise above the condescending, arrogant contempt that most of his colleagues seemed to hold toward natives of the subcontinent.

This was the first day of Benet's group psychotherapy sessions. After the upsetting confrontation with Warren Blackwell, Benet was eager for another chance to test his skill as a therapist. He opted to skip breakfast at the officer's mess and amble on over to Building Q, the hospital's administrative center. It was rumored to have been named after Lord Quentin Quigley, the British Colonel who first negotiated with Calcutta officials to take over the hospital for use by the Allies.

66

The group therapy room was on the second floor of the hospital's only large building, a giant in a field of *bashas*. It was the first time Benet had been in the large brick edifice since the interrogation following the death of Calvin Brothers. It was even uglier than he remembered.

When the U.S. Army Air Force converted the Indian establishment for use as an Army hospital, they stripped away all the inside finishing, and painted the rooms and hallways moss green, the floors beige. Furniture was at a minimum: occasional tables and desks, wooden chairs with rattan seats. The windows were covered on the outside with wrought iron bars. Benet wondered if the bars were part of the previous hospital or if they'd been added on by the Army's construction crew.

The psychologist stationed himself at a huge, bare-topped metal desk and took a sheath of papers out of his briefcase. He looked over the names on his list, soldiers who'd been recommended by the doctors in charge of their wards or who were directly under his care in the Neuro-Psychiatric Ward. More might be added, or some who'd been assigned might not come today if their physical conditions did not allow. He'd find out. There were six names, each followed by a brief handwritten note.

Group List for September 12, 1944/ Clinical psychologist in charge: Lt. Richard Benet.
Ted Sturke- age 20, hepatitis and bronchial infection. Carried his buddy a mile on the Ledo Road to discover when he reached his squad that his friend was dead. Guilt-ridden, wishes he had died. Blames himself that his friend didn't make it. Unable to sleep, no appetite.
2. Miles Fletcher ("Fletch") - age 19, severe malaria. Sole survivor of a flight over the Hump. Nearly starved to death, lived with the Chindits for six months, went native and experienced delusions of grandeur with the natives thinking he was a god. A facade of cheeriness masks depression. He's trying hard to get better but can't seem to think clearly and often has flashbacks of the crash.
3. Gus St. John - age 22. Imprisoned in Rangoon for several months. Starved, tortured nearly to death. Is suspicious of everything, afraid the food is poisoned, avoids contact

with the men. He claims that the others
persecute him, talk about him etc. May need
individual counseling.
4.   Isaac Martinez (Ike) - 21. His first
assignment was guarding a ridge near
Myitchina. He had to bury two of the original
six patrollers, carry another soldier weak
with dengue fever. Two suicide attempts.
5.   Warren Blackwell - 24. Has been trying to
work the system for a release for three
months. Recent accident that resulted in death
of a Hindu boy has thrown him into a manic-
depressive state. With medication, he could
interact and eventually be able to benefit
from group therapy.

At 0845 hours, shortly before the group session was scheduled to begin, Silas Lowell came into the room. The psychologist recognized him as his joke-cracking seat partner during their endless train trip from Bombay to Calcutta. "Si" was just as short and fat as Benet remembered him, but this time the Sergeant wasn't smiling. His normally ruddy complexion was white and drained. He moved like a frightened rabbit. Benet looked up from the list of his patients.

"Lieutenant, sir, excuse me for barging in like this," began Si, "but there's a situation that someone needs to address and I cannot locate Mac or Kopriva or anyone for that matter. I've questioned the orderlies, those that know a little English, and they claim to know nothing about it. There are men in Ward 30 in pain, sir, and we will not have enough morphine to treat them and as far as I know there will not be any supply trains coming in for another week and..."

"Calm down, Sergeant. What in God's name are you talking about? What's happened to the men in 30? Has there been an accident? I've got some disturbed men coming in any minute now and I don't need you up here spluttering like an idiot. Now just tell me in plain English what happened?"

Still standing at attention, the Sergeant took a few deep breaths. "Sir, I'm talking about the disappearance of morphine, a very large quantity. One of my duties is to handle reordering of medications and when I reviewed our supplies this morning, I noticed that over half the morphine was gone."

Benet frowned, made a few notes, and glared at Si. "Can you come back at 1200 hours and we'll look into this together? Chances are, there's just been a little rearranging and a portion of the morphine has been placed elsewhere. In the meantime, I suggest that you inform Colonel Mac. I'm sure he will investigate thoroughly. I'd like to help you, but as you can see, I really don't have time for this."

Si looked crushed. "But sir, I'm the one who is charge of arrangement, inventory and reordering. I've got strict guidelines about how much of every medication, every bandage, and every tourniquet. Someone might think I stole the missing drugs."

"Good grief, man, don't you understand that I have a group to lead? Keep looking for the Colonel; he's bound to be somewhere here on the base." Benet glared at Si and lowered his voice. "My group is due any minute. I'm trying to create a calm, non-threatening atmosphere for them and your hysteria is making that impossible. Report back at 1200 hours. Now get lost."

As if to punctuate his ultimatum, Benet glanced up at the large wall clock on the wall across from his desk. It read 0900 hours exactly. Just before the arrival of Ted, Miles, Gus and Ike, Si trudged from the converted classroom.

The quartet of men stood at the door, each saluting Lt. Benet and announcing himself.

"Ted Sturke, sir. Merrill's Marauder's."

"Sturke" was too small to have carried a dog for a mile, much less a man, Benet remarked to himself. He stood very erect, as though he were about to head up a parade. It's a wonder he didn't have back problems as well as bronchitis.

Even before the patient gave his name, Benet knew which one was Gus St. John. Sunken eyes; a blank, drained expression; and slouching shoulders revealed the man's suffering. On top of that, he was ridiculously thin. In a barely audible voice, Gus spoke his name. Following Sturke's example, he chose a spot in the small circle. He literally crumpled into a chair.

Ike was nervous as he checked in, his voice rasping, as though he couldn't get enough air. He looked around anxiously as though a tiger were hiding behind the desk or in one of the corners. Odd, since the room was nearly empty and probably the safest place in Calcutta at the moment. Benet took the swarthy fellow's hand and shook it warmly.

"Welcome aboard, Sergeant Martinez. Think of this room as your safe haven, a ship to sanity. I'm in charge and my only goal for our sessions is to help you. I'm glad you're here today."

The last to introduce himself was Sergeant Miles Fletcher, taller by a head than anyone else in the room. He wore a goofy smile and spoke with a Southern drawl. "So yer the capin of this ship, sir? I thought we were in the Army, not the dang Navy. Ah plum fergot to bring my life preserver and ah never learnt ta swim." He laughed a horsy "Huh,huh,huh" that triggered sniggers from the assembled company. Benet welcomed the laughs. It was pretty lame, but better weak humor than none at all.

Benet took a deep breath, wondering how he would achieve the right level of informality to keep the men comfortable and yet maintain discipline. As Professor Dinegar, his role model at Ohio State University, would put it, he'd learn by doing. Except for Gus, who stared at his lap, the men were looking at him. Did he detect wariness or was it just expectancy?

The silence had lasted long enough, so he jumped in. "Welcome men. We're going to be very informal here, so when you come in on future Mondays, sit anywhere you like." Benet glanced at his roster. "Has anyone seen Warren Blackwell?" he asked. Blackwell was on the list to join the group, as he was recently reassigned to the A-section of Ward 55. "A" was for the soldiers who were less mentally and emotionally unstable. The "B" room was referred to as "The Madhouse."

Blank looks met the psychologist's question. He felt a twinge of anger that no one told him Blackwell wouldn't be attending group therapy. Just like Mac, whose "command" grew sloppier by the day.

"OK, this is the U.S. Army Air Force group psychotherapy meeting number one. As you know, I'm Lieutenant Benet, clinical psychologist. Today we will tell stories, true stories, your stories. You have three responsibilities here. Number one, be honest. The purpose of our sessions is to help us deal with what we've been through, to get it out and move beyond, to look at life in a positive rather than a negative way."

After he started talking, Ted, Miles, and Gus avoided looking at him. Only Isaac met his concerned gaze. *I want to help you*, he voiced silently to the men, hoping that sincerity came through in his voice.

Benet raised his voice for emphasis. "I won't prescribe techniques to elevate attitudes or grow stronger in character: each one of you will do it in his own way.

"Rule number two, you must swear to keep what is exchanged in this room during these sessions completely confidential. Any breach of confidentiality will be dealt with by Colonel McDermott, who reports directly to "Vinegar Joe" Stilwell. You know who I mean, the

General in charge of the land route across Burma. As you know, they've changed its name from 'the Ledo Road' to 'Stilwell Road'."

Even Gus looked up at the mention of the tough-as-nails leader, who'd marched 113 people out of Burma, 100 miles in 21 days, not losing a single one. Stilwell loomed larger than life: a curmudgeonly infantry man who wore his World War One helmet for special effect.

Fletch raised his hand. "Sir, may I guess what our third rule is?"

"Why of course, Fletch, what is our third rule?"

"We need to lissenup. Every fella gets to have his say."

"Right, Fletch. We're talking about respect. I don't care if you're bored or you don't want to be here. Your duty is to listen to the other guy; to let everyone have a chance. You've heard of the Golden Rule? Do unto others as you would have them do unto you. I'm not saying it's easy but that's what I expect and that's what I will demand. OK, who wants to talk first?"

To Benet's surprise, Fletch didn't volunteer. The four men looked at their therapist. The time was getting on, as they'd used up twenty minutes of the ninety. Benet would have to call on someone. "We'll go alphabetically, by first name. OK, Fletch, tell us about you."

Fletch sat up straight, pulling his lanky frame out of a slouch. Unlike the rest of the men, he was far too tall for the metal chairs. "Well, I reckon I'm jest about the only man here from south of the Mason-Dixon line, grew up on my pap's farm outside Durham— that's in North Carolina—had dreams of studyin' for veterinary. Always did love animals—wild, farm critters, cats and dogs, birds, you name it. When the call came to help our country win the war, I and jest about every fella in the county enlisted."

If they all rambled like Fletch, there wouldn't be time for everyone. "Fletch, that's a good start," interrupted Richard. "How many of you did what Fletch did, enlisted rather than waiting to be drafted?"

The three others raised their hands. "That was the thing to do, wasn't it? We love our country and we want to protect it and our families. We're patriotic, courageous, not afraid to fight for what we believe in," said Lt. Benet.

Gus stared at Benet. "What about you, Doc? Did you volunteer?"

"Well, I was already enrolled in something that I believed in. Unlike anyone in my family, I was in graduate school at Ohio State University. My dream was to teach young people, to set them on fire for learning. I'm 33, an old man compared to you. I got my Ph.D. in

71

psychology and my draft notice the very same day. I was glad to serve America, but life as I knew it had to be put in the deep freeze. But we're not here to talk about me. Fletch, what happened to you in Burma?"

The goofy smile vanished and Fletch looked as though he'd been slapped.

"I think I told everyone my story already but here it is again. I was part of the Flying Tigers. It was my second flight carrying supplies over the Hump; we hit a monsoon rain and couldn't see a thing. Suddenly we lost altitude and that's all I recall. Maybe my position on the right side of the plane saved me. I was guarding a mule to keep him from kicking through the plane's wall.

"Toward the end, I was holdin' on to old Jack's neck. That was the mule's name, Jack for Jackass. Anyway we landed in some kind of rice field. Not sure it was rice, but it was a bog. When I came to, a few hundred yards from the smoldering carcass plane, Jack was gone and I knew all my buddies were dead."

11

Tears trickled from Fletch's eyes; his lips turned down at the corners; he began to tremble. The men looked away, no doubt worried that they too would break down when their turns came. It was time for Benet to intervene.

"That's OK, man, it's not going to be easy for any of you to tell what you've been through. You don't have to get everything off your chest all at once. Let's all practice a relaxation exercise. You may close your eyes or leave them open. Breathe deeply. Inhale slowly ... in, in, in; now exhale very, very slowly. Let's just do this for the next few minutes. Then we'll go on to Gus."

The room became still. Benet closed his eyes. He heard the mingled breathing of his group, and outside the window, the cawing of birds. They were probably the large raven-like creatures he'd been observing ever since his arrival at the hospital. The breathing technique was one he'd used on himself for many years. It never failed to calm him. He hoped the effect would be the same for Fletch, Gus, Ike, and Sturke.

"OK, open your eyes now and take one final very deep breath. Now, Sergeant St. John, we are ready to hear from you."

Gus started to say something but was interrupted by a loud, harsh cough that emanated from deep in his chest. Fletch went to the water cooler and brought Gus a tin cup of water.

Gus's voice was faint. Finally he began: "After being separated from my patrol, I was a prisoner in Rangoon. I was best at reconnoitering and that's what I was doing when I was captured. There were land mines everywhere and a huge explosion behind me. I'm not sure if the men in my patrol were killed or not. I never saw them again. I tried to find a way out of the jungle but even if I'd been able to, I had no communication with headquarters in Myitkyna. The natives found me first."

With a deep sigh, Gus continued. His voice had grown softer and once again Richard had to ask him again to speak up. "I was tied up and marched along with other Americans and Europeans to a place that makes hell seem like a vacation resort. We were locked up in a native prison. Most days we got a handful of rice. Some days, nothing. There was just enough water to keep us alive. We worked on building walls and digging pits from morning 'til night. If you stopped from exhaustion they lashed you with whips or beat you with canes. We weren't allowed to talk to one another."

Another cough interrupted Gus. "I wanted to die; we all did. Every bit of hope was beaten out of us. The bastards made sure we couldn't end the torture. They took away anything that could have been used for suicide. I got so I couldn't imagine a life after the prison. I knew that no one at home would ever understand what I'd been through and that I would hate them for not understanding.

"I hated myself and I wondered why I'd been born. All I wanted to do was to escape at night by sleeping and every morning I awakened with a sense of dread and fear. All I could think of was how I was lower than the wild pigs that came by to watch us laboring, lower than the monkeys and hyenas, the ants and spiders. I envied them because they were free. I tried to kill myself by eating dirt but a guard caught me and beat me unconscious. The next day, I still had to work twelve hours in the blazing sun. I came to realize that there were worse fates than death."

"OK, Gus, that's enough for now," Benet intervened. "I appreciate your candor. I can hardly imagine what you went through. You'll be able to tell us more as time goes by, but we've got only another half hour. It's your turn, Ike."

"W-W-Well, I'm n-n-not useta sp-p-peakin in-in public," Ike managed to get out. "I I was f-f-free but all m-my buddies d-d-died." The soldier had begun to sweat heavily. He looked at Benet with a silent appeal.

"Would you like me to share what happened to you with the guys here?" asked Benet. "If you're nervous talking in front of them, you can just listen, talk only when you feel like it, and rely on me to help you."

Ike nodded his head. "Y-Y-Y-Yes. I n-n-n-never ust-ta st-st-stutter but but after th-th-the jungle t-t-time I I I s-s-started."

Benet understood how death and isolation in the jungle could rob a man of his reason or at least of his ability to express his thoughts coherently. Some soldiers, such as the late Calvin Brothers, lost their speech entirely. Others sank into lunacy, such as a pitiful case isolated in Ward B. The soldier ripped off whatever clothes were put on him and sat crouching naked in the corner of a cement cell. In an effort to keep Ike from ending up like that, Benet did his best to tell the man's story for him.

"Ike was the lead soldier of an intelligence patrol," he began. "Three O.S.S. men and three tank soldiers were posted west of

Myitkyina on a ridge overlooking the Japanese encampment. Just before the Allied takeover, the Japs initiated a grenade attack. The men were outnumbered and they wanted to keep their presence a secret.

"They escaped injury and raced down the north face of the ridge, hid in caves, and waited out a monsoon to try connecting with their patrol. Their food was gone and they had nothing but bark and insects to eat. They became separated and wandered for days. Ike here had dengue fever, malaria, insect and rat bites. He was lying under a tree, alone, waiting to die, when the reconnaissance team found him..."

"Hey Doc," interrupted Fletch. "When did this fella tell you all that? He don't talk so good and the way you're tellin' it, he's got total recall. Was he the only guy you found of the lost patrol?"

"Good question, Fletch. The day after we found Ike, we found his best friend Ralph trying to start a fire to cook a mongoose he'd trapped. Ralph had managed to keep a notebook describing everything for a report in the event they got out alive."

The group was silent as all imagined the plight of the straggling patrol members. No doubt every man could imagine himself in that scene. If there was anything Benet would remember about his time with these men, it would be their sad faces.

Gus seemed to be taking an interest in the stories. He stared at Benet with deep eyes, a look that conveyed suffering beyond tears. Benet struggled to control his own emotions.

"How come Ralph ain't here?" Gus mumbled. "Looks like he should be, seein' as he's the one kept the diary."

"Ralph needed intensive care," Benet replied quickly, "I heard that the medics took him to the 20th General Hospital where they have a better blood bank and larger morphine supply." The truth was that Ralph died during the medical airlift from Myitkyina. Benet made a private decision never to mention that fact, certainly not to Ike.

The closeness of death was a realization Benet shared with his patients. He, as the therapist, the healer, was supposed to maintain professional objectivity. Sometimes Benet wondered how he could do this. In a mystical transfer, he managed to avoid cynicism by pouring his heart out to Rita each day. It was almost as though feeling thoughts of love warded off the chill of death.

Gradually, the men began talking among themselves, an activity that Benet desired. Part of the healing that might come for them would be through interaction and the realization that they were kindred spirits. Not for a minute did Richard suppose that he had answers. At best, he hoped to tap into the higher selves of his charges, to help them find inner strength and, despite everything, the will to go on living.

"What I'd like you to do is notice when you're remembering those stories. Just notice. If you feel like talking about it, that's what this group is for. It is perfectly normal to be deeply affected by what you lived through. It will take time to get over it. Remember that nothing any of you have said is to go outside the group."

The men squirmed in their chairs. Gus, Fletch, and occasionally Sturke, were carrying on whispered conversations.

Benet stood up to regain attention. "If you'd like, you can come to my office in the next couple days to talk with me in private." He cleared his throat, and the chatter stopped.

"We'll be back here Wednesday and if I can arrange for a vehicle, we'll take our first tour of the city on Friday. It will be more or less a route outlined by the American Red Cross. Any questions? No? Okay, put your chairs back against the wall and head for the mess hall."

Silas was standing right outside the door, just as he'd promised, but before Benet could talk with him, he had to make sure the men were out of hearing range. The wall clock had stopped at 1100 hours but Benet's watch read only ten minutes until noon, the official end of the group session.

Five minutes later, Benet and the Sergeant were descending into the cellar level of the Q Building. It was silent except for the sound of their Army-issue shoes on the linoleum floor and a distant "scritch, scritch."

"Si, what's that scratching noise? Is this building infested with rats?" Benet stopped in order to hear better. "Listen. Don't you hear it?"

The younger man scratched his crewcut. As both men stood listening, it occurred to Benet that the nickname he'd like to give Si was "Silo," a combination of "Silas" and "Lowe." He'd think of some tactful way to introduce it—maybe when they went out sightseeing next Wednesday, that is if Si were assigned to him.

Finally Si heard the sound. "Yeah, this place is real old. I'm sure all kinds of critters make their homes in the walls. I heard a rumor that it dates back to the Punjab War and the cellar was used to hide soldiers and arms. Well, anyway, we're almost at the supply room. I've got the key."

There was only one problem with Si's explanation, Benet thought to himself. How could they possibly hear rats through the cinderblock walls? Benet noticed that the walls were an ugly yellow, the same color he detested from the Psych Building of Ohio State University. He half expected to walk past the rat lab, where he'd spent too many hours while working on his dissertation. The "scritch" started up again, bringing Benet back to the present.

"It sounds as though we've got rodents in the wall," Richard commented. "This place is so old, it's no surprise. Someone told me that the original hospital was established around the turn of the century. It's probably seen many generations of rats."

"That's no rat," Si exclaimed. "It sounds more like a giant monkey. Who knows, maybe part of this basement was closed off. Well, anyway, Doc, here we are at the refrigerator room." Silas pulled a large ring of keys from his pocket and unlocked first an outer, then an inner door. He reached around inside the door and turned on florescent lights. A blast of icy air greeted them.

"We gotta move fast as we'll get numb in a hurry if we stay in here long, Doc." Si pointed to some metal shelving labeled "Pain Suppression." On the top shelf were large bottles of aspirin with simple black and white labels. Unlike the aspirin in stores, they were Army brand. Analgesic salves and ointments lined the second shelf. The third shelf had just half a dozen vials labeled "Morphine."

The Sergeant waved his arm toward the empty shelf, all the while looking intently at Benet. "Just last week, this was full. Why the rush on morphine? Now do you believe me?"

"Yep, I see what you mean, Si. I see why you're worried about this, but there's got to be an explanation. Maybe we're shipping morphine out to the field hospitals. Maybe we've had more amputations and surgeries at the 20th General Hospital. Did you do as I asked and track down Mac, I mean Colonel McDermott?"

"Well, sir, I did, but..." Si's voice trailed off.

"Yes, and what did he say? You did ask him, didn't you?"

"Um, well, um, I waited for an hour. You know that pip-squeak Kopriva, the sneaky so-and-so he keeps by his side? He was outside Mac's *basha*, sort of guarding it, and he said the Colonel was ill and not to be disturbed."

The two men were shaking with cold. "I've seen enough in here and my feet are going numb," Benet stated. "Let's continue this conversation outside."

They walked out of the refrigerated room back into the hall, Silas locking the two doors behind him. He forgot to turn off the light, so he had to open the doors up again, turn it off, and re-lock. A large rat scuttled by their feet. It disappeared down the hall into the shadows.

"You're right, sir, there are rats down here," said Silas. "At least one rat. It looked huge."

"Sergeant, we don't have all day. Stick to the business at hand. In answer to your question, I know who you are talking about. Everyone knows Lieutenant Kopriva. Do you mean to tell me you only talked to that fool, not the colonel?" Benet knew as soon as he asked that this was the case.

"Sir, the colonel was meeting with General Stilwell. He couldn't be interrupted and besides, I didn't have an appointment. Lieutenant Kopriva said that it would be any minute and I kept expecting to get in a word or two. Finally it was time to come to the group psychotherapy room and report to you."

"Hmmm. I'll look into this myself, Si. You did your best. Better go line up for chow. Report to me before Friday."

A brisk salute, and the short, stubby man was gone. Benet ambled over to the officer's mess. Something was distinctly fishy about this situation. He hadn't let on to Silas, but it was highly unlikely that "Vinegar Joe" Stilwell had slipped into the hospital without the officers being briefed. What's more, Kopriva, the skunk, had behaved oddly. It was as though he were trying to hide something.

If some culprit were stealing, it would be best to find out and stop him. If supplies were being shared with another hospital, he needed to know. The medical supply inventory was outside his jurisdiction, and he might be sticking his neck out. Nevertheless, Benet would speak to the elusive hospital director at the first opportunity.

12

As he did every night, Benet ended the day with a letter:

Calcutta, India
20 September 1944

My dearest,
*It was another sweltering day here at the hospital and I don't
have much to report other than moving to new quarters, which I
described rather fully to you in yesterday's epistle. Apparently the
clinical psychologist who was supposed to be my basha mate came
down with dengue fever and is still in Fiji. He was too sick to make
the journey, so it looks as though your adoring husband will have
complete privacy for the foreseeable future. The better, my sweet, to
write you at all hours while listening to our military radio station.
You know, don't you, that you are my first thought every morning
and my last image at night before fatigue wins out and I collapse
with relief to dream of you, just you.*
*Remember how I wrote to you after Monday's psychotherapy
session that I thought the men would improve much more rapidly if
they had hobbies? Of course, they didn't like the idea and said I must
be thinking this was the Boy Scouts. Well, I ignored their skepticism
and forged ahead with my ideas. Well, 'mirabile dictu', as Professor
Dinegar used to exclaim, Fletch took me literally and now has a pet
cat. Can one call a cat a hobby? In Fletch's case, one can and does.
The striped orange creature looks like a miniature tiger, though I
suspect it is some hybrid variety of alley cat.*
*Fletch brought his feline friend (he's named him "Nelson") with
him to the group on Wednesday. The cat is somewhere between
being a kitten and an adolescent. My patient spends all his time
brushing Nelson, making cat toys out of strings and sticks, trying to
get Nelson to play, and finding food that a cat would like. He seems
thrilled to have something loyal to him. The other men passed Nelson
around and petted him, all except for Gus, who said he hates cats. Of
course Gus hates everything. I wouldn't be at all surprised if the
others looked for cats or some kind of creature to adopt. Anything to
snap these fellas out of their utter discouragement and boredom is
mentally healthy.*

Along those lines, we go tomorrow morning on our first sightseeing tour in the city. I told the group that we might have a chance to shop at New Market for Christmas gifts to send back to the states. While it may sound too early to be thinking about Christmas, as you and I know, there is no telling how long a package will take to travel halfway around the world. I have several ideas in mind for you, my sweet, and whilst we amble through the stalls of wares, I will take mental notes so as to give you a complete description of the possibilities.

But even before we shop, my beauteous one, I plan to have our driver take me to Calcutta University. As you remember, Dina Pavri, my friend from the Ohio State days, told me that I should observe some of the university's teaching methodologies. She suggested in particular that I should visit the English Department, where she had many friends. In fact, Dina was an English professor for several years before she decided to study clinical psychology in the states. She was interested in establishing a Guidance and Counseling Department at Calcutta University. Well, at any rate, I will invent some reason why we should make a stop there on our way to the shopping area. Come to think of it, I don't really need to invent a reason. The men will be so glad to get away from the hospital and out on what seems to be a lark (ahem, a therapeutic lark it must be noted), that I imagine they won't care where we go.

But, my beloved, I have rambled long enough and now I must say goodnight.

All my love and devotion,
Your faithful husband, Richard

13

Even at 0750 hours, the day was hot enough to undo the effects of Benet's morning shower. Sweat poured from his face as he walked to meet his charges in front of the Q Building. Would he ever get used to India's scorching temperatures? Sturke, Ike, Fletch, and Gus waited under a palm tree. Benet had joked with the men about not being a Boy Scout leader but that's exactly what he felt like just now. Everyone but Gus seemed jolly. The former prisoner of war smoked one cigarette after another, coughing between puffs. His eyes were more sunken than usual.

"OK, fellas, we're going to New Market. On the way, we'll stop in Calcutta University. I need to look up a fellow student from my graduate school days. I might also try to locate a swimming pool in that area but there may not be time. Swimming will be good therapy for all of us, especially in this heat. All I could get for our outing was a truck. You can pile in the back and have a better view that way."

As he spoke, a dilapidated Army issue pickup arrived in a cloud of dust. That damned Kopriva was driving, Benet noted with disappointment. Kopriva was a fawning sycophant to Mac. Anyone but Kopriva would have been casual about the stop at Calcutta University, but now, he was sure, Kopriva would bring the matter up to Mac and he'd have a lot of explaining to do. No matter. Plans were plans, and he would follow through with what he set out to do.

They set off for Chowringee amidst bullock carts, bicyclists, pedestrians and all manner of automobiles, rickshaws, and wandering cattle. Of the last group, some cows had wearied of the traffic and settled down for a snooze right in the middle of the street. Kopriva drove wildly, Benet thought to himself, especially considering the case of Warren, the young soldier who'd gone mad because of accidentally running over a Hindu boy. But since their survival depended on Kopriva, he kept his comments to himself. No point stirring up the driver.

After ten minutes of careening in and out of traffic, Kopriva pulled up to a complex of white buildings surrounded by a grassy lawn and a wrought iron fence. A sign announced "Bethune Girls' College, Founded in 1848 by the Honorable John Elliott Drinkwater Bethune."

"A Girls' College?" Benet asked Kopriva. "I instructed you to make our first stop Calcutta University." He leaned his head out the window and yelled at the four soldiers in the truck bed. "Just stay put, men. I don't think we're at the right address."

Kopriva looked at Benet with a weary expression. "This is the only Calcutta University I know. The Girls' College is one of its branches. The specialty here is English, so you can probably find someone who knows your friend or at least who can tell you how to find her."

Benet changed his mind about leaving the men with Kopriva. Instead, they entered the college grounds and walked *en masse* toward what looked as though it might be an administrative building. Before they reached the imposing edifice, Benet practically ran into an attractive girl with long blond curls and wide set blue eyes. She smiled brightly at him.

"Excuse me, sir, we're the hostesses. My name is Marion and we're here at the invitation of the fourth year English students for a luncheon. May we help you find your way here at the Girls' College?" The speaker, obviously an American, wore a sky blue uniform. Her companions wore similar garments. They seemed quite energetic. Benet had heard of the "hostesses," whose duties consisted of writing letters home on behalf of the soldiers and assisting them in other ways.

Benet felt like removing his officer's cap and bowing. Instead, he motioned his entourage and tried to explain their unusual appearance on the campus of a girls' college.

"I'm Lieutenant Richard Benet, 12th Airborne Division, Clinical Psychologist at the U.S. Army Air Force 142nd General Hospital, Southern Avenue, Alipore District. I'm hoping to find Dr. Dina Pavri, a professor of literature, whom I knew back in the U.S. during graduate school.

The blond "hostess" looked at Benet as if he were speaking Urdu. It was clear she had no idea what he was talking about. He was about to give up the quest and get back to the men when a strikingly beautiful young Indian woman stepped forward from the back ranks of the hostesses. She was wrapped in yards of orange silk edged in gold brocade. She had the loveliest eyes, other than Rita's, that Benet had ever seen.

The blond director of the hostesses sighed with relief. "Lieutenant Benet, I can't offer any help with your search, but this is Miss Veena Sengupta, our student liaison. She knows all of the faculty members both here at Bethune and at the mother college.

Veena, meet Dr. Richard Benet, psychologist and Army Air Force lieutenant."

Veena placed her palms together at her chin and uttered a soft "*Namaste.*" Benet did the best he could to offer a greeting in kind. He loved the ritual nature of the Indian culture and prided himself on following the local customs.

He could feel his face turning red and hoped the blush didn't show. It was highly unusual for a young Indian lady to talk with an American soldier. In fact, except for the bearers hired by the Army base, there was little chance for American soldiers to interact with Indians at all.

Veena, however, had overcome her nervousness—if she'd had any. She spoke in soft, formal English. "Sir, when did the aforementioned Dr. Pavri teach at Calcutta University? That would help me look up her name, as she is someone I do not know. All of my professors have been there at the main college a very long time and it is most likely that someone amongst them will be able to provide you with information."

While Benet was thus engaged in conversation the men had wandered off and piled back in the truck. Someone had started honking the horn in rude protest for having to wait. To keep the situation from growing worse, Benet would have to cut his inquiry short.

Veena stood demurely, flanked by the hostesses, awaiting his answer.

"It was 1935 or '36. She and I were in several classes together at Ohio State University and became quite good friends. When she completed her Ph.D. and returned to India, we promised to keep in correspondence. We exchanged letters for a time, but I've misplaced her address."

Raucous horn honking, which had stopped for awhile, started up again. That damn Kopriva was going to ruin the outing. If it was one of the men fooling around, Kopriva could and should have stopped him. Of course, it might have been Kopriva himself from what Benet observed. He usually acted like a loon.

The psychologist took a small writing tablet out of his pocket, jotted down the hospital switchboard number, and gave it to Veena Sengupta. He would be very surprised if he ever heard from her.

"Well, Miss Gupta, I mean 'Sengupta,' and you hostessing ladies, as you can plainly hear, the troops are growing restless. Duty calls me. Thank you very much for your time. Have a pleasant morning and I will await a call from you when information is uncovered concerning Dina Pavri."

Apparently, while Kopriva had gone to buy some Indian cigarettes, the patients had climbed into the cab and started the horn honking. At least that was the story Ted, Sturke, Gus, and Ike gave Benet. Worse than a bunch of school kids, Benet thought to himself. The sooner they could get to New Market the better.

Kopriva returned and they were once again weaving through Calcutta's hectic streets. They finally reached the heart of the market place and began to stroll through the stalls of goods. Buying and selling created a busy hum of voices. Benet knew they should not pay the first price quoted, as "Yankees" were an easy mark for shrewd Indian merchants. "Offer them half what they quote to you and you'll still be paying twice as much as you should," the saying went.

Kopriva managed to park the truck and the men piled out onto the filthy sidewalk. The fetid smell in the air gagged Benet. He was tempted to put a handkerchief over his nose, but that, of course, would offend the Indians, all of whom had apparently gotten used to the foul air. The Americans snaked through pedestrians, Benet in the lead, patients in the middle, and Kopriva bringing up the rear. They all stuck close together. The alien nature of everything around them created an odd solidarity.

Mobs of children appeared from nowhere. Even the tiniest child spoke some English as he or she frantically tried to sell colorful necklaces, small wooden instruments, or embroidered purses.

"You buy for sweetheart, *sahib*?" an urchin pleaded. The child held up his toothpick arm draped with strings of beads." You buy from me. No mommy, no poppy, no sister, no brother. You buy from me, *sahib*." The unluckier children had no wares to hawk. Their pleas were even shriller. "*Baksheesh, sahib, baksheesh*. No mommy, no poppy, no sister, no brother. *Baksheesh, sahib, baksheesh*." Everyone needed *baksheesh*. The soldiers were millionaires in this land of famine, this city of homeless, starving people.

Once Benet and his men reached the shops, they were able to escape the constant bombardment of requests. Despite the fact that Benet found him despicable, Kopriva was quite helpful when it came to finding their way around.

"Ah, here it is," Kopriva exclaimed, "Punwani Brothers." Under a large wooden sign announcing the shop name, a caption read

"Established 1918: Specialists in Indian Ivory ware, Brassware, Carved Wooden Tables, Boxes, Trays, and Souvenirs."

14

As they stepped inside the shop, a stout, turbaned gentleman dressed in tan and gold leggings and *curta* greeted them with a small bow and closed palms to chin.

"Welcome, *namaste*. I am Harish Punwani, one of the seven Punwani brothers. You are now seeing Calcutta's finest handmade crafts by its best artisans. You will not find better anywhere else in Calcutta, nor indeed anywhere in all of India. You have anniversary, birthdays, Christmas, New Year, Easter, any other gift day? A gift from India is indeed a treasure. Please look at every section and also go to the second and third floors. Our clerks speak perfect English and will help you find anything that does not meet the eye."

They would need help, Benet thought to himself. The shop's interior was very dim. The thick smell of musky incense filled the air. He blinked several times, trying to adjust his eyes to the relative darkness.

"I want to send my mother an ivory elephant," said Fletch. "Where would I find one?"

Harish pointed to the stairs in the far right hand corner of the shop. "One flight up and you will find not only ivory elephants but intricately carved bullock carts, boats, powder boxes, letter openers, chokers, bracelets, necklaces, brooches, napkin holders, cigarette holders, cribbage boards, chopsticks and more. Just ask any of our clerks and they will most happily tell you about the maker of every item."

Ted, Gus, and Ike, followed by Kopriva, had already started up the stairs. Benet yelled out. "It is 1130 hours. Be back down here at the entrance by 1200 hours and we will go to an excellent Chinese restaurant for lunch. Do you hear me? 1200 hours!"

Half an hour would allow time to view only a fraction of the Punwani Brothers' extensive wares. The shop was stuffed with tens of thousands of items for sale. Benet, feeling his need to keep tabs on the men, resisted the desire to roam. Someone like Gus might just slip away. The psychologist would station himself by the door. As he waited for his troupe, he studied a sign; "Hindu Gods and Goddesses" posted near the store entrance.

Another of the Punwani brothers noticed Benet looking closely at a small ivory figurine and rushed to his side. "Ah, I see that you admire Lakshmi. She is the goddess of wealth. Note her four hands and her stand of the lotus flower. All over India, she is worshipped. Next month we will be celebrating her festival, Diwali. The meaning is "festival of lights". On this day, all houses are cleaned and made as bright as possible."

This Punwani, taller and thinner than his brothers, handed a tiny Lakshmi to Benet. "This one, she is three inches tall but also we have the four-inch and five-inch Lakshmi, if you would rather have a larger figurine."

"Well, thank you very much, but today I am just looking. My pals will be coming down any minute and I can come back to buy souvenirs at some more convenient time."

"Ah, but *sahib*, we may not have such fine carving as these figurines. They are made by a craftsman who is old and quite ill. It is said that his son will take over the family's business and the son is not the artist his father is. Why not buy today? Have you a wife, *sahib*? The American ladies, I've been told, very much admire these ivory artifacts. While you are deciding, I will order some tea for us."

Before Benet could refuse, Punwani summoned a tiny Anglo-Indian boy who promptly brought a tray of steaming glasses of strong black tea. Next to the small glasses was a bowl of sugar cubes.

It amazed Benet that Indians drank hot tea on even the sultriest days. Americans would have chosen ice cold drinks, but then, there was much in India that made no sense to him. The psychologist sipped as the merchant continued to promote his wares.

After a few minutes, Benet had to admit feeling much restored by the tea. He picked up the Lakshmi figurine. It was exquisite. He knew that Rita would place it on her vanity table alongside a few small carvings she'd purchased.

"How much?"

"For you, *sahib*, she will be special price of five dollars."

Benet winced. He'd lost a dollar last night playing poker and had just seven dollars left before his next paycheck. He spotted a long, curved ivory letter opener with a cavalcade of miniature elephants marching across one side of the blade. Pointing, he asked Punwani, "What about this piece? Could you add it in for the five dollar total?"

Punwani rolled his eyes to the ceiling. "For this fine letter opener alone, my best price is four in American dollars. For you, however, I can make a special deal. Both the Lakshmi figurine and the letter opener for seven dollars."

Richard could imagine using the elegant ivory opener for Rita's letters. Ivory articles were very rare and with time might become even more so. "I will pay six dollars for both," he offered.

The Punwani sibling winced and softly groaned.

"Six-fifty, my last and best price. But with this I lose money. Please not to tell my brothers, as they will be angry. They will accuse me of robbing the store, of giving away our merchandise for free."

Benet felt extravagant. After all, Rita was working at home saving for their future. On the other hand, he was sure that Rita would want him to buy the ivory figurine, that she would want him to open envelopes, especially those from her, with the ivory elephants on parade.

"Six-fifty. I'll take both the figurine and the letter opener."

Kopriva and "the gang" clambered down the stairs just as Benet was paying Punwani in dollars rather than *rupees*.

"Keep the change," Benet said. "Think of it as a symbol of the American G. I.'s good will toward Indians." He was hoping the men would notice his tip and be equally generous.

Fletch walked up to the cash register with an armload of wares. "Hey, Doc, issat one lil package all ya got? I guess I'm buyin' more than anyone else. Hey, Doc, what about that swimming pool? Are we gonna git ta see it today?"

"Sorry, old man. We won't have time on this jaunt. I promise that I'll take care of this on my own. We'll have the matter settled in a week or so."

Sturke, Ike and Kopriva all bought marble replicas of the Taj Mahal, which Benet promised to visit with them in an upcoming outing. Gus was the only man who'd made no purchase at all. When Benet questioned him, a baleful look was the only answer.

The psychologist thanked the Brothers Punwani and herded his soldiers toward the door. "We'll go to lunch at the Cathay Restaurant. It's famous for Chinese cuisine. I think you'll like their egg drop soup..."

Kopriva cut in. "This isn't what you might have had at home. It's Indianised or you might say 'Bengalised.' It has many more spices, a lot more fish."

He looked quickly toward Benet. "I think we should go through the maidan first. I've heard it called 'the green lungs of Calcutta.' I've heard that before it became the firing field for Fort William, it was all jungle."

One of the Punwanis had been eavesdropping and chose this moment to jump in. "My grandfather remembered when the maidan was a dense jungle infested with tigers and many other breeds of wild animals. Sometimes during seasons of too little rainfall, one of the tigers would become a man-eater and claim several victims before someone killed the beast. Legend has it that the tigers who learned to hate and fear humans were taken by *goondas* and trained as guards to hide criminal activities."

The patients gathered around, obviously fascinated to hear about India from a native Bengali. Benet looked at his watch. He had to have Ike, Sturke, Fletch, and Gus back at 1500 hours; it was already 1200 hours.

"*Goondas?*" Sturke wondered aloud. "What the hell are *goondas?*"

"Have you heard the term *hooligan?*" asked Kopriva. "Or just think of *goondas* as criminals. They are social outcasts who've taken to crime as the only means of ..."

"Kopriva, we're running late," interrupted Benet. "Get in the truck. I'd like a word with you. Men, pile in the back. After the Sergeant and I have a little conference in the cab, we'll be on our way to lunch."

Once the two of them were alone in the cab, Benet felt himself growing angry. He turned toward his junior officer with an accusing look.

"Who's in charge of this group? You or me? I am perfectly capable of giving the men an orientation to Calcutta. Their impressions of the city are important to their recovery. I don't need you to talk about social outcasts. You don't seem to understand that these fellas are feeling bad enough. They are feeling like social outcasts themselves. Learn to button your lip; do what you've been assigned to do. Drive!"

Kopriva glared at Benet. His lower lip was trembling and his eyes were full of hate. His expression said "You son of a bitch," but his words were simply "Yes, sir. Excuse me, *sir*. Shall I deliver your patients to the Cathay Restaurant or the India Palace?"

The sarcasm around the word "patients" was not wasted on Benet. Damn it, thought Benet, why Kopriva had to go along on his outing was beyond him. On the other hand, since the expedition was arranged through Mac's orders, having Kopriva along made it easier for the colonel to spy on Benet. He'd had to talk to Mac for twenty minutes to convince him that a tour of Calcutta's "safe" regions

89

would be therapeutic for the men. The thought that Mac didn't trust him to take the group on his own rankled him.

They drove south toward the Chinese restaurant. Forgetting about Kopriva and his obnoxiousness, Benet took in the view. Bicycles were ridden by white-garbed Indian men; pedestrians scurried through the chaotic traffic carrying all manner of burdens, little motorized hybrids scooted about—could they be taxis?

As the natives never made them move from the road, cattle impeded their progress. The creatures lay in the middle of the busiest thoroughfares chewing their cuds, unruffled by the traffic roaring all around them. Kopriva maneuvered the truck to Red Road, which turned into Casurina Avenue. Still within the maidan area, they passed a race course.

"Hey Doc," Fletch yelled through the window that separated the truck bed from the cab. "Is this where they used to have the tigers?"

"So they say," Benet answered. "We're passing through the Calcutta Maidan—as Kopriva told you, also known as 'the green lungs' of Calcutta. Before Fort William cleared out this area for field artillery practice, it was a jungle. The natives probably shot the tigers."

"Aw, how could they kill such noble critters?" Ike asked.

Fletch looked at Ike with a condescending smile. Of the four, Fletch fancied himself the brains of the group. "Well, look, to the Indians' way o' thinkin', tigers are just like vermin to the farmers, on a par with rats and mice. Besides, a tiger without his territory becomes a killer, a man-eater. Haven't ya'll heard of man-eating tigers?"

A loud voice came over the megaphone from the race course. Kopriva slowed the truck down so they could see what all the commotion was about. Surrounded by a throng of natives, a tall Indian stood on a raised stage. He seemed to be exhorting, urging the crowd to strengthen its resolve. The name Gandhi was repeatedly mentioned, each time inspiring cheers from the onlookers. People shouted, clapped, and waved their fists high in the air.

There was something familiar, thought Benet, about the speaker. He couldn't quite place the memory, but he was certain he'd seen him before.

"Hey, Kopriva, switch lanes, so I can see better. I need to know what's going on and I think I recognize the rabble-rouser."

Kopriva kept driving in the same lane. Hadn't he heard?

90

Benet spoke more forcefully, "We don't have to be back at the base for hours, and we still have more than enough time for lunch."

With the grim look of a man who hated being given orders, Kopriva complied.

The speaker's exhortations were interspersed with chants. Mingled with Indian dialects were English phrases.

"Brits Quit India! Brits Quit India! Brits Quit India ... Yankees go home! Yankees go home!... Reclaim the hospital buildings! Out with Americans! India for Indians!" The speaker continued in a native tongue.

As clusters of passersby were drawn to the scene, the crowd grew larger. It seemed as though the truck might be engulfed if they didn't move out soon.

Kopriva shifted into gear and began to head away from the racetrack. "Whatta bunch of hotheads. Crazy bastards don't have nothing else to do. Boy, I'm starving. Let's get some chow."

"Yeah, we're hungry enough back here to eat a cow. One of them sacred cows would do," Ike yelled through the cab window.

"Wait," Benet protested. "I think I know that speaker. I can almost make out what he's shouting..."

It was too late. A street-sweeping truck roared up behind them and the driver slammed impatiently on the horn. Clearly, they had to get out of the area. Just as the sea of people at the maidan vanished through the rear view mirror, Benet flashed on the speaker's identity. It was Ravi something, the tall Hindu that was always coming to the 142nd to see Colonel McDermott. If he was really a city official, as Mac had told Benet, what was he doing out here in a park giving public speeches? And what was that about taking back buildings? Something quite strange was going on between the hospital and Ravi. Benet was determined to get around McDermott's secrecy and find out the truth.

15

In 1944, winter came early to Findlay, Ohio. In fact, it started before Halloween. Rita let her class build snowmen. She gave them black construction paper to make cutouts of spiders and witches' hats. During recess, they decorated their snow people with them. Thanks to Richard's daily letters, she got through most of the school week without a crying jag. On Friday during lunch, however, she found herself at the breaking point. She and Evelyn, a first grade teacher, were alone in the lounge. Everyone else had gone to The Coffee Cup Cafe for lunch.

Both teachers opened lunchboxes and took out food from home. They sat forlornly at the white formica table looking out at blowing snow. Evelyn's eyes were puffy; either she was allergic to something or she'd been crying. Rita wondered how to open up a conversation. It might encourage Evelyn to confide in her. It sometimes helped to know that others were feeling just as bad as you were.

"You know," Rita began, "the war news is so discouraging, it seems as though nothing will ever be normal again. Am I the only one that senses an air of desperation surrounding everything, a sort of grasping at whatever happiness we can squeeze out of each day?"

"You read my mind," Evelyn said. "You live for letters from your Richard and I keep hoping my marriage to Jack can survive our separation. And I don't just mean his loyalty being tested. I'm also worried about my own. It looks as though we've both seen happier days."

Rita nodded in agreement. "It's hard to believe how much better life seemed in October a year ago. Do you sometimes feel that you're just going through the motions? I can't remember a time when I didn't have the war preying on my mind. But, unless I *act* upbeat, the children get to quarreling and the day becomes torture. It's a strain."

The lounge door burst open and with it came the chatter of Washington Elementary School's faculty. The intimate conversation ended, but Rita felt she had gained a new friend in Evelyn. They smiled at one another and washed out their coffee cups.

"Well, back to the fray," Rita quipped. "Say Evelyn, how would you like to learn to play bridge? We've been meeting every Thursday night at Mary Jane's, and Eleanor is teaching us."

"Sure thing. Let's talk next week."

The afternoon bell sounded and Rita went back to her classroom. She looked in amazement through the large plate glass window at the back. The snow, which had been blowing sideways, was now a blizzard. No sooner had her children come into the room when an announcement sounded over the P.A. system.

"Attention teachers. Because of the snow storm, school will be dismissed in one hour. Parents have been notified to pick up their children at 1:30. We're asking for volunteers to stay with the children whose parents can't get here right away. The weather forecast calls for continued severe blizzard conditions."

The children were excited at the chance for a holiday. Rita helped them gather up their coats and mittens. They still had half an hour before dismissal, so she started reading to them from *Why be a Goop?* As squirming and excited whispering increased, it became apparent that a story wasn't going to hold their interest for long. Normally Rita would have no trouble at all controlling the class, but she found it hard to share their energy. In a way, she envied their enthusiasm. She felt discouraged by the prospect of another dull, lonely weekend at home with her parents.

Sharon waved her hand in the air. "Teacher, teacher," she shouted.

"Mrs. Benet," Rita corrected. "Remember, it is more polite to use peoples' proper names. Yes, Sharon, what is it?"

"Can we make more hats and pipes to take home? Then we can make more snow people and dress them up for Halloween? Can we, pleeeze?"

Sarah chimed in, "Pretty pleeeze, Miz Benet. I'll pass out the scissors!"

"Oh well, why not," Rita said, reaching around behind her desk to a shelf of art supplies. "Here's a stack of paper, Sharon. We don't have enough black to go around, so some of you may have to use other colors. Be sure to draw what you are planning on the paper first. And remember that you might also need to take turns using the scissors."

The room turned quiet as 24 heads leaned over desks. In the next twenty minutes, each student produced two or three cutouts. The children were still engrossed when 1:30 p.m. arrived.

"OK, children, I can see that you've made some wonderful snowman accessories. Remember, last week we said that one meaning of 'accessory' is a piece of clothing to go with an outfit, something like a hat, a scarf, or a pair of shoes. Sarah, please pass around the basket for scissors and have people put the paper scraps in the same basket. I'll sort them out. When it warms up and your mom and dad let you go out to play, make a snow person or animal. Your homework is to write a story about the best thing about snow days."

The dismissal bell interrupted, then Rita continued. "Only the bus students can leave. Everyone whose parents pick them up just stay seated until they get here. Remember, those of you leaving right now, make sure you have your coats, hats, and mittens. We're probably going to have a few snow days, so take everything with you that you might need."

Well-trained, the students taking the bus lined up by the door. Rita checked to make sure coats were buttoned and hats were on securely. "Goodbye, goodbye. Have fun this weekend but don't forget to write your stories."

Sharon, at the head of the line, hugged her before walking out.

"You're the best teacher in the world," Donald said.

"Yeah," Robert agreed. "Thanks, Miz Benet, for helping me learn to read. My Dad says that you've given me a future."

"I love all of you," Rita said. "But it's time to shoo, shoo." She waved them out and went to sit with the remaining children. One by one their parents came by to take them home.

By 2:15, Rita was alone. The storm outside had grown fierce. Ordinarily, she would clean the boards and tidy up before the weekend, but with the bad weather, she would just clear out.

Rummaging through the boxes in the cloakroom, she found a pair of rubber boots to put on over her Oxfords. She stuffed her lesson plans and the week's papers to grade in her satchel tied a scarf over her head, and, locking the door behind her, went outside to the parking lot. The last of the busses was heading out, wasting no time. The green bomb, as she called her Packard, was covered with a thick coat of snow.

As though he'd been waiting for her, Fred Eckles, wrapped in a bulky sheepskin coat, emerged from nowhere. Armed with a broom, he began sweeping the snow off her car.

Rita didn't want to encourage her boss's attentions, but she could hardly object to his help. The windows had to be free of snow. How else would she be able to drive home safely?

"You are too kind. I owe you a favor, Mr. Eckles. I hope you're as nice to your wife as you are to the faculty. You look after us like we were your children. Thank you very, very much." Rita mentioned

Mrs. Eckles whenever Fred started paying attention to her, hoping that this would discourage him from getting ideas.

"Ah, Mrs. Benet, think nothing of it. I want the best teacher on our faculty to get home safely. You know, I get nothing but glowing reports from the parents of your students. It was downright amazing how you taught Robert to read, working with him like that during the lunch break and after school. Besides, I'm helping all the teachers clear off their cars. You take care of yourself, you hear, and just let me know if you need anything."

He held open her car door, and Rita slipped into the driver's seat. She pulled the door shut, flashed a perfunctory smile toward Eckles, and backed cautiously out of her parking spot.

Most of the teachers were leaving at about the same time, and despite what the principal said, she saw no evidence of his helping anyone else with snow removal. She remembered Evelyn's remark that Fred Eckles no longer wore a wedding ring. He could be a wolf in sheep's clothing for all she knew. At any rate, she didn't trust his motives.

It was a harrowing drive on slick roads. Finally home, Rita slid the Packard to a stop and wearily climbed up the porch. Calling out her greetings to anyone who might be at home, she headed upstairs to change out of her school clothes. A few minutes later, Rita came downstairs wrapped in a chenille robe. She hugged the cup of hot chocolate her mother handed her, sat down at the kitchen table, and gave a long sigh.

Ruth smiled and patted her daughter's shoulder. "You know, dear, your father and I would like you to go to church with us this Sunday. It will help. I know all this worrying about Richard is hard on you, and..." Rita was shaking her head.

"Mother, I appreciate your concern, but I really need to catch up on sleep over the weekend. I don't know quite how to explain this to you, but I'd rather spend time reading the books that Richard and I used to read together. There's one he liked most—the collection of poems by Rumi."

"Well, dear," Ruth sighed, "I know that Richard always seemed to be caught up in those mystical things like philosophy and psychology. It's rather amazing he turned out so well. The poor fellow didn't have much help from his family. They were always working and couldn't take the time to give him training or education. But you had a better example and were raised properly, in the church. You can love Richard without swallowing everything he believes in."

"Honestly, mother, I give up. You'll never understand."

The wind was still howling, the snow coming down fast. She doubted that they would go anywhere over the weekend on icy roads.

Her dad had gone out to shovel the walk, knowing it would get covered up again before he was done. As he opened the front door on his way out, he commented, "It helps to shovel it along the way, otherwise, it will be too heavy to lift."

Mother and daughter moved into the living room. Ruth settled into the green stuffed easy chair that her husband had just vacated. But Rita, who was determined not to get trapped into another long, dull evening in the living room, thought better of it, and walked to the staircase. She was still listening, but planned to make a getaway before her father came back inside.

"Here's just an example," Ruth said as she picked up a worn, leather-covered Bible and located a page in it. "Let me just read you a few verses from Psalm 90. I think it will put our problems in perspective."

"Mother," Rita interjected, "couldn't you read this to me tomorrow? I think I'm coming down with a sore throat. I promise I'll listen to your Bible lesson then. I forgot to check yesterday to see if there was any mail for me. You know that's the day the mailman came so late I'd already gone up to my room. Did you forget again and put my mail with the bills?"

"I'll tell you, dear, about the mail after you listen to just these two verses. You know, Psalm 90, the one that begins 'Lord, thou hast been our dwelling place in all generations.' Men are compared to grass which is renewed in the morning and fades and withers by evening. Now this is the part that you must take to heart:

For all our days pass away under thy wrath,
our years come to an end like a sigh
The years of our life are threescore and ten
or even by reason of strength fourscore;
yet their span is but toil and trouble;
they are soon gone, and we fly away.
Who considers the power of thy anger
and thy wrath according to the fear of thee
So teach us to number our days
that we may get a heart of wisdom."

96

Ruth looked at her daughter expectantly. "Well, dear, don't you find it inspiring?"

"Um, yes, mother, but I don't feel well. Maybe I'm coming down with a fever. I'm going to try to sleep in tomorrow and Sunday, so please go to church without me. If anyone calls, tell them I'll call back. Oh, yes, as I said, what about the mail?"

"Nothing came but the *Saturday Evening Post,* but the postman—that nice young Olson—said that he would be happy to bring your letters from Richard to the school so you could get them earlier in the day. He's so friendly that I invited him in for a cup of coffee. You'd already retired to your 'bailiwick,' as your father calls it."

By now, Rita was drooped over the banister, one foot on the bottom step of the staircase, now beginning to feel more tired than she could ever remember.

"Mother, I'm about to collapse. It's bedtime for me. 'Nite, Dad." She blew a kiss in to her Dad, who had given up on shoveling snow and was nodding off in his easy chair.

"'Nite, Mom." She leaned over to hug Ruth and kiss her on one soft, wrinkled cheek.

The third floor of the Collins' home was cold and dark. The furnace system barely functioned there, and yet Rita loved the privacy. She burned candles, lit incense and, as she was planning to do now, occasionally smoked. She opened a window a tiny crack and lit a Camel. The snow had stopped and the air was sub-freezing. She put her cigarette in the ashtray she kept hidden in a desk drawer and went to the closet for a sweater.

She'd started a letter to Richard yesterday and she would finish it the next day. For now she just wanted to smoke and read Rumi. The book was buried somewhere in the closet, so she pulled out a lined tablet and a pen and tested her memory. All she could remember of "The Guest House" were two verses.

This being human is a guest house. Every morning a new arrival. A joy, a depression, a meanness, some momentary awareness comes as an unexpected visitor ... Welcome and entertain them all!

The cigarette butt discarded, ashtray hidden, teeth brushed, flannel pajamas donned, Rita snuggled under a down quilt. On the other side of the world, Richard was probably just getting up.

The thought of India excited Rita as she imagined its heat and color; she longed for the warmth of Richard next to her. Wonderful as his letters were, they couldn't make up for his absence.

How slowly time passed. If *only* she could wake up and find out that the war was over. If only she could remember a time when life was joyous. Of course, if she could spend the night in Richard's arms, it wouldn't matter what was happening in the world. They created their own universe.

With that pleasant thought, she drifted off to sleep.

16

Ravi Ghosh thanked the gods for the night he met the hospital director. In no time at all, he had Colonel James McDermott where he wanted him. Opium arrived through the Rangoon connection delivered by the notorious *goonda* Bagh Singh. The American Colonel was a regular customer.

Such a perfect arrangement. Not only was Mac conveniently supplying Ravi with morphine, saleable to the Japanese at great profit, Mac had also introduced his mistress, a nurse named Clara to opium, thus doubling his demand.

Ravi relished his own cleverness. He knew the importance of appearances. It all happened easily, he told himself, because he looked like an upper-class intellectual whose intentions must surely be as respectable as his well-cut London-tailored suit. He could pass himself off as anyone he wanted to be.

Unlike the true *goondas*, Ghosh was from a middle class family. His father, a municipal tax collector, died in the collapse of a building on Ravi's ninth birthday. As a boy, Ravi did not get along well with his mother and kept himself apart from his two siblings. Lonely and troubled, young Ravi sought out friends from the street. Outwardly polite, he attended Bangabasi Collegiate School, making high marks and never causing trouble.

But the outward Ravi was a cover-up. His real passion dwelled in money and power. Achieving his goals necessitated crime. Never directly involved in extortion, beatings, or murders, he assigned less shrewd *goondas* to carry out his wishes. He grew enamored with violence as a way of accomplishing his ends, and he eventually dropped out of school.

Unbeknownst to First Lieutenant Richard Benet, one of Ravi's most trusted spies doubled as a bearer at the hospital. In fact, he was Benet's dependable Sanjay. It was through him that Ravi learned of McDermott's alcoholism. Sanjay's twin, Shubi, had helped set up the fateful walk that led Mac to the opium den.

It amused the Bengali that these Yankee soldiers and their officers thought they conducted their affairs in private. They might as well have been living in a house of glass. In India, everyone knew everything about everybody, and the hospital was no more private than if it had been an open-air encampment in the maidan.

To continue his operations, Ravi needed a messenger, someone to navigate gracefully between Indian society and the hospital. The maidan was where Ravi would find his courier. He smiled to himself, feeling confident. It would be an adventurous, freethinking Indian student, a lovely young lady—a bit of a rebel, an idealist devoted to the cause of India for Indians.

This someone, Ravi sensed, might appear at one of his patriotic forums. As often in Ravi's life, he hadn't long to wait. The perfect messenger appeared the very next day at an open-air gathering. Ravi eyed the speaker even as he scanned the crowd. He clapped when the crowd did, playing the part of an activist. In actuality, he barely listened. He was there for one purpose only: to recruit.

When he spotted a lively girl, laughing with her friends on the outskirts of the crowd, Ravi moved quickly. Something about this young woman's expression and the gleam in her deep brown eyes assured him that she would be daring enough. To his relief, she seemed eager to talk with him.

"*Namaste, sahib.* I'm Veena Sengupta, reporting for the Bethune Girls' College newspaper."

"*Namaste*, Miss Sengupta," Ravi said with a slight bow. Are you a political activist or are you merely curious about this brazen crowd? I see you have a notebook. Perhaps, you are not really a student but a detective for the Americans sent here to record the speaker's message?"

Veena laughed, "I am hardly anything for the Americans. I think we must discourage them from feeling too much at home in our country. They might not be quite so bad as the British, but truly we do not need foreigners of any country here. India has enough people of her own. The newspaper is a project for my journalism class. We are compiling a column titled 'Views from the Man on the Street.'"

The crowd grew more frenzied, their cheering louder, their banners waving more wildly. Ravi shouted above their voices. "You want to know my views on the Americans who seem to be everywhere infiltrating? I believe we must oust them."

Veena wrote on a small pad. "You've given me an idea. I'm entitling this piece, 'How long can we tolerate foreigners? Calcutta residents voice their views on America's military presence.'"

As she wrote, Ravi admired her soft, feminine face, the slender form he imagined under her blue *sari*, her obvious intelligence and way with words. How very bold, how very unusual, how refreshing,

Ravi commented to himself. A modern young woman not over-powered by tradition. This was a good sign.

Meanwhile, the speeches continued to blare. The first speaker stepped down from the wooden platform that served as a stage. His replacement was one of the infamous Chatterjees. Indians resented the family for their ill-gotten wealth and property, riches that were second only to that of the famous Birla patriarchy.

"I'm inspired by the patriotism of Sundas Bose," one Chatterjee brother said. "Now is the time for all of us to fearlessly speak the truth. We want our country back. The Allies are using us as a pawn on their giant chessboard. They do not care what happens to India or her people. At first we believed that the Americans would be an improvement over the British, but now we know better." When the crowd roared its agreement, Veena and Ravi joined in.

Chatterjee rambled on, advocating the overthrow of any foreign influence. Ravi finally recognized the speaker. It was Anil Chatterjee, the youngest of eight brothers. He yelled into a megaphone, "We need a small army and one by one we will take back our buildings, regain them for the uses they had before foreign occupation. "India for Indians ... India for Indians ... India for Indians, *jai hind*, glory to India, *jai hind*, glory to India!"

The chant was taken up by the ever-increasing crowd, many of whom carried signs in Hindi or Urdu reading "Americans go back to Uncle Sam," "We will take back our buildings," and "Go back where you came from."

Ravi moved closer to Veena, close enough to smell the delicate rose fragrance that she wore. "How would you like to do something besides write articles?" he asked in a low voice. "What about doing something that would make a real difference in the independence movement?" He knew he was being too familiar, but he hoped that Veena's passion for freeing India would override any alarm she might feel.

With Ravi following closely, Veena shifted toward the outskirts of the crowd. Her friends Arundati and Chitra were nowhere to be seen. She'd lost them, which was perfectly fine, as they would meet back at the college commons before suppertime. She felt sure no one would hear her talking to Ravi.

"Now, *Sahib*, what exactly is it that you want me to do? My family has warned me not to become deeply involved in politics, but I cannot stand by and let my country be ruined. Some of my professors feel that a woman's place is not always in the home, especially not for a young, well-educated woman. They have influenced me quite strongly. Do you want me to write articles for a bigger audience such as *The London Times*? My English professor would be delighted were I to try something so daring, but it would upset my parents no end. I would have to change my name and assume a different..."

Veena seemed to be getting carried away with her imagined journalistic debut, Ravi decided. "You might have to assume a different identity," he said, "but I assure you that this assignment does not involve writing. It is far more active and maybe just a little dangerous. I need for you to serve as a courier to the 142nd General Hospital and to report whatever you observe each time you visit. I would give you a package and you would report your findings directly to me."

"That sounds like something I could do," Veena said. "What would I be carrying and what sort of thing would you want me to observe?"

"I can't reveal the content of these packages, Miss Sengupta. I can assure you that it is not a risk to you unless someone else finds it. The contents are to remain sealed but you have my word that they are directly related to our regaining the hospital grounds, which are much needed for the Calcutta health system."

Veena seemed to waver. A slight frown passed over her perfectly symmetrical features. "Mr. Ravi Ghosh," she said, "my curiosity always gets me into trouble. I can only hope that perhaps this time it will help me."

"You would have to trust me on this," Ravi said, "and just believe that your mission would be of utmost importance. Of course, if it is too much to ask, there are other students, particularly a young man I know, who would be more than happy to take on this mission."

"Please just call me 'Beeni,' no more 'Miss Sengupta,' please," Veena commented. "Having said that, you must know that I do not question the importance of secrecy. I will be perfect for your task, as the American soldiers are far less likely to suspect a young woman than a man. So many of the men students my age have become *goondas* or joined criminal tribes. It seems that young men nowadays are immediately suspected of something illicit."

"Well, Miss Sengupta, I mean Beeni, I suppose you're right. It will be much easier for you to perform the second part of this job, and that is, paying careful attention—you might say even spying—to the officers at the 142nd General Hospital."

"Yes," said Veena, "I could pretend that I'm just being friendly, and of course, curious."

Speeches had ended and the mob was drifting across the fields toward Red Road, which bordered the maidan. Veena trailed after Ravi. People pressed in from all sides. They had to walk quickly to keep from being crushed. Everyone talked nonstop, in tones of anger and determination.

"I already know someone from the hospital," Veena announced.

Ravi stopped in mid-smile and faced Veena. "You must be mistaken." He looked at his watch and continued walking.

"No, really," protested Veena. "I do know someone, an American. I met him on campus. A Lieutenant Richard Benet, a psychologist in charge of the Neuro-Psychiatric Ward. He was looking for a former colleague of his who was supposed to be teaching at Calcutta University. His patients were in a truck waiting for him and kept honking the horn quite rudely. He was nice enough, however, and I know he'd remember me."

"How is this going to help us?" Ravi asked. "Just because you saw this American once doesn't mean that you can fabricate a reason to find him at the hospital. We must be realistic. Time is running out."

"But my plan is very realistic," said Veena. "I could go to the hospital for a paper I'm writing, a report or study. I'd know just what to say. Please do not talk with the young man you are thinking of. I am the right person for your task. I want to help my country."

"OK, Miss Sen..., I mean Beeni. You've got the job. Let's meet here at the race track tomorrow and go to Gajendra Grande Restaurant for lunch. I will explain exactly what I need for you to do. Oh, and Beeni, you must not tell anyone. Please go to a shop and buy something so you can tell your friends where you've been. If anyone finds out that you are with me, all will be ruined."

He handed her a five-*rupee* bill. "Have several bags with you. Say they are purchases you couldn't resist."

"Oh, but I don't need anything, and I can't take money from you," Veena protested.

"Please, do not question me. Just look as though you've had a wonderful shopping trip. If you don't need anything, buy little gifts for your friends. No one ever minds receiving a present from a friend."

17

When Rita Benet entered the faculty lounge she met a typically bustling Friday scene: sack lunches being opened, soup heating up on a hot plate, teachers making plans for the weekend.

"Hey, Rita, how about coming over tonight to play bridge? I heard from Evelyn that you're in a group already and would like to practice as much as possible."

Mildred Simpson's bright smile made the offer hard to refuse. Rita didn't know the fourth grade teacher that well but she'd heard nothing but complimentary remarks about how good she was with students.

"Well, yes, that sounds nice," said Rita "but I'm not sure you want me at the bridge table. I'm a rank beginner, and I do mean rank."

"Oh phooey, we're all still learning," Mildred assured Rita. "If it makes you feel any better, I just found out that the convention I'd been calling 'deadwood' is actually 'blackwood'."

"Gosh, I haven't even gotten that far. The only bridge convention I know beyond just simple bidding might be 'no trump,' and even that is pretty shaky."

"Not to worry, dearie. We just play for fun. I'm having a couple girls from the neighborhood over—Madge and Lorraine. I think you'll like them—and they're in the initial stages of learning bridge. You'll fit right in. We'll have dessert and coffee and see what cards the bridge gods, or should I say 'goddesses' deal to us. I live at 15 Center Street. Come by about eight."

Going to Mildred's would be fun. Not that Rita was particularly keen on bridge, but she really liked to socialize with teacher pals. Besides, it was a cheery alternative to sitting with the folks for yet another evening or stretching out her letter writing to Richard to last for hours.

After lunch, the children were already in the classroom before the bell rang. "Guess what, third graders?" she exclaimed. "You've worked hard all week, so I've decided not to start our math review until Monday. We'll do art projects all afternoon until 2:30, and then I'll read you more of *Alice in Wonderland* until the bell rings.

"Yea, no work!" Donald said to no one in particular.

"Just a minute, young man," Rita scolded. "Our art program is part of learning. This is not kindergarten. If you can't control your remarks, I'll give you the math review to work on right now. While we're painting, you may sit at the table outside in the hall and start on these workbook exercises." She picked up a workbook and started walking toward Donald's desk.

"I'm sorry, Miz Benet," Donald pleaded. "I'll be quiet. I promise. Lemme paint with the class. Pleeez."

"OK, Donald, but I'm not going to warn you again. No speaking out. Raise your hand if you have something to say." All faces were turned to her. She put on her sternest expression. No smile and a steady, piercing stare. That was the effect she hoped for, anyway.

"And that goes for the rest of you." The room became totally silent.

"OK, if there are no questions. I'll pass out materials and then give you some suggestions for what to paint."

She distributed white construction paper and a watercolor painting set to each student. The small pimento jars she'd saved last summer were ideal for holding water. She appointed Sarah and Patricia to fill the jars from the water fountain located just outside her room and give one to every two students, who would share.

In another twenty minutes, every child was deeply involved in painting a picture of home, a tree in autumn before its leaves fell, or a family pet. For the less advanced, those who were having trouble with painting, Rita substituted a basket of crayons. Some students took a long time with one painting. Others worked quickly, requiring several more sheets of paper.

"Good work, third graders," Rita announced at 2:35. " Make sure you write your name at the bottom right hand corner of all your art. Row by row, starting with row one, closest to the door, bring your paintings to the side table where they can dry. We'll be using them in the book you'll be making to take home to your family before Christmas vacation. Then, let's clean up our supplies. As soon as you've finished, come sit in the reading circle and we'll pick up where we left off with *Alice's Adventures in Wonderland*."

The cleanup was accomplished with a minimum of noise and bickering. In another five minutes the children were seated on the carpeting around Rita's storytelling chair. After just a few rearrangements such as moving Donald away from Alvin and quieting a few girls who insisted on giggling, she began.

"Remember how last time, Alice was sitting by her sister on the riverbank when a white rabbit runs by and takes a watch out of its waistcoat. Does anyone remember what the rabbit says to itself?"

Alvin raised his hand. "I think it's something like. 'Darn! I'm late'."

"That's very close, Alvin. It's actually 'Oh dear! Oh dear! I shall be too late.' Remember, last time we learned that Lewis Carroll wrote this almost 100 years ago as Christmas greetings 'from a fairy to a child.' The rabbit looked at its watch and commented 'I shall be too late.' Nowadays we don't speak so formally."

Patricia waved her hand in the air. Before Rita could call on her, she blurted out "Can we hear more of the story?"

"Yes, Patricia, I'm just getting to that. Remember that you must wait until I tell you to speak. You can't just raise your hand and blurt out. OK, Alice, who's never seen anything like this rabbit with a waistcoat and a watch, is running after it across a field. It pops down a large rabbit-hole under a hedge..."

The dismissal bell sounded and Rita closed her book.

"Good listening, boys and girls. We'll continue with Alice's adventures on Monday after our big math review. Get your coats from the cloak room; check for hats and mittens; if you have them, put them on. As soon as everyone's lined up at the door, you're all dismissed. Have a good weekend."

Several of girls hugged Rita around the knees. "Goodbye, Missuz Benet," said Patricia. "You have a good weekend too. My Mommy says you're the best teacher at the school and I'm very lucky to have you."

"Why thank you, Patricia. That's very nice. Tell your mom I appreciate her saying that."

The last child having departed, Rita breathed a weary sigh. She sat at her desk and finished next week's lesson plans. Though tired, she was less exhausted than usual on a Friday afternoon. She was looking forward to getting to know Mildred better and to meeting new friends. Fifteen minutes later she was home.

The aromas of beef stew and chocolate cake met Rita at the door. Much as she longed for the privacy of her own home, she'd have to admit that it was comforting to have a snug household to return to every night. Ruth Collins stood by the gas stove, aproned and red-faced from the heat. Wooden spoon in hand, she stirred a huge pot of vegetables and beef in a rich tomato sauce.

"Hi, sweetheart. You're home early for a Friday, and you don't look so worn out. Was it a good day at school?"

"Mama, any Friday is a good day because of its being the last day of the school week. I'm keeping the class in line and it seems like that's the main thing the boss—that excuse for a principal Mr. Eckles—cares about, more how orderly everything looks than how much the students learn. But as far as that goes, I think these children are learning a lot. I've gained their respect and they pay attention. Mmmm. The stew smells wonderful. Can I eat early? I have an invitation to play bridge at Mildred Simpson's tonight."

"Sure, dear. We can eat whenever you like. Your Dad said he had to work late to balance the books. I'll save his supper for later, so it's just us two."

"Oh good. I'll put my feet up and take a nap, then get dressed to go out. Just call me when you're ready."

"The stew can be ready any time. I'm going to set the table now. Why don't you just come downstairs and I'll serve us. Do you want me to wake you up at 5:30, just in case you doze off."

"Good idea, Ma." Rita hugged Ruth, kissed her on the cheek, and trudged upstairs. The dresser top was empty, so just as she'd feared, there was no message from India to enliven the evening. Well, there was always the hope that she'd get two letters on Saturday. She'd just collapse for awhile...

Gale Collins arrived home just as his daughter Rita was leaving. They met at the door.

"Hello and goodbye, Daddy. I had to eat supper early because of going out to play bridge with some teacher friends. You can have my piece of chocolate cake. The bridge hostess said we'd have dessert before playing cards."

"Fine, dear. We'll miss you tonight."

"I know, Daddy. I'll miss being with you and Ma. I promise not to sleep away half the day. Maybe we can all spend the afternoon together. Let's listen to opera tomorrow on the Texaco Hour. I have cutouts to make for school and Ma can bring her sewing." She hugged her father.

Gale Collins gestured toward the road. "It's a little slick out there, some patches of black ice left from the storm last week. Drive safely and be sure to keep your car doors locked. At the courthouse, they were talking about some strangers in town with Nazi ties. Findlay isn't the safe little town it used to be."

It took less time than she'd calculated to drive from Center Street to Lincoln Avenue, and Rita arrived at Mildred's house five minutes early. She thought about waiting in the car until eight but realized how silly that would be. It was below freezing, and with gas rationing, she could hardly keep the car motor running. No doubt Mildred could use a little help in getting things set up, or maybe she could review her 'no trump' knowledge.

Like many young wives in Findlay, Mildred was living in her parents' house. Rita rang the doorbell and waited, taking in her surroundings. Mildred's place was a large brick Victorian-style home complete with turrets and white gingerbread trim. A large house for one, even though that situation was only temporary. Mildred had explained that her parents were in Michigan helping her mother's mother—Granny Simpson—move into a nursing home, and that for the next month Mildred would be the sole occupant.

For a second time Rita pushed the button next to the front door. Maybe the doorbell was out of order. The cold was beginning to make her shiver under her wool tweed coat. She'd "dressed down" for the bridge night. Looking at her brown wool pleated slacks, she hoped the others wouldn't be in dresses.

At last the front door opened. "Oh, Hi kiddo, hope you haven't been standing out here forever. Come in, come in. Let's keep the cold outside."

"Millie, sorry to arrive ahead of time," Rita said, as her hostess closed the massive front door behind them.

"Please don't think anything of it. I would have answered sooner, but I was in the kitchen. It's hard to hear from there. Sometimes you have to ring more than once." Mildred was still in her skirt and blouse from school, Rita noted.

"Give me your coat and I'll hang it in the foyer closet." Mildred said, holding her arms out. "Madge and Lorraine aren't here yet. But since you are, I have to tell you about a new worry. Promise you won't say anything to the other girls. I don't want to start a rumor."

"What...?" Rita began.

"Just follow me," said Mildred, walking down the hall past a staircase that led to the second floor. Just before the kitchen was a door off to the left-hand side. Maybe a bathroom or pantry? Rita thought to herself.

"We're going down to the cellar," Mildred said, flicking on a light switch. "The stairs are steep. Watch your step."

"I hope it's not mice," Rita said. "I have a real fear of rodents."

"You mean mouse-o-phobia?" Mildred laughed. "I wish it were something that simple, and I could just make an appointment with the exterminator." They'd reached the bottom of the stairs. Mildred pulled a string to turn on a bare bulb overhead.

Rita's eyes adjusted to the dim basement light: A workbench and tools hanging on the wall; an oversize wooden wardrobe covered with dust and adorned with a mirror blackened with age dominated one wall.

"This isn't so bad," she said. "Our basement's much more of a mess than this."

"Shhhhh." Mildred whispered. "Come over here and look where I'm pointing. "For the past week, there's been a stranger living in Thelma Shunter's basement."

Rita peered through the half cellar window. The view across to the adjoining house looked directly into another window. Anything beyond the glass panes was indistinct, veiled by some type of thin curtain or blind. A faint light from within illuminated the snow-covered easement between the two large homes.

"I see what you mean," Rita said. "Maybe Thelma needed the money and so she took in a boarder."

A shadow passed in front of the curtain. "No, I thought that at first," Mildred replied. "But I keep thinking that it might be one of those Nazis hiding out. You know, they've been talking about it on the radio. I've hardly slept at all this week worrying about what to do. But there's the doorbell. Madge and Lorraine are here. Please—not a word about this until we have another chance to talk in private."

18

After enjoying Mildred's walnut cake and freshly-brewed coffee, the four women gathered at the bridge table. Mildred not only was the perfect hostess, she knew how to keep score. On the fresh linen tablecloth, she had laid out tallies and two decks of playing cards.

As was her custom, Rita took mental fashion notes. Madge, a single gal who worked at a factory in Dayton, was the most dressed up of the four. She'd come to Findlay for the weekend to stay with her cousin, whose husband had just shipped out to England. Her short blond hair was held back with a green ribbon that perfectly matched her green dotted Swiss shirtwaist.

"I have to wear overalls and a bandana every day for my job," Madge said when complimented on her outfit. "It's pretty gritty, so I like to dress up whenever I get a chance."

Lorraine was a first-time mother with a year-old baby. Her husband, she explained, had joined the Marines the year before, right after his twentieth birthday. He was sent to Guadalcanal and he longed to see his new daughter. Lorraine wore slacks that looked just like Rita's except that hers were charcoal gray rather than brown.

"OK ladies," announced Mildred. "Let's try to keep table talk to a minimum. It's not fair to review the rules while someone is deciding what to bid. Do the best you can and remember that we all make mistakes. That's really the only way to learn."

Madge opened the bidding with one club. Lorraine passed. It was Rita's turn. She knew that Madge's bid indicated a thirteen or fourteen point hand, but the minute she blurted out, "Two no trump," she was sorry. She held eighteen points in her hand, but one of those points was based on a singleton. From what she remembered about counting points, one never counted a singleton in the no trump convention.

Mildred looked at her hand, frowned, and in a quiet voice said "pass."

To Rita's surprise Madge bid "three no trump." Probably Madge expected her bid to be a slam, but after Lorraine quickly passed, so did she. She'd heard that one should play a hand for all it was worth, but for her, it was going to be hard enough to make three tricks over the six required for book.

The next ten minutes felt like an hour to Rita, but to her relief, she and Madge made their bid. When the other women congratulated her, Rita insisted that she'd just been lucky, that she really didn't know what she was doing.

"That's not true," Mildred said. "You lack confidence but your instincts were right. You're lucky. Some people lack card sense. They have to work hard to get what you already have. The confidence will come in time. OK, girls, whose turn to deal next?"

In answer, Lorraine slid the deck of cards to Rita, who started shuffling. "Fine," Mildred said, "while you're dealing, I'll record the score. Rita, if you're really my friend, you'll give me some decent cards this hand!"

Not only were Mildred's cards decent, they were good enough for a grand slam, which she and Lorraine bid and made. From then on, Rita had very few points for the rest of the evening. She and Madge were severely trounced. Bridge was not so exciting if all you could do was pass and slough off cards. Thankfully, the evening was drawing to a close. There was still the letter to write to Richard before her head hit the pillow.

The proper "thank you's" said, Mildred's guests were gathered at the front door to leave.

"Rita, could you stay a minute longer? I need to talk with you. I'll reheat the coffee, and we'll have a cup."

Rita knew this would be about Thelma's boarder. As much as she longed to go home, she couldn't very well say no to helping Mildred. Helping her do what, she wasn't sure. She took off her coat and flopped into a plush red living room chair.

"I didn't want the others to hear any of this," Mildred said. She carried in a tray with sugar, cream and two steaming cups of coffee. "Part of me says that it's none of my business who Thelma Shunter has staying in her basement, but the other part feels like it's my patriotic duty to see what's going on over there and to report anything suspicious."

Rita took a sip of her coffee, which she'd cooled down considerably with an ample dose of cream. "I agree with you, Millie. Is there any way you could just ask Thelma? If she is harboring someone suspicious, of course she wouldn't tell you the truth, but you might be able to tell a lot from the way she answers."

"I've tried, and she changes the subject immediately. 'Of course, I don't have a boarder,' she sniffs indignantly. 'Vy vould I do such a thing!'" Mildred did a great job of imitating Thelma's thick German accent.

111

"You may think this is a little far-fetched," Rita said, "but why don't you bake a cake and we could take it over? We could call on her the day after tomorrow and I could pretend to be using her bathroom, meanwhile slipping downstairs to look around. That walnut cake you served tonight would be perfect."

"Why would I be bringing a cake to that old grouch?" Mildred asked. "Don't you think she'd really suspect something then?"

"Speaking of the cake, could you bring me another slice?" Rita asked. "No, I think she would be touched. It's obvious she's a woman who loves to eat. Look at the size of her. Besides, you could say something like...you didn't mean to offend her by asking about someone in her basement. Just explain that you've never stayed in your parents' house alone and sometimes you imagine things."

"Hmmm," replied Mildred. She disappeared into the kitchen and returned with two big pieces of walnut cake, white and spongy with a glossy vanilla frosting. "Here you are, Rita dear. Aren't you glad we don't have to watch about our weight? Having husbands overseas is a very effective diet."

Rita took several small bites of cake, then stood up and paced around the living room floor. "Didn't you once tell me that your house and the Shunter house have exactly the same layout?" she asked.

"Yes, as a matter of fact, the floor plans are identical, but I don't see what that has to do with..."

"You'll see," Rita interrupted. "I'm going to test how long it would take me to sneak down to the cellar while you kept Thelma busy." Before Mildred could comment further, Rita strode from the living room to the hall and to the cellar door, which was right next to the bathroom door. She opened the cellar door, flicked on the light, and walked down the creaking wooden stairs. Curious about the "secret window" Mildred referred to, she turned on the overhead bulb and proceeded carefully, as there was clutter everywhere. She spotted a window and stopped in her tracks. The faint, tinny sound of a radio broadcast was coming from the basement next door. Was the announcer speaking German? Was that German music? There was much to investigate here, but for now, she would get back upstairs to her friend.

Mildred had finished her cake and was tidying up the living room. She looked at Rita with a puzzled expression. "It took you forever," she said. "I'd have to give Thelma a whole baking lesson at that rate."

"You won't believe this," Rita said, "but I think there really is someone downstairs next door, and I think he's there right now."

"Did you see a light?" asked Mildred.

"No, but I swear I heard a radio coming from over there." I thought at first you were nuts, but now I think we absolutely must call on Fraulein Shunter. You can take the cake, maybe bring her some recipes, and I'll do the sleuthing. Instead of this Sunday, let's schedule our 'house call' for next Saturday; that would give us the whole school week to make sure we plan everything exactly right."

"But what if we do find something?" asked Mildred. "What then? I don't think we could exactly contact the local police."

Rita smiled. "I'll talk with Madge. She told me her brother works for the F.B.I. in Dayton. If we should find anything, we can let them handle it."

"And if Thelma decides to unlock the family rifle closet, I'm coming over to stay in your guest room," Mildred quipped. Her jovial tone didn't match the look in her eyes.

19

Calcutta sweltered under one of the worst heat waves in memory. Daily temperatures topped 110 degrees. More casualties from Burma were admitted to the overcrowded hospital. The overhead fans in Ward 55 did little to relieve the steam bath atmosphere. Extra beds occupied every available space, and the sheer number of bodies generated heat. Handling the most extreme emotional casualties of the China-Burma-India war effort, Lt. Benet worked overtime. One day blurred into the next.

The frustration of the CBI arena, its miserable diseases and weather, drove more men to psychological exhaustion each day. In addition to tending new patients, Benet invested great energy into his original core group. At first, the psychologist hoped that Gus could be rehabilitated by being with the others in group therapy, but shortly after the field trip to downtown Calcutta, the young private slid deeper into a world of his own private misery.

When Gus threatened to commit suicide, Mac tried to have him transferred to the 29th General Hospital. More deaths at the 142nd would reflect quite badly on McDermott. At the 29th, Gus would be given electroshock treatments and shipped home as soon as transportation became available. But no action had been taken on Mac's request and Gus stayed on at the 142nd.

Benet felt irascible and frazzled. Monday seemed like yesterday, but it was already the weekend. Many of the enlisted men took up heavy drinking, and depression was widespread. The psychologist still wrote daily to his wife, but he'd nearly given up on sleep.

Sunday evening found Benet stationed by Gus's bedside. Since the night a few weeks ago when Benet left Warren under Mahmood's careless watch, he'd been dressed down by Mac *and* Peterson. Their message was: "Never, never leave Indians or Anglo Indians in charge of anything at all." He'd been told that this kind of carelessness could get him court-martialed.

Subdued by the reprimand, Benet had been spending extra hours trying to get to the root of Gus's depression. By now it was clear that Gus could not join the other traumatized or mildly disturbed patients for field trips, movies, swimming (once they located a pool) or any of the "R and R" activities. In group sessions, Gus would mention his intention to drown himself in the Hoogly River.

"I don't want to live," Gus announced to the group. "My life had turned to shit when I was just a kid and it's gone from bad to worse ever since. Only a fool could be happy. Life's just not worth living."

Benet sighed. He found it incredibly sad that one just barely twenty years old was so cynical, so hopeless. "There's a difference between being unhappy and wanting to end your life," he said. "Being in Calcutta, none of us can forget the fact that unlike the people who go to bed hungry every night, we're damned lucky."

"Doc, yesterday I saw a dog carrying something. When it got closer, I swear that cur had a human hand. I nearly threw up."

"I know, I know," Benet sympathized. "Just when we think we've seen the worst, Calcutta comes up with new horrors. But that doesn't mean that being happy—or at least willing oneself to live—is a crime. Only a damn fool cocoons himself from reality. It takes courage to be happy. It takes courage to live."

Later, alone with his patient, Benet argued with Gus for the better part of an hour. "No one is asking you to go around grinning like an ape. You just have to quit trying to do yourself in. It's been said that some people can't manage their emotions. That's a bunch of baloney."

"I never said it's impossible to control feelings," Gus said. "What I said is that my life is rotten and it has been since I was born."

"You're not that different than many people, Gus. You've had a rough time, but you can manage your thought processes. What I mean is, you can decide to change your mind and through force of will, do just that."

"That's easy enough for you to say," Gus mumbled. "I get so damn mad that I want to kill anyone who even looks at me. They don't know what I've been through. I hate them for their stupid idiot faces. I wanna smash them."

Gus buried his face in his hands and began to sob. Having never seen a man so wracked with grief, the psychologist was nearly overwhelmed with pity. He sat silently by the bedside, letting the soldier vent his sadness. When the sobs quit, Gus blew his nose loudly into a handkerchief.

"You can talk with me about what happened in the jungle," the psychologist began quietly. "You've been through hell, but you survived. You're safe now; everyone here wants you to get better."

Gus remained silent. The regular flapping of an overhead fan was the only sound. The air was filled with a hospital smell—musty, medicinal, faintly sweet. Benet suppressed an urge to fan himself with a folded newspaper. He resisted the desire to go to the nurses' kitchenette for a cup of coffee. He would sit, just sit, until Gus started talking.

"Something happened—" Gus began. Benet sat and waited. Gus's silence gave over to a rush of words. "I'm ... I'm not sure I can talk about this. I'm, I'm... something must be wrong with me, really wrong with me. I did something I shouldn't have, or maybe I should have. I don't know what's right anymore. I'm confused; I wake up at night and can't stop thinking that I'll be punished. I'll never feel all right again."

Benet chose his words carefully. "You say, 'Something happened.' Something always happens, Gus. We think we're the only ones in the world who've done or seen or indulged in something, but there's nothing new under the sun, especially the scorching Indian sun. It will help you to unload that terrible burden, that weight on your mind. I'm here to listen. That's my job."

Benet wanted Gus to feel safe with him; maybe he should reiterate the ironclad tradition of confidentiality. He'd mentioned it repeatedly in group therapy sessions. It was a given in the doctor/patient relationship, but in Gus's fearful, embarrassed state, it was unlikely he would assume anything of the sort.

"Listen, Gus, your secret is safe with me. I can tell that whatever this is, it's eating away at you. The situation will only grow worse if you can't talk about it. If you feel ashamed of something; you need to unburden. It's what they call a 'confession' in the Catholic Church. I'm not a priest. I can't grant absolution, but I can assure you that there's nothing wrong with you. It may take some time, but you can get on with your life. You can pick yourself up and dust yourself off."

Gus sat up ramrod straight against the bed pillows. He shot a poisonous look at Benet. His eyes were narrow slits. "Godammit, you stuck-up egghead," he said. "You don't know what you're talking about. All of you so-called psychologists never had to eat bark and worms just to keep alive, to fight bugs and rats in the jungle, and to be treated like whores. You're full of shit."

Gus raised his voice until he was practically shouting. "Just 'dust myself off', he says, 'dust myself off.' I was raped, you fool, butt-fucked, used up and thrown away." Having confessed, Gus slumped against the pillows, the blood drained from his face.

116

Benet took several deep breaths before speaking. "What happened to you must have been horrible, Gus. No wonder you're angry; no wonder you feel that I've been dismissing your pain. I'm sorry for what you went through. Let me assure you, that you aren't the only one who's been raped by the enemy. It isn't as though you had a choice. You can get beyond this. What's happened is in the past. All you have is right now. The war will end and you'll be able to put all of this behind you."

Gus looked directly at Benet. His voice lowered a few decibels and the anger had faded from his face. "Doc, you still don't understand. I see you have a wedding band on. You're a married man, right?"

"Yes, and don't think it's easy to be faithful here in the midst of brothels and loose nurses." He'd nearly mentioned the rumor that Mac had cornered the market on nurse Clara, who allegedly charged for sexual favors. Instead, he added, "We're all human; we have physical needs."

"OK, Doc, I'll level with you. I wasn't alone in that Burmese jungle. My best buddy John, he was with me. Everyone else got swallowed up in the green hell. We were both fucked by the enemy, slapped around, and thrown away out in the middle of a jungle. Me and John, we were gonna die nowhere the hell in Burma. But then a funny thing happened. It turned out that we loved one another."

Gus's voice trembled. He was having trouble controlling his emotions. "The Japs crept up on us one morning and shot at us. Johnny took a bullet for me. He was shot through the head; I held him as he died."

"Yes," Benet said. "I'm with you. Your lover was shot and what happened next?"

Gus continued. "Things got worse. I was given to this hulk of a Samurai Jap officer who kept me as a kind of house pet, a sex toy, at the prison camp. Finally his General put a stop to it and I was thrown out with the other prisoners to work. Everyone knew about me by then. I was branded. If any of the others had had hidden weapons, I would have been stabbed in the back."

"It must have been truly awful," interjected Benet.

"Yeah, Doc, I can't even find the words to describe it. The fatigue, the starving, the sexual abuse—none of that was as bad as the mental part. I missed Johnny. I wanted to cry for him, but we had no privacy, so I held it in. I was an outcast, hated by the enemy and scorned by my fellow prisoners."

"I can see how alone you've been," Benet said. "I can understand that you need to feel less alone. I haven't had to endure anything like what you have, but I think I can comprehend how you must feel. I'm not judging you, Gus. On the contrary, I admire you for being able to pour all this out. There's a saying that the truth will set you free. You're on the right track, Gus."

"Yeah, Doc, but what if the fellas in my unit, that is if I ever get back to them and if any of them are even still alive, what if they find out? They'll have nothing to do with me. I'll be treated like dirt. I've heard them talking about queers and sissies. If I go home it'll be just the same. It's as though I'm still in prison."

"Gus, look around you. It's not as black and white as you seem to think it is. There are all kinds of guys here and because sex and love don't officially exist in the Army, no one knows what's beneath the surface. Some of my patients have had homosexual experiences for the first time, figuring that it was better than risking the clap from Calcutta's ladies of the night."

"Well," Gus said. "I see what you mean. But if nobody's asking or being truthful, it keeps a fella on pins and needles. On top of that, now I gotta worry what you think of me."

"I'm not here to judge," said Benet. "Let God do that, or Shiva or Mother Earth. My only goal is to help you cope with your feelings, Gus, and to help you become more stable."

"Sure, Doc, but you don't know what it's like to have people look down at you because you happen to like men. They make all kinds of assumptions—that you're weak, dishonest, cowardly. But Johnny was braver than our unit leader. Johnny was a patriot, ready to die for his country. Instead, he died for me."

"I see what you mean, Gus, but you're wrong that I have no idea what it's like to be scorned. Believe it or not, some of the officers ridicule me because of all my letter writing. They call me a sissy and worse. I'm a small, short fellow and I grew up having to fight bullies in the neighborhood and in the schoolyard. My revenge was to outsmart the bastards."

"I'm not smart," Gus said. "I'm confused and I don't know how I'll be able to tell my family that I love men. That is, if I ever see my family again, if we ever get out of Calcutta."

"You will see your family again, Gus. The Allies are making great gains and by this time next year, we should all be back home. You'll figure out how to tell your parents when the time comes. Or you'll move away and they won't have to know. You underestimate your intelligence. I can tell that you've got a sharp mind."

Gus closed his eyes and leaned back on the pillow. His breathing slowed and he appeared to be half asleep. Benet continued. "Look, we're stuck here together and often we live more like family with our buddies than we did with those we left at home. Here in the CBI, it seems that the Army doesn't inquire very closely into our personal lives. As long as it's not a distraction to the ranks, as long as they've got good fighting units, they don't care if a guy does it with his dog. It's no accident that we're called 'the forgotten front'."

Gus missed Benet's attempt at humor. He was dozing. Benet looked at his watch. It was 0400 hours, just enough time to return to the *basha* for a few hours' sleep.

Outside the hospital, the air felt fresh, even a bit cool. Benet knew that it was only the contrast with the hot box atmosphere he'd been in that made it seem that way, but he relished it nonetheless. Wild dogs howled in the distance. Their howls were particularly high-pitched, as though the pack found something to kill. Perhaps it was a smaller, weaker one of their own kind. Or maybe it was a tiger. Though it had been many years since most of the Bengal tigers had been driven out of the city, an occasional intrepid beast still wandered about.

Just as the canine howling subsided, another sound pierced the darkness—a human cry that verged on hysteria.

20

Following the cry, a woman's laugh pealed through the night. Another sound, a man's voice, accompanied the sounds of mirth. Instinctively, Benet slipped behind a sal tree, grateful that it was a moonless night. It would not do to be seen.

When his eyes adjusted to the darkness, he realized that he was ten feet from Mac's *basha*. Why, there was Mac himself, strolling along the path with Nurse Clara. Benet was surprised that Mac knew how to laugh. In public, he never cracked a joke, never displayed more than a wan smile. The men agreed that he was completely humorless.

Benet strained to hear what the two were saying. He thought he heard a mention of "opera," but what would Mac and Clara have to say about opera? He listened more intently. The word was not "opera." It was "opium."

Walking arm in arm, the pair grew closer. They stood caressing, a couple feet beyond Benet's sal tree lookout post. Lt. Richard Benet's mind raced. Why would Mac and Clara be discussing opium? It was known that drugs were smuggled into India from Burma. But what did that have to do with the hospital?

Clara and Mac stepped inside Mac's *basha*, the door slammed shut, and all was quiet once more. Benet walked quickly to his own *basha*, mulling over his glimpse into Mac's "other" life. Were Clara and Mac dealing in opium? Had he heard correctly?

There was talk, of course, of an opium ring operating from Rangoon, Burma. The illegal drug trade was one of many operations run by the *goondas.* It was even possible, Benet thought, that some of the hospital workers were also part of the city's underworld. In Calcutta, anything was possible.

The psychologist was operating on sheer adrenaline, and for some reason, Gus's lengthy confession caused his imagination to run wild. What if McDermott was really a drug dealer just pretending to act as hospital director? It was never entirely clear to Benet why Mac had been chosen to head up the 142nd General Hospital. It was said he'd been in charge of a heroic mission in the Burmese jungle, something to do with Myitkyina. But the man was terrible with personal relationships. McDermott paid little attention to the hospital. At times, thought Benet, the Army's idiotic way of operating seemed downright Byzantine.

Relieved to reach "home" at last, Benet unlatched the *basha* door. Too weary to remove anything but his shirt, he slumped onto the hard, narrow mattress. He envisioned himself back in Ohio with Rita, stroking her soft cheek and silky black hair as she breathed gently next to him. Before he could imagine further, he was asleep.

Benet dreamed that he was on a bridge high above a roiling river. The bridge lacked guard rails. He knew he had to walk across but doubted that he could keep his balance. A plunge to the waters below would surely result in death. Swimming to a safe place was not an option, as the river seemed to have no shores. There were sharks and other dangerous creatures circling through the water...

21

It was 0530 hours and just barely light when Sergeant Silas Lowell tapped on Benet's *basha* door. Living in such close quarters, the hospital personnel all knew quite a bit about one another's habits. Normally, Benet was awake by this time and beginning his day with a brisk constitutional around the hospital grounds.

When there was no answer, Silas walked around the perimeter of the *basha* and peeked in the window. There was Benet stretched out on his narrow bed, completely clothed and dead asleep. Silas tapped on the window and still failed to get a reaction. It looked as though he'd been on a drinking binge, but the Sergeant knew Doc was not a drinking man. The psychologist drank alcohol when social convention—as in meeting with a superior—seemed to necessitate it. When his fellow officers were getting drunk at the club, Doc was writing letters to his wife.

When his knuckles ached from tapping on the window, Silas finally remembered that Doc had been in a marathon session with Gus yesterday. Who knew how long that had gone on? It may have been an all-nighter. It was clear that the psychologist was not going to wake up any time soon, so Silas decided that he would act without direct orders.

He walked away from Benet's quarters, stopped in his tracks, turned around and walked back. Why not leave an explanatory note? It would have to be brief, as time was running out before he had to report for duty. Silas took a small tablet and the stub of a pencil from his shirt pocket and began to scrawl.

Dear Lt. Doc Benet:
Tried to wake you up so you could go with me, but you were dead to the world, so decided to act alone. I am running an experiment to check on the hospital's morphine supply. If I'm right, I might be able to solve the mystery. I know that detective work isn't part of my job description, but I have a hunch and I need to follow up on it. Faithfully yours, Sgt. Lowell."

He slipped the note under Benet's front door and walked back to the path. It was now 0600 hours, and he would have to get everything done before hospital personnel were up and about.

Silas walked back to the dirt path toward the Q Building. There were just a few natives lurking about in their white *curtas*. Lately it seemed as though the Army was hiring dozens more Calcutta natives. He could be sure of not being seen by anyone. He slipped around to the side, where a sunken staircase led to the cellar. He'd made a point to leave it unlocked last night in order to avoid going in the front entrance.

Silas realized that someone might have locked the cellar after he'd left. He knew that if he got caught trying to break in, he'd have trouble explaining why he was acting without orders. He broke into a nervous sweat. Breathing was difficult. He'd have to lose those ten extra pounds he'd gained since beginning his Calcutta duty.

To his relief, the door was still unlocked. Sweeping the grounds with a glance, Silas was relieved to see no one. He let himself into the dark corridor that led eventually to the medical supply room. He'd "borrowed" a key from Benet's desk, as he was sure the doctor would approve of his investigation. After all, he had tried to tell Benet. It wasn't his fault the psychologist overslept.

The light inside the basement of the Q Building was dim but Silas knew exactly where he was going. Today was Friday, and a new shipment of morphine would have arrived on Monday. On Wednesday, Silas had emptied all the container cartons, put the medication in sacks behind the medical sanitation supplies and replaced the cartons with lumber bits from a construction project near the hospital grounds.

If any of the medical staff found the cartons filled with rubble rather than morphine vials, the logical response would be to contact him to report the situation. If, on the other hand, someone was depleting the supply illegally, they might rummage around to find where the vials were. He or she might suspect that someone else was dipping into supplies.

It was a cat and mouse game at best, but Silas felt strongly that Colonel Mac's tall Hindu visitor might be at the root of this. The Colonel's friend, a Ravi something, had been at the hospital every day that week. On Thursday, a young woman who identified herself as Ravi's daughter visited Mac. She claimed to be writing an article on American medical practice for her college literary magazine.

Feeling his way around a corner that led to a dark hall, Silas realized he'd entered a different door than the one he'd planned. He would have to retrace his steps and figure out the correct path. The cellar was a labyrinth, but he would try every hall and eventually find the correct one.

As he groped his way about, Silas reviewed his suspicions. Mac escorted the "daughter of Ravi" around the 142nd spending an extraordinary amount of time in the Q Building cellar. He also noticed that Mac had locked many of the doors that led to the medical supply room.

Was this to keep anyone from knowing what went on? Might an exchange have taken place? When the young woman left, she was carrying a picnic basket covered with a checkered cloth. She had arrived empty handed. It was extremely odd.

Silas reached the medical supply room and located the morphine cartons. They were still filled with bits of wood. It was impossible to tell if anyone had touched them. The test was yet to come. He went to the cabinet where he stored the solutions and cleaning cloths he used to sterilize medical equipment. He'd started keeping them there because the native janitorial staff would use them for routine cleaning. Whenever he tried to find the cloths, he knew his stash had been raided.

When his eyes were better adjusted to the dim light, Silas located the cabinet, inside an obscure closet. The door was slightly ajar, which was not how he remembered leaving it. Sometimes the night wind rattled through these old buildings with fury. Maybe last night's strong breezes opened his closet. He stepped inside and reached to the shelf just above his head. He ran his hand along the rough wood, feeling for the cloth pouch.

Silas touched the edge of the heavy cotton material and thought he could feel the outline of a glass vial. He removed it to make sure he'd found the morphine. He'd carefully placed 24 full containers in the pouch just nine hours earlier. If they were still there, he was one step closer to solving the mystery.

Before he could make sure of anything, Silas heard the door creaking further open and footsteps behind him. He turned around and saw a familiar face. Before he could act, a pair of gloved hands tightened around his neck. He kicked mightily and tried to scream, but to no avail. Silas Lowe, the life strangled out of him, crumpled to the closet floor.

22

Benet had just closed his eyes when the alarm clock's *brrrinnng* interrupted his sleep. In his repose, he'd been in the jungle with a map and a compass. He could survive. He could forage, hunt and camp, but he needed a map. He lay in bed for a moment, trying to recall more of the dream.

As soon as Benet opened his eyes, Sanjay appeared. The Indian held his palms together at his chin, and bowed his head. It was a pleasant greeting, Benet thought. He might try to introduce it in the United States when he got home.

"Good morning, *sahib*. I understand that you are having very hard nights working with the patients. I have everything in readiness for your meeting."

"Ah yes, Sanjay. Good morning. I'm glad you're here to assist me. In just twenty minutes, I have to be at the officer's mess. An important meeting with the top brass."

Having taken a quick trip to the bathroom, Benet bumped into Sanjay outside the door. He'd get to the meeting on time even if he had to run, and by the looks of things he would. Sanjay shook out the wrinkles from Benet's dress uniform.

"It will not do to appear rumpled, *Sahib* doctor sir. All you need to do is be jumping into these garments and you will be most presentable."

Benet decided he would ride his bike to cut down on the time. It was just as well that he hadn't showered. The Calcutta steam bath removed any feeling of cleanliness in no time at all. Lt. Benet pedaled vigorously around the periphery of the hospital grounds.

He remembered the all-day bicycle jaunts that he and his cousin Cletus made from Findlay to Dayton. It was lucky that he'd grown up bicycling the country roads in rural Ohio. One never knew what skills might come in handy.

Benet was a strong cyclist. He covered the half mile to the Officer's Club in four minutes. Panting, he leaned his bike against a palm tree and mopped his brow with a handkerchief. In an effort to catch his breath, he walked evenly toward the heavy wooden door of the white stucco building. Though it was unlikely, he hoped that Peterson had not beaten him here.

An Anglo-Indian girl, dark-featured but fair-skinned, sat at the reception desk. She was chewing gum with a vengeance and filing her nails. Her fuzzy, untended hair looked as though she was having a morning like his, Benet thought. Busy with her manicure, she did not look up.

Benet cleared his throat. "Has a General Peterson signed in this morning?"

The girl opened a worn leather binder and traced her index finger down the page. "Peterson?" she asked. Then, as though a number of Petersons had been streaming into the Officer's Club all morning, she asked grumpily, "Would that be General Oley Peterson?"

"Why, yes," Benet replied, "that's the very Peterson I'm supposed to be meeting right now. I'm Benet, Lieutenant Richard Benet. The General said he might be running late." Benet looked at his watch to dramatize his point. The gesture was wasted. The girl had already returned to her nails and chewing gum.

"Actually, Lieutenant Beard, you're the one who's late. General Peterson is waiting for you in the library."

"That's Benet, Lieutenant Richard Benet," he corrected her. "Thank you." He wanted to add "for nothing," but the sarcasm would have been wasted. She was applying bright red polish to her fingernails.

Benet found Peterson sitting at a small table reading *The Calcutta Times.* At the psychologist's entrance, the big-boned General rose to his feet, dropping his newspaper to the floor. He extended his right hand and the two men shook, as if completing a deal.

"Howdeedo, Lieutenant Milay."

"It's Benet, sir, starts with 'B,' rhymes with 'today.' Pleased to see you."

"Sit down, sit down. I keep hearin' good reports about yer work with rehabilitation 'n morale buildin'. Summatha men tell me that you are popular and have quite a good bedside manner. It's very important that the men like as well as respect their officers, especially in dealin' with such a delicate matter as their mental health. I hear that ya kept that Sgt. St. John from becomin' anutha casualty."

"Oh, you mean Gus? Yes sir, he was so traumatized by imprisonment in Rangoon, he'd just about lost his will to live. I've had several all-night sessions with him, the most recent a couple nights ago. It's been a bit hectic. I apologize for being late to our meeting."

"Not ta worry, Lieutenant. I hadn been here long a'tall. Yer to be commended. Ya saved one of our men."

Peterson grimaced before continuing. "Ya gotta know, any suicides reflect quite badly on tha Neuro-Psychiatric arm of tha medical corps. Tha private may nevah be one hunnard per cent, but whatever ya did, I think we gottum away from tha edge. Do ya agree, Lieutenant?"

"Yes sir, although he may need to be watched for some time. I'm not sure he'll be fit for a return to duty any time soon." Or course, Benet didn't dare tell Peterson the real "problem."

Sexuality was a taboo subject within the hospital or, as far as he knew, anywhere in the military. He felt a certain irony about Gus's "confession." It was the unburdening to Benet that gave Gus hope and strength, and the fact that Benet clearly did not think less of him for his sexual orientation. To the psychologist, it made no difference at all. If, however, he was "discovered" by Mac, Gus knew he would be scorned.

"Well sir, I suppose I did. But as you know, there's nothing like being a good listener. Gus has been through a lot, but he has a strong spirit and..."

"Lieutenant," interrupted Peterson, "I hope ya brought your appetite. I ordered breakfast fer us." He snapped his fingers. "Shubi, bring it in."

The Indian bearer entered the library with a wheeled cart, from which he set up a small table. Moving swiftly, he covered it with a white linen cloth, flatware and dishes. Then he put out a steaming pot of tea, buttered toast stacked on a platter, boiled eggs in porcelain holders, and a small rectangular tray of bacon and sausage. Two china tubs held marmalade and sugar cubes. There was no milk for the tea, as all dairy products in India were considered impure and therefore off limits.

The Indian poured their cups of tea and started to serve them.

"No thankya, Shubi," said Peterson. "The Lieutenant and I will help ourselves. Let us have an hour of privacy, as we have some biznus to discuss." Shubi bowed slightly, touched his palms together under his chin and left without a sound. They were alone in the library.

"Ya know the sayin' here in the subcontinent, Lieutenant. 'The walls have eyes and ears but 'specially ears.' I hope ya like tea. As we all know, the coffee here's so wretched, it's far safer to jes stick with tea, which the Indians make quite well. I b'lieve for the most part, it's imported from England."

"You're right about sticking to tea," agreed Benet. "I've grown fond of the drink, even though we never had it back home in Ohio unless one was sick and then it was chamomile tea or rose hips. But of course, with all the British influence still in India, it seems quite the thing to do, drinking tea, that is."

He paused a moment, wondering about the propriety of what he wanted to ask. "Um, excuse me if I'm being nosy, sir, but we psychologists are an inquisitive lot. Wasn't Shubi the bearer for Mac, I mean Colonel McDermott? I'm pretty sure I've seen him before with the Colonel."

Peterson acted as if he hadn't heard the question.

"Lieutenant, please have summa this delicious breakfast afore it gets cold." The General forked out crisp bacon strips and a couple sausages onto Benet's white platter. He lopped off the top of his soft boiled egg, salted and peppered it, and began to spoon it out.

Relieved that he wouldn't have to figure out the egg procedure on his own, Benet followed Peterson's example. He'd never had eggs served this way. Once he started eating, he realized how ravenous he was. There had to be more to this meeting than just having breakfast, but for now he just enjoyed it.

"Umm, quite delicious." The higher one's rank, the better the food, Benet thought to himself.

Peterson seemed equally famished. Like a human vacuum cleaner, he'd already polished off the egg, three slices of toast and a large amount of sausage. He swilled three cups of tea to Benet's one. "Benet, this is *entre nous,* but ah removed Shubi from the service of Colonel McDermott. My bearer was injured in a bus accident and Shubi had jes resigned his position with Mac. He told the personnel office he was movin' to Delhi to help his agin' parents. The real reason was that Mac mistreated him. I found a replacement bearer for Mac and convinced Shubi to continue workin' for tha Army with me as his boss."

Benet poured himself more tea and, at Peterson's insistence, ate the last four sausages. He was not surprised to hear that Mac had acted badly toward Shubi. He hadn't forgotten the nasty shove he'd once seen the hospital colonel give Silas when he thought his orders weren't followed quickly enough, and assumed no one was looking. He imagined that Mac was capable of great cruelty.

128

With a shock, Lt. Benet realized that he hadn't seen Silas for a couple days. Men were being transferred left and right. He liked old "Silo" and would have wanted to say goodbye to him.

"Speaking of our Colonel Mac," Peterson continued, "I have a lil mission for ya, top secret and extremely important. I trust that ya'll maintain complete and utter confidentiality, Lieutenant Benet?"

"Yes sir, of course, sir."

Even though the library was still empty and the elusive Shubi had not come back to clear their breakfast, Peterson leaned toward Benet and lowered his voice to a whisper. "I need for ya to find out who is really runnin' the hospital. It's clear that Mac has not been doin' it fer some time. There is somethin' quite fishy 'bout the medical supplies as well. Large amounts of morphine 'pear to vanish and I cannot find out from the surgical ward where it is going." He looked at Richard with a troubled expression.

"Yes, General," Benet said. "I've been hearing about trouble with our medical supplies. It's at the top of my list to investigate. I've just been so busy with my cases."

"Do ya remember the Sergeant—short, stubby fellow by the name of Lowell—who was in charge? He said that morphine was given to the field surgeon's representative in exchange for dressings 'n bandages, but I have no proof of that."

"*Was* in charge?" asked Benet. "I know Si Lowell. We crossed the subcontinent at the same train from Bombay. In fact, I've been rather missing him. Was he sent home? Has he been transferred from medical accounting to another duty? Si wasn't big in the brains department, but he did an outstanding job with the inventory. He'd mentioned the morphine situation to me. Did Mac learn about that and give him the boot?"

Peterson's wide brow furrowed and his freckles appeared darker. "No, Lieutenant. I have grim news. Silas Lowell is no longah at tha hospital."

"But I saw him just a couple days ago. He and I were going to try to investigate the missing supplies. He said he had a few ideas, but he wanted my supervision. What happened? Did he have to leave for a family emergency? He said that his mother was quite ill and that if she died, he would have to fly home right away. Apparently he's the only..."

"We think he's gone AWOL," Peterson paused. "Or, that he's been murdahd."

23

The breakfast meeting with Peterson was the first of many that Benet would have. As the Military Police investigated Si's disappearance, Benet followed instructions to observe McDermott more closely. It occurred to him that he was being recruited as a spy, but somehow that didn't bother him. The edge of danger it gave to his job was oddly appealing. In a way, it was like dealing with yet another patient. The difference was that this one was in charge of the hospital rather than a patient in the wards.

Mac had trained his new bearer to say "*Sahib*, Colonel not in," whenever Benet came around. McDermott turned the weekly medical staff briefing over to Kopriva. There were no chances at all to observe the Colonel.

A week after the first chat with Peterson, Benet was summoned to a follow-up. They met on a Tuesday night at the Officer's Club for an after-dinner drink. Lt. Benet, who seldom drank, ordered a rum and coke. Peterson took his usual, scotch on the rocks.

"I'm afraid I have nothing to report," Benet said. The Colonel is more of a "empty uniform" than ever. As of now, the medical supplies are accounted for. Nothing's been tampered with. It seems that Lt. Kopriva is now in charge of the inventory. In fact, he seems to have taken over all of McDermott's functions. The Colonel is, how shall I put it ... 'dating' one of the nurses. He seems to 'entertain' her nightly."

Peterson ordered another scotch from the waiter, who looked like a double for Sanjay. Try as he might, Benet could not tell some of these natives from others. He politely refused another rum and coke. Ever since the sherry evening at McDermott's *basha*, he'd learned to make one drink last all evening. Drinking wasn't part of his self-image and besides, he'd seen too many men in this forgotten theater of the war turn into boozers.

"Ah, yes, Benet, it's commin' nawledge that Mac entertains Nurse Jacobs in his *basha*. She's tha latest, et any rate, and tha longes' lastin'. But do they go owt on dates as well? If so, ah'd like fer ya to trail 'em on one a their outins. We, and by that I mean tha medical administration, have a hunch that Mac mighta gotten in verah deep with tha natives."

"Do you mean with that Ravi character?" Benet asked. "Ghosh seems to pop up every now and then and his comings and goings have no logical explanation. Every week either he or this sweet young thing, a college student named Veena, comes to have lunch with the Colonel. It's funny to see them in the officer's mess, especially when none of the officers have very easy access to Mac. It's almost as though some kind of exchange is going on."

Peterson swilled down the last of his third scotch, "Yer beginnin' to get tha pitcher, Lieutenant. We need confirmashun but we think ther might be some illicit activity goin' on." Peterson paused, then lowered his voice, "He jes mite be an opium addict."

"A what? An addict?" Benet asked. "Opium isn't exactly available to American military personnel. With all due respect, sir. I deal with a lot of soldiers in addition to those that I counsel directly. They may be addicted to alcohol and they may visit brothels in the off-limits area; they may have offbeat sexual preferences, but I haven't seen any cases of opium addiction.

Benet hoped he wasn't giving away Gus's secret, but to his relief Peterson did not seem to pay much attention to his mention of 'sexual preferences.'

"Yer absalutly right about mosta tha men," Lieutenant, "but we're talkin' 'bout someone who's powerful, protected, 'n secretive. Mac's a personal frien' of Gen'ral Joseph Stilwell 'n ya may not know this, he's even served as one a "Vinegar Joe's" trusted advisors. He helped plan tha Ledo Road strategy."

"But the man's an alcoholic," the psychologist exclaimed. "I don't see how he even functions. Emotionally, he seems to have checked out a long time ago. He's washed up."

Suddenly, Peterson changed his mind and ordered another scotch on the rocks. Benet decided to throw caution to the wind, and ordered another rum and coke. Here at last was a senior officer who valued his opinion. The moment was not to be wasted.

"You know, sir," Benet said, "I just recalled something unusual that happened with Mac last month. In a rare appearance at the club's communal dinner table, he boasted that he'd been entertained royally at an upper caste home. I wonder if it could be the home of that Ravi Ghosh."

"I've nevah before known Mac to have anythin' to do with tha natives," Peterson reflected. "Does this Indian fellow evah mention his biznus? We try ta encourage good relations with tha Indian citizens, but as far as ah know, tha good will only goes one way— from us ta them. Maybe ower Mac's a secret diplomat."

"Hmm," mused Benet. "That seems highly unlikely. As far as business, the only thing I've been able to glean is that Mac once helped the Indian's nephew with learning some English phrases."

"Have you evah met the nephew?" Peterson asked.

"No, apparently he was about to leave for a university in America as soon as the war ended. Oh, there is something else. At one point, the Indian said he was on a planning board for a new hospital in Calcutta and he wanted to see how the 142nd operated. None of what he said was very convincing."

Peterson looked at his watch. "Lieutenant, yer doin' a decent job despite little to go on 'n a nebulous task at best. Jest find out whatcha can. Havin' said that, ah notice that it's past 2300 hours and I'm sure we both have a busy day tomorrow. Ah'll be checking back with ya."

The Officer's Club was nearly deserted when the two men shook hands and stepped out into the hot, sticky night. A solitary night bird trilled. Peterson's driver was waiting to take him back to the 20th General Hospital, where the Neuro-Psychiatric Branch Headquarters was located and where Peterson lived.

Benet returned to his *basha*, rubbing his temples to soothe their throbbing. Downing a couple aspirin, he turned on the overhead fan. Supplied with onion skin paper and Parker pen, he stationed himself at the room's all-purpose table. The fountain pen was a graduation present from his faculty advisor Dr. Dinegar. That was another lifetime ago. He sighed and began writing.

India
5 November 1945
Dearest:

The first and only thing of importance which I have to tell you is that considerable mail came today, including numerous glorious letters from you. Since I am writing this late at night, it may be a hybrid. It isn't that I'm particularly lazy, but rather that bad lighting, bugs, and lights going out give me a severe pain and interfere with my clear thinking. Tsk.

About 3:00 this afternoon (or as they say in the Army 1500 hours) I suddenly realized that I had started blowing my nose, and without the slightest warning, or reason that I can think of, I find myself in possession of a full-fledged cold by this hour, 11:45 p.m. your time. That makes me mad as hell, for I've been so darn careful all along. I guess I'll just have to grin and bear it. Capt. Seeger is just getting over a cold, and Phipps has been bothered, too. So perhaps it is just that I should join them.

It pleased me to learn that you liked my very personal letter of last month. I was worried that it might have gotten lost, and wondered just how I could duplicate it, since such letters depend upon mood for proper expression. My irritable moods of late are not conducive to the trends of sentiment that I really feel toward you -- in fact, you are the only person, rather the thought of you, who restrain me at all. Otherwise, I would be a pretty cynical little cuss. On all sides of me I see a gorgeous and luxurious nature infiltrated with a vermin termed 'man' who constantly makes his odious presence felt in various unpleasant ways. Such as telephone posts across rice paddies.

Last night's show (darn it, I didn't have time to include it in yesterday's letter) was Ann Southern in "Mazie Goes to Reno" and outside of a pretty trying plot, it did manage to get a little fun across to the audience. The newsreels and G.I. shorts are usually worth more than the main feature.

Well, darling, I shall write you at greater length tomorrow, after my sightseeing day with the healthier boys of the Neuro-Psychiatric Ward.
In the meantime, all my love
A big kiss and hug,
Richard.

24

On Wednesday, Benet awakened before the alarm clock sounded. This was a part of the schedule he enjoyed, for it brought the weekly sightseeing tour. He, as well as the men, welcomed the temporary escape from the hospital.

At last week's briefing with Peterson, who was now covering for Mac, Benet had proposed taking his group to the Jain Temple. To his relief, the General said yes. Also known as Parashnath Mandit, the Jain Temple was actually not just one but a complex of temples. Benet heard from those who'd seen it that the Jain complex was even more beautiful than Agra's Taj Mahal. His entourage would comprise Gus, Fletch, Ike and Sturke.

When the psychologist arrived at Q Building, he saw that the men had beat him to their meeting place. They were leaning against the Q Building in the tiny shaded area under the roof's edge. This would be the third Wednesday outing and their first time swimming. It had taken the efforts of General Peterson to finally secure rental of a municipal pool.

"Congratulations for being punctual," Benet said. "Sit down here at the picnic table and listen up before we begin today's adventure."

"Doc, we don't need a briefing before swimming," Fletch protested. "We all got our suits along and we all know how to swim. Let's get outta this dump ASAP."

"Culture before athletics," Benet said. "Before we go swimming, we'll tour the Jain temple. Lieutenant Kopriva was unavailable to be our driver, so we'll also experience the Calcutta Municipal bus system."

"Ah, c'mon, Doc," said Fletch, "you ain't afraid ta drive around Calcutta are ya? We'll all back-seat drive."

"Yeah," said Sturke. "We'll look ahead and yell if we see sacred cows on the road. There's extra trucks around, and we'd trust our lives with you, Doc. Besides, if you chicken out, I'll take over. I learned to drive in New York City: I'm used to bad traffic."

"Enough jabbering," said Benet. "Just what I don't need is a bunch of back seat drivers. Our designated truck is in the shop getting a new transmission, so it's out of the question. It's only half a mile to the bus stop, and we need to look for bus Number Three. Remember not to give anything at all to beggars."

Fletch interrupted, "Yeah, yeah, we know that, Doc. We weren't born yesterday."

"Let me repeat," Benet said. "We'll go to the Jain Temple first, then to the municipal pool, and after that to a Chinese restaurant for lunch, my treat. But wait, we can't start just yet."

Holding forth at one end of a picnic table, Benet opened his copy of John Barry's *Calcutta 1940* and began reading aloud:

...we come in sight of the Temples. These are four in number, the most important being that dedicated to Shree Shree Sheetalnathji, the tenth of the twenty-four Jain deities. Access to this Temple is gained through a lofty three-storied gatehouse, flanked on either side by crouching lions. A marble tablet in the handsome portico beneath records that the Temple was built in 1867 by Rai Budree Doss, Bahadur..."

"We're not a scholarly bunch, Doc," volunteered Gus. "I vote we just go see it. We'll forget everything you just read before we get there. Let's get on to the bus!"

"OK, you lunkheads," said the psychologist. "This will be our buddy system. Gus and Fletch are one pair; Ike and Sturke another. You're responsible for keeping track of one another, and I'm responsible for keeping track of you all. Please be careful."

They strolled along the dirt path that encircled the hospital grounds. A group of nurses and several privates had gathered together to watch an Indian and his performing monkey.

The small gray creature, dressed in a red jacket with black and gold trim, wore a red conductor's hat topped with a black plume. It stood on its hind legs and strutted awkwardly to the flute playing of the owner, who squatted nearby. Next to the monkey's owner were two skinny little boys dressed in dirty rags. The children held out tin cans for donations.

Benet saw the men reaching into their pockets for *rupees*.

"Hey, remember what I told you. We'd all like to give *rupees* to the poor but we can't. Move along or we'll miss our bus. If we do that we'll run out of time for the lunch I've planned after the temple and swimming."

The mention of food was enough to keep the men from lingering. Gus broke into a song "I been workin' at the horse-pital," he improvised, "all the livelong day. I been workin' at the horse-pital and I want to get away."

The others joined in, making up new verses. They soon reached a sign for Bus #3. It pulled up in a few minutes, a big red double decker. Benet led the way, putting the correct number of *rupees* in the collector's box and checking behind him for his foursome.

The psychologist and his charges stood in a cluster, holding to the overhead leather straps hanging from the ceiling of the first level. Benet had studied the directions with his bilingual map and compared it with a simplified drawing he'd sketched of their route.

Every seat was taken. The men stood in the center aisle wedged in with dozens of locals. The Indians looked at them as though they'd just landed from another planet. Next to Benet was a boy of ten or twelve holding his mother's hand and clutching an English textbook.

The bus lurched and rocked its way along Upper Circular Road. It passed two ornamental pillars, one bearing the inscription in English: "Road to the temple garden of Rai Burdree Doss, Badhadur, Mookeem to His Excellency the Viceroy." Benet referred to the Barry guidebook. "This marks the entrance to Halsi Bagan Road," he announced to the men.

"You soldiers from ze hos-pit-all?" asked the boy. "My *babu* say the hospital is soon belonging to Alipore District. My *babu* say the people army will be taking it back for Calcutta."

"Shush, Prosunno," said his mother, a handsome woman in a magenta *sari*. She looked at Benet apologetically, folded her hands together and nodded her head toward him.

"*Namaste, sahib* G. I. My son speaks too boldly. Please to forgive him. His father says no such thing. He must hear this nonsense at school."

"Never mind, madam," said Benet. "Children are known for speaking anything that comes into their heads." Benet looked down at Prosunno. "Young man, you speak very good English. Did you learn from your teacher?"

"Yes, American sir," said Prosunno. "We are having English lessons every day and I am the best of my class. I hope to go to your country to study. I am wanting to become a lawyer when I grow up."

Prosunno's mother looked down at the boy and repeated her shushing. "We must pay attention, as do not want to miss our stop." She turned to Benet. "Where is it you are heading, if I may ask?"

"We've been told we must see the Jain Temples. I've got a camera to take photos of my men to send to their folks back in the states. We're also going to tour around a bit, as much as these fellows will pay attention."

"We also are getting off at the Temples so you may follow us."

No sooner had the woman said this than she rang a bell for the driver to stop. Dozens of passengers got up and rushed for the doors. Squeezed into the mob, Benet, Sturke, Gus, Ike and Fletch followed the mother and son down the platform.

The five Americans and two Indians stood at the corner of Halsi Bagan Road and Badridas Temple Street.

"Well, now you see where you are, right by your destination. But, I urge you to come back at moonlight," Prosunno's mother said to Benet. "When you can do so, it is truly spectacular. You can arrange it with the Temple authorities. Of course, the Jain Temple is magnificent at any time of night or day. And now we must go. Good luck, American soldiers."

She started walking away, pulling Prosunno along by his hand.

"Mama, can't we go with American soldiers to the Jain Temple? I am having many questions about America."

"No my dear, we cannot. You know we are meeting your uncle for tea. He always has special cakes for you. Come along."

"Goodbye and God speed," Fletch called out as he waved to Prosunno.

Sturke guffawed. "God speed? What the hell does that mean to an Indian?"

"Yeah, man," Gus added. "You shoulda said something like, 'May Shiva protect you' or 'May you escape Kali's wrath.'"

Benet led his troupe toward the temple entrance, a three-storied gatehouse flanked on either side by crouching cats.

"Stop here and sit on the wall near the stone lions. I want to get a photo of you four."

Using his box camera, Benet snapped a couple photos of Gus, Sturke, Ike and Fletch. He would include the group picture in his monthly report to Colonel Mac to illustrate the activities he was providing for the men. It wasn't that he cared about getting a promotion, but he felt it necessary to disabuse Mac of the notion that he didn't work hard enough. Being responsible for four patients in downtown Calcutta wasn't exactly easy.

Sturke looked at the lion on the right. He pointed to the big cat's sneering lips. "This reminds me of someone we all know. Now who does this resemble? I'll give you a clue. It has two legs instead of four."

"You you m-mean Mu mu Mac?" stammered Ike.

Everyone except Benet guffawed. "I think our colonel is a tiger, not a lion," he said. "There is a certain similarity in the eyes. Let's get along. There's a lot to see. We want to spend time inside the temple."

As they walked into the garden just beyond the gatehouse, Fletch nudged Benet. "Doc, are you saying our colonel is a beast?

This elicited loud guffaws from the others, who started to chant, "the beast of Bengal, the beast of Bengal ... our hospital is run by the beast of Bengal."

Though secretly amused, Benet forced himself to put on a stern expression. Followed by his crew, he stepped through the Jain Temple complex's massive open gate. "Shut up and look," he told the men.

He waved his arm upward and as he did, his men stopped joking about the "beast" and gazed at the walls and ceiling. Every inch was covered with squares of colored glass or mirrors, arranged in graceful designs. The sounds of traffic outside had disappeared. Colored glass oil lamps were burning from countless niches, shelves, and corners.

"Jeepers," exclaimed Gus. "It's like being inside a magic lantern."

They walked through vaulted rooms, each more intricately decorated than the one before. White-garbed Jains in attendance at the temple were sweeping the floor in front of them as they walked. They wore gauzy rectangles of cloth over their mouths.

The usually garrulous men fell silent. Benet felt pleased. He wanted them to feel they'd gotten completely away from the hospital and, for a short time, from the U.S. Army Air Force.

"Who are these Jains, anyway?" asked Gus.

Benet read aloud from a pamphlet he'd picked up at the temple entrance: "The Jains are a religious sect founded by Mahavira Vardhamana, presumably started in Marwar in the 6th century B.C. The Jains say that regard for life is the highest virtue.

"Cloth masks are worn so as not to harm any insects that might fly into the mouth," he continued. "You will notice that the Jains constantly sweep the floor as they walk so as not to accidentally tread on insects or small animals. All Jains are vegetarians. The most devout of the sect do not eat potatoes or onions as digging them up might harm worms in the surrounding earth."

Not to be outdone, Gus read from his copy of the guide pamphlet: "The priests are famous for never using mechanized transportation, preferring to sweepingly walk all over India to their postings from the monasteries in Western India."

As they walked from room to room, the calmness made talk seem unnecessary. It might not help a group of heavily booted tank gunners get back their fighting spirit, Benet thought to himself, but for Fletch, Ike, Gus and Sturke, the Jain temple was good medicine.

They reached the temple verandah and followed along a railing of filigree-worked metal into yet another sanctuary. The ornate carving and the play of light and color were dazzling. Large mirrors, glittering chandeliers, and multi-colored crystals made the walls seem alive.

The psychologist and his patients next entered an enormous circular room with vaulted ceilings and a dazzling play of colors. Beams of light, filtering in through a multitude of distant windows, created a feeling of movement. They stood in awe, looking upward.

Ahead of them stood a candle-lit altar encircled by gilded pillars. Three images graced the altar. The men paused in the center of the room. No one spoke. It was like nothing any of them had ever seen.

Benet continued his role of tour leader. "And this room, according to Barry's guidebook, is the 'Holy of Holies'." He pointed to the altar. "We have here the images of Anand Swami and Gatan Swami. However, I'm not sure who the deity in the center is. Obviously, he is important, as he is wearing a gold necklace. And look: someone has placed a garland of fresh red roses around the neck."

"Do you suppose that's the chief deity of the Jains?" Gus asked in a whisper.

"You know, it just might be," said Benet. "There are so many gods and goddesses in this country, I can keep only a very few in mind, and just when I think I've heard of every religion or sect, another pops up. Speaking of gods and goddesses, there are twenty-four Jain deities. Obviously we won't have time to visit all of their shrines."

Gus looked at his watch. "Doc, it's already eleven hundred hours."

Leaving the Jain Temple complex, Benet and his men walked several blocks to a Calcutta municipal swimming pool, where the

U.S. Army Air Force had arranged a temporary membership for personnel on duty in Calcutta. After obtaining locker keys and changing into their swim suits, the men spent an hour in the water.

Soldiers from Calcutta's other two military hospitals were also enjoying the Olympic-sized pool. The water was clean and the entire facility was pleasantly well organized. Fletch and Gus swam laps. Ike and Sturke got into a splashing contest.

Though Benet was pleased to see how much his patients enjoyed the physical activity, he felt slightly worried. Fearing that the men might notice his bow-leggedness, he stayed in the water the entire hour. When their allotted time was up, he made a point to be the last one getting out.

Eating at Chang Foo's Chinese Restaurant was the highlight of the outing for everyone except Ike, who became embarrassed when trying to order. Whenever he was nervous, his stammering increased. Finally Gus started speaking for him, which only increased Ike's humiliation.

While the others picked at the egg-fried rice and spicy Kung Pao dishes, Ike was sullen and silent, barely touching his food. In his planning, Benet had imagined the restaurant experience as a celebratory meal. Instead, it was a letdown. He silently cursed himself for planning too ambitious a day.

At fifteen hundred hours, they boarded another bus and soon arrived back at the hospital.

Lt. Benet dismissed his gang of four, then went to his office in the Q Building Annex, another of the rambling *basha*-type edifices that dotted the hospital grounds. On the days he spent with the men, he had supper at the general mess hall rather than the Officer's Club. It had been recommended in his job description that he be with the men in less official capacities. Mingling, the psychologist assumed, was supposed to make him more approachable.

Most personnel had taken the afternoon off. The hall was dark; the doors closed and locked. As Benet turned a corner and approached his office, however, he heard talking and footsteps. Ahead of him were a tall Hindu man and a young woman. They were leaving his office, Number 300.

Benet felt a surge of anger. Things were going from bad to worse. As if he didn't have enough to deal with, were there now sightseers or spies infiltrating the hospital? Was he the only one even attempting to maintain some kind of order?

"Hey, what's going on?" he yelled. "What are you doing in this building?"

The Indians turned around and greeted him with "*Namastes.*"

"Oh, so sorry, Dr. Benet," said the man. "I am Ravinath Ghosh, a friend of Colonel McDermott's and this is my student Veena Sengupta."

"You may call me 'Beeni,'" said the young woman.

Smiling graciously, Ravi continued. "We heard about your interest in Indian culture from the honorable *sahib* Colonel McDermott, and thought that perhaps we might invite you to a moonlight tour this evening. We envision it as an education in the name of cultural enrichment, if you will."

"Oh," said Benet, "I see. Forgive me if I seemed rude. We Americans are not used to seeing people other than military personnel on the hospital grounds. Sadly our contact with local inhabitants of Calcutta consists mainly of our bearers, maintenance staff, or the mess hall workers."

That wasn't quite true. Benet thought he'd seen the tall Hindu in the Q Building before. The young woman also looked slightly familiar. Hadn't she been at the campus of the Bethune Girls' College? He remembered back to his question about Dina Pavri. An Indian girl said she would be on the lookout for Pavri. It may well have been Veena.

Benet briefly considered going but then thought better of it. "Well Mr. Ghosh, Miss Sengupta," he said, "thank you for your kind offer but I'll pass. Just now I cannot think of anything that I'd like to see by moonlight or any other light. I am behind in some work that must be done, so if you will excuse me."

Ravi bowed very slightly. "Yes, I understand. Our offer stands. Now I must escort Miss Sengupta home to her family. We wish you a good evening." Veena flashed Richard a charming smile and then the two were gone.

25

Benet's intention was to entertain Rita in each letter, not to present conundrums or share things that might upset her. He opted not to tell Rita about his encounter with Ravi and Veena. After clearing his desk of forms and reports, he began to write.

10 November 1944
142nd General Hospital
Calcutta, India
   My Dearest, This has been a busy day, filled with taking my "better adjusted" patients on an outing to the Jain Temples; a municipal pool, where they swam—therapeutic benefits, you know— and to a Chinese restaurant. I am a bit done in, and at this golden hour of afternoon, missing you very much. Instead of giving details about the outing, I will give you a picture of what I see out my office window...

   The natives are working like little beavers in the rice paddies, clipping away with their sharp little scythes. The rice seems to be of two varieties, one a half foot taller than the other. They gather armfuls of it, as it is cut, eight or ten stems coming from one common pod, and gently lay it on the ground. These various armfuls they gather into bundles, tie two bundles to either end of a five-foot stick, and then put the balanced stick over the shoulder and manfully lug it to the communal barnyard. I have been wondering just how property is owned over here, or how it is rented, or just what the arrangement is.

   Right now I haven't the vaguest idea, but I do know that thoughts of you keep my mental health intact, my dearest. Otherwise, I could not bear every day here in India—on the other side of the world from all I love best. Just as I counsel the men, my mottos are 'Live and learn' and 'This too will pass.'

   In a country as bountiful as this, it is difficult to believe stories told by my friends of sights they have seen themselves in Calcutta: hundreds of starving natives cluttering the streets, sinking to the ground, wailing bitterly, right in broad daylight.

   While I am complaining, another aspect of India comes to mind: their cursed transportation system. Even today, as we bussed home, we saw a passenger train puffing along and its coaches were loaded to the steps with natives—just riding—no business, no pleasure—just going back and forth. Some strong force should kick them to hell off the trains during times like these and get down to work. But it seems that only the poor women work, and there lies some hope.

But in this district, their stupid adherence to centuries-old religious practice has relegated women to a position similar to a breeding sow, and she is rarely seen except heavily clothed with a cloth drawn over her face. Of course, they have prostitutes, but they form a separate caste and do nothing but practice nature's oldest profession until syphilis eats them away.

Last night, M/Sgt. Davis got quite a thrill (he is in the first basha from mine) when he awakened to hear a sniffing just outside his net. The howls of jackals had been disturbing the boys for some minutes, and they sounded close, but no one knew they went through the bashas looking for food. I slept through the whole episode...

Benet folded the letter and put it in an envelope. He would finish before he went to sleep tonight. Here in this land of so many people with seemingly nothing to do, he found it ironic that he was always watching the clock. It was six o'clock, or—as the military would have it—eighteen hundred hours, and he must leave for the mess hall now or miss dinner.

Placing his latest Rita letter in his shirt pocket, Benet splashed water on his face and toweled off. As he strode briskly along the path from his quarters to the mess hall, he noticed the sunset, even more spectacular than usual. He took his pocket diary out to make a quick sketch. He labeled the circles, lines and squiggles so that when he and Rita were together again, he could more accurately tell her about it.

This is the moon, he wrote, *with only the rim and shaded portion a cool gold-silver.* The evening star was indicated by an asterisk. A curved line stood for the horizon. Above the curved line, Benet wrote a description of colors layering up from the earth: pink, pink to amber, amber to blue-green. Below the curved line, he drew rectangles indicating *bashas*, circles indicating ponds and two areas marked "rice paddies." At the bottom of the drawing were two parallel lines labeled "Walk from the mess hall."

The sunset's palette had faded into gray by the time he finished his notes and reached the green wooden building that served as mess hall. This was a facility where both officers and the non-comms could take their meals. The food was erratic, ranging from mediocre to disgusting.

The psychologist bounded up the worn steps and across the verandah. Once inside, he grabbed a tray, plate and utensils, and walked the food line. The servers, white-aproned and capped, were nearly out of the evening's fare—pork and beans, rice and scrambled eggs. Looking at the dregs nearly killed Benet's appetite.

A cluster of officers sat at "his" corner: Andy Anderson, Lt. Seeger, Lt. Moriconi, Master Sergeants Hosenkamp and Scruggs. Red Cross nurses Ellen Colony and Kay Glist were just pulling their chairs out from the table as Richard walked up.

"Hey, hey, Doc Benet, we'll see you another day," quipped Ellen. She had taken to speaking in rhymes.

Kay rolled her eyes and groaned. "Lt. Benet, I think my friend here might need to join your psychotherapy group. India has at last affected her mind, robbing her of what little reason she possessed. I ask you, how can such a fruitcake be in charge of critically ill patients?"

"Well you know, ladies, that humor is the best medicine. It doesn't matter if the jokes are feeble: the patients will love them anyway."

"Wait a minute," Ellen protested. "What's this about 'feeble.' I haven't heard any brilliant humor coming from our resident clinical psychologist."

"Come on, you nut," said Kay, "we gotta scram. Clara's shift ended about five minutes ago and you know that brat never waits a second after time's up."

"Bye, guys 'n gals," said Kay. "We'll see ya next week." She raced after Ellen, who was already out the door and halfway down the stairs. "Wait up, Speedy."

"Silly geese," said Hosenkamp.

"You're right about that," Benet agreed. "We could sure use our sweethearts and wives here, but at least these are women with shoes." When seen at all, most Indian women were barefooted.

Gradually the men were leaving, and the mess hall was nearly empty. The psychologist stared at the cold beans and fake eggs on his plate. He forced himself to take a bite. "Food and nothing more" was the best one could say about such a meal. The lights dimmed, then grew brighter, a sign of the usual nightly fluctuations in the electrical generator.

In addition to Hosenkamp, one of the remaining dinnertime stragglers was Ed Scruggs, a fellow Ohio native. Ed had attended two years of college before being drafted. He cornered Benet at every opportunity to discuss his emotional problems.

Scruggs had poured out his entire story more than once. He met "the love of his life" during freshman year of college, and she'd promised to wait for him. So far, she had, but he was terribly afraid that she would run out of patience.

That was just one topic Scruggs foisted on Benet. When it wasn't his love life, Scruggs wanted to hash over diversified subjects such as an officer's responsibilities, Mormons, and the strengths and weaknesses of the Army's educational system.

Hosencamp turned in his cafeteria tray. He yelled across a couple tables, "Hey, Doc, you missed tonight's meeting. The enlisted men are s'posed to contribute ten *rupees* to the Christmas party fund. Some fellas were mad at the idea. They said no go to the whole thing. I guess we hafta have an official vote on it. Wadya think?"

Before Benet could answer, Clara Jones sidled next to him and threw a sultry glance toward Scruggs. "Hi there, you two heartbreakers. Too bad you're both taken. I'd choose you two over the whole army of lunkheads around this dump."

Clara managed to look glamorous even in a starched white uniform. She wore her nurse's cap at an angle over her unruly black curls. Her large hazel eyes radiated spirit and intelligence. Benet wondered why she was single.

Ed Scruggs rose to his feet. "I'm takin' off," he said. "Gotta study for a big test in the morning. Night Doc Benet, Nurse Clara."

"Bye, Scruggs," Benet said. "You ace that son of a bitch. Remember, you're a cut above. Number one, you're from Ohio. Number two, you're college material."

Pressing closer, Clara gave Benet a flirtatious look. While the nurse didn't exactly make Benet uncomfortable, he didn't care to be alone with her. He'd heard tales about Clara's three dates a night. He knew for a fact that she spent most nights at Mac's *basha*. It was none of his business, and he certainly didn't judge anyone on a moral basis. Still…

"Um, I need to finish up some work, Clara. Are you OK?"

"Well, not exactly," Clara said in a barely audible voice.

While some of the married officers carried on wildly, dating the nurses or slinking off to brothels. Benet's love for Rita kept him loyal. If this was going to be a test, Benet knew he was strong enough to pass. Clara seemed to want something from him, and, whether he liked it or not, it was clear that he was going to learn about it.

Aside from the cleanup crew, the psychologist and the nurse were the only two people left in the mess. Benet looked at his watch, a Timex that Rita gave to him last Christmas. In the meantime, Clara started weeping. She leaned her head against his shoulder. Her sobs grew louder. Despite his intention to remain aloof, Benet put his arm around her shoulder.

"Oh, Lieutenant Benet, forgive me," Clara cried out. "I didn't mean to break down. Please don't tell anyone about this. I'm so upset, I can hardly think. I can hardly talk. She wailed loudly and clung to Benet for several minutes. Finally she stopped and took several deep breaths.

Benet pulled out a clean handkerchief and passed it to Clara. He disentangled himself and walked over to the cooler to get her a glass of water. "What is it? Can I do anything to help?" he asked in a professional voice.

When Clara said nothing, he added, "All of us hate being stuck in Calcutta: it's enough to make anyone weep."

As if proving his point, Clara broke into a fresh round of sobs.

He pretended not to notice. He wanted her to regain control, to listen to him. "I promise that anything you tell me won't go beyond here. But I think it best if we walk out to the porch, out of hearing of the kitchen crew."

Though the workers couldn't be seen, he knew that they were listening. A few of them understood English.

"OK, let's go outside and sit on the porch," Clara suggested. She dabbed at her eyes with a handkerchief. "I'm in hot water. I need your professional opinion."

"Well," Benet said, "I'm not sure I can help but I can be a sounding board." He kept from adding a quip about Clara's well-known energetic "dating habits." She was upset enough already. It was better to say less rather than more.

The nurse sounded desperate, and Benet was a kind man. They sat in two wicker chairs that happened to be on the screened-in porch. The screen was torn in several places. Mosquitoes, on the lookout for new flesh, were buzzing around them.

"I'll smoke a cigarette," Clara said. "That'll help ward off the insect world, at least for awhile. I know you have to get back and write a letter to your wife back in Ohio."

"What are you talking about, Clara?"

146

"Doctor, everyone knows about your writing. Everyone else is out drinking, but you're in your quarters penning mushy love letters. Don't worry, this won't take long." She crossed her legs and gave Benet an earnest look. "You'll keep what I say to yourself, right?"

Benet nodded, "Haven't I convinced you of that? Of course I will. This is my job. I hear confessions all the time. I don't judge and I never let anything leak outside. I deal only with how to relieve suffering. Nothing less, nothing more."

Clara puffed a smoke ring into the air, then began. "I managed to get myself in a mess." She paused before continuing. "I guess you may not know that I'm not three-date Clara anymore. I'm seeing a lot of Mac. He's the only one I'm seeing."

"Seeing?"

Clara sighed and lit another cigarette. "Well, it is more than seeing. You might say we're having an affair. Believe it or not, Mac said we might be able to make a pair someday. I don't want to spend the rest of my life playing the field."

"There's nothing wrong with that, Clara. It's perfectly natural. But—I know I sound like an old fogey—you need to be careful with Mac."

"Sure, I know that," said Clara. "You're a happily married man, Doc. Don't most people long for what you have? Never mind, don't answer that."

"Most people, unless they're seriously damaged or emotionally hurt, long for some degree of happiness and stability with a partner. I'm one of the lucky ones, but I'm not at all sure that marriage is the only way to find bliss. There's no guarantee that if a person is unhappy before marriage, they'll be cured afterwards."

"Well, Mac is a very unhappy person. I know that."

The lights went out in the mess hall behind them. It was growing late.

"Sometime the gloom spreads, like a disease," said Benet. "Are you here to ask my advice on whether or not to keep going with this man?"

"Doc, I'm afraid. At first it was wonderful whenever we were together. Mac can seem harsh, but he just needs someone who understands him. He lost his father when he was twelve. His mother became an alcoholic."

Clara lit another cigarette and continued. "He confided that he hasn't told anyone else about this, that it's all behind him. But his

147

addictions tell me that he is still very sad about everything in his childhood."

"What addictions?" asked Benet. "I know Mac drinks, but I didn't know about drug use." Actually, Benet did know, but playing dumb was the way to get more information. The ploy didn't work.

"I mean his alcoholism," Clara lied. "He's addicted to alcohol. Lately, he's turned against me. He's been rough, frightening, and constantly sarcastic. I can't stay with him but I can't leave him either. I don't know what to do." The nurse buried her face in her hands.

"I think you know the answer, Clara. When you can't stand it any longer, you will decide to get out of the affair. It sounds to me as though you're paying too big a price. This can't be helping your self-esteem. Has he hurt you physically or just emotionally?"

"Oh my God," moaned Clara. "It's worse than you imagine. I've got some bruises on my arms from where he's squeezed me too tight. But it's not that. It's... It's..."

Benet put his hand lightly on her trembling shoulder and patted her in what was meant to be a brotherly gesture. "You won't tell me anything I haven't heard, Clara. Besides, you don't have to tell me."

Clara blew a cloud of smoke into the night air. "In a way, I'm being threatened with blackmail. Mac knows some things about me that would result in a dishonorable discharge. He could ruin me. He says that if I leave him, he'll tell that officer from the 20th General Hospital everything. You know who I mean... Sanderson, Paddington, or something like that."

"I think you mean General Peterson," said Benet. "Are you sure that disclosure of this 'secret' would ruin you?"

"Yes. I can't really go into it. Anyway, it was a stage and it's over."

"What about telling Mac that you can only be with him him once a week? If he says he'll report you, just tell him you'll talk with Peterson yourself. An Army career is the only thing Mac has in his life. I'm pretty certain he wouldn't do anything to endanger it. If you decide on that course, you may consult me again and I'll help you prepare your case to present to Peterson."

They sat and talked a few more minutes. Clara took Benet's hand. "Thank you, Lt. Dr. Benet. Your Rita is a lucky woman to have such a good listener and wise husband. I can't tell you how much you've helped."

Ten minutes later Benet was back in his *basha* and dressed for bed. He had just enough energy to finish writing to Rita. He sat at the wooden table and using the notes he'd made earlier, finished his earlier sketch.

Under the sketch, he resumed the letter:

The above diagram is a rather crude effort on my part to illustrate what I have often mentioned to you, the wonderful beauty of a sunset in Bengal. The pink is a pink, not a red or crimson color, except for the extreme edges of the few fragmentary clouds that are revealed against the horizon. The very atmosphere seems to take on the colors I have written in above. You will have to experience the view to appreciate it. It is similar to one's most sacred associations with the little white church in the vale. Your mind pauses, or your soul, for a fraction of a moment, and the vain earthly troubles of man seem transitory and insignificant. Watching the Bengali sunset is a nightly sacrament for me; a baptism that strips me of ego and bathes me.

Sweetest girl, I've enjoyed this so much, these few minutes with you. I look forward ever and constantly to that wonderful moment when I'll feel your eager and willing arms around me.
Until then, most faithfully,
Your obedient husband, Dick.

26

Rita arrived at eight in the morning, and they were to go to Thelma's house at nine-thirty. The sweet aroma of baking filled the kitchen, and Mildred's face was flushed from the heat of the oven. Over her slacks and sweater, she wore a red-checkered apron.

"You and my mother are natural born cooks," said Rita. "I think my mom would rather be in the kitchen than anywhere else in the world. Me, I like to get out of the kitchen as fast as possible." She looked toward a large round metal canister with a handle sitting on the countertop. "Oh, that must be the *piece de resistance*."

"Yes, that's my 'good neighbor' cake for Thelma. I finished last night by ten, but then I was inspired. I'd misplaced the molasses cookie recipe for weeks, but all of a sudden there it was under the silverware holder. So, after the cake was done and frosted, I made the dough last night, rolled out the cookies this morning, and just finished baking them this morning. Three of my students have birthdays this week, so I'll keep them for that. But I made dozens. Maybe we should try them to make sure they turned out."

Mildred put several cookies on a plate between them and poured them each a cup of coffee. "Let's make sure we know what we're doing. I hope you wore quiet shoes."

"Yes," said Rita. "I'll be stealthier than the family cat."

"I telephoned Thelma yesterday," said Mildred. "I told her that I discovered a book of hand-copied recipes in an old trunk in the attic. Since my parents are gone, I'd have no other way of knowing if they were any good than actually trying them out. To make a long story short, I said in my nicest 'good neighbor' voice that I wanted to bring her a surprise from my kitchen."

Rita looked at Mildred incredulously, her usually smooth features wrenched into a mask of feigned alarm. "Don't tell me she just said 'Oh fine, come on over, and we'll have a chat'."

"No, she didn't say anything at first. To tell the truth, I don't think any of the neighbors have ever wanted to call on her. I said a silent prayer as I waited. Imagine my relief when she said 'yes' and that any time after eight in the morning would be fine. She said that she'd have a fresh pot of coffee on the stove. Oh, and guess what," Mildred continued. "Yesterday I noticed big boot prints in the snow leading to Thelma's back door. Strange…Thelma gets so few visitors."

"Speaking of sinister events, won't Fraulein Shunter be suspicious if I'm along?" Rita asked.

"I thought of that. She knew that we both worked as teachers at Washington. I said that we were painting props for a school play and that I'd already invited you to come over at eight-thirty so we could work together. To my relief, she said that you were most welcome."

"But what if she hadn't invited me? That would have ruined everything."

"My dear Rita, you underestimate me. Teaching fourth graders makes one very creative. Of course, I'm sure the same is true with teaching third graders."

"We become wealths of creativity," agreed Rita. "Anyone who deals with kids should be able to pull off 'Operation Thelma."

"In answer to your question, I would have told her—when she mentioned the pot of coffee—that I couldn't leave you at home alone to work while I went off gallivanting. I could tell that Thelma, despite her grumpy exterior, was really kind of sweet and obviously very lonely.

Rita looked at her wristwatch. "My goodness, it's already time to start our mission. I'll put my coat back on."

"I'll carry the cake," Mildred said as she got ready to leave. "Remember to drink lots of coffee. Then you can say something like 'coffee goes right through me,' before you excuse yourself."

"Mildred, you've thought of everything. If they drafted women into the Army, you'd be a general by now."

By nine a.m., Mildred and Rita were seated in the Shunter living room conversing with the large, broad-faced first generation German spinster, who spoke with a thick German accent. A bit odd, thought Rita, for someone who'd lived in America nearly all of her life.

Mildred led the conversation, asking Thelma about a gallery of framed needlework hanging on one wall, about the marble-topped end tables that surely must have been family heirlooms; and about her late sister Lois who, until one year before the war, had shared the house with Thelma. Rita glanced at her watch. It was nine fifteen and the subject of baking hadn't even started. Their hostess was getting out some family photo albums of Lois and her when they were growing up.

"You ladies please excuse me," Rita announced. "Coffee goes right through me, and I have to find the powder room. Thelma, I'll catch up on the photos when I get back. Could you tell me where–"

"It's right down ze hall, second door. Don't go in the first door. Zat's zee basement and there's hardly any light. I vouldn't vant you to trip and fall. And I sink I have rats, big black ones. Second door, OK?"

"If you'll excuse me," Rita said. She removed a sanitary napkin from her pocketbook and conspicuously placed it in the pocket of her cardigan sweater. Thelma and Mildred started talking about recipes, a topic that Mildred could sustain for hours. Not that Rita had hours; she planned to hurry downstairs, look for anything fishy, take careful mental notes and rejoin the trio. If Thelma asked her why she took so long, she'd look a bit embarrassed and say that her period had just started.

Rita found the bathroom, turned on a light and closed the door as though the room was being used. Next, she found the stairs that led to Thelma's cellar. Very quietly, she closed that door behind her, flicked a light switch on and then off. In the few seconds between flicks, she got her bearings enough to feel her way downstairs in the dark. Should Thelma and Mildred happen to walk by the door that led to the cellar, Thelma might notice a light under the door.

At the bottom of the steps, based on the configuration of Mildred's cellar, Rita groped for a string that turned on the overhead light. She found it and was suddenly bathed in a pool of weak light. Because wartime scarcity made excessive consumption of anything, even electricity, ill-advised, most Americans were using 25 watt light bulbs whenever possible.

Mildred must have been imagining, Rita thought to herself. This just looked like an ordinary basement. All kinds of carpentry equipment lined the walls. There was the workbench upon which Thelma must have crafted the coffee table that they'd admired in the living room. "Vith my own hands, I made zis," she'd proudly announced.

Straining her eyes, Rita walked further into the gigantic room. It was so musty, damp, and chilly, only a mole would feel at home. Suddenly a draft swept through the semi-darkness and as it did, Rita made out a single bed, a desk and chair and a bookcase. She walked over to what looked like a student apartment. Over the bed was a felt pennant advertising Findlay College—An Ohio Tradition.

Oddly, there were no papers or notebooks on the desk. If Thelma was taking in students, why had she become so angry with Mildred for inquiring? The fathers, sons, brothers, and uncles who'd volunteered or been drafted left behind empty rooms. Money was scarce. It was no surprise that since the war began, many people who would not ordinarily consider doing so, had been taking in lodgers.

Rita had almost decided that her investigation was a failure when she noticed the well-stocked bookcase opposite the bed. The books had leather covers and most were embossed in gold. The elegance of this piece of furniture didn't match the austerity of the room. She ran her fingers along the volumes and started to remove a copy of Plato's *Republic*. As soon as she did, the entire bookcase opened in a circular direction to reveal a hidden office.

Time had to be running short. Rita prayed that Mildred could manage to keep Thelma in the living room talking. In the meantime, she committed every detail of this hidden bailiwick to memory. As though the "student" had recently been using it, there was a ham radio already turned on.

Rita donned the earphones and listened. A male voice, speaking German, came across.

"*Grunwald, Grunwald...Sind Sie da?*"

(Grunwald, Grunwald...are you there?)

"*Arthur...Gott en Himmel! Was ist los?*"

(Arthur...God in Heaven! What's happening?)

Rita said nothing. She trembled at the thought of Nazi spies lurking in Thelma's basement.

"*Sheiße! Grunwald...Sie Werden dieses antworten!*" The voice grew angrier and louder. "*Gott en Himmel!*"

(Shit! Grunwald, you will answer for this!...God in Heaven!)

Very quietly, Rita placed the earphones back on their rack. Before leaving, Rita noticed a small black leather-bound book with a Nazi swastika emblazoned on the cover. She almost picked it up before realizing that her fingerprints could be traced. If this was some kind of spy operation, she could be putting herself in danger.

Adjacent to the book was something that, based on what she'd read in an issue of *Life*, looked like a teletype machine. Peering closer, she read but did not understand the following message:

Bericht benötigt für Produktion der Gummireifenfabrik in Dayton, Ohio...Schick schnell wie möglich. Heil Hitler!

(Report needed for production of the Rubber Tire Company in Dayton, Ohio. Send as quickly as possible. Heil Hitler!

A clumping sound came from above Rita's head. That had to be Thelma, possibly angry and coming to look for her. Time to get back to the coffee klatch, and there was not a second to waste. She

153

hurriedly shoved the revolving fake bookcase back into place and entered the "student" room.

She accidentally knocked over a small tin wastepaper basket and stooped down to pick up the trash strewn across her path. There was a letter addressed to Art Grunwald. Sticking the letter in her pocket and pulling the light string, Rita felt her way upstairs. Her heart was pounding and she'd broken into a sweat.

Tiptoeing into the bathroom, she flushed the toilet, turned out the light and went into the living room. Thelma stared at her and Mildred feigned a worried expression. A stack of albums lay opened up on the handmade coffee table.

Before Thelma could ask a question, Mildred began "Good grief, Rita. Have you been sick? We've been through all of Thelma's fascinating albums and I've learned enough of her family history to write a book."

Rita felt herself blushing, which was just the effect she was hoping for. "It's my period," she said. "It started early for some reason, and yes, I was a little sick, but I'm OK now. I'm sorry you two were worried."

Thelma's look softened. "Vould you like an aspirin?" she offered. "A glass of vater? You do not look so vell, Miss Rita."

"No, no, I'm fine. Really, I'm fine."

"The morning is getting away from us, Thelma. We must get back to my house and begin making props for the student production." Mildred held out her slender hand to shake Thelma's plump one. "Thank you so much for your hospitality, and when you do get a boarder for your student apartment, send him or her over for dinner sometime. It's been said that I'm a marvelous cook."

Thelma watched as her guests trod across the snow to the house next door. After waving goodbye at the door, the large woman shuffled back inside and banged the door closed.

They were nearly at Mildred's door, safely out of earshot. "Mildred, you won't believe what I discovered in the basement. We've got to get in touch with the police."

"Shhhh, we can't talk about anything until we're inside with the doors locked."

Rita clutched the letter inside her cardigan pocket. She was still absorbing the scene next door. She had broken into a jog and had to be stopped by Mildred, who put a gentle but firm hand on her elbow.

"Thelma may still be looking at us. Don't act rushed. You can tell me everything in another few minutes."

154

During the visit to Thelma's, it had resumed snowing. The two teachers slowed down and pretended to look at the large snowflakes drifting through the air. All along Center Street, the front yards sloped down to the sidewalk, so it was necessary to walk carefully to avoid slipping. Yesterday's snow had turned to ice under the fresh layer that had fallen overnight. Treading lightly, they reached Mildred's front porch and stepped inside. Mildred locked the door behind her; she and Rita went to the kitchen, a room where no windows could be seen from next door.

"You were down there long enough, kiddo," Mildred began. "You can't believe how hard it was to keep Thelma from getting suspicious. By the way, instead of mentioning the light in the cellar, I asked her if she'd thought about taking in boarders. She said she could use the extra income and that she might be getting someone soon."

Rita described what she'd found in Thelma's cellar. She pulled the letter out of her pocket only to find that it was an empty envelope. "Let's check with the registrar at Findlay College. They can tell us if Arthur Grunwald is really a student. Look at the postmark. This was sent from Munich."

"Yes, you're right. Too bad the letter wasn't still inside. I'll go call the college. It's not noon yet and sometimes the administration works a half day on Saturday."

Mildred walked into the bedroom to use the telephone, leaving Rita to glance through the latest issue of *Life*. The cover featured a photo of Paul Sarringhaus, Ohio State University football star. Richard predicted that the halfback would go far, and here was proof.

Just as Rita was getting into the Sarringhaus article, Mildred returned. "Well, it took a while, but I finally got through to the registrar's office. There were very few people working but a helpful student assistant found a Miss Jones who searched the records. There is not an Arthur Grunwald anywhere in their files."

"I'm not surprised," said Rita. "Remind me. Did you say that Thelma admitted to someone living in her cellar?"

"She weaseled around the question, not exactly saying yes or no. Finally, she claimed that she was between boarders, that it was hard to find a student who wasn't too noisy and who paid the rent on time."

"OK, so it's obvious that Thelma is hiding the communications stuff," Rita said. "We've discovered something, something really big, and it can't be good. I'm still in shock. We've got to notify the police and the sooner, the better."

Mildred got up from the deep-seated armchair and paced over to the window. Both women looked out at the whirling snow. The storm had hit in earnest. "If we call the local police, Thelma will know we turned her in. I have to live next door to this woman, and I'd hate to have her mad at me. I know you think I'm being cowardly, but..."

"Wait," exclaimed Rita. "This is bigger than the Findlay police. We need to notify the F.B.I. Your friend Madge, our bridge player. She lives in Dayton when she's not here visiting. Let's call her and find the F.B.I. office there. We could tell them what we know and ask to remain anonymous."

"I don't know," Mildred said doubtfully. "Thelma might still suspect us, especially me. You're right, though. We have to do something."

"Look up Madge's number. I'll make this call." Rita took a small spiral notebook and a pencil out of her brown leather purse.

Mildred went to a small writing desk in a corner of the living room, opened a drawer and took out her well-used address book. "Ready to write? You can reach Madge at 30215."

An hour later, the call had been made to the Dayton Federal Bureau of Investigation. Mildred opened a can of Campbell's Chicken Noodle and fixed lunch for the two of them.

"Let's hope that's the end of it—at least for us," Rita sighed. "I'm ravenous. This soup hits the spot."

"I don't know about you," Mildred said, "but I'm burning with curiosity about exactly what is going on. I'm afraid to get any closer to this affair, but on the other hand I'd love to know the outcome."

"I could always call back," Rita offered. "I could say that we will continue working with the F.B.I. and provide more information on Thelma as we observe her."

"No, there might be too big a price to pay for that. We can just listen for her arrest on the news."

"Or we can never hear anything and just always wonder," Rita said. "But look outside. It's a regular blizzard. The snow is blowing sideways at 100 miles an hour. If I wait any longer I won't be able to drive home."

Mildred looked into the hall closet and produced an umbrella. "You can hold this over your head as a shield," she said.

Rita bundled up and gladly accepted Mildred's offering. "I hope we did some good," she told her fellow teacher. "I'll see you in school Monday."

"Right, girlfriend," said Mildred. "And remember, we can't talk about it in front of anybody. It's as though none of this ever happened."

27

Ravinath Ghosh was a man of many faces. Whichever of his identities he assumed, he had a knack for attracting followers. Long ago, he'd abandoned the home and religion of his parents, deciding that he would devote his life to winning back India for Indians and to gaining a private fortune. Very quickly he learned that in order to gain power, he needed to deal with the *goondas*.

In Ravi's mind, there were two main strata of *goondas*. There were those who, through bad luck and family misfortunes, turned to crime in order to survive. That category was the vast majority. Then there were those not from the lower castes, men such as himself. His kind realized that the power they needed to overthrow the tyranny of foreign oppression was available only through using *goondas* to perform certain unpleasant tasks.

At exactly the same time Benet was viewing the sunset over Bengal's eastern skies, Ravinath Ghosh was standing in his doorway admiring the colorful panorama from another part of the Alipore district.

Ravi was dressed in his best clothes. This was a special evening, so on his head he wore a military looking hat, much like that of American G. I.'s but worn more squarely. Though his eyesight was fine without them, he wore clear reading glasses for a more distinguished appearance.

Ravi stood at his door awaiting the evening's guests. He felt both grateful and optimistic. If all went smoothly, tonight would mark the setting in place of a plan to take back the general hospital for India.

Contrary to the story he'd concocted for Benet, the house belonged to Ravi's parents, both of whom had been killed during the 1934 earthquake. The building they were trapped in caught fire. An electrical cable was soaked in water from an overflowing canal. The resulting conflagration incinerated the building and everyone in it. Ravi, as one of two children, was left in charge of the estate.

Because Ravi's married sister lived in Alahabad, the house was left in Ravi's care. At first the young bachelor maintained the grounds and interior of the palatial stucco home. Before long, other interests distracted him. When he became involved in the underground fight for India's true independence, he'd let the garden run wild.

Several peacocks that used to strut proudly around the verdant yard died from neglect. Ravi created a small army of city guerilla fighters and utilized the house for headquarters. He was the "brains" of his movement. Tonight he was holding a business meeting and party for a second tier of freedom fighters—volunteers that he'd recruited at his public rallies.

His sidekick Shubi doubled as an Army Air Force employee. When a name was needed for Ravi's group, Shubi suggested "Ravi's Avengers." The name stuck. The men and women involved during the earliest days recruited others and in a few short months, the ranks swelled. Ordinary people were frustrated by the government's failure to act decisively. They welcomed a chance to make a difference by becoming "Avengers."

Had an omniscient observer been stationed at the entrance of Ravi's headquarters that night, he would have seen an odd assortment of guests entering, people of different ages and castes. And yet on closer examination, the observer would realize that these people were not really so disparate. All were Hindus, Calcutta natives, and in some way connected to the Army Air Force Hospital #142 that occupied the grounds of a former school in Alipore.

It was no coincidence that just a month earlier, the hospital's director had his first experience with opium. Ravi's intent had been to undermine the command, to distract and infiltrate the 142nd. Though it was not his purpose, he would not have cared that Mac's opium indulgence hastened the man's self-destruction.

Ravi abhorred foreigners. The British, he felt, should be set on fire and toasted to ashes. Even those Americans who tried to be civil and expressed sincere interest in Indian culture were a nuisance, about as welcome as termites or mosquitoes.

It had taken no time at all to gain control of Colonel McDermott. With satisfaction the Bengali recalled luring the Colonel to his house and tricking him into smoking the pipe. The rest had been even easier. Ravi could now collect medical supplies to sell to the Japanese. It was a perfect exchange. Mac needed opium; Ravi needed the hospital's medical supplies. It was that simple and that effective.

Another key to Ravi's great progress was Veena. The young woman's charm and beauty made it easy for her to gain access to the hospital. She smuggled opium to the Colonel. He gave her bottles and jars of medicine, and she carried the medical supplies back to

159

Ravi. Keeping nothing for himself, Ravi, in turn, sold them to the Japanese. Proceeds went to support the independence movement.

"Veena the Courier," Ravi called her. Tonight she brought with her some fellow college students to join the cause—rebellious boys who had to fib to their conservative families in order to attend meetings. The boys' anger at the foreigners in their city could be well harnessed. They joined people of all ages sitting on cushions scattered about the red, green and purple hand-woven carpet. Everyone was chatting nonstop.

Depok, the older of the college men, turned to Veena with obvious admiration. "I still can't understand how you manage to come and go at the hospital? Don't they have security guards? Is it not astonishing even to these obtuse Americans that here is a young Indian woman who is not keeping her place as a propriety-bound future wife and mother? 'How can she be so bold, so brash?' they must wonder. What is it like when you have a mission to perform?"

"You mean when I'm smuggling drugs in and medicines out?"

"Yes," answered Depok. "Not how you carry the goods. That would be easy enough. What do you tell the soldiers when you enter the grounds? Surely you are a startling sight to them. I've heard that the hospital has very few women and no Indian women workers at all."

Veena smiled proudly. "Easy. You may not know this, but I am a writer for the newspaper of Bethune Girls' College. I have started a myth that I am writing a story about military hospitals. I stroll about at will, talking with patients and doctors, pretending to take notes. They know and like me. I am confident that no one suspects my real reason for being there."

"Hmmm," said Depok. "You seem to know exactly what you are about. But I still am wondering how does this get you to this Colonel hospital director? Don't you have to invent more myths to accomplish the reason you came?"

"Ah, but you haven't heard the extent of how this plan works. My partner in this infiltration is Shubi Roy, the Colonel's personal bearer."

"Bearer?" asked Depok. "You mean servant?"

Veena laughed. "The Americans don't like to think of themselves as having servants. They imagine that they are too kind and good. Hah—they disguise their arrogance by using the term *bearer*."

"Very well," said Depok. "I'm with you so far."

160

"Shubi knows ahead of time when I'm coming, as we have a 'lips to ear' communication line through the Indian employees of the hospital. He takes me in to the Colonel's office, where our exchange takes place. The Colonel takes the package with opium, checking the amount. He unlocks his bottom desk drawer and takes out the morphine packages plus whatever else Mr. Tamiyaka—he's our Japanese buyer—has requested. We both check the accounting. Often I have to ask Colonel Mac for some additional payment in the form of American dollars. Then I leave the office and report to Ravi. It's that simple."

Depok's face was filled with admiration. "Of course, you must learn from Shubi about the hospital director's growing inattentiveness? And you use him to arrange the next drug exchange?"

"Yes, yes. Shhhh. Ravi is beginning his talk. And there's Shubi coming in now."

Veena pointed to a small Indian with a sharp nose, gleaming eyes and a stiff, upright stance. Everything about Shubi conveyed determination. Like most of the men in the room, he wore white leggings and *curta*. He squeezed by people to sit cross-legged on the floor near Ravi's podium at the far wall.

Chatter stopped as Ravi stepped before the audience of twenty or so people. His bearing was regal. Before speaking, he scanned the room with dark eyes, taking inventory. The audience, still growing, had now reached over thirty. He smiled, took a deep breath, then began.

"Good evening, my fellow Bengalis. Need I tell you how very pleased I am that all of you are here tonight? It is a most auspicious sign, proof that we are united in our devotion to Indian independence. Our other members, we might even call them our 'army,' are here in spirit. They must diligently stay with training and therefore could not be physically present. We have been talking about taking back our school for many months. The time for action is drawing near."

Ravi held up his right hand and pointed his index finger toward the ceiling. "I have chosen December 31 on the American calendar, as for them that is a big holiday, New Year's Eve. It's like our April 15th. Their Army administrators will have many festivities and entertainment for the men. There will be bands, dances, parties. Many of the soldiers will drink too much alcohol. For us, this provides a perfect opportunity.

"As I have mentioned before, the ineffective director of the hospital is not really in charge of the 142nd; he is not in charge even of himself."

Scattered laughter sounded from a few listeners.

Ravi continued. "He has fallen most completely into the clutches of opium. This American, known as 'Mac' by his colleagues, is given over to evening debaucheries. He is conveniently unaware of what is going on throughout the buildings and grounds.

"When we execute our plans for the takeover, the importance of *Sahib* Mac's whereabouts cannot be underestimated. I have left the job of monitoring this hospital director in Shubi's capable hands. He will make sure that the Colonel is smoking opium that night. Not only that, he will do his best to see that Mr. Mac is occupied with his lover, a nurse who has also taken up the opium habit."

The crowd applauded and started to chatter about the beauty of Ravi's plan and the foolishness of Americans. The talking soon reached a loud din. Finally, Ravi struck a brass gong behind the podium.

"Quiet—please, I beseech you. We will have music and feasting after business is concluded and then you may joke on your own time. Tonight's work is serious and demands your complete attention. You must listen most carefully."

Once again silence prevailed, and Ravi continued. "The officer who actually oversees the hospital is now a Lieutenant by the name of Dr. Richard Benet, a psychologist. This man spends all of his free time writing letters to his wife back in America. He does not drink or go to the Officer's Club. The one entertainment in which he partakes of is the nightly movie, but Shubi has learned that there will be no movie on New Year's Eve.

"It is essential that *Sahib* Benet is not in the hospital wards on the night of December 31. Shubi has volunteered to let me know exactly where this Benet will be located that night. I must ask all of you for I am wondering what we can do about this troublesome Benet. He could ruin our plan."

"Kill him?" offered Abu, a friend of Depok's.

Ravi glared at the young man. "We will not be advocating violence. This is to be a peaceful takeover. If as a last resort violence must be done to achieve our ends, our army will take over. That is their job. And now, are there any *reasonable* suggestions?"

Sitting toward the back of the room on a hassock was Dr. V. S. Aziz, a professor on sabbatical from Calcutta University. Like others in the room, he was passionately devoted to taking back India for Indians.

Aziz raised his hand and after a nod from Ravi, stood up. Heads turned to look at the bespectacled scholar. He was considerably older than most of the others and spoke with an air of iron-clad authority.

"Esteemed *Sahib* Ghosh," began the professor, "my brothers and sisters united in this noble mission of purifying our country by shaking the British and the American yoke; I must pose a question. We are hearing about this hospital takeover, but I for one find it quite vague. We will be needing more details, the who, what, where, and when. You will notice that I do not include 'Why.' The 'why' is crystal clear to us all. On this New Year's Eve, we know that we need to remove the acting director, this Benny or, um, Benet. Other than that, who will do what?"

Aziz sat down, and everyone started asking questions:

"Do we truly have an army of supporters?"

"Have we paid 'friends' in the district police force to back us up?"

"What do we do if the American Military Police start shooting?"

"What will happen to the patients in case the hospital has to be destroyed?"

Ravi sounded the gong. "Silence, everyone. Just calm down. Do not think of this as invading an enemy country. Our job is simply to reclaim the building—not destruction, but occupation. Shortly after midnight of the American New Year's Eve, our forces will surround the hospital. A large contingency of volunteers will proceed to empty contents of the administrative offices into boxes.

"Benet will have been removed, kidnapped if necessary. We will announce to any American who confronts us that we are reclaiming our land and buildings to use for an Indian hospital."

Applause broke out and Ravi hit the gong to command attention.

"If you recall, however. I asked a question. Let us review. Shubi will see to it that the so-called director of the hospital—an opium addict—will be oblivious to what's going on. To repeat, the only other officer we have to worry about is Benet. Surely one of you must have a solution to the impediment of Lieutenant Doctor Benet. Miss Sengupta, you've met the psychologist. What do you think?"

Veena stood up. "Depok and I had an idea. It's rather extreme but it just might work. If you want to hear it, I will let my friend explain."

"Yes, of course," Ravi said. "We must hear all good ideas and consider them and that way we will find the best. You college students are often wiser than your elders. We will be listening."

Depok stood up and walked to the front of the room. "Veena has talked with this Benet and learned that he has a great fascination with temples and Indian deities. It will not be difficult to draw him out of the hospital that evening with the promise of seeing a special treasure."

Murmurs of agreement rippled through the room. "Ah, yes," said another of the college students who'd come along with Depok. "Why not lure the American with the promise of viewing the jeweled statue of Ganesha. There's an old rumor that such a statue is hidden in a secret room of the Jain temples."

Shubi's sixteen-year-old daughter Sushmita was normally shy. The girl had clung to her father the entire evening, wide-eyed and taking in all that was said. Given confidence by the crowd's excitement, she stood up and exclaimed, "Better yet, we could have someone promise Benet that he was to see the largest image of Kali in the world. We could instead take him to the *goonda* den on Ratan Neogi Lane."

"What do you mean, 'the *goonda* den'?" asked Ravi. He knew exactly what the girl meant but pretended otherwise. "I've heard such places exist but never known of an actual address. Tell us more, please."

Sushmita continued. "I'm not sure of the actual address, but I've heard from girls at school that the *goondas* have taken over an abandoned *godown*—a warehouse—and that one of our classmates, a very poor girl whose parents had died, was kidnapped, taken there and sold to a brothel."

At the mention of "brothel," people stared at Sushmita. Ignoring the stares, she finished her story.

"We don't really know what happened to poor Chitra but the person who told us about our friend was a teacher we liked and trusted. He made us promise not to give out his name, as the *goondas* would most certainly have slit his throat." She drew a finger across her own throat to emphasize the need for confidentiality. "I beg all of you here not to mention how this information reached you. Anyway, that is what I know." She sat down abruptly and took her father's hand. Shubi, proud of his daughter, was smiling.

"Thank you, Sushmita," Ravi said. "I will seriously consider your plan. However, we do it, we will stage a New Year's Eve outing for *Sahib* Benet, a little expedition, if you will. It does not matter if the lure is a glimpse of Ganesh, Kali, or a lesser god. Anything will do as a ruse. We will investigate this den of the *goondas* and find a believable escort. We need someone that the American trusts to see that he vacates the hospital and is contained in this *godown*."

Depok spoke up. "I know a little bit about this place. Sushmita left out the best part. The *goondas* keep a guard tiger to help contain prisoners. We could leave Benet there quite effectively until our takeover is complete."

"I could arrange the New Year's Eve invitation," Veena said. "Doctor Benet likes to talk with me about India's deities and he's also mentioned that he wants to return to visit the Jain temples by moonlight. Do we know if there will be a full moon on December 31st?"

"Yes," Shubi volunteered. "It will be very full and bright. You can speak of both the Jain temple and the hidden treasure to Benet. I will suggest to Colonel Mac assigning Dr. Anderson to cover Benet's watch that evening. The Colonel is so indifferent about anything to do with the hospital, he barely knows what's going on. Leave that arrangement up to me."

"Yes," agreed Veena. "The hospital director is what the Americans call 'an empty uniform.' Several of us will have a car waiting as we talk to Benet. If necessary, we will force him to go with us. However, the psychologist is most anxious to learn about Indian culture. It's likely he will believe we are in earnest. Even if he has doubts, he will not refuse the chance to see the treasures of India that we'll describe to him. Most definitely, we will be able to get him out of the way." She looked directly at Ravi, adding "The rest is up to you and your army."

"I myself will go in search of the derelict *godown* on Ratan Neogi Lane," offered Ravi. "I have complete confidence that I can deal with these *goondas*. Veena, when the time comes, I will trust you and your friends to see that Benet is contained as long as needed. Fortunately, I have the financial resources to pay for the *goondas'* cooperation. We may even need to employ their guard tiger."

165

28

The official business part of Ravi's gathering was over. A troupe of sitar players entered the meeting room. Soon, the sound of contemporary *ragas* filled the air. The guests got up and stretched cramped limbs. Following a signal from their host, they gradually filled the dining room of the mansion.

A long table was laden with traditional Bengali cuisine. Huge trays were laden with Ravi's favorites: river fish—Hilsa and Rhui—rice, spinach, lentils, and vegetables cooked with onion, garlic and tomato. For dessert, there were puddings and sweets made with yoghurt or cheese. Tea and punch flowed freely.

There was no alcohol in sight. The few young men who wanted to smoke cigarettes slipped outside into the garden. Ravi himself liked to smoke and occasionally he drank whiskey, but in this company, he refrained. It was important to keep the respect and admiration of everyone present. To be seen breaking ancient taboos would be incredibly foolish. He had not worked this hard to risk anything going awry.

Once the dishes and remaining food were cleared away, the tables were shoved to the back wall. Harmonium and tabla players joined the sitar players. Sitting cross-legged on the floor, the musicians began a concert for Ravi's guests.

The younger crowd thought the music was a bit too formal, too classical. Abu impolitely rummaged through the bookshelves to locate Ravi's fine record collection. A boy of no more than fourteen, Abu found an upright record player and whistled to his friend.

"Hey, Depok," yelled Abu over the classical music coming from the imported troupe. "*Sahib* Ghosh's musicians are too old-fashioned. How about giving them a break and letting us play jazz and swing?"

"Yeah, yeah," chimed in others. "Let's have swing."

"But I've already paid these musicians." Ravi protested. "All this money I've spent, all this work." His protests fell on deaf ears. Record albums flew through the air toward Abu. Deftly catching each one, he called out the titles and asked which he should play.

Ravi sounded the gong. He stood atop a chair and shouted. "Please listen. You can play records later. I beg you to let the musicians perform. You can request other numbers from them.

They have been paid to play the entire evening. I have a dancer who is scheduled after three more numbers."

His pleas were drowned out by the strains of "Ice Cold Katie," "So Long, Sarah Jane," and "Jealous." By the time Ravi had walked over to apologize, the offended musicians had already packed up their instruments. Wild strains of jazz floated through the air and men were dancing alone and with one another. The girls sat on the side and giggled at them.

As the musicians straggled out of the crowded room, a bewildered young Indian lady entered. It was Andra, the dancer Ravi had hired. "Humph," she snorted. "We thought we were hired to play at a respectable party. This is just a pack of *goondas.* "

"This was to be a respectable party," said Ravi, following the musicians to the front door. "It's just that the young people have too much energy to sit and listen to classical music. Oh, please do not be offended. Take some of these trays of food. Here, take them all." He pushed a tray of banana fritters toward them.

"Take your fritters and drop dead." Andra flung the tray aside angrily and fritters flew in all directions. The guests who were dancing soon trampled on them and started skidding. This caused the girls in the sidelines to laugh more uproariously.

The musicians slammed the front door behind them. "What the hell do they know anyway?" Ravi asked no one in particular. He nearly slipped on a mashed fritter. "Hey, Depok. Find Teddy Weatherford's Waikiki. That album has Reuben Solomon and his Jive Boys. You gotta hear it."

The men continued dancing to their admiring audience of young women. Ravi joined in. Everyone sang along to "Last Time I Saw Paris," "Blues in the Night," and "St. Louis Blues." At midnight, Ravi turned off the record player, rang the gong and stood on a chair to address the revelers. The room fell quiet and people sat on the floor, exhausted but attentive.

"OK, my fellow Bengalis. The party is now ended and you are free to go home. Our victory when we take back the hospital, will be an important step in freeing India. Our weapons are fear—which we will instill in the foreigners on the night of December 31st—surprise, ruthless efficiency, and fierce devotion to our cause, a free India."

The guests began chanting, "Free Mother India, India for Indians, Free Mother India."

"Do not forget," shouted Ravi, "that we must not speak of the plan outside this room. The value of surprise cannot be underestimated. I leave this slogan with you: *Sher I Azad Hind.* In English, it would be 'Tiger of the Free India.' Keep that in your hearts."

By one a.m., the last guest had left. Ravi had hired some helpers from his late father's extended family. He gave them the signal to begin a clean up. Not entirely satisfied with the way this important night had gone, he walked out to the garden and sat on a stone wall.

As he often did, Ravi looked up at the night sky, studying the constellation Orion. A shooting star fell toward earth, just as it had months earlier when he and his men had been camped on the outskirts of Calcutta. At that time, the hospital takeover was little more than a dream.

Ravi was pleased that his plan cut across castes and social strata. The guests of this evening's meeting would no doubt scorn the scraggly men who comprised his "army." They would scorn the *goondas* of Ratan Neogi Lane, thugs who were essential to his plan. But the world, even in India, was rapidly changing. If need be, *goondas* and respectable folks could learn to work together.

Ravi knew that the hospital takeover might not be what the evening's guests envisioned. Things could become violent. If the Military Police of the Americans were called in, Ravi's army had weapons and explosives ready to use. There might be some deaths on the enemy side, and perhaps even in their own ranks. There was a saying Ravi's father liked to quote: "The end justifies the means." The shooting star was an omen. Tonight Ravi knew that his father had been right.

29

Though it served as vital link in the China-Burma-India Theater of operations, Calcutta, India was geographically on the periphery. The Allied effort in Calcutta comprised military staging areas and rehabilitation hospitals. In the former, munitions were assembled and sent to Kunming, China. In the latter, men and women had to "hurry up and wait." The waiting grew long and burdensome.

Alcoholism and visits to the red light district were on the rise. In an act of uncharacteristic friendliness, the hospital director invited Benet for a night "on the town." It was the first time Mac had been anything but rude and condescending. Astonished, Benet at first refused. Later he decided that going along just to observe might be educational. His was an "intellectual curiosity," he told himself. Not surprisingly, the evening included a foray into the off-limits section of Calcutta. When he returned shortly after midnight to his quarters, he sat down and wrote a vignette.

UNDER THE VILLAGE PALMS
or
Why Not? It's Been Going on a Long Time
by Richard Benet, 1944

The Officer on Duty and the Sergeant of the guard called for me at the club and I joined them with alacrity, for we were about to visit the village brothel area -- on business, not pleasure.

We drove into the darkened village about 10:00 o'clock at night. The road was dusty and bumpy; the jeep creaked and heaved its way along. Every other blackened shop had an open kerosene lamp flickering in the front, revealing skirted shapes sitting quietly on benches and sleeping boards. A musty odor saturated the air, drenching our spirits. Forty-fives jutted from the hips of the OD and the sergeant of the guard. The twentieth century was moving into a community sagging under the dreadful burden of a thousand years of unchanging superstition, poverty, and human degradation.

The old, rotted and gutted by the termite TIME, was confronted with the modern, strong, self-sufficient, scientific, and hard. The ancient gave way as the bow of a ship cleaves through the water, and just as the waves heal the wound made by the passing, so did the

169

ancient soul of this village close in and around us. We were a foreign excrescence struggling vainly in its age-old shadows.

We rounded a corner and came to a stop before the narrow lane leading into the compound. Several natives were standing in covert watchfulness before another of the nameless "confectionaries" which scar the streets. They knew that we were the Americans, representatives of the mightiest nation the world has ever known; we were all rajahs; we were veritable giants; our thundering silver bombers roared their song of death in a fierce battle chant over the quiet of their homes every morning. They were not impressed. They simply watched. Some day we would leave as we had come, in a jarring burst of flaming exhausts, and then once again they would pad barefooted over their rice paddy trails, safe from the chattering, clanging trucks that jerked madly over the roads.

The Sergeant rudely shoved aside an unprotesting Indian soldier who blocked the path. Our flashlights made tentative jabs into the gloom of the bamboo-sheathed alley. Silent palms were outlined against the darker blue of the sky. The stars mutely shamed us. But we walked warily on, unsure of our footing. The trail turned and debauched into a courtyard with a suddenness that appalled us. We blinked in the sputtering light from the open lamps.

When our eyes had accustomed themselves to the semi-darkness, we saw that we were surrounded by heavily clothed seated figures. They were the "beebies" and were waiting for trade. They said nothing, for they knew that we were the American patrol. We walked around the circle, flashing our glaring lights into their faces as they stiffened on the ground. One especially attractive, well dressed girl did not pause in preening her hair. It rested on her head in marcelled waves like a blue-black glistening crown.

"May I touch it?" I asked, curious to know if it were set in grease. She said nothing, but at my gesture leaned forward slightly. I hesitantly touched her head, careful not to disarrange her hair dress. The spun hair was soft and silky and dry.

I followed the OD and the Sergeant of the guard to the first of the closed compartment doors. "Open up, open up!" the Sergeant shouted in a lewd tone. There was a rustle, then silence.

"Open the Goddamned door before I break it down," he yelled and kicked viciously at the flimsy bamboo. Apparently fastened only with a bamboo string, the door sagged away from the sill. Our combined flashlights lit up the interior. An Indian poked his head from under a dirty sheet which covered the bed.

170

"Let's see the beebie," the Sergeant raucously commanded. The man half lifted the sheet, revealing the upper part of the black woman.

"More, damn you." The sheet went all the way up, and the half naked backside of the "beebie" flashed for a moment before the sheet dropped. The Sergeant laughed.

The courtyard was closed on three sides by the compound building, which was continuous, being separated only by bamboo sheathing. The fourth side, forming the square, consisted of a solid fence. The door of the next compartment before which we stopped was open and no one was inside. The room was about six by eight or ten feet with a seven foot ceiling. There was no flooring.

The ground was not the true color of ground. It was black; worn shiny and hard by countless footsteps. Vermin, rodents, sweat, excrement, filth, waste, human misery had left their imprint in the floor upon which some girl was faltering through a living hell -- the sordid sop of a depraved appetite. How had this happened? How, indeed?

Furtive figures could be detected silently slipping from stealthily opened doors, soon melted in the shadows without a backward glance. I approached one of the compartments from which the culmination of an illicit union had resulted in this skulking retreat. Through the half-open doorway, I could see a miniature woman adjusting her girdle of abundant cotton cloth more firmly about her slim hips. She deftly tightened the flow of the sari over her shoulders, throwing her tiny breasts into high relief. Childish hands of grace smoothed the folds of the skirt and softly patted her hair, which was drawn tightly over her head and tied just below her ears.

The girl stared at me with frank curiosity and with perfect self-confidence. "Ahhhh...." her voice trilled like a bird's song, "American." The consonants were blurred, weakened, more melodious than when spoken by a Westerner. As the last tonal effect of "American" hung tingling in the pensive night, she began to laugh in a high metallic key which made me want to box her ears. I spoke to her sharply, "Mulam English?" She shook her head in a pert negative and answered, "Nay mulam."

"Mohammedan?" I questioned.

In a gush of words, she shrilled, "Nay Mohammedan, nay teek. Me Hindu."

"Teek," I smiled, "Hindu good. You pretty Hindu." Despite her lack of knowledge of the English language she understood the *universal language of praise all too well. With no more invitation that that she glided to the doorway, stretching her hand to me in supplication. I eluded her momentarily by backing hastily. She laughed again and shook her head wisely. In alternative English and Bengalese we conversed for five minutes, neither knowing more at the end of that interesting period than we had at the beginning, but we were becoming acquainted.*

Several times I inquired, "How much?" and tried to make her understand that I wanted a distinction between Indians and white men. But her response of "Two annas," four annas, one rupee" seemed irrelevant and unwitting. Her attitude indicated that she wanted me to touch her, but under the circumstances, it was not difficult for me to refrain.

The OD loomed out of the shadows and suggested that we continue our checking. As we went from compartment to compartment our experiences varied, but the squalor of the rooms did not. The accommodations were usually a dirty pad, stretched on the black floor. Beside the pad were two small jars of ointment. A cracked earthen bowl of water set across from the lubricating oils, and near that was a raised mound of earth, disfigured with ashes. Above the ashes, the tarnished brass bowl in which the "beebie" prepared her meal of boiled rice.

Despite the known fact that the American and British patrols would be active at 10:00, a number of local residents had determined to exercise their libido regardless of possible interruption. About half the stalls were occupied or had just been used. As we approached one door, a Hindu broke from it and ran through us, as we scattered before his dash.

The door remained ajar and we looked curiously inside. This compartment had a large open oil lamp and was clearly lighted up. Rolling from side to side on a raised bed was a black woman. The bed sheet had been pulled around her body. A continuous stream of moans issued from the bundle.

"Hey," the Sergeant called. Louder moans. More wriggling. "What the hell goes on in here, you bitch?" the soldier wanted to know.

Some spark of indignation stirred in the poor wretch. Without turning toward us, she said low and distinctly, "Jow!"

With an outraged lewd curse, the Sergeant seized the door, crashing it to the doorframe with an obscene parting benediction. The OD and I stood by without a word.

We were informed that there was still a further brothel compound, deep inside the labyrinth of stagnant ponds. We stumbled along in the darkness lighting our way with flashlights, walking on the ridge between two cesspools. A sheeted Hindu slipped down the bank ahead of us and stooped before the water, dipping into it with a bowl. He washed his hands fastidiously, then drank deeply and spat into the pond.

To our left we noticed a block-like structure, apparently constructed from huge quarried stones. A Stygian aroma assailed our nostrils and we blanched, faltered, and strode recklessly up the gravel path to look inside. It had no roof, was so built that some degree of privacy was insured. Open at four sides, the walls projected in such a way that the cubes couldn't be seen from the walk.

Defecatory indications lay heaped everywhere, but since the subject squatted on a flat surface, we were puzzled as to just what benefit was secured from the latrine's use. However, the ways of these people have not been revealed to us, so we passed on, noting as we went that a rain would drain the accumulated feces into the adjoining ponds.

In dimensions and general appearance, the second area was like the first, except that it was deserted. Lack of business, a British Sergeant told us. The girls were all purchased for the purpose of prostitution, he added, or were widows who had no other means of living. They were Hindus, but he was vague about whether men other than Hindus visited them.

We returned to the first compound and found that the situation had not altered materially. The "beebies" were still waiting, squatted in the darkness. The group surgeon once had occasion to examine five of these women for venereal diseases. All five were afflicted with a running soreness caused by uncleanness. Signs of gonorrhea were present in each case, and two had symptoms of incipient syphilis.

This institution is, therefore, a social cancer in the community, but no control is attempted except that maintained by the Allied armies. Military restrictions do not cure, nor even prevent, infection. The ideological myth of continence is promoted by the army on the theory that stating a thing makes it so. Ergo, black is white, and never mind the evidence of your eyes. This state of affairs often results in an occasional disease tersely written in orders "for cause," and terminating in Privacy for an NCO.

Before leaving, the eldest woman and the madam of the establishment invited us into her compartment. Two British Sergeants were seated on the edge of a huge bed, while one of them fanned a sleeping child.

The madam faced the not-too-bashful OD, clinging to his arm, simpering that American officer very rich, and sing-songing, "With you, not a rupee, not too annas, for notheeng. Just love, you and me?" Her arms slipped around his neck and she raised her legs, throwing her full length against his bosom.

But American officers are made of stern stuff; the OD extricated himself from her warm clasp, muttered a threat to me, "One word of this and..." I followed closely behind his retreating, hulking back, only to find that the bedeviled woman had leaped on me.

In a panic, I tripped, shook her loose, and began to run. As we retraced our steps to the jeep, in considerable confusion, mocking laughter, tingling in space, floated in the night air after us. They were sure of themselves, we were not. Our Sergeant was befouling himself with filthy curses, but we heard him only faintly.

In the security of my own jeep, I sat for some time in serious thought, then I walked out into the night for a breath of fresh air.

Benet finished his story and pulled the last page from his typewriter. It was after one a.m., and he could hardly wait to collapse into his narrow bed. A knock at the door broke through his exhaustion and caused his heart to pound.

Who could it be at this hour?

"*Sahib, sahib.* You are needed in Ward 55. Your patient Meester Warren is most agitated and says he will be killing himself. Please come quickly."

Benet gathered together the pages of his story and stuffed them into his jacket pocket. It would not do to have anyone read them. He ran toward Ward 55.

30

Accompanied by Sanjay, Benet walked carefully though the darkened wards of sleeping patients. At least, some were sleeping. Others tossed about, moaning. A few were sitting with heads back, looking wide-eyed at the ceiling. Considered a danger to others, Warren had been moved to a section of the hospital for the most desperate patients.

Ever since their first confrontation, Benet had been troubled by the young man. Warren was now primarily under the care of Lt. Andy Anderson, an M.D., and therefore authorized to prescribe drugs. However, Benet was still involved in the case. He'd gone to see Warren several times a week, to listen and provide continuity.

According to Andy, Warren often asked for "Dr. Benet, the cow doctor." When Benet came to Warren's room, the latter shifted from friendliness to hostility without warning. One night he wanted to beat Benet to a pulp; another afternoon he called his doctor the brother he'd never had.

Warren gave Benet several versions of his past, from being raised on a farm in northern Ohio to growing up on his uncle's ranch in New Mexico. As his mind seemingly unraveled, his bellicose tendencies seemed to grow stronger. Like many of the patients in Ward 55, he imagined that someone was after him.

Tonight Warren was lying fully dressed on top of the covers of his bed. His arms lay tightly at his sides. His body was stiff, his eyes open and glazed. Even though he wore a coat, he was shivering. Sanjay, who'd accompanied Benet, took a blanket from the closet and covered Warren. The bearer then sat cross-legged in the corner.

Benet took a chair next to the bed. "Hi there, Warren. I hear you've been distressed. You've had these bad spells before and you've gotten through them. We're all sick and tired of living here, and before too much longer, we should all be on a ship headed back to the States."

Warren turned feverish eyes toward Richard. "Well, speak for yourself. I won't be going anywhere, except maybe to the burning *ghats*. I'm not going to live much longer. You're a letter writer, Doc. Can you write my last will and testament?"

"No, Warren. I won't write your will because you're going to live. Last time I was here to talk with you, we discussed your plan to finish college on the G. I. Bill. You said that you wanted to go to Ohio State University to study Biology. Remember?"

Warren flung off the blanket. "I'm too damned hot. What are you people trying to do to me? I never mentioned going to college. I'm a farmer and I told my mother that I'd come home and raise cows. Didn't you say that you treated cows, doctor, tended to their psychological problems, their emotional illnesses, their neuroses and psychoses? Biology, schmiology. That was another Warren Blackwell, Doc. I ain't college material."

"OK. I'm obviously confusing you with that other Warren."

"Yeah Doc, I'm one of those future farmers of America. F.F.A. Except I'll be dead. This fucking hospital is a dangerous place and I'm scared to death. You know the natives are planning to blow it up with us in it. We'll be blown to smithereens, charred to a crisp, barbecued. I'd prefer to end it now and just get it over with. You people can't watch me every minute. One of these days you won't be looking and I'll be dead. Here today and gone tomorrow. Ha, ha ... I've got the last laugh."

With that, Warren started guffawing hysterically. His laughs turned into a deep, rattling cough. Benet handed him the glass of water that was on the bed stand.

"You're very agitated, Warren. What is the trouble?"

Warren frowned at the glass in his hand, then put it down. "Everything is the trouble. Get that water away from me. They're putting arsenic in my water, small amounts all the time in order to gradually poison me. I'm just like an insect with a pin through my heart and they are having a big joke on me." Warren broke into another fit of coughing.

"Now listen," Benet said earnestly, "the only people who come into your room are Dr. Anderson, the nurses, and me. We're not putting poison in your water. Think about it. We'd lose our jobs if we killed off our patients. We'd be fired."

"You don't know about the gnomes," protested Warren. "They sneak out from the cracks in the floor. They piss in my water. They pull out my hair while I'm asleep. I wake up howling with pain and when a nurse comes in to check on me, the bastards hide. They're fiends from hell, gnomes with pig snouts. The nurses all think I've gone crazy. I can tell by the smirks on their faces and the way they talk to me. As if I were a five-year-old." He started to sob. "It's so humiliating."

Richard attempted to sound calm. "Warren, you're just imagining this. You've got a good head of hair. I can't see that any of it is missing. It looks like it's all there, and I'm sure the water's safe to drink. Here, I'll drink the water to prove it's not poisoned. Would that convince you?"

"No, don't," Warren shrieked. "It won't do any good to have two of us dead. After the night invaders have finished me off, you'll be the only one who can tell what really happened. You want to see the hair they've pulled out? My God, every night, I'm awakened by horrific yanking. Just wait till you see this..."

Warren leaned over and pulled open the top drawer of the nightstand next to his narrow bed. Sure enough, there was fine brown hair that matched that on his head. No scissors were allowed to the patients, so it couldn't have been cut. The damn fool must have pulled it out himself.

"Believe it or not, Warren, this war will be over and you'll be going back home. The nightmare will end and you'll be able to return to your loved ones. Do you ever write to your family? Do they know what a miserable time you're having?"

"They wouldn't care if I killed myself," Warren said in a barely audible voice. "My parents never wanted me. I was just another mouth to feed, a burden. After my brother died, they blamed me. But I didn't push him in. It just happened."

Last week Warren had recounted the drowning death of his younger brother, Jeff. They'd gone along with their uncle on a fishing trip. The two boys wandered off and lay face down on a boulder overlooking an inlet to see if they could see the magic trout that were supposed to live in the pool beneath.

"Jeffrey and I argued," Warren said quietly. "We were wrestling. He just slipped and fell into the deep water. There was nothing I could do."

"Yes, accidents happen, and as you said, you were just children. Your uncle should have been watching young boys, especially near water. I believe you, Warren. But, that was then and it's over with. You have the rest of your life to live now. Some of your buddies didn't make it out of the jungle in Burma. You need to live for them."

Warren started to howl, and Benet realized that he'd said the wrong thing. But dammit, it was true. Just being alive in this godforsaken outpost was a gift, especially considering how most of the poor souls in India were one bowl of rice away from starving.

Warren finally regained some control. He blew his nose loudly in the handkerchief Richard handed him.

"Doc, two things you just don't seem to understand. Number one, I never told my uncle that Jeff drowned. I just said I didn't know what happened, that he must have gotten lost. There was an investigation, but no one ever suspected that I knew anything. I pretended to be sad about losing my brother, but what I really felt was guilt, as though I caused his death.

"Number two, you say I should write to someone who loves me back home. Easy for you to say. I've seen that photo of your wife. Everyone talks about Rita Benet's picture, and you've got her right in your pocket. Hell, I wouldn't be here in the nut house if I had someone waiting at home. Don't you see that nothing matters anymore? I don't have anyone and if I never came back, I'd be just like Jeff down at the bottom of the lake. I'd be disappeared."

"That's not true, Warren. I bet you have friends you went to school with. Haven't you ever had a girlfriend, a handsome fellow like you?"

"Nah." He paused for a long time. "Ya know, sometimes I think maybe I pushed Jeff off the rock. I couldn't swim to save him, but I could have yelled for my uncle. I let him just vanish, and I never told anyone how it happened."

"Warren, we've been over and over that. You were just a little boy, and you were too frightened to tell anyone. It sounds as though you had to be on your own a lot and it was too much responsibility. But you can't do anything about that, and you gotta stop blaming yourself. That's all gone. Whatever happened, happened. Think about now."

Benet fought a desire to leave and continue his talk with Warren another day. The room had grown unbearably hot. At least Warren was no longer talking about suicide. Still, his emotional state was precarious. A hasty exit by Benet might plunge this troubled man back into despair.

Hoping that Warren would notice, Benet took a drink of the "poisoned" water. He removed his jacket, putting it over the back of the padded desk chair.

Warren was quiet for a minute before speaking. "Ya know, Doc, now that I think on it, there was a girl who really liked me, and I was sweet on her. I used to walk her home from school. Nancy Williams was her name."

Benet looked at his watch. It was growing late. There was a small cot next to the opposite wall, too tempting to resist.

"I'm listening to you, Warren. I want to hear about Nancy. I can help you write a letter to her tomorrow. Now I think I'll lie down and listen. You continue talking."

It was no longer the Warren of violent fears who spoke. A calmer personality seemed to have emerged.

"Nancy told me things she never told anyone else. Know something, Doc? We always said we were going to get married when we were old enough. She wanted a lot of kids. This wife of yours that you write to every day, has she borne you any children?"

Benet answered from his supine position on the cot. "Mmm. You mean Rita, my wife Rita, the love of my life. We met when we were children. We never loved anyone else. We married when we were in college and were planning to start a family while I finished my Ph.D. Turned out we couldn't have kids, so before the draft brought me over here, we tried to adopt a baby. But I'm sure you aren't interested in hearing all this..."

"Doc," said Warren, "I'm sorry I've been treating you like a turd. I was wrong. You're not a bad guy at all. It's good for me to hear about someone with a more normal life, anything besides talking about this fucking hell hole, this fucking war. I'm beginning to feel more like living. I know you're just doing what the Army pays you to do by baby-sitting me."

"Mmm," said Benet. He nearly burst out laughing. What a ludicrous picture the two of them must have made. Patient and counselor stretched out in adjacent beds, chatting through the night.

As always, after the sun went down, so did the base generators. One small, dim lamp was all that kept Warren's room from being completely dark. Benet peered through the gloom to see if his charge had dozed off. Warren's eyes were closed, but every so often they opened wide. As though talking in his sleep, Warren murmured, "Please don't leave me, Doc. I won't make it on my own."

"I'll stay with you through the night," Benet murmured. "In the morning, Dr. Anderson will be taking over. I'll see you're moved to a sunnier room."

"Doc, I want to send a letter to Nancy. She swore she'd wait. I promised I'd write, but I was waiting for her to write first. Nancy, Nancy... Nancy...." His voice trailed off.

Benet enjoyed a moment of self-congratulation. He'd never heard his patient mention "Nancy." If Warren felt there was someone

179

who cared if he lived or died, it was more likely he would be able to find the will to live. He, Benet, would have made a difference.

"That's the idea, Warren. Just get back in touch. I'll have Sanjay bring you some stationary tomorrow so you can write to Nancy. I know she wants to hear from you. Be sure to write your APO address so she can write back. You'd be surprised to see how mail lifts a man's spirits."

The only answer was a snore. Benet, intending to write the day's letter to Rita, crept softly out of the room. Letters, after all, were what kept him sane. In order to revive himself, he walked briskly up and down the long hall of the isolation ward.

Though still exhausted, Benet was now thinking clearly. Sitting on the floor outside Warren's room, he wrote three pages, signed it "from your loving husband, Richard," folded it up and put it in his uniform jacket pocket. He'd mail it after his meeting tomorrow with General Peterson.

When he reached in his pocket to deposit the letter he'd just completed, his hand touched some folded papers. Growing very sleepy, he pulled them out. It was his story "Under the Village Palms." No matter. Perhaps he would send that to Rita as well for safekeeping.

There was always the danger of her misunderstanding the story, but she did trust him completely. After all, he'd made it clear that he was not a customer at the brothel; he was there just as an observer. His visit was strictly in the spirit of professional interest. At any rate, he was too weary to continue his internal dialogue.

Benet tottered back into Warren's room and sat down on his cot, removing his shoes. He stretched out on the narrow bed, covered himself up with his jacket, and was asleep in less than ten minutes.

Warren crept out of his hospital bed. But this was a different Warren than the one Benet had just talked to. He was furious, outraged, and insulted. That jackass Benet was a fool. The pretentious stuffed shirt had believed the shit he'd made up about Nancy. There was no Nancy. Warren lifted up his mattress and took out the butcher knife he'd stolen from the kitchen. It would be so easy to cover Benet's head with a pillow and plunge the blade into that idiot's heart.

The only problem would be his own escape afterwards. At the end of the hall, an armed watchman kept vigil. Warren slipped the knife back under the mattress and looked over at the sleeping psychologist. He was sick of Dr. Benet's air or superiority. How he would love to show him up for what he was—a weak-willed phony.

Light from a full moon shone through the barred window, illuminating Benet. It shone on the jacket that served as a makeshift blanket. Something white was half out of one of the jacket's pockets. Warren slipped his fingers around the top of the packet. Moving without a sound, he carried the folded pages over to the lamp next to his bed.

A smile broke across Warren's face as he read Doc's story so stupidly titled "Under the Village Palms." At last he had something on Benet, something he could use against him. It would be better than suffocating his jailer. He memorized Rita Benet's address: "311 Center Street, Findlay, Ohio."

Warren slipped the papers back into Benet's pocket and got back under the covers of his own bed. He could hardly keep from laughing out loud. He congratulated himself. He would mention the Palms story and use it to break up Doc's marriage, a perfect way of getting even with the man who made his life so miserable.

In the morning, Warren planned to ask Sanjay for writing materials to send a note to the fictitious Nancy. Instead, he would write to Mrs. Rita Benet. His letter would reveal that her beloved husband was a frequent customer at the lowest brothels in Calcutta. He would explain how he personally had admired her picture, as her husband showed it off to anyone and everyone. He'd write how he hated to be the bearer of bad news, but that she ought to know. As Benet slept, Warren composed the letter in his mind.

31

"Well, Lt. Benet," boomed General Oley Peterson, "how good ta see ya again, sooner I'm sure than either of us expected. I have some startlin' news about our Mac McDermott. But first, woncha order some breakfast?"

Benet felt unkempt after his nearly sleepless night with Warren, but he tried to look and sound alert. The two men were alone in a private room at the Officer's Club.

"Thank you sir. It is an honor to be invited to breakfast. I have felt for some time that Colonel Mac had problems that were getting the better of him, but I've had my hands full with my patients, so I suppose you might say I've turned a blind eye."

An Indian knocked lightly on the door and stepped into the meeting room.

"*Sahibs*, may I take your order?" The morning shift waiter bore a remarkable similarity to Sanjay, Benet noticed. Perhaps he was related. The Indian stood immobile, a white towel over his right arm.

Peterson's frowned. It was clear that the niceties of a breakfast together were not the point of this meeting.

"Ah yes," Benet said. "A pot of strong black tea, milk, toast and marmalade. That should do it."

"No eggs or sausage, *sahib*?"

When Benet shook his head in dissent, the waiter backed gracefully out of the room, closing the door as he left.

"Lieutenant, tha shit's hit tha fan," announced Peterson. "Your Colonel, 'cause of his expensive opium habit, is respon'ble for medical supplies vanishin' from our hospital."

"My God," Benet said. "You mean he's stealing to support his addiction? As bad as Mac is, I never dreamed...."

"Tha's bad nuff, but he jes might be connected ta deaths at tha hospital. Lieutenant, surely ya musta been suspicious."

The waiter returned with the psychologist's breakfast and a thermos jug from which he refilled Peterson's coffee cup. Benet used the time to compose his thoughts. Even though he'd done nothing wrong, he felt guilty. Why hadn't he notified the military police about the loss of medical supplies? He should have reported to someone above Mac that the 142nd was going to hell in a handbasket. Instead, he'd waited. He'd acted solely on the assumption that in the military, one survived only by unquestioning assent to authority. In his heart, he'd known that such deliberate blindness might be dangerous.

"Lieutenant?" asked Peterson. "Are ya with me?"

"Yes, General Peterson. I'm with you. Are you referring to the murder of Sergeant Lowell? I thought MPs tracked down the Indian janitor who stabbed him. I assumed they turned the perp over to the Calcutta police. Weren't his fingerprints on the knife? Wasn't it decided that the same janitor had been stealing our medications and selling them?"

"Drink yer tea, Lieutenant, afore it gets cold." Peterson smiled grimly. "Yer on the right track. This does hafta do with Silas Lowell, the man put in charge of the medical supplies. The story went that Lowell was 'bout to find out who'd been stealin' morphine 'n in order ta shut him up, the 'medicine thief' killed him."

There was a knock at the door and Peterson's second-in-command, Lt. Luigi Marinelli, popped his head in. "Excuse the interruption, General, Lieutenant, but I'm just reminding General Peterson that his briefing with General Stilwell is at 1200 hours. Sir, shall I set up our files in the Peacock Room?"

"Marinelli, ya know what to do. Jes do it. Order a lunch fer the General, and please, no more interruptions. Lieutenant Benet and I'll be finished here in about twenty minutes."

Marinelli saluted smartly, backed out, and closed the door behind him.

"Yes, now ... where was I?"

"The Indian janitor confessed to killing Sergeant Lowell. You were saying that it seemed almost too simple."

"Right. There was somethin' not quite right 'bout the confession. We asked our friends on the Calcutta police force 'bout the janitor. What was his name? He had a Christian name, somethin' like George?"

"It was Fred. He'd been raised in a Catholic orphanage and had made a living working for Americans starting when he was sixteen. That's when they can no longer take care of the orphans, I've heard."

"Yes, 'n Fred was an orphan," said Peterson. "But we digress. Back to the night a the crime. The man'd almost dis'peared into the *goonda* neighborhoods when our Military Police accosted him. He admitted the crime right away. Matter of fact, his confession seemed too sudden, too easy. It was 'most as though sumun would kill'im if he didn't take 'sponsibility for the murder."

Benet finished his first cup of tea, then took a large bite of toast and jam. "So you think he was hired as a hit man?" he asked. "Who would want Silas dead? Everyone liked the guy. His only fault was telling really bad jokes, but he worked hard, never said a mean thing about anybody. It just doesn't make sense."

Peterson lit a cigarette and offered one to Benet.

"No thanks. I gave it up for my wife. She hates cigarette smoke. OK, sir, how about this? It wasn't Silas; it was his job, taking care of our medical supplies, knowing what came in, what went out. He once told me that supplies were missing and I told him to just keep better track. He knew too much. If our derelict Colonel Mac found out that Silas knew about his dirty little secret, he'd for sure want him shut up. But killed? As much as I can't stand Mac, it's hard for me to believe that he's a murderer."

The waiter slipped into the conference room, refilled Peterson's coffee cup and poured more tea for Richard. How many cups had Oley Peterson consumed, Richard wondered. The man seemed to live on cigarettes and coffee.

"Thank ya, Mohan. We'll not be needin' anythin' else. Please put a 'Don' disturb' sign on the door."

A slight bow was made and the waiter disappeared. The director of the 20th General Hospital lit another Camel and inhaled deeply. He blew the smoke out in thin, precise rings.

Benet sighed. He felt a profound weariness at this whole sordid affair. "Well," he exclaimed, with more energy than he felt. "Now that I think of it, I haven't really seen Mac for quite a few days. He is having an affair with one of the nurses, I suppose you already know about that."

Peterson puffed on his cigarette and nodded.

"She cornered me after dinner one night and seemed desperate to talk. Of course, because I'm a psychologist, people always want to confide in me. At first I thought she was making a pass, but she was truly distraught."

More smoke rings. "Hmm," said Peterson. "Did she talk about McDermott?"

"Yes, she said they wanted to see if they could be a couple and that Mac needed someone who understood him. She indicated that she could see through his beastly exterior to the 'good' McDermott inside. But I could tell that she was holding something back. She acted frightened."

"And wadja tell her, Lieutenant? What was yer advice?"

"I was talking to her as a friend. I suggested that she get out of the relationship when she decided she could no longer stand being in it."

"Wadja s'pose she wuz mos' upset 'bout? The thing about which she couldn' talk?"

"OK, sir, I have an idea, but would you venture a guess from the story I've related?"

"First of all," Peterson began, "I reckon our nurse Clara is afraid that Mac'll slap her 'round if she tries ta leave him. The man thinks a women as sub-human, even though I'm sure with Clara he's tried to disguise his contempt for her. Secondly, I 'spect that Clara's has adopted the opium habit jes like Mac. Tha's was prob'ly what she was ashamed to tell. Fer all we know, he may be blackmailin' her."

"General, that was my guess, opium addiction. From what I've heard about the nurse, she would try anything. From what I can tell, the combination of Mac and opium has just about done her in."

"And yer prob'ly wondrin' what I need from ya, Lieutenant. I don't 'spect you ta untangle this situation. Tha's my job. I'm a career Army officer, so there's nevah a time to let up. Ya know, this damn war'll end someday. I hardly need ta ask, Lieutenant, but I assume you're goin' back to civilian life."

"I promised my wife I'd find a college teaching job after I get home. Before I answered the draft, I had an offer in Huntingdon, West Virginia. Also, we plan to adopt a baby. Rita never quits looking, but without a father in the home, no agency will allow a couple to adopt."

"Ah yes. Doc, you're a damn good psychologist. The Army could really use ya. But I gather an Army career doesn't interest you. Oh well, Lieutenant, of course I wancha to keep treatin' yer patients with the swimmin' field trips and group therapy sesshuns. Try ta have your bearer report the coming' and going' of Mac and his nurse. Talk ta Clara as much as possible. See wacha can learn."

"I understand," said Benet. "I'll report to you every few days."

"And Lieutenant, Mac could find out that I've been talkin' with ya. So be careful. Watch yer back."

A knock at the door was followed by Marinelli's voice. "General, sir, it's time for your next appointment." Both men stood up and walked to the door. Thunder rumbled in the distance. Another monsoon rain was on the way.

Peterson shook Benet's hand. "Remember ta be careful and don't talk 'bout this to anyone. I'll be checkin' with ya each week.

185

"Yes sir, thank you for your confidence in me." Benet headed toward Ward 55 to talk with Fletch, Ike, Gus and Sturke. A few raindrops splattered his face, and soon he was running through a torrential downpour. The Army-issue poncho he carried for such emergencies would cover nearly every inch of his uniform. He donned it quickly and rolled up his trousers to keep them dry. If only that were the worst problem he faced, he'd be grateful.

Peterson was depending on him. To do exactly what, he wasn't sure. Or perhaps he was—to spy, pry and watch his back. This Calcutta assignment was turning into a nightmare. It would be the height of irony to get through the last gritty year in reasonably good shape only to get killed by a fellow officer. Benet would write tonight to Rita, as he always did, but he would carefully avoid a depiction of the latest situation. More than anything else during his tour of duty in Calcutta, this whole picture stunk.

32

During the first weeks of December 1944, it snowed every day. In Findlay, Ohio, no one could recall a fiercer winter. Icy roads and blizzards kept people indoors and businesses closed. At Washington Elementary School, "snow days" were becoming the rule rather than the exception. Rita still wrote to Richard every day, but it was becoming harder not to complain. She needed to keep her head high. Wasn't that what her absent husband was always telling her?

Right before Christmas break, the weather cleared enough to get in a few days of school. Early on Friday, the local radio station, WINX, announced that public schools would open at the normal time. Rita had been awake for hours and was dressed and ready to go even before the radio news.

Outside her bedroom the sunrise turned the sky peach and gold. Sitting at her dressing table, Rita buried her nose in the bouquet of white roses that Richard had sent to her to commemorate their first date. Since their separation a year ago, he'd sent flowers for every holiday, birthday, and anniversary.

Roses made the endless waiting more bearable. In low moments, Rita would bend over them and smile at the story behind their delivery. During one Sunday dinner, her Aunt Gay let out the secret. At the beginning of each month, Richard would send his sister a money order to use at the florist shop. Gay called the florist and ordered blossoms sent to her brother's daughter. If there was no special occasion that month, Gay would save the money to buy a grander bouquet the next time.

Rita sat in her chilly bedroom feeling the soft petals with her fingertips. In many ways, she was grateful for school. The children in her class were excited about Santa Claus and getting to stay home. For those whose fathers and uncles had arrived back from the war, it would be an especially joyous time.

She did not begrudge those families that were now complete, back together again and whole. And yet her heart ached at her aloneness. She loved her parents, of course, but living her life around theirs, like a maiden aunt, made her feel old and used up. Adding to her dejection was the fact that all of her household effects were stuffed in the two rooms adjoining her temporary bedroom.

Her mother called from downstairs. "Rita, dear, are you all right? I heard noises from your room in the middle of the night, and I've been wondering if something was wrong. I didn't want you to oversleep and miss work."

"Yes, Ma, I'm fine. I'll be right downstairs."

Rita disliked the "inspections" that went with her departures. She slipped into her tweed wool coat. This might save her from the predictable lecture about how thin she'd grown. Perhaps she could just breeze through the kitchen, wave a quick goodbye and dash out the door.

Her mother, however, thought differently.

"You know, dear. That coat could be updated very simply. It's still in good condition and tweed is always smart. I might be able to find a velvet collar at Lamont's. Our neighbor Mollie has a sewing machine that she loves to use, and she could place it just right. We could manage a remodeling with not much expense.

"Ma, Lamont's is a fabric store. I don't think they have velvet collars. Thanks anyway for thinking of it."

"We'll see about that," Ruth sniffed. "Sit down, dear. How about some oatmeal? I just made a pot. You'll feel so much better if you eat breakfast."

Rita's place at the wooden kitchen table was set with a new red and white checked place mat. On it were carefully arranged a white cup and saucer, cereal bowl on a small platter, a juice glass, napkin, and silverware.

"I hate to seem ungrateful, Mom, but I'm about to melt in this kitchen. It's like an oven. I'll take a rain check on the oatmeal. I forgot to make lesson plans for today, so I've got to leave right now to beat the children to my classroom. They're a handful these days."

Ruth sighed. "That's all the more reason for you to eat breakfast. Your papa's already left for the court house. He has to balance the city's public service accounts for this past quarter."

"Poor Daddy, always working so hard."

"That man was born to work. And you, driving yourself too hard because you don't want to mope about Richard not being back home for the holiday. Ruth brushed away tears with her apron. You will be home on time this afternoon, won't you?"

"No, I'll be home late, just a little late. Mr. Eckles called a meeting of the entire faculty. But there's a bright side. The meeting is about having a longer Christmas vacation because of the weather."

Buttoning her coat and wrapping a wool scarf around her neck, Rita walked out to the kitchen porch. After stepping outside, she turned around, returned to the kitchen, and gave her mother a hug and a kiss on the cheek. Wartime was hard for all of them, and she didn't want to make her mother's day get off to a bad start.

The sun was out, lighting up banks of snow that blanketed every front lawn. Rita drove the green bomb slowly out the drive and north toward Washington Elementary School. She'd had plenty of practice snow driving during Richard's graduate school years at Ohio State University. Toledo's winters had been severe and its big city traffic was far worse than Findlay's.

The deep snowfall of last week had turned Center Street into a wintery showplace. The icy street was deserted except for a lone school bus lumbering slowly ahead of her. Rita took time to notice the environs. Most of the homes dated from the last century, large Victorian two- or three-story mansions with deep verandahs, white lacy trim, shutters, and turrets. Snow covered every lawn, several of which were graced with snow men and women.

The neighborhood's glacial beauty lifted her spirits. Forgetting her pensive mood of earlier this morning, Rita started looking forward to the day ahead. She parked the green bomb in the faculty lot, and hurried into the school. Normally she would have been irritated when Sharon and Robert came into her classroom too early, but today she let them help her with planning the day's activities.

Filled with a Christmas play by the sixth graders and an all-grades assembly and singalong, the day flew by. Just as Rita suspected, the three o'clock faculty meeting focused on snow days. Christmas break would be extended until January 19th. Because heating bills were impossibly high, Mr. Eckles told his teachers, the extension would help the school budget. The long break would give all of them time to plan their lessons for the rest of the year. Eckles would check their plans during the last week in January.

As the principal rambled on, Rita's attention wandered. Why was it that school administrators and maybe all bosses everywhere felt that a meeting had to be lengthy to be respectable? The morning's clearing had ended, and a few snowflakes floated through the air. In five minutes, it began snowing in earnest.

Mr. Eckles looked out the window and finally brought the gathering to a close.

"If no one has anything else to bring up, the meeting is adjourned. Have a Merry Christmas and Happy New Year, everyone. Stay healthy, and come back next year prepared to continue being the best teachers in Hancock County. And remember to pray for our

men who are still in harm's way defending our country. May they
return home safely and soon."

Applause was followed by shuffling of chairs. Evelyn rushed
over to Rita with a gaily wrapped present. "Sweetie, here's a little
something for under the tree. Also, if you're not busy, we're getting
together a couple tables of bridge tonight at my house. We'd love to
have you!"

"Why you rascal," said Rita. "I'll have to give your present to
you for the New Year. This is very kind of you. I'd love to play
bridge, but I promised my mother I'd be home for dinner. She's
fixing something special and I promised I'd be there."

"Ah shucks, we'll miss you."

"Count me in next time, Evie. You and your family have a
wonderful Christmas."

It was nearly dark by four-thirty p.m. as Rita maneuvered
carefully over the icy streets. She was greeted with the aroma of
meat loaf and baked potatoes. After dinner with her parents, she fell
asleep on the couch. It was hard to make herself get ready for bed,
but once she did, she felt wide awake.

A good thing, too, as she still had a letter to write. Propped up by
pillows in bed, Rita filled her fountain pen and began...

December 19, 1944
My Darling:

*Vacation has started and I am very glad for it. A cold has started
too. I just hope I can head it off.*

*Your December 8th letter came today, a day behind your
December 9th. The present mailman is Billy Wells (recently
discharged from the Army). He is very friendly and accommodating.
I hope he stays on. Did I tell you that he calls me when there's a
package from you at the post office so I can pick it up on the way
home from school? If I can't come by, he uses cross-country skis to
bring it to me after his shift is over.*

*My children at school really outdid themselves, particularly
since we are supposed to neither give nor receive gifts. Evelyn got
alarmed about it this morning and asked the principal what to do. He
said, "Take them and keep quiet!"*

*My classroom gave me a three-pound box of candy and a white
silk scarf. Good shopping for children, I'd say. In addition, I got a
little bottle of Yardley's toilet water, a bottle of Wrisley's cologne,
boxes of stationery, handkerchiefs from three people, and four pretty*

rose-shaped cakes of soap in a setting of green leaves. The little rascals must have really saved their pennies. I came home feeling like I must make some kind of gesture, so bought 37 Christmas cards and have them ready to mail in the morning.

One of my children said he wished you were here to help me eat candy. Of course, I do too, but since you aren't, I wish I could get it to you.

There are a lot of places I feel I'm not doing what is expected of me. I don't know whether they (the administration) know it or not. I'm not proud of my teaching. I don't even take care of my room at home decently. And I'm not kidding when I say the last two years have added more than two years to my age in looks. I certainly haven't the right to complain, but I'm fed up to the gills. I hope a vacation gives me a brighter outlook.

I am getting Christmas cards from people I haven't heard from in a long time. I saw Don Renninger on the street. He didn't recognize me but I stopped him a moment. He seemed to know about you but didn't say how. He has a discharge, sends his regards and hopes that you get home soon.

Hurry home, my love!

Lots of hugs and kisses,

Rita

P.S.

Lucky I forgot to seal this last night! I'm enclosing the front page of today's paper. As you can see from the headlines, Thelma Shunter was arrested! Apparently she is accused of harboring her cousin, a Nazi spy named Heinrich Shunter. He was posing as a Findlay College student with the phony name Arthur Grunwald. Of course, the spy is under arrest and we all are waiting to read more news about what happens to him.

I am happy that Mildred and I might have helped bring that about. The arrest, I mean. Remember how I told you in a letter about our basement mission and call to the F.B.I. It's thrilling to think that we helped, but of course there's no way to prove it.

It's silly of me, I guess, but I don't want you to mention this in any letters you write to our parents. Some people are touchy on the issue of Nazi sympathizers, and Thelma has a lot of German American friends who are coming to her defense. Just between you and me, though, I'm proud of my little bit in helping the war effort. And now, I really will mail this, along with a big hug and kiss.

191

33

A few days before Christmas, Rita finally gave in and went to St. Andrew's Cathedral with her mother. It wasn't a regular service but an Evensong. She'd finally relaxed a bit from the daily grind of school, and it was pleasing to notice the result: her mother's lighter spirits. Ruth introduced her daughter proudly to Pastor Shepardson.

"You remember my daughter Rita. She and her husband Richard Benet have been living in Toledo while he finished up his Ph.D. He's in Calcutta, India at an Army Air Force hospital, in charge of a mental ward."

Shepardson shook Rita's gloved hand. "We're so glad you're here tonight. I hope you'll be with us for our celebration of Christmas. The traditional music will be magnificent and the service will be lovely."

"Pleased to meet you, pastor. I apologize for not being here since my wedding two years ago. I have to correct what mother said. Richard is in charge of the Neuro-Psychiatric Ward, not the 'mental ward'."

The chapel was packed with most of Findlay's Episcopalians. Shortly after her marriage to Richard, Rita had decided that she was a Deist, which she described to Evelyn as "one who accepts the existence of God but does not subscribe to any particular religion." But for tonight, she would accommodate her mother.

Chords pealed out from the newly-tuned organ. "Turn to page 102," Ruth whispered. Mother and daughter blended their alto voices with the congregation's singing.

Once in royal David's city stood a lowly cattle shed,
where a mother laid her baby in a manger for his bed:
Mary was that mother mild,
Jesus Christ her little child...

The hymn brought tears to Rita's eyes. She remembered singing it as a child in Sunday school. She'd attended faithfully until she was thirteen, when she decided church was boring. Her mother tried for a few months to bring her daughter, as she put it, "back into the fold." That was years ago, but Rita's memories were so vivid, it might as well have been yesterday.

Pastor Shepardson droned on and as he did, Rita's mind wandered. She reviewed the past eight months. When Richard received his draft notice and she subsequently moved back to the home of her childhood, she assumed that she would not be expected to attend church.

At first, nothing was said when she chose to sleep late on Sunday. That ended, however. Ruth Collins began reminding her daughter that she should not be neglecting her "spiritual development."

"But Ma," Rita had protested, "I'm taking care of my soul, just not in a traditional way."

The organ pealed mightily as another Christmas carol was launched by the choir. Rita's skepticism dissolved as she joined in the festive, reverent spirit around her.

> *Oh come all ye faithful*
> *Joyful and triumphant*
> *O come ye, o come ye*
> *To Beth-eth-le-hem...*

Though she hardly considered herself part of "the faithful," for this one night Rita could envision Bethlehem. As she had during her childhood, she pictured a cold night, a deep, velvety black sky, and a dazzling star casting light on a manger. She closed her eyes and thought of the tender scene within—infant Jesus, his parents Joseph and Mary, and their entourage of animals and wise men. The story came back to her in detail. In her early days, she and her cousins had acted out the miraculous birth of Christ and that night. The organist played introductory chords and the congregation sang.

> *It came up-aw-on a midnight clear*
> *that glorious song of old*
> *From angels bending near the earth*
> *To touch their harps of gold...*
> *Peace on the earth*
> *Good will to men*
> *From heaven's all gracious king*
> *The world in solemn stillness lay*
> *To hear the angels sing...*

When the last verse was finished, Pastor Shepardson gave a brief homily and then invited the congregation to the parish hall for punch and cookies. Rita spotted Evelyn three rows ahead. It was funny seeing her school colleagues out of context. They looked so much more relaxed.

"Do you mind coming along with me to the reception, dear?" Ruth asked. "I'd love it if you would. The guild has been baking for weeks. There will be punch and every imaginable kind of cookie: gingersnaps, Danish wedding cookies, toffee bars, shortbread, and macaroons."

The congregation moved slowly to the back of the chapel, which to the outside world was the front of the church. Rita recognized many faces from her past, folks she hadn't seen for years. Everyone wore a smile, and all were headed toward the reception.

Arm in arm, Rita and her mother walked outside into the freezing air, down the front steps and into the brightly lit church hall. It was a moonless night, crystal clear and studded with stars. Rita looked overhead, half expecting to see the star of Bethlehem. She was doing this just to humor her mother, she reminded herself. No need to get carried away.

"Too bad papa is home with a cold," said Ruth. "He would have loved this. I hope you're enjoying this, sweetheart, and not just pretending for me. We're headed toward the party. The real reason you'll enjoy it, dearie, is not just for the cookies and punch but for the chance to see friends and neighbors from your not-so-distant past.

In the meantime, Ruth spotted friends from her church circle group. They were gathered next to the lavishly decorated giant fir tree, and she walked across the hardwood floor to chat with them. The ladies were all wearing small hats with veils and all holding cups of frothy punch in their right hands.

Evelyn walked over to join Rita "Long time, no see," she quipped. "Isn't it great to be free from seeing those little darlings every day? And we don't have to see them again until next year!"

"Yep," Rita agreed, "and just think, by this time next year, God willing, we'll have Richard and Jack here to celebrate Christmas with us. The war will be over and the world will be safe again. I'm so grateful that we live in a country that's free and strong. That's the best Christmas present anyone could ask for."

Evelyn, munching on cookies, nodded in agreement.

"You know, Evelyn," Rita continued, "at the risk of sounding selfish, my favorite gift will probably be at the post office. Richard bought an ivory necklace for me. He'd been looking for one ever since he arrived in Calcutta. He found it in time for me to put it under the Christmas tree. I'm going to the post office first chance possible to see if it's arrived."

"I see," Evelyn remarked. "That does sound lovely."

Rita headed to the refreshments table and filled a platter with cookies. She carried the treats back to Evelyn, who'd now been joined by Gladys, who taught at Findlay High School and lived in Evelyn's neighborhood.

"Gee, thanks for waiting on us, Rita," said Evelyn. "Can you believe that Gladys expects Sam back from England by the first of the year? Some people have all the luck."

Evelyn turned to Gladys. "Rita just told me that Richard bought an ivory necklace for her in Calcutta, India, and it might arrive tomorrow! Ivory jewelry. Can you imagine?"

"I'm going to be at the post office when the doors open," Rita said. "What about you, Evelyn? Has your fiancé given you a hint?"

"Jack's last V-mail mentioned a cuckoo clock from Germany," said Evelyn. "Yesterday a box arrived that looks clock-sized. It's under the Christmas tree at home. Mom's giving me a permanent tomorrow morning or I'd come with you to the post office. Do me a favor, kid, and telephone me after your early morning trip downtown. I can't wait to hear when your present arrives."

Exhausted, Rita decided to bid her friend farewell. "Sure thing, Evelyn. Gladys, nice to see you again. Have a wonderful Christmas, you two."

Rita held her mother's arm as they walked across the parking lot to the Packard.

"What a beautiful evening," Rita said. "I'm surprised that I really did enjoy it."

"Yes, Rita. Thank you so much for coming with me. I knew you'd have a good time. Evening services are something that St. Andrew's does well. It must be nearly eleven o'clock. I imagine you'll be sleeping in tomorrow."

They got in the car, which took its time coming to life. Rita gave the ignition a rest and tried for a fourth time. At last, the Packard revved up. Too weary to converse, mother and daughter drove home through dark, snow-packed streets. Inside the house, they spoke in whispers. Gale Collins was a very light sleeper and it was important for him to recover in time for Christmas day.

"Thanks again, Ma," Rita said, giving her mother a goodnight kiss on the cheek. "You'll be surprised to know that I'm getting up early. I want to be first in line at the post office. Richard's present for me just might have arrived, and I don't feel like waiting until it's delivered with the regular mail."

"I understand, dearie. Sleep well and sweet dreams."

34

When Rita arrived at the post office five minutes before the nine o'clock opening time, there was already a line snaking from the double doors to the icy sidewalk. She took a place at the end, right behind Ann Eckles, wife of the Washington Elementary School's principal.

"Guess we all had the same idea," said Ann.

"You mean getting our packages before Christmas and not after?" asked Rita.

"Yes. With this terrible weather we've been having, they're saying everything is slowed down. Only five more shopping days."

"Richard's in India," Rita told Mrs. Eckles. "I sent his presents in October and he already has everything. I hope they do something real special for our men in India and for our soldiers everywhere in the world. Who would have believed that the war would last so long?"

"I know." Ann said. "It's dragged on forever, but we must all make sacrifices to keep our America's democracy secure. As the saying goes, 'Freedom isn't free'."

The post office doors opened, and a cheer arose from the waiting crowd. The line turned into a stampede. Once inside, people reshuffled into another queue. Rita secured a place near the beginning.

A large middle-aged woman with fat cheeks and a bulbous nose called out from the window, "Next?" Her voice sounded raspy, as though she might be coming down with a cold. She sneezed three times, in quick succession.

Rita tried not to get too close. "Anything for Gale or Ruth Collins? Or for Mrs. Rita Benet? Same address for all three of us: 311 Center Street."

The post office lady walked away from her window and disappeared into a back room. "Nah, no packages, but I can give you your letters. We're backed up, lots out sick, so anything we can get out early is a big help." She handed Rita several envelopes and a copy of *Life Magazine*.

"Thanks and Merry Christmas," Rita said, walking over to a free counter on the wall opposite the post office boxes. It was possible that Richard's package had been lost or stolen. She sorted through the mail: A letter from Marilyn, who had moved with her husband to

Toronto, and two Christmas cards addressed to her parents. There was no package. Rita's only mail was an airmail letter sent through an APO address.

Her husband's handwriting was beautifully even and graceful, always in black ink. This missive was addressed in pencil. The writing on this envelope was large and childish, like something by one of her slower students.

"What on earth?" she wondered aloud. God forbid that it was bad news about Richard. Had he contracted a jungle illness and become too sick and weak to write?

Rita ripped open the envelope. Oblivious to her surroundings, she stood at a counter and read the wobbly handwriting in disbelief.

Dear Miz. Benet or may I call you Rita,

I'm a patient of your husband's here at the 142nd General Hospital in Calcutta. You might think I'm crazy, but I ain't. When the Army don't know what to do with us, they stick a label on us—'shell shocked,' 'emotionally unbalanced,' 'burned out' or some such insulting term. It turns out the ones making the labels are the crazy ones.

If you didn't already git your husband's story Under the Village Palms, you will. It jes so happened I read that story one night when he was put in my room to guard me. He thought I was asleep but I just pretended to be.

The story he wrote just happined to be out and I jes happined to read it. Never have I seen such a piece of filth. But you, Miz Benet, will see this for yerself if you haven't already. Why would he send this to as nice a lady as I can tell you are? He's the one that needs sickiatric help.

Alright, I'll git to the point. It's not just that his story is nasty and vile and deserved to be torched. It's full of lies. I'll explain. Your husband goes out every night into the hell holes of Calcutta even though it's not allowed. He could be court-martialed. I heard about that night the officers went into the worst off-limits slums. Don't believe for a minute that he was just observing. They was all paying customers. He was in jest as deep as the bums he writes about.

I know when he's back he won't tell you the true story, and believe me, I hate to be the one to tell you all this. But I seen your photographs in his office and I can tell you are a fine, upright lady and pardon me for mentioning it but a beautiful lady as well. You deserve better.

198

*Like I said, that piece of—I won't say it—that your husband
wrote should have been burned or torn up into little pieces and
flushed down the toilet and I could kick myself for not doing it when I
could. I've been worried about it ever since. I decided that the best
thing to do was to tell you in a letter because if a man will deceive
his wife once you can be sure he'll do it again.*

*God forgive me if I am speaking out of turn but I knew that
unless I wrote to you, the truth would be buried forever. I got your
address from an envelope that was also on the table with that dirty
story and after I'm home I may come by to visit you as by then I'd be
surprised if you decided to put up with a lying, cheating husband.
You deserve the best. I'll be glad to help you any way I can after the
war is over.*
Wishing you a Merry Christmas,
your admirer
Warren Blackwell

The day before Warren's letter arrived, Rita had received "Under
the Village Palms." She'd put it in a file with her husband's poems
and essays. She re-read Warren's message in disbelief. How dare he
send her such a letter? Certainly Warren had made everything up.
Obviously, it was a crude attempt to hurt her husband. And yet, how
could she be sure?

"G'bye now," Ann Eckles called out to Rita as she left the post
office. Rita, fighting tears, waved back.

Rita leaned against the counter. What if Warren attempted to
track her down when the war ended? Did Richard have any idea that
Warren hated him so much, enough to send her this nasty letter full
of lies? And, God forbid, what if Richard had actually behaved as
Warren suggested?

Leaning over the counter as though she were sorting out her
mail, Rita struggled to regain composure. She read Warren's letter a
second time. In spite of her determination to keep a brave front, she
started to cry.

A deep voice behind her said, "Mrs. Benet, can I do anything to
help you?"

She turned around to see the mailman, who sometimes delivered
letters to the door. This was the last straw. Rita's stomach churned,
her head was pounding, and she felt too weak to stand up. She felt
dizzy.

The next thing she knew, the mailman's strong arms were holding her up. People had gathered around them. Someone asked if he should call a doctor. Rita wanted to disappear. She shoved the embarrassing letter in her purse, as her thoughts raced through her mind.

"No, please just go about your business," said the mailman as he led Rita away from the gawking crowd. "By the way, my name's Tony," he told her. "I'm the one that brings mail to your house and calls your mother from the post office when a package arrives from India."

They ended up in the post office's cavernous, brightly-lit sorting area. Rita sat down in the room's only chair. Tony brought her a glass of water and knelt by her on the floor.

Rita finished the glass's contents before answering. "You've been so kind, but I need to go home. I'm fine now, really..." She stood up but Tony grabbed her hand and gently pulled her back down into her chair.

"Mrs. Benet, I think you're more upset than you'll admit. I dunno what the bad news was, but I don't want to know. I've seen lots of people receive a shock in the mail. Once a man had a heart attack after opening one of those bad news letters..."

Rita interrupted, "Don't worry. I'm not going to have a heart attack. Thank you for your concern. Now, I must go."

Tony stood in the doorway, his head nearly touching the top. "I've got to tell you, Rita Benet, that you are the most beautiful woman I've ever seen. I know I may be speaking out of turn, but I'd like to take you out to dinner at the Phoenix."

"I'm a happily married woman," said Rita. "That's an insulting suggestion. Now let me by." She rushed through the door, thankful that Tony backed off.

The drive home was a blur. Even though she should toss the letter from Warren into the fireplace and burn it, she knew that she'd end up keeping it. When the war ended and her husband had been home for a while, she'd get to the truth. She wanted desperately to believe that Richard was being faithful to their marriage vows. Surely "Under the Village Palms", was, as Richard told her, written from the bystander's perspective. Clearly, Warren was demented and wanted to stir up trouble. She felt that her vacation was ruined. There was no one she could confide in. Only Evelyn would understand, and Evelyn had troubles of her own.

Gale and Ruth were out for day, probably Christmas shopping. Relieved to be alone in the house, Rita left a note for them on the table saying she was asleep, that she might be coming down with the flu, and to please wake her up in time for supper.

Rita climbed upstairs to her chilly bedroom, put on flannel pajamas, and crawled into bed. If only she could have talked to Richard for reassurance, if only she knew when he was coming home, if only she knew for sure that this demented Warren character was harmless. Though she hadn't spoken to God in many years, she prayed for strength to live through these tormenting doubts and for Richard to come home soon.

35

New Year's Eve at the 142nd General Hospital was a scene of revelry. A military band played Benny Goodman numbers. Men were drinking and carousing, dancing with nurses or one another.

A number of the men were involved in a talent show that Lieutenant Anderson had organized, complete with music and dancing routines. A few of the nurses participated, but many of the women's roles were acted, in slapstick fashion, by men. Another group of soldiers participated in a quiz show run by General Peterson.

The sole exception to the atmosphere of merriment was that surrounding Lieutenant Richard Benet, spending the night as Acting Officer on Duty. Far from the celebration, Benet sat alone in the Q Building at a wooden desk in a first floor office.

Several officers had dates with nurses and were going out to dinner at restaurants in the Alipore district. Benet's nemesis, the so-called director of the hospital, was missing as usual. No doubt supplied with opium, Mac and Clara were most likely having their own party in some unused building on the hospital grounds.

Benet was mid-way through a letter to Rita. He paused to swat twenty or thirty little blue bugs, then described the Indian way of celebrating the New Year...

...For Bengalis, the New Year is in mid-April. They call it Bangla Naboborosho here. On this day, everyone goes to a shrine near the Howrah Bridge. ...(you'll find the bridge on the Calcutta map I sent you last month). Shopkeepers and businessmen take their new account books to have them blessed! They also take their little images of Ganesh, the elephant headed god, who is supposed to guard their interests. Whether or not they have their miniature Ganeshes blessed is unclear to me.

Outside the hospital, it is just another sweltering night in what Rudyard Kipling called 'The City of Dreadful Night.' The hospital is located in the better part of Calcutta, however. If you were here, my dearest. I'd hire a horse and buggy to take us to my favorite Chinese restaurant, and later we'd go to the Officer's Club to dance ..."

Beyond the relatively wealthy Alipore district, which contained blocks of upstanding middle-class houses, millions of starving natives slept on the street. Their festering, diseased limbs were barely covered with flesh. Many would not live until morning.

Flickering through the night were small fires made by the street campers. Around the meager fires were huddled bodies. Some areas contained terrace rows of brick foreign-built dwellings for factory workers. These squalid neighborhoods had a few street lamps, under which people sat on their haunches and gambled with cards.

Iron-blue smoke drifting from the fires did nothing to mask a vile stench emanating from uncovered service privies. Near the dimly lit areas, gray figures stole about, gossiping or quarreling. Scratching in corners for garbage were mangy dogs, their coats nearly bald with undernourishment. Beyond the sitters and dogs lay the deep, unspeakable darkness.

At midnight, fireworks exploded all over the hospital grounds. Loud cheers issued from the Officer's Club and the enlisted men's Recreation Hall. Champagne glasses clinked, soldiers, nurses, and civilian personnel stationed at the hospital welcomed the arrival of 1945.

36

Ravi heard new rumors that the United States Army had plans to occupy the hospital property for an indefinite time in the future. It was just as well to oust the foreigners as soon as possible. In the darkness surrounding the hospital grounds, shadowy figures were congregating. The tall Hindu's army comprised a mix of *goondas*, business men with connections to the Calcutta underworld, and a dozen or so dissident college students. These sub-groups were united in their goal of facilitating the birth of Indian independence.

Stealthily as tigers in the jungle, Ravi's volunteers formed a human ring around the hospital perimeter. The goal was to reinstate Indians at the 142nd before the end of the month. The volunteer soldiers were well supplied with guns and explosives. Weapons were to be used if necessary.

As the ragtag army stationed itself in the shadows and behind walls around the hospital, Benet finished his New Year's Eve letter to Rita. He was about to leave his post for a late drink with the fellows at the Officer's Club when Ravi Ghosh and Veena Sengupta appeared. They'd brought him a pot of tea and a basket of Indian sweets.

"*Namaste*," said Veena, "or as you Americans say, Happy New Year!"

Ravi poured Benet a cup of tea.

"We heard from Sanjay that you were homesick and that you would be all alone during this festivity. We brought you the favorite treat of Ganesha, the elephant god, son of Parvati and Shiva."

"And here they are," said Veena, "treats made according to my mother's recipe."

Benet was pleased. This midnight visit confirmed his notion that Indians could be capable of touching acts of kindness. How much better to have a cultural exchange than to be part of a drunken brawl. Benet prided himself on being one of the less-resented Americans.

"What a surprise." he said. "Did Sanjay tell you to bring me refreshments on New Year's Eve?...Mmm, these dumplings are delicious."

"Not dumplings—they are *modakas* that I baked myself," Veena said. "The filling is coconut and dried fruit. The outside is made of rice flour. The sweetness comes from jaggery, made from drying the juice of sugarcane. My mother learned to make them from her mother."

"Delicious, and most appreciated," said Benet between bites. Reaching for his second *modaka*, he realized how hungry he was. "But I don't know what I did to deserve my own private party." This was a bit of madness, Benet told himself. He was beginning to think that living in India loosened his grasp of reality.

"Ah," Ravi said, "Sanjay told us you might welcome some company. He also said that you most generously gave him the night off to be with his wife and children. However, he is with us to wish you Happy New Year."

No sooner was his name spoken when Sanjay stepped from the dark hall into Benet's office. He was dressed in his usual white *curta* and jodhpurs. Around his shoulders was a shawl, as if he planned to go out for the evening.

"*Namaste, sahib*. I know that you told me to spend tonight with my family, but you are like family to me. Ravi, Veena and I have a surprise for you. I told them how much you wanted to see a Bengal tiger."

"Thank you, Sanjay. "I'm touched by your kindness, but I promised General Peterson that I would stay on base until zero six hundred hours. Besides, I've recently learned that there are no tigers left in Calcutta and that to see them one must go to the zoo."

Sanjay flashed a knowing smile Benet's way.

"Oh yes, that is what foreigners are told, and though you Americans roam some distance from your military base, you do not know all there is to know. Believe me, any Calcutta native is familiar with this magical location. It is not a closely guarded secret."

"Well..." began Lt. Benet.

"And *sahib*," interrupted Sanjay. "As you know, cats are nocturnal beasts. Now is the perfect time to view them."

As Sanjay continued talking, Ravi poured more tea into Richard's empty cup and Veena offered Benet more sweets.

"We are having our own New Year's celebration for Dr. Benet, are we not?" asked Sanjay. "*Sahib*, I remember how your are telling me that you hoped to visit Corbett or Royal Chitwan national parks. So I talked to Shubi and Shubi talked to *Sahib* Mac and obtained permission for a substitute to take over for you while we are taking you to the Tiger Temple of Calcutta, a most magnificent treasure of our city. Very few Americans have seen it."

"And Dr. Lieutenant Benet," said Veena. "Also as part of this Tiger Temple, there is a ruined vault inside which is a most sacred jeweled statue of our revered god, Ganesha. You see, that is why I baked for you the *modakas*. There are guards near this Ganesha but Ravi has gotten a special license for you to view it. This treasure is known to no Americans at all, and very few foreigners have seen it since the year 600."

"I am honored," said Benet, "but I cannot leave the grounds until I'm sure this is truly authorized and also until I see my replacement. I would love to go, and at some future time when everything is in order, I will."

"But *Sahib*," argued Sanjay, "we must leave immediately. I told the temple watchman we would arrive by one or one and a half hours after midnight. Already we have used one half hour. Here is the note from *Sahib* Colonel Mac granting his permission. I brought it from Shubi. Your Mac was perhaps drinking a little too much alcohol so his writing is a bit wobbly, but it is official, you can be sure."

Benet studied the paper in Sanjay's hand, and, though wobbly, the writing did look authentic. There it was: "...*Kopriva is to relieve Lt. Benet at zero one hundred hours.*" He could hardly believe his good fortune. Imagine how much he would have to write to Rita about this adventure.

"Well after all," Benet said, "it is New Year's Eve. I may never have such an opportunity again."

"Very wise, esteemed Doctor," said Ravi. Veena smiled as she picked up the tea things and prepared to leave.

Sanjay took the wool shawl from his own shoulders and handed it to Benet. "This is a present from my wife's family for you, something by which you will be able to remember India. So now, come, come with us. We will take you to these most wondrous sights."

"But Kopriva's not here yet. I can't just leave."

As if he hadn't heard, Sanjay placed the shawl on Richard's shoulders. "There you are, *sahib*, a *brahmin* tourist for the night. Please come with me. A taxi awaits us at the hospital entrance. We will take it to the Jain Temple and walk from there. The night is calling."

Ravi moved next to Benet's desk. He seemed taller than usual, almost menacing.

"As you may know, Lieutenant Dr. Benet," he said, "Your Colonel and I are very close friends. He asked me to sit in until

Lieutenant Kopriva arrives. He will be back after his date with a Red Cross nurse. As you may have heard, he and the nurse are having quite a romance. It is a night for romance, for adventure. I promise you will have the latter. Go, I will keep guard until your replacement arrives. Leave. Enjoy this special night."

Benet was flanked on all sides by his Indian visitors. There was nothing to do but give in. "You're right. I would not want to miss seeing tigers. Let's go."

Taking one last *modaka* from Veena, he walked out of the Q Building with Sanjay.

Lt. Benet and his bearer passed the Officers Club, the recreation hall, and the silent *bashas* to the pillars of the hospital entrance. Richard pushed open the iron gate, which should have been locked. Things were certainly getting lax, but if they weren't, he could never have been able to break away so easily. This outing was going to be something he'd always remember.

"See, just as I said, our taxi is waiting." Sanjay pointed toward a clunky black sedan with its engine running. Richard noticed that Veena had slipped away and also that the car was a black jeep in an advanced stage of dilapidation.

"But this isn't a taxi, Sanjay. Taxis are yellow or black and white. I'll go back and telephone Yellow Cab for us."

A horn sounded from the waiting auto. A woman about Veena's age stuck her head out and waved. "Hello, Sanjay. Hello, Lieutenant Benet. I'm Veena's best girlfriend Janaki. Ravi said I could go along to keep you company."

"Doctor Benet," said Sanjay. "I am seeing that you are skeptical so I will be explaining. We of India have our families nearby and it is quite normal for us to serve as taxicabs for one another. When we say "taxi," we are not necessarily referring to a Yellow Cab but friends who have agreed to help us travel about this vast city when it is too late to walk, and not at all safe."

Indicating the dangers of Calcutta, Sanjay crossed his index finger across his throat.

Benet slid uneasily into the back seat of the "Indian taxicab." Sanjay introduced the driver as "Nathan" and the other front seat passenger as "Raja." Benet was wedged between Janaki and Sanjay.

At breakneck speed, "Nathan" drove out of Alipore and they headed north, past the maidan toward the Jain Temple. The Indians chattered nonstop in Hindi. Only Janaki occasionally spoke in English to Benet. She had a beautiful smile, Richard noticed. Her

207

dress puzzled him, as she wore khaki jodhpurs and a long shirt, almost like a military uniform. Her head was covered in the traditional way, but with an olive green *pashmina* shawl rather than the silk of a *sari*.

Nathan, or whoever he was, turned around to talk with Sanjay. Benet had seen that profile before. He'd heard that voice. The heated conversation around him continued. It seemed as though he'd become invisible to his escorts. Benet leaned his head back and closed his eyes, hoping that his relaxed appearance might lead his "hosts" to think he felt comfortable. He racked his memory for where and when he had seen the man they called Nathan.

"Well, here we are," announced Sanjay. "Now begins our short hike."

Was it Benet's imagination or did his bearer sound less cheery, more businesslike? He had no idea where he was. To himself he admitted the foolishness of going along with these people, but he couldn't very well escape at this point. Alone in Calcutta, not knowing where he was, he wouldn't stand much of a chance of staying alive. Though less despised than the British, Americans were definitely out of favor.

Janaki stayed in the car. "Sanjay and Lieutenant Doctor, Nathan and I have a small errand. We will let you out here and meet you in the room of the jeweled Ganesha." She flashed another of her dazzling smiles at Benet. Her headscarf had fallen to her shoulders and Benet saw that she wore a khaki turban underneath.

The black auto sped off and Sanjay led Benet down a narrow, dimly-lit lane. They stepped around piles of garbage and ill or sleeping people using the street for a bed. The miasma burned the American's nostrils. Pretending to sneeze, Benet put a handkerchief over his nose.

Sanjay was jogging ahead. "Hurry along, please. We will be late and the temple watchmen change every two hours. The second shift will not let us in and we will be stranded here all night if we do not keep to schedule."

Benet noticed with a chill that Sanjay's speech now included no "*sahibs*." Gone was the air of deference. The psychologist pulled the shawl he'd been given more tightly around his shoulders. A squishy feeling under his foot turned out to be a half-eaten dead rat.

"This better be worth it," Benet yelled. He was nearly out of breath. "I feel like we're in the middle of nowhere. Shouldn't our taxi mates be back with us by now?"

Sanjay did not answer. He was so far ahead that Benet had to run to keep him in sight. He suddenly recalled where he'd seen Nathan's face before. "Nathan" was Narendra, Ravi's nephew. He had once come to the hospital to talk with Mac. That was before Mac became so reclusive. He'd actually introduced the young man to Benet.

Sanjay finally stopped, and Benet caught up with him. "*Sahib*," he announced, "Here we are at the Tiger Temple. We do not have time to see it before we go to view the sacred Ganesha. We will be seeing it afterwards, if you do not mind. Let us push forward to the treasure of treasures."

"OK, fine, Sanjay. You lead and I'll follow. No doubt this will be the highlight of my time in the subcontinent."

Benet could see no temple; in fact, he couldn't see much of anything. They were in a horrific slum. The psychologist nearly tripped over a dead body. Remembering Sanjay's finger across the throat, Benet resisted an urge to hold Sanjay's *curta* so as not to lose track of him. If he lost Sanjay, he would be consigned to oblivion. No one here would understand or help him. They would take his money, his military ID, strip him of everything, and he would join the living dead on the streets and in the gutters. He would be nobody.

Sanjay stopped at a small door, barely discernible in a brick wall. "And now *sahib*," he said firmly, "we are here at last." He opened the door, pushed the psychologist inside, and followed closely behind. For five minutes, they descended a narrow staircase before entering a small prison of a room.

Hearing the click of a lock, Benet knew for sure that he been tricked. He took the handkerchief away from his nose. While better than the poisonous atmosphere outdoors, the air was nonetheless foul. An earthy smell told Benet that they were underground. Along with Sanjay, he might as well be buried alive. But no, that wasn't quite right. Sanjay knew his way out and Benet did not.

37

As Sanjay and Benet approached the end of the hall, a door opened. Three turbaned Indians surrounded the psychologist and tied his arms behind him.

"What?" yelled Benet. "What is going on? Sanjay, call off these thugs. Tell them we're just here to view the jeweled Ganesha."

"They are just doing their job," Sanjay replied. His face was grim, his voice raspy. "I am sorry for your misfortune, but you were our final impediment this evening to taking back our grounds and buildings. Surely you must know that the 142nd General Hospital is property stolen from the city of Calcutta. And now, Yankee, it is goodbye. I must go to meet Nathan and Janaki as we three are needed in the takeover."

"But, Sanjay. You can't just leave me here. There's been a mistake. Call off these bullies!"

"Sorry, but my loyalty to India makes me turn a deaf ear. Do not waste your pleading words on these *goondas*. They will not understand you. The more you protest, the worse you will be treated."

Benet struggled, but his hands and arms were tightly bound.

"Help me! I will reward you. Tell them to let me go!" he shouted.

"Regretfully, Yankee, it is I who must go." Sanjay spoke in a low voice. He sounded almost sorry. "The Ganesha was a fiction, but perhaps you will have a chance to see a tiger. Yes, I think I can promise you that. Happy New Year, Lieutenant."

With a sarcastic bow of the head and hands folded in an ironic *namaste*, Sanjay departed.

Benet was now a captive of the three *goondas*. Even though his mouth had gone dry and sweat poured down his temples, he struggled to appear calm. The thugs pushed him along until they reached a small, windowless room lined with wooden planks. The fattest of the three huge men punched one fist into the palm of the other hand, as if to illustrate what he would like to do to Benet.

The thinner, bony thug walked over to Benet and sneered. He muttered something in Hindi, then put his thumbs in his ears and waved his fingers out on either side. He peered directly into Benet's face and growled. The Indians were obviously having a good time at his expense.

"Shut up, you bastards," said Benet, feeling a need to talk despite the fact that he couldn't be understood. "I know what you're up to. You think you're going to blow up the hospital. But I'm getting out of here. I know a checkpoint in Alipore where I can quickly alert the Military Police. You might as well let me go. Someone is on the way right now and you could get killed."

This was empty jargon, of course. No one knew where he was. No one was on the way. These lummoxes didn't understand a word he said. Nonetheless, it was better to keep speaking in a defiant tone.

The growler leered down, mocked Benet in unintelligible words, and spat. As the psychologist screwed up his face in a vain effort to clear away the spittle, his tormenter prepared to send another spray.

"*Prasad, Prasad ...*" One of the huge men grabbed the growler's arm. The fattest *goonda* escorted him toward the door. All three were leaving.

"Hop-pee No Year," the *goondas* said in unison. They left the room, banging the door behind them. Benet heard an ominous clank, as though a chain was being secured. Spittle stung his eyes and mixed with his own sweat. His prison had no windows, and he wondered idly if he would run out of air to breathe.

Benet felt energized by the sheer hopelessness of his plight. An odd phenomenon, he noted to himself. If he were to survive, he had to conserve his strength, both emotional and physical. Leaning against a wall, he slid down into a sitting position on the floor. He closed his eyes and thought of Rita, waiting for him at home in Findlay. He thought of his patients—Sturke, Gus, Ike and Warren. He would get out of this trap no matter what. Drifting in and out of a light sleep, Benet waited for what seemed like hours.

The door crashed open. The tallest *goonda* re-entered Benet's cubicle, followed by Sanjay. When Benet tried to speak, the *goonda* slapped him across the face. Each time he tried to communicate, the slaps became more violent. Benet stared ahead. For several minutes, the room was completely quiet.

Sanjay broke the silence. "It will give me great satisfaction, Lieutenant Doctor American, to speak my mind. I am wasting my words, as I am, of course, talking to a dead man. Nonetheless, it will be good to know that you have been disabused of the notion that we Indians are saps and hapless victims of your American oppression.

"We are planning a New Year's surprise, not for just you, but for all of you presumptuous Americans. By morning, your sacred hospital grounds will be freed from thieves and impostors. We are waiting no longer. Ravi Ghosh's independent army surrounds what you have so wrongfully stolen from us. Thanks to your colleague Andy Anderson's knowledge of the electrical system of the hospital, we will, if necessary, take him hostage and use his skills to blow up the hospital and everyone in it.

"When you return, if you return—which is extremely doubtful— your Neuro-Psychiatric Ward may be a charred pile of rubble. Your friends and patients may be but distant memories."

Benet didn't want to accept what he was hearing. "But why, why...?"

"Your Colonel Mac is why," Sanjay answered. "At first he was most useful to us. He supplied us with medications sought by a certain Japanese gentleman. We sold Mepracine, Atabrine and morphine to General Tanaka. All of the money went to help the cause of Indian independence."

"Ah yes," said Benet. He looked at his torturer to make sure the *goonda* wasn't gearing up for another attack. But the Indian, leaning slouched against a wall, looked half asleep. Apparently it was OK to talk. "Now I understand why Ravi Ghosh was a permanent fixture at the hospital. He was the connection, the link between your Japanese customers and the hospital. But I still don't understand what Mac had to do with all of this."

"How could you not know that this McDermott is a weak and evil man," Sanjay exclaimed. "He is an addict and a murderer. It was Mac who saw to it that we obtained morphine that we needed for the Japanese general. In return, we supplied your Mac with opium to support his habit. It was even better for our purposes when his consort—I believe her name is Jacobs—also became an opium addict."

Benet thought back to Clara's breakdown at the mess hall. It all made sense now. She'd been too embarrassed to tell him the worst. It was even possible that Mac had blackmailed her, vowing to kill her if she threatened to leave him.

Sanjay continued. "Mac, as you call him, played right into our hands. Though unintentionally, he was also helping our most noble cause. Ah, so perfect an arrangement ... but now has come the time for action. We shall reclaim what is rightfully ours and we will do it this very evening. And you, Benet, must sit here tied up and able to do nothing."

Benet spoke as forcefully as his exhausted state allowed. "It would be easier for you and for everybody if you just waited. Sanjay, the war will soon be over and the China-Burma-India Theater of operations will close down. We Americans will be leaving your country; we'll be giving your hospital back to you. Why cause death and destruction?"

The *goonda* raised his hand to slap Benet, but Sanjay kept him from it. The former bearer paced back and forth. "Yes, Benet, you wonder 'Why now?' Do you not recall the murder of Sergeant Lowell and the accusation of an Indian man as the culprit?"

"Yes, that was very strange. It seemed as though a perpetrator was needed very quickly and that the Indian confessed too easily."

"Agreed," said Sanjay. "Think about it. There was no motive for the Indian man to kill the Sergeant. Clearly, he was framed. You see, Ravi Ghosh pretended to be a friend to your Mac. He knew that it was Mac who strangled Silas Lowell."

Apparently Sanjay wanted Benet to know everything. He continued: "Mac said that he would kill anyone who knew about his addiction. He also needed to insure that no one learned about his cozy little opium/morphine exchange operation. What he didn't know was that the Indian employees of the hospital were all spies for Ravi Ghosh."

"So Silas Lowell was the man who knew too much?" asked Richard. "He had to be silenced or..."

Sanjay interrupted. "Yes. Ravi learned from one of his spies that Lowell was murdered by none other than your Mac."

"But you have no proof other than a spy's word. I detest Mac, but I don't believe he is a murderer." Actually, Benet could believe anything about Mac. However, he felt such an admission would weaken his own cause. "As I said, you could avoid bloodshed and death on both sides by simply waiting until we all go home to America, and surely that will be soon."

Sanjay frowned. "There is more here than meets the eye," as you Americans would say. "Unlike you people, who must always be following your first impulse, we Indians know it is best to look beneath the surface."

Benet hoped that by keeping Sanjay in a conversation, he could somehow avert destruction of the hospital. While he talked with Sanjay, he tried to figure a way out of his prison.

"Yes," said Benet. "I have always admired that trait in your people. But I too look beneath the surface. What proof did you find that we framed the Indian who stabbed Sgt. Lowell? What evidence do you have that the Colonel is a murderer?"

Sanjay grimaced. "For such an intelligent man, how little you have realized about our country and our people. I learned a fact most interesting from Shubi, the bearer of your Colonel Mac. The corpse hanging in the latrine last October was a sentry in Mac's squadron in Burma. He had to be eliminated because he knew too much. Your depraved hospital director made it look like a suicide."

"I don't believe this," Benet protested, but the truth of the matter was that he could believe anything about Mac. The situation was even worse than he feared. As he thought back to the hanging corpse, it was quite believable that the death had been made to look like a suicide.

"Whether you believe it or not, it is true," Sanjay proclaimed. "I know everything. Sergeant Calvin Brothers, the so-called suicide, had witnessed Mac treat his own men most savagely. On a nighttime mission to Burma, Brothers witnessed Mac strangle his buddy in a fit of anger and it was shortly after that when Brothers became mute."

"How did you learn all this?" asked Benet. "Wasn't Brothers at the 20th General Hospital under the care of General Peterson's staff?"

"You seem to forget, Benet, that I have many friends on the hospital staff. Shubi observed intimate details of Colonel Mac's life and relayed them to me. Like me, and like all the local employees of your American installations, we Indians are working for a cause, that of our country's freedom from British and American interference. My friend Ram, at the 20th General Hospital, has also kept me informed. And now, because there is nothing to lose by telling you this, I will finish my story."

Though Benet felt completely desperate, he spoke boldly. "If you go through with your irrational plan, there is much for your side to lose. I will escape. Our Military Police will keep the hospital from being destroyed. We have the cooperation of the Calcutta police force."

Sanjay laughed. "Just keep thinking that. By the time you escape from your prison—that is if you escape—the coup will be complete. And now, for your amusement, I insist on telling you the rest of the story."

The Indian continued. "Amazingly, Calvin Brothers survived an explosion and weeks of wandering in the jungles of Burma. He was rescued and brought to Calcutta for rehabilitation, first at the 20th and then the 142nd hospitals. The recovery progressed rapidly and Brothers was very close to regaining his speech. Mac knew that

Brothers had probably seen him murdering one of his own men. To keep Brothers from ratting on him, Mac saw to it that he conveniently 'committed suicide.' But now, Lieutenant, I must be leaving you."

Benet made one last attempt to talk his way out. "If you'll free me, I will see that Mac is brought to justice. I promise you that before the war is over, our personnel will be out of the hospital and it will return to its previous use. I can work as your ally. You don't need to follow Ravi's orders. He's brainwashed you. Please—let me out of here."

"Benet, you are wasting your words. You might as well be accepting your fate. There is much work ahead of me and I am staying too long." Followed by his *goonda* companion, Sanjay walked toward the door.

"I'll get out," shouted Richard. "I will contact the Calcutta police. You'll pay for this."

The Indian left, banging the wooden door sharply. A key clicked in the lock. Benet shouted Sanjay's name a few times before he surrendered to his profound aloneness.

38

As if addressing a particularly thick-headed patient, Benet talked to himself very deliberately. "I have to get out of here, wherever 'here' is."

In his mind, the psychologist retraced the route they'd taken to this ruin of a warehouse, this *godown*. He acknowledged the fear that coursed through his body. He went from sweating to shaking with chills. His throat was tight, his breathing shallow. He resisted an impulse to shout for help. It might bring the *goondas* back.

Benet gave himself a pep talk. "There's no time for this. Fear will drain my energy, use up my batteries. Can't waste a breath. Try one thing, then another. Get out of here. The *goondas* may be stronger but I'm smarter. Big is good, but smarter is better."

Thankfully, Sanjay hadn't turned off the bare overhead bulb before leaving. Benet struggled to release his hands from the ropes that bound them. The chair he was tied to nearly fell over. He realized that it was essential to stay upright. His chances of escaping would be far less if he were lying on the floor.

Being careful not to topple over, Benet walked his chair backwards to the rough cement wall. Tomorrow, he would write a letter to Rita. He would joke about this New Year's Eve debacle, comparing his journey to the wall as that of a giant human centipede.

He positioned the back of his chair against the wall and began rubbing the ropes against it. He was careful to touch the ragged surface with the ropes only and not his skin. The sawing worked. At last one of the ropes broke. By wriggling his wrists, applying all his strength, Benet managed to free his hands.

"Rita, I'm coming home," Richard chanted to himself. "I'm coming home. Wait for me, wait for me, wait for me."

He repeated this over and over as he searched the room for a way out. If only there was a hidden exit, a tunnel, or secret door.

Benet ran his hands over every inch of his cell and found nothing. Finally he decided to move the room's one piece of furniture, a wooden desk shoved against the wall. Under the desk was a square of tiles. Smashing the wooden chair that had so recently been his prison, Benet snapped off one of the chair's legs. The splintery end of the chair leg served as a crowbar and before long, he had lifted all the tiles. To his despair, there were wooden planks underneath.

The overhead light, a bare bulb hanging from a chain, began to flicker. In Calcutta, this signaled the failure of electrical power. Without any light at all, Benet might as well prepare to die.

"Oh no," Benet shouted. He could feel himself cracking up. He was acting like one of his more disturbed patients. "No, no!" He yelled himself hoarse. He tore at his hair. He jumped up and down on a wooden foundation.

The lights went out at the same time the planks gave way.

Benet was alone in mud and darkness. When he tried standing up, his head hit the top of what felt like an earthen cave. He tried to think of what advice he would give his patients in such a predicament. *Keep moving, keep moving, keep moving. Find a way out. Go ahead. Do whatever it takes to get the hell out. Don't give up...*

Benet imagined Rita's photograph. Though right now it seemed as if he had no future, he composed a letter in his mind to her. Once he got back outside, he would somehow manage to get across Calcutta. He would find his way back to the hospital, and in the future, he would recount tonight's ordeal to his wife.

I have to survive to tell this story.

But for now, he had to find his way out of the pit. Using his arms to pry at the ceiling, Benet searched for an escape. He alternated arms to give one a rest while the other was working, but still his arms began to ache. His knuckles were swollen from pounding, his fingers bloody from clawing.

At one edge of his prison, Benet found a softer area of the ceiling and at last broke through. Using every bit of strength he could muster, he managed to hoist himself up into another dimly-lit cell of this labyrinth.

He groped his way along what seemed to be an endless tunnel. Faint light was coming from an unknown source. Benet looked at his watch, which had stopped at twelve hundred hours. It was probably still night, and with luck, he could find his way out before dawn. Somehow he'd find a way to the hospital before disaster struck.

Benet thought he'd seen an Air Force Military Police installation somewhere between Russo Road and Southern Avenue. The MPs could rally massive forces to infiltrate the 142nd before Ravi and his troops arrived.

For the first time since he'd left Q Building, Benet allowed himself to feel hopeful. He continued groping along the walls. To his

217

amazement, an iron grate opened at his push. Just as he was about to step through it, a deep roar sounded from the other side.

Benet slammed the grate shut and latched it securely. One more step forward and he might have become dinner.

Standing in awe, he watched through the grillwork as a magnificent Bengal tiger paced back and forth, its tail twitching from side to side. The tiger stood six feet tall at the shoulder. Its long claws clicked against the floor, each click and scratch diminishing Benet's hopes of escaping. Despite the danger, Benet marveled at the tiger's magnificence.

He did not marvel for long, however. Time was running out. Benet considered his options, which were few. He thought of crawling his way back to his original prison. By so doing, he might save his own life. On the other hand, if he back-tracked it might assure destruction of the hospital. He would be responsible for hundreds of deaths of both staff and patients. There was no contest. He had to go forward, but how?

As if in answer, the tiger roared.

Suddenly the door of the outer room opened. A tiny, wizened Indian entered carrying a pail of raw meat. When the man clicked his tongue and cracked a whip, the tiger backed into its corner. Was this the tiger's trainer? Benet concentrated. He wracked his brain. He knew that this could well be his last chance. His smattering of Hindi would now be put to the test.

"Hello. Are you the owner of this tiger? May I pass through? I am a doctor and have to report to my hospital on Southern Avenue in a very short time."

The Indian was throwing pieces of meat to the huge cat. The beast seemed ravenous. Holding dog-sized carcasses between its front paws, the tiger chomped fiercely. This must be a special guard tiger owned by the neighborhood *goondas*, Richard decided. If this were true, the tiger trainer was low in the chain of command. He might be ignorant of Ravi's hospital takeover plan.

The small man wore a *dhoti*, once white, but now tan with age and dirt. Perhaps, Benet thought, he was an untouchable. Whatever the case, he could probably be bribed. At least it was worth trying.

"I must get through," said Benet, pushing the gate slightly open. To his astonishment, the tiger's keeper answered in English.

"No, you cannot pass. Any who come here are prisoners of Ravi Ghosh. This is his guard tiger. Mast-ali is a fine killing machine

218

when I give the signal. You must stay here until *Sahib* Ravi Ghosh decides to release you. It is not my decision."

Benet emptied his pockets of coins. The total was 30 *rupees*, won in last night's poker game.

The tiger guard jerked his chin up, indicating a negative response. "Not enough," he grunted. "What about your watch?" He pointed to the Bulova on Benet's right wrist. It had been a Christmas present from Rita. He hated to part with it, but if he didn't, he might never see her again.

"OK, if you'll call off the guard tiger, I'll give you all my money and the wristwatch. But I also need to know in which direction is Southern Avenue."

The Indian frowned. "For that, more money."

Benet pulled out his Parker fountain pen, a birthday present from Rita. This also was painful to give up, but the Indian could walk away at any time, leaving him alone with no recourse.

"The pen is very expensive, will get you much money in the marketplace. This is everything I have. Now please, let me by."

"First you hand over the money, watch, and pen through the grating. Then I will chain Mast-ali and direct you to the road outside."

Benet wanted to argue that first the tiger must be chained, and then he would hand over the loot. Instead, he followed the Indian's wishes, all the while silently praying that he would keep his word. Quickly, he handed over *rupees*, wrist watch and pen.

Sure enough, the Indian waved his whip in the air and Mast-ali grew docile as a house cat. The trainer proceeded to unlatch the gate and at the same time threw Mast-ali a chunk of meat. The cat lay down and started gnawing.

The Indian pointed to the door ahead and indicated a left turn. "Go," he said. "Go to the end of the building. You will come to stairs. Climb up, open door, and jump. Not far to the ground. Go to the end of Russo Street. You come to Southern Avenue."

Before the tiger was finished with its snack, Benet was out the door and halfway down the hall to what he hoped would be freedom. He came to the hall's end and clambered up the aforementioned stairs. Opening a door to the outside world, he jumped to the ground and started running.

Benet raced past sooty houses of the factory workers, down poorly lit lanes, on a road so foul smelling that he gagged. Running until he was near collapse, Benet came to Russo Street. Instead of the

219

mile to Southern Avenue that he'd calculated, it was more like two miles. Once at Southern, he turned left.

The Military Police station was exactly where Benet thought it was. As it was open 24 hours a day, the small office was brightly lit. He let himself in and faced the officer on duty, a handsome black man nursing a cup of coffee and looking bored.

Benet imagined the impression he must make. His uniform, minus his cap, which had fallen off long ago, was dirty and ripped. His hands were bleeding from banging and clawing his way out of the *goondas'* den. He caught a reflection of himself in a window. His black wavy hair was sticking out on every side. What's more, he was still out of breath. He inhaled and exhaled deeply a few times before speaking.

The MP checked his watch and then looked at the disheveled man standing at his desk. Benet saw from his nametag that he was Sergeant Sherman.

"Good God, man, what can I do for you?" asked the Sergeant.

Benet saluted. "I'm Lieutenant Richard Benet, clinical psychologist, in charge of the Neuro-Psychiatric Ward of the 142nd General Hospital. A renegade Indian group is planning to take over the hospital tonight. You need to order a police force to defend it A.S.A.P."

Sherman stared at him with a skeptical expression. "Man, are you sure you're not one of the N-P Ward patients? Pardon me, Lieutenant, but you need to get a grip."

The Sergeant got up, walked to the cooler, and came back with a tall glass of water for Benet.

"Now why don't you just slow down a minute. Have a seat and tell me exactly what's going on."

Benet gulped down the water as though he'd crossed a desert.

"If it's just the same, I need to remain standing. The hospital where I work is about to be taken over by an Indian insurrectionist group."

Sherman stared and reached for the telephone. "I'll have to believe you, Lieutenant. Just one thing: how do you know this?"

"It's bizarre. I was alone on duty in our main admin quarters, about to be relieved and went out with Indians I thought of as friends. It was a fraud. They stuck me in a locked room."

"They what?"

"I know this sounds like science fiction. I can hardly believe it myself. There is an old factory nearby. It's a sort of criminal headquarters. I was trapped by *goondas*—you know, what the Indians call thugs—I just barely escaped."

"Yeah, I can tell you've been through something. I'll call my commanding officer and we'll send a helicopter. It's on Southern Avenue, right?"

Benet looked at the wall clock. It was 0300 hours and the Indian's takeover might already be underway. It wouldn't be light for another two hours.

"May I borrow a Jeep to get to the hospital?" Richard asked. "I may be in time to keep the *goondas* from using explosives."

Sherman was already dialing the phone. He tossed Benet ignition keys and pointed with his right hand. "First jalopy on this side. Help will be on the way. Be careful, Lieutenant."

The Jeep started right away and Benet roared south on Russo to Southern Avenue. The streets were deserted. A few bodies lay on the sidewalks outside stuccoed garden walls. He wondered if they were dead or alive. It was shocking to realize that dead or dying Indians seemed a normal part of the scenery. The famine in Calcutta was so bad that trucks drove the streets just before dawn to collect the dead.

All was quiet and dark in the direction of the hospital. Richard parked the Jeep a block away. He would approach the buildings on foot.

221

39

Ravi Ghosh congratulated himself on making sure that Benet was locked up. That busybody psychologist might have thrown off the entire plan. The tall Bengali slipped unseen into the hospital grounds. The sentry had his back turned when Ravi darted by the massive pillars of the hospital entrance and jumped into the shadows. It was half past three. By this time, nearly all the staff and patients were asleep.

Ghosh checked in Lt. Anderson's *basha*, the location of which Shubi had pointed out earlier. Anderson was known for his complete knowledge of the hospital's electrical system, a knowledge that might prove useful. Shubi was a key informant as well as an active participant in the morning's scenario. Anderson was not in his quarters. Perhaps he was on duty.

Ravi would look further for Anderson and then send Shubi out to alert the forces of his makeshift "army," who would begin to move out all the equipment from Building Q, the heart and brains of the hospital. Plan One was to give a signal, when the army would probably occupy the hospital and refuse to leave. That was the preferred method of takeover. However, Ravi doubted things would be that simple. He must hold Anderson hostage in case his first plan didn't work.

As Ravi walked the Q Building's main hall, he thanked the gods for power failures. The recent outage made him nearly invisible. He had planned to meet Shubi near the medical supply room to tell him when to alert the volunteer army. Operating on sheer memory, he groped his way along.

In the early hours of 1945, Anderson had shifted watch duty to Lt. Kopriva, who sat glumly at a desk in the glass-paneled lookout post. Kopriva was none too pleased about spending New Year's Eve in the bowels of the Q Building. In fact, he was mad as hell. When he heard a door opening and closing at the far end of the hall, he snapped out of a doze, took his .45 revolver out of the holster and stood up.

"Who goes there?" he yelled into the darkness.

No answer. Perhaps he imagined the sound. Using a flashlight he'd found in the desk drawer, he walked slowly and quietly down the hall. He kept his revolver ready.

222

Ravi flattened himself against the wall and waited until Kopriva was a few feet away. He put out one foot and tripped the American. Kopriva pulled the trigger of his .45 just as Ravi grabbed him from behind. As Kopriva struggled, Ravi, who was taller and more powerful, punched his thumbs in the pulse points behind Kopriva's ears. In short order, the Lieutenant passed out.

Ten minutes after Ravi entered the hospital grounds, Benet drove up to the gate in a borrowed Jeep. Surely the military police would be arriving soon, but in the meantime, Benet would take action. As much as he detested Mac, he would go to his quarters, wake him up, and tell him what was happening. Before he could act on such a plan, however, a shot reverberated through the night.

Benet could only guess what happened, but no doubt the hospital takeover was already underway. The sound came from the Q Building. The officer on duty must have fired at one of the Indian insurrectionists. Instead of going to Mac's *basha*, Benet ran back toward Q Building. Without a weapon of any sort, he was not sure what he could do, but he knew that whatever was done to hold off the Indian forces, it would not be done by Mac. It was now up to him.

The psychologist felt dizzy with fatigue, his legs ached, and his head pounded. Operating on adrenaline, he ran to the Q Building and slipped in a door near the main hallway. It was nearly dark, but he knew his way.

Through the shadows, Benet could make out a window. This had to be the duty station. It looked as though no one was there. Perhaps Indian forces had already captured the building. He would check the office and then notify Mac.

Benet opened the station door. Crumpled at his feet lay Henry Kopriva, unconscious but still breathing. Just as he was checking Kopriva's pulse, a low hum announced the generator's reactivation. The hall of the Q Building suddenly lit up. A second hum pulsed, louder than that of the generator. Benet fervently hoped that it meant the arrival of Army helicopters.

Benet caught a glimpse of Ravi Ghosh striding down the hall. Kopriva would have to fend for himself. Benet left the duty station and stealthily trailed behind Ravi. If the Bengali tried anything, Benet would hold him off until the Military Police arrived. That is, if they arrived.

Apparently, the generator in the Q Building was the only part of the hospital electrical system that was operating. All around was total darkness. Benet stalked the Indian along a dirt path leading to the *bashas*. He tried to move without making a sound. A night bird cawed from one of the palm trees towering overhead.

Ravi had disappeared behind a grove of palm trees next to Mac's *basha*. Benet knelt down behind some shrubbery. He heard rustling and then a soft banging that might have been a door opening and closing. Could Ravi have entered Mac's quarters? If that were the case, was Ravi entering to force Mac's cooperation or to tie him up? With the takeover underway, what possible further use could Ravi have for Mac?

And where were the police? As Benet crouched in waiting, ready to act, he berated himself for not being more forceful at Sherman's office. Could it be that his request was ignored and that forces weren't being sent after all? Unlikely, but possible. The situation had grown so outlandish that nothing would surprise him.

He was wrong. When shouting and a gunshot pierced the air, Benet had to stifle a shout of alarm. Next, he heard the banging of a door followed by the sound of running. Someone was escaping from the *basha*. Benet waited a few minutes, then entered.

Benet found a flashlight hanging by the front door and clicked it on. It looked as though a hurricane had swept through the place. Furniture was overturned, a whiskey bottle was smashed on the floor, the window was wide open and its curtains torn down. Some-one was crying. Clearly, these were not the sobs of Mac. They had a distinctly feminine sound.

Benet shone the flashlight on a form huddled in the corner of an inner room. Whoever it was appeared terrified. The cowering figure wore only a sheet.

"Clara?" he asked.

"Oh Richard, thank God you're here. Mac and I had it out. I'd just told him that this was the end, that I was going to quit seeing him. He went berserk. He tried to strangle me."

"Clara, I want to hear about this another time. I must get some answers. Was a tall Indian just here? Did something happen between him and Mac? I've go to act fast. The entire hospital is in grave danger."

Clara pulled the sheet more tightly around her and crawled from the floor to the side of the unmade bed. Her face looked bruised and swollen.

"Mac beat me up," she whimpered.

"What a bastard," Benet said. He sat down on the bed beside Clara and put an arm around her shoulders.

"Yes, there was an Indian man here," Clara said quietly. "In fact, he interrupted us in the middle of the fight. He demanded money that Mac owed him and said he had to have the keys to the central power station. Mac refused, ordered him to leave, and then shot at him."

Benet stood up. "So Clara, did Mac's bullet find a target? What happened? Where did they go?"

"The Indian was too fast and powerful," said Clara. "He karate-chopped Mac's arm aside, grabbed the gun, and started to chase him. They're both are out there somewhere."

"Clara, are there any guns in the *basha*? Before I go out to find Ravi, I've got to be armed. Surely Mac kept another revolver hidden away."

The nurse clutched the sheet around herself like a *sari* and walked to the dresser. She took out a .45 revolver and handed it to Benet.

"Here. It's loaded with enough bullets to kill both of those evil losers."

Benet took the gun and tucked it inside his shredded jacket.

Despite wearing only a sheet, Clara seemed to be regaining her composure. "I heard Ravi say that he was going to the wards, to the medical supply closet. I'm pretty sure it's locked. Mac was the only one with access. You probably need this."

She handed him a key. "I've got to get back to my *basha*, she sobbed. "God, what a nightmare. I hope this isn't an omen for the rest of 1945."

"What happened to our Colonel Mac?" asked Benet.

"Ha!" Clara laughed bitterly. "Mac is a rat deserting a sinking ship. He is probably somewhere outside the limits of Alipore now. I hope he's disappeared into Calcutta. The city will consume him and no one will be sorry."

"Clara, before you go back to the women's *bashas*, please listen to me. You're got to alert the other nurses that there's about to be an evacuation. Ravi Ghosh and his forces are trying to seize the hospital. The Military Police are supposedly on their way. If any of us are to survive, the MPs our only chance."

"Good grief," Clara shrieked, "Why aren't they here? Here we are fumbling around in the middle of the night with no backup and no one in charge."

"I'm not sure why they're taking so long," Benet said. "But since Mac's missing in action, I'm taking over. I'll deflect the Indians as long as necessary."

"And as soon as you get out of here," Clara said, "I'm going to get dressed and swing into action. I've recovered enough to be useful."

"You just try to keep your friends informed but calm," Benet said. "I'm going to track down Ravi. It'll be a game of cat and mouse. I'm not sure which of us is the cat and which the mouse."

Clara gave a mock salute. "Sure thing, Doc. Now if you'll just get out of here..."

"Just one question, Clara. Why, with an entire hospital to overtake, would Ravi be going to the medical supply room first? Do you have any explanation?"

"Yes," replied Clara. "It's about a debt owed by Mac. The Indian supplied him with opium and in return was paid with medical supplies which he sold. Mac was weeks behind in payment. My guess is that the Indian wants to collect on the morphine owed him before leading his coup."

"Thanks for everything, Clara," said Benet. "You just pull yourself together. Leave right now. As long as we have the cover of night, I think we can keep safe." Benet began walking toward where he'd last seen Ravi.

Clara called out after him. "Look at your watch. It's almost morning."

Benet stared for a moment at his bare wrist. He did not tell Clara that he traded his watch to save his life. He jogged to the hospital's main wards. The medical supply room was in a small annex connected to the wards by an enclosed walkway. Ravi could be just ahead of him or he may be behind. He could be anywhere.

Two things gave Benet an advantage over the Indian. Benet possessed a loaded pistol. He also had a key to medical supply room, which, if Clara was right, would be the Indian's first destination.

If he could reach the med room first, he would unlock it and hide behind the file cabinets lined up outside the door. The door was heavy and closed automatically unless a person held it open. Once Ravi walked in, Benet's plan was to quickly lock the door from the outside.

That done, the Indian could yell and scream all he wanted, but no one would hear him. Unlike the trap room of Benet's captivity, the med room had no hidden exits. It was grimly appropriate, thought

Dr. Benet, for Ravi to be entombed with the medical supplies he'd been pilfering. The plan firmly in mind, Benet moved soundlessly through the halls.

A small domestic cat raced by, meowing loudly. Benet noticed that it was the animal that one of his patients had taken in as a pet. He recalled the patient's name, Fletch, and wondered where he was on this crazy morning.

Benet was trying to think of the cat's name when a pair of arms grabbed him from behind. The grip was incredibly forceful, but Benet kicked and screamed. His hand found the handle of his revolver, which he planned to use when he fought his way free.

Both the assailant and Benet fell to the ground. Benet pulled himself free, and rolled over on the other man. The attacker was shorter and smaller than Benet. He looked like one of the *goondas* that had been in the bogus taxi. Undoubtedly he was acting on Ravi's behalf. Benet felt strong hands around his throat: He could hardly breathe. The ordeal of the last five hours was catching up with him. He began to lose consciousness.

"Give me the key," snarled the attacker in Hindi. "Give me the damned key!"

Benet was still pinned to the ground, but he could move his arms. Finally he identified his assailant as Mahmood, one of the hospital orderlies. He reached inside his shirt pocket but instead of the key, he pulled out his gun and stuck it between Mahmood's eyes.

"Let me go or I'll blow your brains out," Benet yelled.

After another wrestling bout, both men got to their feet. Mahmood unsheathed a knife and tried to stab Benet. He spit out a stream of Hindi expletives.

Benet tripped Mahmood and, as the Indian scuttled onto the floor, shot at his feet. His goal was simply to scare the man. Killing an Indian in his own country, no matter what the circumstances, was definitely not a good idea.

"You miserable God-damned cur." Benet shouted. "Try anything else and I'll aim higher than your feet." Mahmood disappeared into the shadows.

Benet, revived by a fresh surge of adrenaline, checked the medical supply room lock to make sure it was secure, and fastened two extra latches at the top of the door. He stationed himself behind the nearby file cabinets. If Ravi had to fiddle with the lock before entering, Benet would have more time to strategize. He hoped that Ravi hadn't already been here, found the door impossible, and decided not to waste any more time before calling in his volunteer troops. There was no way to know, nothing to do but lie in hiding near the supply room door.

He must have fallen asleep. The next thing he knew, he heard Indian voices coming closer. My God, that was Sanjay's voice, thought Benet. His former bearer was leading Ravi to the supply room. The voices were accompanied by the clanking of keys. Apparently Sanjay had stolen a master set from the Q Building.

Benet drew himself into a tighter crouch. Sanjay might wonder why the door was double locked then search for an enemy. That was absurd, Benet told himself. As far as Sanjay knew, the psychologist was still trapped in the *goonda's* den or perhaps consumed by their guard tiger.

Benet couldn't make out what Ghosh and Sanjay were saying. When he heard the Indians enter the room, he peeked cautiously around the edge of the file cabinet. Sure enough, they were inside. He would have to trap Sanjay as well as Ravi Ghosh. It seemed heartless to include the bearer who'd served him so well. On the other hand, Sanjay had betrayed him.

Benet moved back into the shadows and listened. As far as he could tell, the Indians were on the other side of the door. The clink of jars and the sound of cardboard boxes being dropped meant that the Indians must be emptying supplies into a container. That was good. Their backs would be toward him.

There wasn't a moment to waste. Benet held the key in his right hand, ready to insert it in the lock. He stood up very slowly, pushed his body against the door to slam it, and immediately pushed the key in the lock, turning it to the right.

Angry curses and yelling issued faintly from the other side of the supply room door. He heard the clink of a key from the other side of the lock. He doubted that it was possible to unlock the room from the inside, but he wasn't sure. Fortunately there was a deadbolt on the outside. Richard slid it securely into place. Then, just for extra protection, he used his remaining strength to push a file case against the door.

As Benet walked outside to a silvery gray dawn, he heard the whir of helicopters and a whining siren. On this first morning of 1945, a miracle: help had finally arrived. Even if Ravi's army was waiting to capture the 142nd, America's military might would prevail. Reaching his *basha*, he collapsed on his bed. In less than a minute, he was asleep.

When Benet awakened two days later, he lay in a hospital bed. General Peterson sat at his side. Apparently, said the General, Benet's alarm to the MP's triggered a chain of events that saved the hospital from a potentially violent takeover. Without Ravi Ghosh to keep them motivated, the Indian volunteer corps dispersed. The MP's fired guns into the air and there was much scuffling, but injuries were minor.

Ravi Ghosh and Sanjay Roy, reported Peterson, nearly suffocated in the medical supply room. Once they were out, however, they managed to slip away from the MP's. Colonel James McDermott fled to somewhere in Calcutta and could not be found.

40

Ten months later, on October 1, 1945, the U.S.S. Cardinal left the port of Bombay for San Francisco. The huge transport ship became a floating city; its inhabitants, hundreds of soldiers vacating the China-Burma-India theater of military operations. Among them were the staff of the 142nd General Hospital, with a few notable exceptions, and a handful of patients. It would take up to three weeks to complete the journey. The days at sea assumed a soporific monotony.

Benet continued to write daily letters to Rita. He described the jade green waters of Malacca Strait, and passage through the South China Sea, the Philippines, and San Bernardino Strait. Benet also informed his wife Rita of the ongoing poker, cribbage and gin rummy games. He wrote about seeing inexplicable phosphorescent lights in the nighttime ocean. Within his missives, Benet created a post-war travelogue, highlighting the occasional war ruins that came into view—remnants of barbed wire littering an island beach, equipment carcasses accompanied by a buoy that held a sign announcing "Wreck."

They were 5,500 miles from San Francisco—"Frisco," the men called it—and Benet found himself unable to sleep. He was haunted by the memory of December 31, an event they now referred to as "the New Year's Eve Surprise." In his letters, he'd downplayed the horrors of that night, dismissing it as a "misunderstanding" that "kept him on duty all night."

If only he weren't seasick, he could keep his mind in better order. Possibly it was the combination of eating two desserts at dinner and drinking beer with the fellows afterwards, but whatever the case, Benet felt increasingly queasy. As the ship lurched and tossed through the night, he fought yet another wave of nausea. At 0300 hours, he put on pants, shoes and jacket and slipped past his snoring bunkmates to the ladders that led topside.

After ten minutes of pacing the deck and breathing in the cold, salty air, Benet felt better. He stopped, leaned against the guard rail and stared out at the ocean. The sea appeared as an endlessly vast gray slate. A pale golden column of light, reflecting the full moon, slashed down the middle of the field of slate. It was lonely, eerie and beautiful. Benet stood for a long time gazing at the ocean and thinking of Rita.

When he returned to his cabin, not only did his stomach feel calmer, his fatigue was gone. There was little point in trying to catch more sleep before the 0500 wake-up call. He pulled out his fountain pen and stash of writing paper, propped up a flashlight, and wrote the following:

February 5, 1944
Dearest Rita,
   It is indeed wonderful that the Army takes care of our mail even as we are sailing home. Writing to you is almost as much of a comfort as receiving your sweet letters. There are no words which can fully describe how I feel about my incomparable Rita. Will it be enough to say that you have been, are and will be my only love?
   I've complained to you about my living quarters throughout this long, weary separation, but here in the stinking hold of the ship, they (the conditions) have reached a new low. There are thousands of us here in this maritime metropolis, and we are warehoused in shelves. I'm lucky in that I have a bottom bunk, which makes it easy to slip out for a midnight stroll.
   Yes, my darling, I've taken to walking at night, to breathe in fresh sea air and also to have a chance to compose my letters to you in peace and quiet. For you see, precious one, writing a letter in this place is a task complicated by a dozen fellows trying to get my attention. So if my letters seem incoherent, don't worry.
   Top off my gastrointestinal distress with the fact that I have had my worst day of poker since donning khaki, and you will find a man greatly perturbed. I have never seen so many straights, flushes and full houses licked in my life. Almost enough to make a man swear off—and I would if there were any other thing to do that so successfully filled the time.
   Sending my love across the ocean,
   Your devoted husband,
                    Richard

By noon of the Cardinal's tenth day out, the ship reached the Philippines and by late in the evening, the men could occasionally see city lights through the darkness. The next day, word got around that Luzon was just off port. Benet hurried to the main deck for a view and remained there for over an hour. He spotted two mountains to the southeast, their tops obscured by clouds. In one of the straits, the men witnessed more signs of war. An island was pockmarked

231

with charred stains of fire. Remnants of barbed wire fortifications floated along the beaches.

Benet joined others on deck for whale watching. Kopriva, who seemed a different man—friendlier and more humane—since the "disappearance" of Mac, was the first to discover a series of spouts off the port. The whale watchers yelled out each time they detected the backs of the leviathans. Benet swore that he'd counted fifteen.

The morning's excitement over, Benet strolled to the recreation lounge and settled into a game of gin rummy. He and a very young Sergeant named Mickey Raus were the best players. Soon it was evident to all that they were evenly matched. Vaguely bored with the whole scene, Richard started mentally calling his opponent "Mickey Mouse."

"Doc," interrupted a voice, "I've gotta tear you away from your cards for a minute here. Something's come up." Gangly, red-haired Lloyd McKaye was a captain who'd befriended Benet during their first days of the Pacific crossing.

"I'll be right with you, McKaye. Had enough gin rummy to last me the rest of this vacation. Mickey Mouse here can hold the fort. He's the real card shark of us all."

Raus glared at the psychologist but said nothing. As Benet threw down his hand of cards, so did the others. Burton, to the left of Raus, gathered them up and started shuffling the deck.

"Hey Blackwell," Raus yelled to an enlisted man lounging nearby. "Come on over. We need a fourth."

"Why the hell not?" Blackwell asked no one in particular as he shuffled over to the table to sit in Benet's place.

"So what is it, old man?" Benet asked McKaye when they were out of hearing range of the card players.

"You know how damned hot it is in the compartments?" asked McKaye.

"Yep, of course I do. A regular inferno."

"Last night I told a couple enlisted men they could lie on the floor of the lounge. By 0200 hours the entire floor was covered with about 50 of them. I said they should just get used to sleeping in the hold, but my words fell on deaf ears."

"I'm not surprised. I'll give the men a pep talk tonight and a warning. Peterson comes around occasionally to inspect. If he finds them all sprawled out in the lounge when it's supposed to be mopped, we'll all be dressed down and probably even punished for the rest of our crossing."

Benet delivered a lecture to the "lounge lizards" at 2200 hours. To his astonishment, it worked. An hour later, the floor was clear of dozing soldiers. Having completed his letter-writing task earlier in the day, he went to bed in a calm state of mind. Unfortunately, his seasickness returned and after just three hours of sleep, he was wide awake.

Rather than thrashing around any longer in his bunk, Benet decided to escape for some fresh air. Clouds obscured the moon, so he literally groped his way up the narrow ladder out of the ship's hold. Once deck side, he took a few deep breaths of damp, heavy air. It smelled like rain. Storms at sea had a way of going from almost nothing to gale force in no time at all. He would stay close to the lounge so he could duck inside if it started to pour.

He turned his thoughts to Rita, waiting at the end of the voyage. He imagined the joy of their reunion, the incredible comfort of feeling, after so many godforsaken solitary nights, those lovely arms wrapped around him. They would not be able to get enough of one another. Life would be one endless honeymoon.

A north wind picked up, splattering Benet's face with fat drops of rain. So much for thoughts of home. Like it or not, he would have to go back down to the hold. When he stepped inside the dimly lit lounge, he heard a loud, metallic clank. An enlisted man with mop and bucket stood in a dark corner of the room.

"Hey, you there," Benet called out. "You the night shift? This place sure needs a good cleaning!"

The man kicked his bucket aside and stepped forward a few inches. "Yeah, Doc," he said in a surly tone "I'm cleanin' some dirt, but I won't be moppin' no floor. You ruined my cousin Warren, now I'm gonna give *you* an attitude adjustment."

As the stranger moved still closer, Benet got a better look at the short, ill-featured man. He'd seen that face somewhere before. Was it in the mess hall? Had the stranger visited Warren in the Neuro-Psychiatric Ward, or was he the soldier who filled in at the card game earlier? Whoever he was, Richard would have to calm him down before someone got hurt.

"Warren was a sick man. I did what I could to help him."

"Ya wrecked him, that's whacha did, you idiot egghead sunofabitch so-called psychologist. I'm his flesh and blood and I'm gonna make you pay for fucking with him."

"What's your name, fella?" asked Benet. "First tell me who you are, and then I'll explain what happened with your cousin. He's being well taken care of at the 20th General Hospital in Calcutta. Any day now, he'll be on his way back home, and you'll be able to see him."

"Shit, man, you don't need my name. It won't do you no good because, ya know, you'll be outta the picture. But since you asked, it's Bob—Bob Blackwell."

Blackwell trudged toward Richard with heavy steps. He reeked of alcohol and held a hypodermic in his hand.

"I've got an injection for you, Doc, like the shots you put into Warren, 'cept this ain't no tranquilizer. It's air, just like all the hot air you spouted to Warren. You and your fucking words screwed him up royally, and now it's payback time."

Before Benet could respond, Blackwell knocked him over and sat on top of his chest. He outweighed Benet by forty pounds, so it was fairly easy for Blackwell to keep his prey from escaping. He pinned Benet's left side to the floor and fumbled with his right arm, all the while holding the hypodermic in his teeth. Richard pushed with all his might, and he finally managed to roll to the right, at the same time loosening his left arm from under Blackwell. With both arms free, he felt empowered.

The psychologist's sense of relief was quickly squelched. Blackwell grunted and heaved them over. Once again he was on top. Blackwell's bulk seemed to spread out further this time, covering the psychologist like a giant blob. The hypodermic needle waved dangerously close to Benet's exposed inner arm.

A vision of Rita flashed through Benet's mind. Somehow he had to get out from under his crazed attacker. If he didn't, he would never see Rita again.

In the meantime, Blackwell shifted his weight in an effort to keep Benet pinned down. He balanced himself with his left hand, placed the intended murder hypodermic in his blubbery lips, and used his right hand as a probe. With one grubby finger, Blackwell jabbed the exposed soft flesh inside Benet's elbow joint.

Outside, it was beginning to rain in earnest. Wind blew the lounge door back and forth. Benet shouted over the din of pounding rain. "Bob, I know you blame me for what happened to Warren." He managed to slide his arm away from the poking finger.

Blackwell growled, but because of the hypodermic held between his lips, he couldn't answer.

"Uunnh" was all Blackwell could manage. He was drooling so much it seemed the hypodermic might slip out of his lip hold.

Unfortunately, all that happened was that some drops of saliva fell into Benet's eyes.

"Bob, Bob, I'm on your side. I'm just as angry as you are about Warren's illness. He was my patient, and I tried, I really did, but I failed him."

"Uunnh. Nnnhgh."

"You're afraid you'll never see your cousin again or if you do that he won't be the Warren you used to know."

Still firmly ensconced on Benet's chest, Blackwell took the hypodermic out of his mouth and held it in his right hand.

"Yeah, he was like a brother to me. We grew up together. He wudda been OK but you damn Army shrinks played with his mind. Ya ruined him."

Benet took a break from struggling. He lay quietly under Blackwell's fat bottom and tried to lure his foe into being sensible.

"Look," he reasoned, "I know you're upset, and I don't blame you. You're disappointed. You're frustrated. I'd feel just the same way if I were you."

"Hah," Blackwell sneered. "You can say that, but you don't know how it feels to be me." He started to cry. "Warren was my only friend in the world, and now he's screwed up for life."

"No, I couldn't possibly know what it's like. You're right, Bob, how could I know? How could I even begin to know? But I do know this. Warren will be sent home from the Twentieth Hospital in a week or so. You'll be the only person in the family who will know what he's been through. No one else—I mean no one—will understand.

"So what's the point?" Blackwell sniveled. "Why should I let you go? I've got no use for you stuckup dumb bastard psychologists."

Blackwell's weight was making it hard for Benet to breathe. Benet felt his strength draining away. He had to convince this oaf that there was an alternative to jabbing him with a hypodermic.

"OK, here's the point. It's better for us both if you let me go. If you kill me, you'll lose a chance to learn how to help Warren. Believe me, I'm the only person on this ship who knows a lot about your cousin's case. I lived it. I was with him for hours. We talked about everything."

"Shit, them's just words. How do I know I can believe you? I oughta just pop your vein with this here needle. Little air bubble'll polish ya off nice and quick while everyone's asleep. I'll jes' slide you overboard and no one will ever know what happened."

41

12 October 1945
At Sea
Dearest Rita,
    I hope this letter will answer some of the questions you must be asking. You recall my writing about Bob Blackwell, the enlisted oaf who tried to kill me, first by attempting to shoot air into my veins with a hypodermic and then by trying to throw me overboard? Thank God, General Peterson came along just in time to keep me from becoming shark bait.

    After my near demise, Blackwell apologized to both the General and me. He explained his behavior with the fact that he'd been drinking. After the General left, I made the mistake of listening to Blackwell's troubles for an hour and then the big dope proceeded to attach himself to me like a leech. I fear I've created a monster. It was better when he hated me.

    Today, however, I'm free of Blackwell. The poor fellow is violently seasick and forced to stay in his berth next to the privy. It would suit me fine if he remained seasick for the rest of our voyage home.

    I'm sure you recall the disappearance, after the failed hospital takeover attempt, of my former 'bete noir' Colonel James McDermott? Well, Mac was declared AWOL and General Peterson took over as Acting Director of the hospital. Yes, Peterson was still in charge of the 20th, but he had a very competent assistant and so managed to direct both the 20th and the 142nd. At any rate, we heard nothing of McDermott and assumed that maybe he'd died at a goonda's hands or withered away in a lowdown opium den somewhere in the depths of darkest Calcutta. Instead, he hid for months at a private residence in Alipore.

    But, the beast (McDermott) crept out of his hole. Or to put it more accurately, the Army dragnet finally snared him. It seems that after the strange disappearance of Ravi Ghosh, Narendra Ghosh (Ravi's alleged nephew) took McDermott under his wing, providing him with a disguise and using him as a messenger for various drug enterprises. Mac was court-martialed and is now on trial for three counts of murder: for a soldier in the Burmese campaign, a hospital patient named Calvin Brothers, and Sgt. Silas Lowell.

But there's more to the story. Ravi Ghosh ran amok with the goondas that had been in his employ. Both Ghosh and my former bearer Sanjay have prices on their heads. The two dropped from sight and allegedly are now operating criminal activities in Ramgarh, northeast of Calcutta.

All of this information is courtesy of good old Andy Anderson, so I can't guarantee its accuracy, but I thought you'd be interested.

But now I switch to a topic of heartfelt interest to me, and that is: you and me. You are aware, my love, are you not, that though you were entrancingly adorable as a young girl, that in mature womanhood you combine all those features which we think most desirable in a wife and companion?

In detailing those qualities, which I personally appreciate, I list your total personality, the YOU which everyone loves. Next, I stand in awe and reverence before your love for me. Again, I am twice confirmed by your graciousness, your consideration, your selflessness. And finally, that which would suffice to make any man happy in such a wife, your physical perfection. Of course, no one quality is separate, and they are all portrayed in your sweet smile, your serious eyes, the grace of your walk, your lovely hands, your charming voice.

I realize that no man is more fortunate than I. No man has more to fight for. No man has more to come home to. You are my wife and my friend. You are beloved by me above all women, all persons, all earthly possessions.

Sending my love across the ocean,
Your devoted husband,
Richard
p.s. What wonderful news that you will be at the Fairmont Hotel in San Francisco to meet me! I dream of a happiness on that fine day for which words are inadequate.

42

On the morning of October 20, 1945, the U.S.S. Cardinal was five miles from the California coast. Like most of the G.I.'s on board, Lt. Richard Benet was up and strolling the deck before daybreak. The anticipation of seeing Rita so enlivened him, he'd slept but little. By that afternoon, the ship would reach San Francisco.

After breakfast, Benet and his pal Andy Anderson stood against the ship rail and gazed at the rocky coast as it seemed to unroll. The air felt crisp and clear against their faces. As the Cardinal grew closer to land, sunlight illuminated the green hills bordering San Francisco Bay.

"My God, can you believe it?" Anderson asked. "American soil, just ahead of us."

"Magnificent," said Benet. "No wonder they call this the Golden Gate. And look, man, we're headed under the bridge itself."

Along with other G.I.'s crowding the deck, Anderson and Benet craned their heads upward to see if there the ship would have enough clearance. As the lumbering ship floated underneath the Golden Gate Bridge, room to spare, a cheer arose.

"Look ahead," shouted Benet, "here comes the welcome party!"

An Army boat, the deck of which held a Women's Army Corps band, sailed nearby. "When Johnny comes Marching Home" was the first of a spirited medley of tunes reverberating across the water.

"There's Alcatraz," exclaimed Anderson as he pointed to a craggy gray outcropping in the distance. "I thought it would look bigger and more forbidding."

"I see what you mean," said Benet. "It seems harmless, like a little rock outcropping basking in the morning sun."

From all sides, ship horns blew hoarse salute. From suburban San Francisco, car horns sounded. Tug boats made "umph" sounds as they floated alongside the Cardinal to Pier 13. Cheers arose from a huge crowd of welcomers. Some people waved American flags. Others, parked in their cars, honked horns.

"Look," cried one of the G.I.'s, "American women. They're wearing shoes!" More music sounded from the pier, where yet another band of WAC musicians were gathered.

Richard Benet stood in a slow-moving line awaiting his turn to disembark. Every so often, the line would tread forward just a bit.

Benet, like the others, dragged a huge duffel bag. United Service Organization relief workers distributed coffee and doughnuts as the men waited to board ferries.

Benet was to take the Ernie Pyle and Anderson was on a passenger list for the Maynard. The two men shook hands.

"We survived, old man," said Benet. "Be sure to write and let me know how you're doing. Give Doris and your little girl a big hello for me. It will take some weeks of debriefing, but by Christmas, I betcha we'll both be used to civilian life."

Anderson gave Benet an awkward bear hug. "You keep in touch, too. Take good care of your Rita. I think she and Doris would hit it off well. They both play bridge. I expect before too long I'll hear that you've gotten a teaching position."

The lines moved in opposite directions, and the two pals waved a final farewell.

In another three hours, Richard Benet reported to the Officer's Quarters and received his pass for a night's leave. As he rode by taxicab up Mason Street to California Avenue, he marveled at the calm, orderly streets. No cattle or rickshaw carts, no barefooted men carrying immense loads, no bicycles slowing traffic. When the cab reached the apex of Nob Hill, it pulled up to the Fairmont Hotel. Before the cab driver opened his door, Richard literally hopped onto the sidewalk. He dragged his luggage out of the cab and turned to face the cabbie.

"I cudda helped you, sir," said the crusty little man who stood by Benet's side. "That'll be six dollars."

Benet gave the cabbie his fare plus a dollar tip and stood for just a moment in front of the Fairmont's gracious façade. He'd seen some of the most spectacular temples in India but none of them looked as beautiful as the palatial hotel looming before him. He paused, wanting to remember every detail of the Fairmont's stone columns: the gilded bay windows, the elegant cream colored awning and the plush red carpet leading to the entrance. Attendants in red uniforms opened the double doors for him and offered to take his bag.

"No, no thank you," said Benet. "I'm meeting my wife and I'm not quite sure when she'll be arriving."

The lobby was full of military men, their wives, sweethearts, parents and an occasional baby or toddler. Benet looked for Rita in the crowd. Thinking that maybe she'd already checked in and gone to their room, he made an inquiry at the reception desk.

A red-haired clerk with a beak nose and bright orange nail polish ran her finger down her ledger page. After a few minutes, she looked up.

"Mmm, no, Officer, a Mrs. Rita Benet hasn't checked in. I do see your reservation here. Mmm, would you like to sign in now? We've got you on the fifth floor. You and the missus will have a great view of the bay from your room."

"Sure thing, I'll go ahead and fill out the registration card," said Benet. "I'll have to borrow your pen, though. I seem to have misplaced mine."

Paperwork done, Benet dragged his duffel over to a red stuffed chair next to a potted palm. He faced the entrance so he'd be sure to see Rita the minute she entered. His sleepless night caught up with him. In a few minutes, his head fell to his chest and he nodded off.

Soon he was asleep and dreaming of Calcutta. He imagined that insects had gotten inside his mosquito netting. He tried to shake them off, but a soft fluttery movement continued to play about his shoulder. He awakened to find Rita's gloved hand on his shoulder.

"Richard, sweetheart, I'm here."

He looked up and broke into a delighted smile. "Rita, Rita, Rita. You look beautiful. Sorry I fell asleep..."

Before he could say another word, she was in his lap and they embraced. Rita kissed every part of Richard's face.

"Darling, you're a sight for my lonely eyes," she said, "but poor you, you're all tuckered out."

Richard rose from the chair, gently lifting Rita to her feet.

"Yes, sweetheart, you're right. I am beat. Let's hurry up to our room." He gave her an intimate smile. "I have a feeling the view just might revive me."

Afterword

While the characters in *Beast of Bengal* are fictional, many of the letters written by Rita and Richard Benet are adapted from an actual World War II correspondence. Volunteer armies such as Ravi Ghosh's ragtag "Independence Fighters" may have existed during 1945, but the author knows of none.

The novel's political events are based on history. On August 8, 1942, the All-India Congress adopted a resolution mandating an end to British rule. Thus began the "Quit India" campaign. Mohandas Gandhi, also known as Mahatma ("The Holy One"), aspired to lead India in *Satyagraha* or peaceful fighting. The movement lost both leader and spirit when Gandhi and the entire Congress were arrested and jailed.

During WWII, the U.S. Army Air Force used Calcutta as the site for several rehabilitation hospitals. Calcutta later became the capital of West Bengal. The actual 142nd General Hospital was located near Southern Avenue in Calcutta's Alipore district. Army Air Force veterans who staffed that hospital still hold regular get-togethers in the Midwestern United States. It goes without saying that their numbers are rapidly dwindling.

After the U.S. dropped the Atomic Bomb, the war officially ended with Victory over Japan (VJ) Day on August 15, 1945. Men and women stationed in the far-flung China-Burma-India Theater of operations were among the last soldiers to return home.

On August 15, 1947, India declared independence from Britain. Lord Mountbatten, viceroy of India at the time, declared that it would be possible for the British to leave only if power were transferred to two independent governments. Thus it was that Britain instituted the Partition that split the subcontinent into the two nations of Pakistan and India with large pockets of Muslims forming Pakistan and Hindus forming the new India. The division was accompanied by unprecedented violence, staggering migrations in both directions across the newly-formed India/Pakistan border, and unprecedented bloodshed. It is estimated that roughly one million people died, and tens of millions of Muslims and Hindus became refugees.

With the Partition, Bengal was divided. West Bengal became a state of India. East Bengal, primarily Muslim, became East Pakistan and in 1971, it was renamed Bangladesh. Tensions generated by the Partition remain to this day.

On the afternoon of January 30, 1948, Mohandas Gandhi walked across a grassy field to a prayer meeting. Hundreds of people had congregated for evening devotions. A Hindu fanatic emerged from the crowd as if he were going to bow before Gandhi. Instead, the assassin fired three shots from an automatic pistol. As the sun set, Gandhi crumpled to the ground. It was the last day of a magnificent life, the tragic passing of an era.

-Elaine Pinkerton
Santa Fe, New Mexico

About the Author

Elaine Pinkerton's passion for writing began early in life. She launched her professional career freelancing for local, regional, and national publications, including *Family Circle, New Mexico Magazine, Runner's World, On the Run, and New Mexico Traveler*. For nearly a decade, she was a writer/editor for Los Angeles National Library.

Inspired by the beauty of New Mexico and the Southwest, she produced two guidebooks: *Santa Fe on Foot* and *The Santa Fe Trail by Bicycle*. Pinkerton's latest work centers on World War II and India. Her late father, Army Air Force psychologist Richard Beard, provided inspiration for *From Calcutta with Love*. The book comprises correspondence between Richard and his wife Reva. The original WWII letters have been acquired by the Air Force Museum at Wright-Patterson Air Force Base in Dayton, Ohio. *Beast of Bengal* was inspired by a letter in which Pinkerton's father discovered a hanging corpse.

Pinkerton lives in Santa Fe, New Mexico with her husband Robert Dinegar, and two cats.